ALSO BY WILFRID SHEED

Fiction

A Middle-Class Education
The Hack
Square's Progress
Office Politics
The Blacking Factory and Pennsylvania Gothic
Max Jamison
People Will Always Be Kind
Transatlantic Blues

Non-Fiction

The Good Word
The Morning After
Clare Boothe Luce
Frank and Maisie: A Memoir with Parents
Muhammad Ali

Anthologies

Sixteen Short Novels
G. K. Chesterton's Essays and Poems

THE BOYS OF WINTER

THE BOYS
OF WINTER

A NOVEL BY

Wilfrid Sheed

ALFRED A. KNOPF

New York   1987

The story on page 43 was actually written at the exact same stage
of the author's life, and met with the exact same fate.

THIS IS A BORZOI BOOK
PUBLISHED BY ALFRED A. KNOPF, INC.

Library of Congress Cataloging-in-Publication Data
Sheed, Wilfrid.
The boys of winter.
I. Title.
PR6069.H396B6   1987   823'.914   86-46319
ISBN 0-394-55874-X

Manufactured in the United States of America
First Edition

This book was set in a digitized version of Janson by
Adroit Graphic Composition Inc., New York, New York.

It was printed and bound by
The Haddon Craftsmen, Inc., Scranton, Pennsylvania.

Design by Dorothy Schmiderer

AUTHOR'S NOTE

Great literature is, of course, timeless.
This novel is set in 1978.

Winter

1

THE winter writers are spread out like pieces in a game; the rule seems to be: no two writers on the same block, and no more than three to a township. On the whole, they don't think much of each other privately; in fact, each believes he is the only real writer in the area and the rest are frauds, but this only leaks out, drunk and piecemeal, over the years.

The workaday convention is that they are all equally great, that their bad reviews are prompted by the same malice, and even—and this is the tricky part—that they are all equally rich. Although some retired out here young and fat with success while others are still waiting for their first score, they all, in the small talk at Jimmy's, rattle on gaily about agents and options as if, for instance, Waldo Spinks and Billy van Dyne were in one and the same business. And although I assume from their relative fames that Waldo could buy and sell Billy many times over, they jostle each other nightly for the tab, with Billy actually holding a slight edge, as befits his lower status in real life.

In winter, it's like a foreign colony in Antibes or Biarritz; the writers' very bone structure stamps them as outsiders. But in the summer this garrison is suddenly implemented by a vast ordnance of ad men, journalists, publishers, patrons-at-large, and the women that go with the above. The writers moan softly about this development and talk of going into hiding. Yet the profiles remain on display at various parties and around the back tables in Jimmy's. A groupie should have no trouble finding them. Even a recluse has to stick his head out now and then to remind you of what you're missing.

If a certain gray bile is suffusing this description, I come by it honestly. For one thing, I am that most displaced of persons, a weekender, forever deciding whether to keep the house open all year, and forever dropping in on people's lives just in time for the feud, the crack-up (why do these things always happen on Saturday night?) and deeply resented for this. "Fred doesn't drink at all during the week," says Mrs. Fred, glaring over the remains of her husband. "We've never been happier," barks Sam, covering the wail from the Ladies' Room.

Worse even than a weekender, I am also the writers' natural enemy, a publisher. As they see it, I am living off their backs, like a rack-renter. It is they who pay for my house, my insulation: if I can just court Waldo Spinks successfully and fend off Billy van Dyne tactfully, the winter is covered. Light work, you might suppose, but not quite as light as it looks. For instance, since Waldo's natural role is to make it clear that he doesn't need me, and Billy's is the exact opposite, my social life can be prickly. How do you claim prior engagements in such a small community, when Billy calls you three weeks in advance? And what do you do with your evenings when Waldo fails to turn up for the fourth straight time? Billy is more congenial than Waldo, at least to start with, but the sonofabitch always has a fresh manuscript on his person (he must rent them) and by eleven o'clock he's sure to be asking for a candid opinion of his place in American letters, and I can't go on saying "time will tell" indefinitely.

Luckily, I have my own little ego to keep me warm. I also believe that I am better than all of them, only with the good taste not to put it in writing. Waldo Spinkses come and go. Routine case, no complications. Acclaimed first novel sucked out of his youth and the Korean War. Nothing much since. Terminally overpriced. Which he blames on his ex-wives. Waldo came at the end of the two-fisted era, when writers were known to boast about the size of their alimony (it was a symbol of risk-taking) so naturally he claims to pay the largest amount in history. On various nights, he has cited three to five ex-wives and four to twelve known children. Whatever his literary merits, he is surely one of our major bullshit artists.

Why do I want him at all, you say? Because with my genius, I believe I can hammer one more blockbuster out of that very bullshit. The problem is to catch him at the right moment, when he's humble enough to seek help, but not so beaten that nobody wants him. So one waits and watches and puts up with his pathetic "I'm doing literature a favor" arrogance. I'll be there when he's gone, I tell myself as I put away his unused dishes one more time. I've buried better writers than Spinks.

If Spinks can stand for the winners, van Dyne makes a slightly less satisfactory loser, if only because he has talent. I published his first novel, *The Little House on Death Street*, with real excitement (not just the usual "we here at Poontang Press are very high on this") and the book demonstrated not only a quality of profound and unanswerable unsalability, but a rarer gift more akin to invisibility. Some quite good writers have this strange knack. They produce good book after book for publisher after publisher and nobody *sees* them. How do you explain this to a man? You, sir, are good but invisible.

"Jonathan!" He is crouched by the fire. "This new one is the best thing I've done so far. Forget *Death Street*. That was commercial, this is literature."

Commercial! I think I'm going to cry. Seven hundred copies worth of commerce is his idea of cheapening himself sinfully. "Bill, you know how it is with quality fiction these days. My bosses go rigid all over every time I mention it. I like your new avocado, by the way."

He shuts his eyes. They are probably filling up with a hate that he can't afford to show. My *bosses*. Editor emeritus to the Beautiful People and I still have bosses, eh? He, Billy van Dyne, at least answers to no one. I can hear him breathing slowly, his soul settling. When he opens his eyes, it is with a warm smile that seems to say "Would you like to sleep with my wife? She does specialties."

This is the man that really *loathes* me right now. Spinks only goes through the motions. He has another publisher at the moment who probably gets the real thing. Van Dyne knows he is better than Spinks, and he knows that I know it too. The amount of bootless flattery I heap into my rejection letters hasn't helped in this matter. Billy believes I really think he's a genius and that I just haven't the guts to publish him. OK, one is used to these misunderstandings in my profession. Even the best of us is considered a weak-kneed sellout by our disappointed suitors. It beats making a scene.

But van Dyne here is a running sore for me, because he has not only talent but vocation. He will go to his grave polishing his craft. I make a mental note, just to ward off insomnia tonight, that if I bag Spinks I'll take another van Dyne with the proceeds.

But not to suppose that our life out here is exclusively literary. Far from it. I have never met a group of writers who talked less about their art. Partly because they don't think the other writers have any, but largely because they are trying earnestly to make something out of the rest of the life that's lived out here. They know they have abandoned huge quarries of experience by moving to the country; and they know further that this small area is overprospected already. So they cultivate handymen and boutique owners and small-town politicians, and they talk about roofing and siding and gypsy moths, trying to make a usable universe out of scraps, stretching a bikini's worth of material over their variously sized talents.

This book is dedicated to them, specifically to four with whom I have had dealings: if you will, picture other writers swirling about in the background like gases in the galaxy and call my book a species of publisher's revenge on all of them. Having played the courtesan to them too long, curtseying to their pretensions and kissing second-rate ass, I would like to show them who's got the royal blood around here, by beating them to the great regional book—roofing, siding, and all.

Actually, there will be precious little roofing in it. One of the punishments out here is the unwavering volume of house talk: people moving in, moving out, renovating, tearing down walls. It is the link between the writers and the handymen, and I sometimes think the writers kick their houses around just so they'll have something to talk about. For myself, I've been a city boy for years, used to sending out for someone to turn on my faucets. And although I know the basic patter for propping up the bar with carpenters (publishers can learn the words to anything—we are a logical extension of crossword puzzles), I don't really listen to them when they patter back. I hire them on what I take to be character, the reading of which is my business after all, and when I get them home I look around with mild, shrewd eyes and say "Well, what do you think?" Perhaps I don't really understand country character, because I lose a couple of hundred a year by this method. But what the hell, it's good will, and I suspect that the writers play it the same way. There's no future in upstaging a handyman out here.

Yes, first of all, the writers. They are still my subject—despite the local richness—not as writers, but actors who've come to the Fair dressed as country gentlemen or fieldhands, as the dream takes them. There are no geniuses around to jam my typewriter, and, God forbid, no poets, but only ordinary citizens who have learned the joists and stresses of the middlebrow novel. These are my meal ticket, and I propose now to see if I can eat my meal ticket and have it too. If all goes well, they'll get their copies (you first, Waldo) and will then have to decide how much my friendship is worth. I picture orgies of hypocrisy, as they wrestle with the vexed question of whether a vile publisher is better than no publisher at all. And then the contortions they will go through convincing themselves they are not in my book anyway, before congratulating me on doing in the others. But perhaps I underrate them.

Purely for background, we have a couple of well-known painters who come swaggering in every night like sailors off the *Bremerhaven*, in wool hats and hairy turtlenecks. They *seem* completely inarticulate, but it's hard to tell because they drink as if they'd been at sea for a long time, and always glaze over in minutes; but they are present in every scene that takes place in Jimmy's. (Incidentally, the painters out here also have a genius for marrying money that has pretty much escaped our writers.

This I believe argues a certain kind of integrity: since, if you think about it, marrying a dog is quite a price to pay for artistic freedom.)

Then there's this man who made a killing on storm windows at twenty-five and spends the whole afternoon in Jimmy's making book on football, and the banker who only hires people who sing barbershop harmony, and the normal complement of ready-made characters that human life coughs up obligingly in every village in the world.

Nobody at Jimmy's talks about politics during the winter because there really isn't enough for a whole conversation: at its heart, Hampton politics consists entirely of schemes to keep people like us out. But in the summer, all this will change. Guys come out to the Hamptons to run for borough president of Manhattan, and they form Artists and Writers committees, and all my boys are there right next to Paul Newman and Leonard Bernstein or whoever we've got that year. Except van Dyne, who suffers agonies of letterhead envy. Christ, he'd sign anything, right wing, left wing, anything to get the old name out there. Spinks says jokingly that van Dyne can have *his* place on the letterheads, that he's tired of running New York City from this distance. Spinks has to make a lot of tough decisions like that. Is he famous enough to start taking his name *off* things, to show a little less profile? Apparently not. He supported not one but two mayoral candidates last summer, explaining his tortured shift at length in several local papers.

Vain prick. They're all vain pricks, I tell you. If you opened every window at Jimmy's, the stench of ego would knock the birds out of the trees. But I, their comic servant, their scheming hunchback, will get even. Limping over my blasted heath, I shall weave such plots as tyrants dream on.

2

TAKE January. This is the heart of the suicide season. All the talk about the Hamptons being lovely in the winter dies in people's throats. The famous potato fields take on a Siberian sullenness, and people who pride themselves on sticking it out all year sneak furtively off to Orlando and Key West. Writers give lectures in Tallahassee that somehow stretch into March. I can't even get a girl to come out on weekends to share my drafty mansion and my three-pound, eight-ply sweaters.

Superbowl Sunday seems to be the breaking point. Up to then a certain locker-room heartiness keeps us going, even those who don't care for football. Then suddenly the light goes out in people's eyes, their faces empty. Their ball has been taken away.

"What about softball?" croaks Archie Munson, our Sportswriter, which means the closest thing to royalty in a saloon.

"You mean right now?"

Munson's phrase would turn out to be fateful, but that night we kicked it around like kittens.

"Sure, why not. You be the front office, Billy. Like when they say 'a member of the Yankee official family'—that's you. Waldo can be the greedy owner who actually thinks he knows baseball."

"You think I don't, huh?"

"Good attitude. Of *course* you know baseball, sir. I'm your general manager, and I ought to know."

"Then kiss my ass, there's a good fellow."

"Done and done. Pete," he turns to the storm-window man, Pete Simmons, "you be the feisty manager who gives unfortunate quotes. That way the time will simply fly!"

Simmons, who is our token plebeian, is only expected to grunt in response. Anything more is gravy. Yet we treat him as a local sage.

"Shit, as if winter wasn't bad enough," he says.

"Jonathan?" I have to be disposed of somehow, since I insist on being there. "How about press relations? Getting those hangnail stories into the paper. Smoothing over the differences between Waldo and Pete."

"You mean they're both fiery personalities who have a lot of respect for each other?"

"Hey," pipes Billy. "You're horning into my turf already. It's the *member of the official family* who says things like that. Adding that 'the day those two stop feuding is the day I'll worry.'"

"No Billy"—I'm sorry, I'm an editor—"you are only an anonymous source. Your job is to say the rotten things the owner can't say for himself. You do Waldo's dirty work."

Note the mixture of Jamesian complexity and sheer simple-mindedness. The key to both is savagery.

"Why don't I use my anonymous power to undermine my boss Waldo as well?" asks Billy.

"Because you will find your anonymous power warming its ass in Toledo, busher," says Waldo.

Billy bares his teeth like Harpo. "I'm sick of working for you, Bighead. Without your money, you'd be nothing, you know that? You're just a neat stack of dollar bills."

"Reaching to the moon, little man."

The subject could have been chrysanthemums, and it would have ended roughly the same way. But the point to stress is that the kidding is completely, tooth-gratingly friendly. Billy and Waldo drink together practically every night, as if they have to keep an eye on each other, and even incoherent with booze, they are always friendly. And the kidding never lets up.

The baseball joke might have come and gone like any other, but Archie wouldn't let go tonight. "This is the best part of the baseball season, talking in the winter. The game itself is a fucking bore, if you want my opinion."

When somebody wants to talk about something we usually let him, because there isn't that much else to talk about. Filling four hours of drinking time with the same guys every night, you'll take most anything that comes along. And Archie is one of our few genuine nice guys. As our sportswriter (semiretired, but the title lives on, like "Senator"), his envies and hostilities were burned away long ago by the sun, and he alone among the group has lived out his dream as written. For some reason this makes people want to please him.

So when I step into the conversation next weekend, there is Susan Rose saying "what about women?"

"I'm glad you brought that up, Sue. I've got a great deal on bunny costumes. . . ."

"I don't just want to be a body, I want to be a person," says Sue mechanically.

"We'll let you talk."

"In fact, I not only want to be a person, I want to be a shortstop."

"A *shortstop?* Jesus."

"You wouldn't say that if I was a man."

"I wouldn't need to."

Sue Rose glares seductively. She must know in her bones that she will never be a person as long as she lives, but as a body only a cad could refuse her shortstop, especially on an imaginary team.

"Would you settle for second base?"

"Only if you guarantee at least two other women on the team."

"And where do you suggest hiding them?"

"How about short second base and long second base?" says Billy. "And talking of which, where do we hide *me?*"

A point. Billy is spectacularly unathletic. He is big enough, but the coat-hanger shoulders move rustily, and he can't even pick up a drink without looking as if he's using the wrong hand.

"Don't worry," says Archie. "This will be that rarest of human events, a friendly game. If I have to bust heads to get it."

"Good luck, miracle man," says Waldo. "Five gets you ten that you can't keep it friendly."

"What do you mean, fuckhead? I can keep *anything* friendly. Even you, shitface. And I'll thank you not to give me such pissant odds."

"I'll take a piece of Archie's action. Look at how friendly he keeps a conversation."

Thus in the cozy winter bar at Jimmy's, the Other Hampton Friendlies are launched. Waldo has played some semipro, Pete Simmons says he pinch-hit once in American Legion—every second player at least would be pretty good. "Jonathan?" Are you still there, you weekend intruder? "You ever play ball?"

They look at me, and I know what they're seeing—three-inch glasses, a belly that has spared itself nothing, a glistening patina of flab.

"With my sister once. She hit me."

Asking me at all is stretching friendliness pretty far. But goddammit, I am the publisher. "Umpire?" says Archie. "You know any rules at all?"

"Sure. Ten bucks for a called third strike, five for a close play at first base." They all wish I'd just go away, but unfortunately I suddenly want to be in this thing. Writers at play, with me in the middle.

"Your prices are inflationary," says Waldo.

"They're negotiable. And look, don't let my blindness fool you. I got a good feel for the game."

It's true. In school I was one of those freaky kids who practically needs a seeing-eye dog but who can get his bat on anything that's thrown. I could even hit the curve, though I preferred not to.

Billy van Dyne needs a publisher more than most. "A friendly umpire. Why not?"

They are stuck. They belong in this bar, I don't. This is not my scene, because I have no scene. Their loathing caresses me. "OK, Jonathan, you're on."

* · * · *

It must be the coldest winter in history. My house is like a mausoleum. I keep the thermostat down, to humor the President of the moment, and to hold the line on oil prices, but even a blast furnace would not keep out these sea winds. The place was built in the last century, and has developed mysterious pores that let in all the cold air that's going and cannot be blocked by modern know-how. (In summer they atone for this and the joint is an inferno.)

So Jimmy's becomes necessary and we flock there as to a Red Cross station on a battlefield. When the winds rake the power lines and Jimmy's 50-watt bulbs flicker, the owner is prepared. A big red-bearded fellow, Jimmy has a personality like a fireplace anyway, and his backup candles and kerosene lamps are actually slightly brighter than the usual Tiffany gizmos. His real fireplace throws hospitable heat in your face as you walk in shivering, and you half expect fat monks to caper up with flagons.

Shivering and stomping off the snow and blowing smoke on your hands—the image of a softball arching against a blue sky takes on a spurious charm. So we resort to it yet again, as therapy. As the weather gets better we won't need it, I hope.

What is really happening, the game beneath the skin, is that Spinks has turned in his latest novel to his old publisher, and I gather from the vigor with which he doesn't talk about it that there may be a snag. A price snag? or has he written his breakthrough, turning-point stinker? He is nicer to me than usual, sending over the odd bottle of wine to my table. Writers are such subtle fellows.

I have a reputation, built on blind luck, for being the best manuscript editor in the business. I am, as you can tell already, far from that. But if you pick the right writers, and keep a trained pedant on a chain in the office cellar, you don't have to edit a thing, and your reputation grows and grows. Waldo's man Jerry Tauber has the opposite label, equally undeserved. He works for the publishing equivalent of a fast-food chain and has to work like a dog to make his line even presentable. If he turns Waldo down, the book must be almost unreclaimable, even by me. Still, I want it. I need a big name, even a retread (most big names are retreads anyway) to spruce up my increasingly, and puzzlingly, stale list.

Van Dyne, little suspecting that his fate is linked to Waldo's, has taken to pouting. I don't blame him. I have thrown every stalling device in the publisher's handbook at him. And though he himself can absorb any amount of failure, I'm not so sure about his wife Monique. As a connoisseur of the latest in bubbly spring waters, Monique has never been a Jimmy's regular, until this January. It could be that the weather would drive any two-footed creature in here, but I have a prickly feeling on my neck about Nikki. I think she wants one of us, Waldo or possibly me. Oh God, why am I so priapic? After my marriage broke up, I went on one of those second-childhood rampages, thinking I'd settle down after a year or so. But I just kept going. It's been five years now, and I still want to sleep with everything in sight.

However, even I do not have the gall to sleep with Monique while turning down Billy. And I can't, in conscience, publish Billy in order to get at Monique. I would feel too damn silly. So a lot is riding on Waldo's publisher Jerry Tauber as he mulls Spinks's latest excrescence. To get the girl and the manuscript and ride off into the sunset—ah, the excitements of a publisher's life.

3

THANK GOD there are other writers out here of a less agitating sort. Ferris Fender, for instance, who hates bars because they lack nobility of spirit and who bats out Civil War novels for me, every two years on the dot. Novels that make you miss that little old war something awful. And there's Cecily Woodruff, who chronicles heartbreak along Park Avenue from her seaside retreat.

Well, I won't say that Cecily isn't exactly agitating. After two husbands, she thinks she might be a lesbian, but would like to make absolutely sure. I am perfectly willing to take her word for it. It isn't just the tweeds or the deep voice, because oddly enough she makes these quite grotesquely feminine. But she must still be the only woman out here I don't want to lay. Mainly because I've read her books, and I just couldn't bear anyone thinking those utterly beautiful thoughts while we were on the job. The moment she reached for a postcoital cigarette, I would scream, "Cut. You can't have her lighting *any more cigarettes.*"

My late-blooming goatlike reputation seems to get me in trouble unknown to other publishers. "I'm blocked," says Cecily. "I need an affair."

"Well it's not part of my normal duties. But maybe I could introduce you to someone. Waldo Spinks just broke off with his girl."

"Ugh." She actually said "ugh." No wonder she's a writer. "You wouldn't really ask me to sleep with prose like that, would you? Besides, I've seen him on the beach and you could make a Navajo rug out of the hair on his right shoulder blade alone."

"You prefer something hairless?"

"Extremely hairless. That's the trouble. I don't know whether men *as such* are too hairy. My eyes want a woman and my ears want a man."

"That certainly complicates my task as a procurer."

"I need masculine dialogue."

"In that case, I know just the lady for you. My ex-wife," says the failed nightclub comic in me.

"It sounds so unprofessional, doesn't it? 'I need masculine dialogue.' But that's what happens if you live out here. You forget how people talk."

"So why do you think so many novelists live out here then?"

"Because we're not serious. If there's more to writing than loping along the beach in turtlenecks, we haven't heard about it. By the way, *you* look hairless."

"Comme ci, comme ça. I'm not *extremely* hairless." I try to summon up all the hair I can. The lecher at bay is a comical creature.

She has a hand on my shirt button. Mind you, it is late January, my standards are scraping bottom, and she is more womanly than she knows what to do with. She teeters: it is still a humorous situation that can go either way. I teeter back. Perhaps one cannot sleep with *any* of one's authors, one knows too much. "A little too woolly for my taste," she says briskly. "Pity."

That's it for now. We're in what the flying people jokingly call a holding pattern. But I have embarrassed her, made her look silly, no doubt intensifying her block. I may have to come back.

Meanwhile, I decide to make *everything* seem silly. "How would you like to play on our new softball team?" I say inanely.

Her eyes brighten. We are a nation of children. "I'd love to. You know, I'm terrific at it."

"What position?" I gurgle.

"Second base!" Oh no, our first clash. Sue Rose has lost her job already. "The thing is I run like a deer and hit like an angel, but the old soupbone is shaky." Her face has already regressed horribly. She is a freckle-faced urchin again and her blond hair turns red before my eyes. I want to clap a little cap on her and slap her butt. "I like your spirit, kid," I say, entering the mad American dance. "You've got it in here." I tap my medium woolly chest. "And that's what counts."

She breaks away and a moment later I see stuff flying out of the hall closet. This I refuse to believe. Scarves, mittens—and she's got it. Cecily comes out triumphantly waving a baseball glove. "Put it here, pal," she says, pounding the pocket. "Let's see what you've got."

Weakly, incredulously, I go into a little windup. Pow! she socks the glove again. "High and outside," she says.

"What do you mean? That was right over the middle."

"Shut up and play ball."

She tosses the phantom Spalding back to me, and I put it in my pocket. I refuse to go the full nine innings with her.

She tries to calm down now, and show that it's all a joke. The merciless recorder of the Manhattan malaise trots back to her position. "Well so much for softball."

"No, but I mean it about the team," I say.

"OK, I'll come out if I can. I'm actually not very good."

"You can't fool me, lady. I know talent when I see it. In fact, I'm our talent scout." I lie, trying to outclown her. That glove in the closet has given her away. Will she try to blame it on a visiting nephew? No. Too much class for that, at least.

I exit, talking literature. Softball has gotten me off the hook; it has put sex back where it belongs. For that matter, it has gotten her off the hook too. The National Pastime can give our other one quite a run for its money. I mutter something about the number of great baseball books. "There seems to be a natural affinity between novelists and the game." OK on balance, but I make a note not to bring up the team with Ferris Fender. He will undoubtedly tap his spikes and spit in his hat. "The Friendlies, what a *comfy* name," she says, as I wade into the snow on her driveway.

1 7

* * *

My next port of call is indeed Ferris, and before you know it, I find myself babbling about softball. If you think writers are crazy, you should meet publishers. Talent scout, I'm a talent scout. I've finally found a niche in the front office.

Fortunately, Ferris, up to his neck in ferns, despises baseball. It seems it came into its own after the Civil War, and is thus part of the postbellum blight. The trouble is, Ferris looks like a ballplayer: not only the sloping shoulders and capable hands I associate with the sport, but the crinkly blue eyes that see the ducks before the other hunters have seen the sun. I once crouched in a blind with one of our hunting authors (just one of my chores), and a South Carolina kid with those same eyes cleaned out the sky while the author was still clearing his phlegm. And dammit, was I a talent scout or wasn't I?

Besides which, Ferris serves 100-proof Wild Turkey and wouldn't respect an editor who didn't match him tumbler for tumbler.

"A lot of Southern boys play baseball," I say.

"Yeah, ain't it a shame. Nothing better to do since Antietam, I guess."

"Look, Ferris. The war is over."

"It is?" The eyes crinkle so much you can almost hear them, like tinfoil. "Then I guess I'm out of business, old buddy."

All that Ferris demands of an editor is that you allow him to get you too drunk to walk. Then he stands up and stretches and says he feels like writing a chapter or two. Of all my authors, he is one of the most taxing.

"Don't you sometimes think the Civil War was overrated?"

"*Civil* War? What war was that?" Oh shit, I've gone and insulted his war.

"I mean the War Between the States."

"Oh *that* war. And what did you say it was?"

"Never dated?"

"Damn right. I still figure if I write about it enough, I can change the score."

Why is he living up here and not down there? Because he

can't stand being around a bunch of losers, he says. "The new South hurts my eyes"—eyes trained on such an impossible vision are easily hurt. "You know, if your mother gets raped by the whole German Army and turns into a whore, it's a damn shame, but she's still a whore. And that's what I like about the South."

Ah, Southern honor. I know the real reason he's up here. He likes those little Northern boys. Improbable as it may seem, Ferris is homosexual, but he isn't licensed to practice in the South. His family would swoon with shame, and his picture would be removed from the Vanderbilt Hall of Fame, or wherever they keep it. The Hamptons are such a perfect sanctuary for deviants that you feel you're missing a trick in not being one. As the Wild Turkey blankets my brain in fur, I contemplate laying in some whips myself.

"Even if I did play softball, I wouldn't play it with that gang at Jimmy's."

"What's wrong with them?"

"They're too rough," says this giant of a man. "No. It's because they think they're writers, and I find that em*barr*assing." He lingers softly over the word.

"Can't you just ignore it?"

"Uh uh. It's like someone pretending to be a priest or a war hero or something. You've got to call him on it."

Actually, on his rare visits to Jimmy's, Ferris is perfectly courteous, although I guess he thinks he's showing disdain. Southern politeness has too many layers for Northerners, who can barely manage one. But I know what Ferris means. He is the kind of writer for whom there can only be one kind of writer—himself.

"All those boys out there, sucking up e*xperi*ence like weevils. I bet you five of them are writing little novels about Jimmy's right now." I blush prettily. "You think anything glorious ever happened in Jimmy's? Anything big enough for a writer?"

"Everyone can't write about battles."

"They can try. How's your drink?" This is not a question, because he's already refilling it. I'm sorry for the poor author whose manuscript I've promised to read tonight.

"No, it doesn't have to be battles, but it has to be *something*. A book is a work of the spirit, man, not the day's crud from the vacuum cleaner. Experience! All most experience does is tarnish your vision."

Ay ay, suh. That's right, suh. His is a military homosexuality. One pictures him buggering his aide-de-camp before charging on Gettysburg. By God, he is a handsome devil at that. Very clean and soldierly. I picture the lucky little aide-de-camp charging ferociously too, ennobled by the general's seed. And then perhaps at San Juan Hill, passing on the same gift to *his* aide-de-camp. And so the Army goes on.

"Hey, easy Ferris. What are you trying to do, kill me?" My glass is brimming over. "I have to drive home through the ice and snow."

"Sleep over. I haven't got company."

"Freddy deserted you for the weekend?"

"For life. He's getting married. They all do."

"Why don't you settle down with some nice steady fag?"

"I can't stand fags."

The old soldier sits in sorrowing profile with the standing lamp casting shadows on him. No accident, I assume. His whole house is a stage set intact from *Gone With the Wind*. He even has a harpsichord in the corner. So far as I know, he has never served in any army, but he has willed himself into the part more authentically than any general I have ever seen.

He is indeed an artist in a sense that the others out here are not. Don't let that stuff about the human spirit throw you. I know it sounds like a lot of Southern gush and mush, signifying nothing but laziness, but Ferris means something different by it. His work is scrupulously restrained and manly. There are no tears at his gravesides, only a muttered "goddamn"; there are no fiery exhortations, only a "let's go get 'em, boys." Tarnishing his vision, in a pig's eye—he has used his own experience to the hilt. His Civil War sounds suspiciously like an Ole Miss–Alabama football game, and all the better for it.

My tongue follows my wandering mind. "Ever play football?"

"I wouldn't lie to you, Jon."

"You mean you did?"

"I only said I wouldn't lie to you."

The booze is making Ferris skittish too. I think I'll stay over and see if he really writes those chapters in this condition or if he passes out like a gentleman. . . . Oh no, I won't. He is reaching for the bottle again—a half-gallon jug that he calls his Carolina hip flask: "you know, if you don't have time for a *real* visit."

I stand up smartly. "You goin', old buddy? A Northerner can't drive on all that bourbon."

"You underrated us once before, as I recall, Beauregard."

"The hell you say." He puts his arm around me fondly and looks lovingly into my eyes. Perfectly normal, but I'm jumpy today. He's not going to tell me he has a block, and that he needs an affair with lots of masculine dialogue, is he?

The funny thing is, I could almost do it. Just as I can't quite sleep with my authors, I half want to sleep with all of them, if it would help. I would certainly hate to lose a masterpiece out of squeamishness.

Ferris releases me. Perhaps he finds my chest too hairy. "Time to get to work. Can't you smell the old magnolia blossoms already?"

"*Make* me smell them, big fellow."

He belts my back and sends it flying. As I right myself and wobble into my galoshes, he says, "Keep 'em hanging, Jon." He sees me out into the snow and stands politely by as it drifts onto his blond hair. He doesn't go back inside until he's sure I've started the car and negotiated the tricky uphill drive. Only then does he return to his magnolias.

4

I SEE I haven't mentioned my last name. What do you think? Spitz, Katz, Murphy? Wrong on all counts. It's Oglethorpe. Scottish Presbyterian, baby, descended from one of Cromwell's jackals who must have strayed over the border on a foggy night and decided the bleakness suited him. Which means with one stroke of the pen that I'm saved and you're damned. Which I believe sets up a nice relationship between writer and reader—not to mention reviewer.

Presbyterianism does give one a certain perspective on life. For my family in upstate New York, it had long since ceased being a religion, but lived on as a useful attitude. It was, bear in mind, a sect precisely tailored to the rise of capitalism and we, its children, are still designed like missiles to shoot upwards. Success is absolutely guaranteed, if you follow the directions, but at a price. Parts of us have been left out in the interests of streamlining. Having fun, for instance, is difficult. It isn't just things like drinking and dancing on Sundays—my daddy could do both at the same time, when he wasn't cornering steel—but the need for *purpose*. When you get drunk, there should be a deal in it. When you dance, there should be a lay in it. And when you fuck . . .

There, I suppose, we should find a resting place, an end in itself. Yet I don't know. Here I am, or just was, humping Mavis Pettit and trying to get her to come to the country. And if I get her there, I'll be thinking of something else. I may not even know what it is, but it'll be there, the purpose lobe will be humming. Churning over love, marriage, self-improvement—some payoff that hasn't revealed itself yet.

It's an unattractive habit but you get used to it. Just as you get used to the contempt for others that goes with it. Contempt particularly for people who waste time, who get drunk with nothing to show for it, who fuck their vital spirit away aimlessly (vital spirit is very big with us); contempt obviously for my authors, each to his own kind, and their ridiculous weaknesses. Although I'm as motherly with them as the next editor, my inner eye is as cold as Cotton Mather's, and their inner eyes know it. Awkward, but it gets results so my God is happy. Of course, I don't spare myself, that would not be cricket: *every* life is a waste, and it ends in Hell. That is one article of faith that I've never been able to shake. Obviously no one is *chosen;* one look at the human race is enough to tell you that. But *damnation* would suit the facts very well. So Hell it is: you may get to choose the location, whether a Hilton or your own place, but that's about it.

"What do you say, Mavis? It's lovely out there in the winter. Very Russian."

"I wouldn't like Russia."

"Well, it's really more like Scotland."

"How about the Riviera?"

"Oh yes, that too."

Mavis is a publicity girl hoping to become an editor, which calls for sacrifices. "Will this trip advance my career?" she says.

"I doubt it. Unless you say something a lot more brilliant than you've said so far."

She pushes my chest up in mock irritation. Mavis belongs to the "treat 'em mean and make 'em keen" school which suits me admirably. I call her birdbrain and tell her that her gorgeous ass has gotten her about as far as it will go—pretty sickening dialogue to an outsider, but then I suspect most real love scenes are, one way or another. Thank God so few of them get written.

"What were you thinking about just now?" she says. "You look so ugly when you're thinking."

"Thanks. Presbyterianism."

"Oh." After what I take to be stunned silence, she says, "I suppose that explains it."

Actually I don't think about it very often. If I did, I wouldn't spend my weekends in the Hamptons. I know it's where the writers are, but cultivating them is an expensive hobby, and I'd make more money and girls in the city. In fact, I go out there partly to fight the demon of purpose. I go out there knowing it's a waste, watching the fish boats come in, and the grass grow, and the houses decay. This is getting you nowhere, I think, triumphantly. Because if there is no purpose, Hell may be a little easier. As I say, getting a Scotsman to drink is child's play, but getting him to waste his time—mastery!

Still, I do want that Spinks manuscript, and that ain't no fish boat.

"You promise I won't freeze to death?" says Mavis.

"That's not what you'll do to death, honey." I have assumed my most persuasive position and am gliding gently. Mavis loves this kind of thing, and will agree to anything, so long as I don't stop. This, of course, gives me a purpose. Damn it to Hell.

February, and still no word on Spinks. I am stalling on van Dyne. Woodruff is still looking for love. Fender is ignoring the twentieth century. Everything seems to be frozen. We need an Event. Meanwhile Archie Munson continues to seek salvation through softball and, is it my imagination? the character of the game seems to alter slightly even before it has begun. Archie talks of importing a sportswriter friend who tried out once with the White Sox.

"Local people only," says Billy.

"Oh absolutely. Bing would be my house guest all summer."

"Yeah, but not out of love. Suppose he sprains a finger and you're stuck with him?"

"I can always find another friend. Look, Billy, I know we've outlawed excellence and I'm for that one hundred percent. But just supposing we find ourselves miraculously winning a game, what steps do we take to prevent it?"

"You can put *me* in," says Mavis, laboring under three sweaters and a head cold. We are having a dreadful weekend.

"Mave played Frisbee for Vassar, didn't you, dear?"

"Almost. Actually, it was mah-jongg for Brandeis."

They look at her blankly. Our strange little foreign legion outpost does not adapt quickly to strangers in the winter. On the summer assembly line it is different. But in winter, the boys grow inward, whatever is eating them burrows deeper.

Why are they here at all? Why is a bum on skid row? These are, of course, not precisely bums, but they have one or two of the secondary characteristics. To a man, they hate social obligations. Unreliability has achieved almost the status of a custom out here. Spinks is the worst on dinner invitations, once failing to turn up for his own birthday party, but they're all pretty bad. Archie invited me to his place for Superbowl Sunday and I found it locked up tight. It turned out Archie was watching it at Simmons's place, because Sim had some malt scotch, and he had forgotten to tell me.

When something like this happens, apologies are perfunctory or nonexistent. What did you expect? An apology would imply an obligation, and we don't do those. To show how Zeitgeist works, I have become unreliable myself, which isn't easy for an Oglethorpe. But it's either that or live in a screaming fury.

A bar is the ideal setting for these gregarious solitaries. There are no obligations in a bar. For instance, Fred Wilkins walked out in the middle of a drink two months ago and hasn't been seen since. Someday soon, if we know our Fred, he'll walk back in as if nothing has happened, and no one will ask questions. I'll introduce him to you, if he shows up in time. He's a married man with two children and a tile business, but nobody's worried about him, at least at Jimmy's. In fact, I fancy him in right field next summer.

Mavis doesn't know, between sniffles, why she's here at all. She wanted to meet writers, but this is ridiculous. She had deluded herself, poor ninny, that Spinks has a certain raw talent; and of course, like everyone who's chanced to sight him, she thinks Billy van Dyne is the most underrated writer in America. Yet here they are talking softball, and not transcending it as great men should but, if anything, sinking below it. Shut your eyes and they could be Veterans of Foreign Wars. She does not understand that baseball must be talked about this way: it is why artists seek it out so greedily. Mavis will never get anywhere.

Billy has decided, in the safety of winter, that he is pretty good after all, and he wants to play third base. Waldo says no, he has been playing third base in his head for a month now and can't change his ways. Archie says, that's funny, he thought *he* was playing third base. I look at Mavis desperately. Can anything be salvaged? "Why don't you *all* play third base?" she says bitterly. "That's ridiculous," snorts Pete Simmons in a sudden squall of disgust. Pete has not spoken before; he only fastens on to one or two ideas a night. "That's simply ridiculous."

I realize that Pete, our man in plate glass, is more possessive of the group than anyone, and is behaving like some advance animal frightening off strangers. Mavis as a good liberal is not used to naked hostility. If this were fiction, she would redden and bite her lip, but everyone knows people don't really do that. The nation's lips would look like hamburger by now. What she does is just sit there. I must take her home at once and build a fire.

"I don't see what's wrong with three third basemen, or two second basemen, or one first baseman, we must be going," I say in one breath.

"Don't go," says Billy. He hates people to go, any people. He won't let you leave his house before hearing just one more record. And he won't leave your house at all until you have to kind of bump him across the room and over the porch. And even then he'll roll down the car window for a last word. It's not that he necessarily likes you, it's just that he fears abandonment as the last train pulls out. He would ask Count Dracula to stay another five minutes.

In this case he has ordered me another scotch even as I make my preliminary moves. Drinking bar scotch is the next thing to joining AA, so I'm not worried about that. But how do we get through the next few minutes?

"Who's that?" says Mavis.

"Who?"

"That. Over there. That blonde woman."

I have taken off my glasses for reasons of glamour and I see only the menacing haze that Sam Spade sees after a knockout drop. "That *woman*, she keeps staring at us." All very sinister in my condition. Back safely in my horn-rims, I identify Cecily Woodruff at the bar. Mavis brightens—a real writer at last. No more softball, ever again.

In fiction I would groan. But I just sit there. In real life people don't do *anything* much, except tip over chairs occasionally. Cecily is walking carefully toward us. She belongs to that healthy division of people who never come in here without a snootful, so I know she's bagged. This winter is getting more desperate than I realized.

"May I join you?" she says. The writers and such periodically occupy a huge table in a corner of Jimmy's, which can be expanded indefinitely to fit more writers and such. It is a kind of tasteless parody, as we all are, of the Algonquin Round Table.

Cecily sits down even more carefully, as if she expected someone to yank out her chair. I await the opening of her mouth with frozen horror. "Cecily, I'd like you to meet . . ." She is paying no attention, but is looking around the table voraciously, as if this were a singles bar and she were cruising it. Spinks she obviously dismisses. Spinks's house guest I haven't mentioned. He is Jerry Tauber, Waldo's sainted editor, and he looks too dispirited for whatever Cecily has in mind (for that I picture something involving a Nautilus machine and several weightlifters). Jerry always looks dispirited, so it tells me nothing about Waldo's book, only that Jerry also comes from a tradition that hates wasting time. Archie Munson? Too nice for Cecily, too much Absorbine Junior and Sloan's liniment. A sportswriter's idea of romance is the opposite of a woman's. I cannot imagine a great lover in the press box.

She is moving her head almost as slowly as this account of it, as if no one was staring back. It would be embarrassing anywhere else, but here it seems normal enough. Pete Simmons?

Her gaze grinds to a brief halt. Pete is tough, swarthy, super-ficially confident. Above all, he is not a writer. Unfortunately he has a girl along, but this would not bother Cecily tonight. Pete's girl is a mouse, whose name you won't ever catch: Cecily would cheerfully beat the shit out of her. On the other hand, maybe Pete cannot be worked into a Park Avenue Gothic? Well, Cecily's face is not *that* legible. I can't read every little word.

She cranks up again, passes Nikki van Dyne, who is talking to Pete's mouse, and lands on Billy. Moves on briefly like a typewriter that runs off the page, and jerks back again. There's nobody left except me, and she's not going to try that again.

So back to Billy. Let me try to conjecture from what I know of her work what she sees in him. I know she can't use his dialogue—in fact he doesn't belong in her books at all. He is an ardent, rawboned kind of guy who'd break every vase on Park Avenue, if you let him loose in that area. On the other hand his talent is delicate, he does women surprisingly well—especially surprising to his wife, I suspect—and he shares Cecily's passion for fiction as such.

In the impoverished dating service we run around here, it might have to do. I know why Cecily's eyes ran off the edge just now. She was looking for Cormac Burke, our one indisputable talent out here and a man of higher quality than we're used to. But Cormac is in the North of Ireland, reporting on the Troubles and no doubt adding to them.

Having an affair out here is like having one on a lifeboat. As noted, there are very few partners to choose from, and also it is hard not to be noticed. What is Cecily to do now, for instance? She can't just go off with Billy. She can flirt with him just enough to annoy Nikki and get them both to leave early. Or, if she gets lucky, she might drive Nikki into flirting with someone else, thus blowing everything apart. She looks crazy enough to do it all tonight.

But first, conversation. "You don't by any chance play soft-ball, do you Cecily?" says Billy, who knows where her eyes have stopped as well as anybody.

"Well as a matter of fact, I'm very—yes." She decides not to go home for her mitt. "Yes, I play and I heard this was the recruiting office."

"Yes, ma'am, at your service. What position would madam prefer to play?"

"Well, they say I'm darling at second base."

Tom Jones, courting over a chicken bone, was more dignified than this. I wish I could help. After all, these are my authors.

Failing that, I resort to my former plan of cutting my losses and yanking Mavis home by the hair, there to render her helpless with rum punch. But this time, *she* orders a drink. It seems Cecily interests her. I guess I can see why. Cecily is big league, like Cormac and Fender. It doesn't show on paper, but her conversation is twice as interesting as the next person's, and would be even if she and the next person reversed lines. Thus she does transcend softball, without once breaking the convention that conversation about it be kept banal.

The flirting is already thick enough to force Nikki to leave, if she's going to. She stays. She looks at me, looks at Waldo. Forget the others. She has made her elimination roughly a hundred times faster than Cecily. That's how it goes with club-soda drinkers. But which of us has she chosen? I feel the lifeboat tipping. She is not so hot that she can't wait. Club soda again. I have a girl tonight, so she talks to Waldo. Since he is by himself, she could go home with him right now, but we don't do that sort of thing. Too many people watching. We are not bohemians, like the artists. Which is the reason most of us send out for visiting firemen like Mavis.

Talking of which—by God, she wants to *sing*. Her last drink was a stinger, a drink that probably turns up under another name in *Paradise Lost* and Dante's *Inferno*, and now, with that honking sniffle, she wants to sing. It is her little offering to the literati of the Hamptons. In fact she already *is* singing, but nobody is paying attention. Good. Perhaps she will stop in a moment. But no, she is looking at me expectantly, nodding, smiling. It's her first friendly sign in hours. If I want to salvage anything from this evening, I'll join in.

"Going to the chapel and I'm . . . urm . . . going to get ma-a-arried" is a lot to ask.

"I don't know that one."

"It doesn't matter"—she skips a beat—"chapel, and I'm, urm . . ."

Peter's mouse picks it up gratefully, and then to my surprise Cecily does too, in a rich contralto that almost transforms it to opera, and then Billy, who has no shame. I smile weakly and mouth along. Mavis's eyes are glistening now. At least I am doing this for a purpose.

The singing goes on relentlessly, and after a while Cecily takes over, because she knows the words to everything and Billy goes "bum bum bum," panting along like a puppy dog. And as Cecily leads us back to the thirties, Waldo joins in heavily, singing everything in waltz time as far as I can make out. As for Archie, he keeps trying to do "Blue Moon," although he only knows the two words, and although Cecily has sung it twice already. My only consolation is that Jerry Tauber, incredibly, is mouthing the words too to please *his* author.

Mavis orders another stinger, and I almost smash it from her hand. I don't want her drunk and silly. But that's how I am going to get her, if I'm going to get her at all. She looks at me woozily. "Aren't we having a good time?"

Well, no, as a matter of fact. Although I am still smiling and mouthing and explaining to Waldo that "Tea for Two" is not really by Cole Porter, my heart is like ice. It isn't just that I love music too much, although I do. ("How about 'Blue Moon'?" says Archie. "Have we done that one yet?")

It's just that my self-loathing is kicking up a bit. I cannot do what these people are doing, I cannot enjoy myself like that. Here my Calvinist deformity cuts me off like a leper. How did *we* of all people think we were saved? Since we were never taught joy, what could our Heaven consist of?

"Pardon me, boy," says Waldo.

"Choo-choo," says Cecily, for atmosphere.

"Is this the Chattanooga choo-choo?"

"Choo-choo," says Cecily.

I am in Hell.

5

THERE'S little more to be said about Mavis. When she called me a killjoy and lugged her blankets over to the couch, I welcomed it. I really did not want my facsimile joy to fool anybody. And I prefer to pick up my judging and sentencing as I go, rather than all at the end. She began snoring immediately, another piece of lowlife I couldn't share. I felt she was doing it to prove a point.

Sunday morning she crept into my bed and apologized for probably making an ass of herself.

"You did? I must have been too drunk to notice."

"What happened after that woman came in?"

"We sang."

"We did?" No one is that forgetful. "Was I awful?"

"Not by Jimmy's standards. Look, everyone gets drunk at Jimmy's. It's the done thing, like being sick in a hospital or dead in a graveyard. It's certainly no disgrace."

Unfortunately, thinking I'm damned sometimes seems to be the form my drunkenness takes. Either way, Jimmy's suddenly seemed like the fiery place, and I didn't want to go there again for a while. The characters in my novel would just have to wait until I felt better. Billy and Cecily, Nikki and whoever, and above all that goddamned softball game . . . even if their plots move on, even if Billy and Cecily sign a suicide pact and Nikki and Waldo stage an underwater wedding, tough apples. I'm not going back in that place for at least a week.

Instead I shall concentrate on the simple pleasures of Upper
Bonac, the village where I actually live. This on a Sunday
means peering into antique-store windows and asking the price
of that stuffed duck over there. In the course of this, I run into
my other world, Ferris Fender, no doubt checking on Confederate fowling pieces for his next book.

"You look awful," says Ferris. "You bin hanging around with
them writers again?" (He calls them "wrahters.")

"Something like that. So what are you doing in here, Bo?
You certainly don't need any more antiques."

"What do you mean, antiques? This is where I do my reg'lar
shopping. Is there some other store you go to for your stuff?"

I hoped he would invite us over for a cup of bourbon, just to
help me through the day with Mavis. The trouble is, the kid
lacks moral center. It was bad enough lying about her amnesia
last night—when she called me a dried-up joyless fart, at least
she had a point of view—but this morning she tried to make
love out of politeness, to pay for her weekend or keep her job or
something, and I felt as if I were unwrapping a house gift: not
too expensive, but good enough for Oglethorpe. It will go with
my *other* bottle of Taylor champagne.

Here we were performing the great regenerative act, what
the Bible so solemnly calls knowing each other, just to pay for a
weekend. Well I know I'm a one to talk about that, holding as I
do the indoor record for trivial intercourse, but at least it usually feels important at the time. She was just conscientious
throughout like a filing clerk. And at the end I wanted to say,
"Here's your change, miss."

Now on top of that, she goes and gets all worked up about
the countryside, exclaiming over icicles and barren landscapes
and stuff you're not supposed to exclaim about, just nod
thoughtfully (obviously Mavis isn't going to win one with me
this morning). For instance, she also carries on all wrong about
the old houses. "When was this built? It looks historical—you
know, as if things happened here once." "Nothing ever happened in any of these houses. People were born, and died, but
absolutely nothing happened," I snap. In fact, I love the
houses, love the town, but for just this gallant un-Oglethorpian

pointlessness. So much care in the design and building, worthy of a great destiny. But the new owners are mostly Summer People or absentee landlords or retired *Time* magazine executives; of the original impulse that built a village here, none remains.

This is the tragedy of backwater towns, the sense that the Holy Spirit has left them and moved on to Las Vegas, the image they convey of an old man looking for a bathroom in the dark. But try to explain it to this horizontally mobile nit from Fun City.

Anyway, that's why I was hoping Ferris would ask us over. If village curios are your thing, you couldn't do better than Ferris. And I could use him myself. An afternoon treading over the dead leaves at Vicksburg, counting the corpses with manly regret, repairing to Stonewall Jackson's tent to plan an even bigger defeat next time, would get my mind off the question of why I work so hard to attain girls I don't even want so that they can massage one membrane for me for a few golden minutes.

But Ferris moves off on his own mysterious occasions. He saw me last weekend, isn't that enough? Too much visiting can contaminate a man. He's bought himself an ormolu clock— where will he put it?—after which he will probably tramp through the woods, sucking on a hip flask to clear his vision. The man is self-reliant to the point of madness.

Meanwhile, there's Mavis. We return to my barn of a house, and I rustle up a batch of eggs Benedict, if that's how you say in your language. I am supposed to be reading an excruciatingly bad translation of a pretty good book on the new-new French philosophers (now that the old-new philosophers have been discredited) and I'm burning to take my blue pencil to it, as others thrust at the *Times* crossword. But tell me, what do you do with a Mavis? Those enthusiastic people have nothing to fall back on. Once they've stopped clapping their hands, that's it.

I am not, of course, being quite fair to Mavis: she said some things to me last night that she is miserably trying to make up for, while anything remains of her career at Williams and Oglethorpe. So she isn't even being her tart city self, but an amorphous nice guy from nowhere. What still puzzles me is my own behavior last night. Group singing is one of the afflictions endemic to bar-life; if I can't talk through it, I occasionally join in just to deaden the sound. But last night simply enraged me. Here was this Mavis making a fool of herself in front of *my* authors, my gang, and what's worse, she was making *them* do it too. I know it makes no sense, but it seemed crystalline at the time, and I told her so, quite brilliantly, I thought, when we got home, and she proceeded to dig her own grave with the company.

"You are the most unpleasant man I ever met" were her last words last night. "I mean, deep down." Quite right. The fact that I had just told her she belonged in the Half-Wits' Hall of Fame—"Our Mavis, always ready with a song"—hadn't, I suppose, helped. But you've got to say something when you're called a dehydrated turd.

Clearly, things would never be the same between us although her lousy job is safe enough. I have ruined the weekends of better women than Mavis, and worse ones too. Right now our joint task was to get through the afternoon somehow, and I must say she cooperated manfully. "I sort of promised my roommate I'd be back early," she said, "to let her mother in."

Good old Mom. "Sure, I understand. But it wasn't quite what I planned, honey: would you terribly mind taking the train?"

"Oh, not at all, I was counting on it." I got the feeling she would even cling to the outside of the train window, if necessary, to get away from here.

It is my pleasure, as editor in chief and junior partner, to drive into town on Monday mornings verging on Wednesday. For special girls, I'll waive the privilege, and drive them home Sunday, but Mavis is far from special. (If she seems in fact spectacularly unspecial, there is a reason: she is actually several girls, a group portrait of one, composed to save you from meeting any others for a while.) Particulars, none. Brown or blond hair, tall or short, younger and younger. Our weekends can flounder on any one of a hundred reefs, the fun is guessing which one. Sometimes the weekends actually succeed, just often enough to keep me going, and no more. I am kept on a tight ration by my Scottish gods.

All of which may help to explain why that very evening, after I had tucked Mavis into her train, I headed lickerty-lip for Jimmy's, just to see what was shaking.

6

WHAT was shaking was mostly Waldo. I'd seen him putting the gloomy Tauber on the train a few minutes ago and the latter had looked like a funeral director taking his leave. But that's Jerry for you. His writers depress him unspeakably, as well they might. If I had his list I'd drape myself in black crêpe. Besides that, nobody looks good on our train platform, which could be a deserted cow pasture.

Still a fellow can hope. And by the looks of Waldo, a fellow can start hoping right now. The big man is staring into space, swirling a large glassful of transparent liquid. An olive swims round and round faster and faster, and then the pool is empty. Waldo calls for another. When Waldo hits the martinis, something is afoot. Like most of our gang, he stays just this side of the alcoholic ward by dosing himself heavily with white wine. Is he mourning or celebrating? I join him at the writers' table, where he has beaten the rush by several hours.

"Jon, I want you to be our catcher next summer," he says, in the new softball language.

"Don't you like my umpiring?"

"It leaves a lot to be desired. But that's not my point. I just think publishers should be catchers, that's all."

"All publishers?"

"*All* publishers. Jenny, get Jonathan a drink here."

I order what he's having. It gets me closer to my authors.

"I can't see Jerry Tauber catching," I say artfully. "I can't see him on a ballfield at all."

"Well, that's true. But if you could, he'd be a catcher, right?"

This is the idiot I want to sign up? Well, yes, I'm afraid so. *Not since "Thirty-ninth Parallel" has Waldo Spinks written such . . . the raw power that brought you . . .* My pale but interesting list needs a jolt of such hokum. So I find myself pursuing the subject of catchers and publishing, the last thing I expected to find myself talking about when I got up this morning.

"As a matter of fact, I did some catching in school," I say. "Being somewhat slow of foot and short of sight, I had to reduce my game to a very small area. Within that area, I was dynamite." Don't get excited now, Jonathan. Jesus, it's only a game.

My nostrils are flaring suspiciously at the memory, but Waldo is not even listening. He obviously wants to talk about Tauber, but he can't find the right tone. Anything he says to me is partway into a business discussion, so he has to come on roaring when he comes. "What do you hear about the finances of Weber and Schnabel?" he says at last.

Well, I know the answer to that one. Tauber's employers are actually blue chip through and through, but this is not the time to stress that. "They could be shaky," I say. "I know they took a bath on the latest Snodgrass epic, and Schnabel's son Otto was a flaming disaster while he lasted there. The crazy kid bought up three religious imprints the year God died, and they had to liquidate all three and turn them into parking lots."

Good. I have given Waldo his story. "That's what I suspected," he says. It's not exactly a roaring position, but it's the best I can do for him. He looks away, the better to sound impersonal. "The son of a bitch can't meet my price."

"Yeah? It figures." Weber and Schnabel have just met a certain movie star's price of $2 million for her memoirs, so obviously they are hurting for money.

"Jerry loved the book, of course. In fact, he was really excited by it"—I picture Jerry's ghastly features lighting up briefly—"but he said his personal position in the firm was not strong enough for him to raise the dough."

The unscrupulous bastard. Jerry runs old Schnabel with such an iron hand that he even got him to fire his own son, after the religious fiasco. Weber is dead, poor man, but if he wasn't Jerry would run him too, with sheer brain megawatts.

"Well it's a matter of priorities, Wald. If you spend two big ones on some Hollywood chippy, there's not much left for the real writers." It's the turn of Waldo's nostrils to flare. "The question is, do you really want to be on the same list as a forty-inch bra and her ghost?"

I can build him up no further. In fact, my own list contains a forty-two-inch bra whom we got for half a million (and please do read *Husbands Ten, Lovers Nothing* when you get a chance), but this is just a game of words and shadows. I raise the gate and he races snorting round the ring.

"You've got a good goddamn point there, Jon. I've worried about that for some time. Weber and Schnabel is not exactly Tiffany's, is it?" I smile demurely. "You guys have a much classier imprint."

"It's the least you can say for us," I allow. End of first phase. Author buttered up, cavorting. Now for the tricky part.

"Of course," I add, "as you know, classiness comes at a price. Weber and Schnabel is a glorified pulp factory; Williams and Oglethorpe is more like a handicraft studio"—unfortunately—"in other words, small."

"I understand that."

"Which means, among other things, that we never have a hell of a lot of cash on hand. We can't compete with the big boys when it comes to flashy advances, so we have to beat them to death with quality."

This is difficult for him, too. It's always difficult to eat shit and smile at the same time.

"We prefer to spend our money on advertising and on the best-read sales force, which may not be saying much, in America. When we get a bestseller, it travels first class."

"I see."

"So if Jerry couldn't meet your price, well we. . . ."

What is the sound of four dots in real life? None of my authors can tell me. In this case, it includes a gurgle as Waldo swabs up his second martini, and the tick of a match against a box.

Finally, "Well it's a little soon to be talking money, don't you think, Jon? It may not be your kind of book, and you may not be my kind of editor. I don't know much about you, Jonathan. But you seem like a"—Waldo's face gropes, Prissy? Pedantic?—"literary kind of guy, and my stuff may seem a little crude to you."

This may be the first understatement Waldo has ever uttered. His stuff is gaggingly, retchingly crude. However, publishers have to eat. "I wouldn't last five minutes in this business, Waldo, if I was literary in that sense, the librarian sense." Quick run through here of Whitman, Miller, Thomas Wolfe, the whole belch bunch, you know the routine. "It would be my mission to enter your style, to live in it and think in it, until we produce the best, the most typical Waldo Spinks book to date."

Ten cents a dance, that's what they pay me. Come on, big boy—let me see your manuscript, huh? Ooh, it's so big.

"Why don't you let me read it just as a friend?"

He stares at me blankly. I can almost see an olive in each eye by now. Whatever we are, we are not friends. "I don't mean that you need my advice—God forbid I should be telling *you* of all people how to write novels—but just to see if I'm the guy who can make it the best Spinks yet. If I can, money should be no problem." I've waited a long time to catch this fish, and I'm really hauling away. "If the answer is no, it won't be a reflection on the book, but on me. Every editor has his limitations. I couldn't have done a thing for *Moby Dick*, for instance."

My own somewhat smaller fish tugs sluggishly on the line. "I'll have to talk to my agent. I don't know if she'd approve of this arrangement."

"Your agent is Mildred Struthers, right? I'll call her in Stonington right now. I've got her number on me."

Impressive, what? Actually, I know Mildred a hell of a lot better than he does. In fact, I even know what she thinks of him. She may be his agent, but she is my ally. "What's the rush, Jon?" he says cunningly. "You need a book in a hurry?"

"Doesn't everybody?" Those torpid eyes had fooled me. I

should have remembered his poker game, which is based on the famous Cobra Mongoose Method. "I thought *you* might want a quick reading," I say lightly, "so you can get on with your business. Otherwise, I may be gone for a couple of weeks."

Something has happened. I feel it. Waldo has changed. It's like a shift in atmospheric pressure. "Maybe I could drop it off at your place tonight," he says quickly. "What have I got to lose?"

I turn round to look at the bar, which is where the new weather seems to be coming from, and there is Nikki van Dyne, standing by herself. Their plot *has* moved on already. My scenario tells me that Waldo didn't come in here to cry over his book at all, but to meet Nikki before the gang arrived. Or so it suits my purposes to believe.

"Hi, Jon, Waldo." Nikki comes on over, lugging her soda water. There is nothing furtive about her. "Billy is working, and I was going stir-crazy."

"Working? Gee, I wish you hadn't mentioned that word. It reminds me of what I should be doing."

"Don't go." She gives me a warm smile. "I'd be insulted."

"Right," says Waldo heartily. "And I don't want Billy catching me alone with his wife."

Sex has been tossed in casually, and we all smile at its presence. Nikki says, "Let's all be alone together," and she seems to mean it, though I don't know how she expects to work it. It will be like scrimmaging with the Dallas Cowboys. I guess I should have left anyway—seducing Waldo's book has been quite enough of that for one evening—but I'm still recovering from Mavis, my pride is limping, and almost anyone who wants me can have me tonight.

Especially Nikki here. She is what? Thirty-two? Which is attractive in itself after Mavis. It means she has pre–Bruce Springsteen references and a vocabulary of at least three hundred words. She also looks as if she may have some secret joke which is sustaining her: possibly her own intelligence. Otherwise she is beautiful in a no-nonsense sexual way. That is to say her beauty is all for use, not decoration. And going to bed with a grownup seems irresistible.

But we can't go on like this. Why doesn't *Waldo* leave? Doesn't he need a publisher more than I need an author? We shall see.

It seems that our needs are precisely the same, no more, no less, because we're both polite to each other, and neither of us leaves. And of course, we've both had two martinis, which can slow these things to a real crawl. A flirtation à trois has a lovely civilized feel to it. She looks into my eyes tenderly, and then into Waldo's, like a softhearted optician. I touch her hand lightly and by God, Waldo touches the other one. To round things off, I beam at Waldo and he beams back at me. What kind of fruitcakes has Nikki stumbled upon? For now, she enters into the spirit of things, but I know she came in looking for a man and will not put up with this foolishness indefinitely.

I, on the other hand, came in looking for a book. Must keep that thought uppermost. I surge to my feet once more, and they both say "don't go" again and I collapse in my chair. Well, my overcoat is heavy. And there's been another change. There's a blast of cold air through the front door and in walks Billy. Groucho dives for the closet.

Would Billy care to join our game? Or will he yank Nikki out by the feet? None of the above. "Hi folks," he says, and plumps down wearily. "Why didn't they tell me writing is almost as bad as work? So how did it go with Tauber, Waldo?"

This is a bit direct for our set. "My people are talking to their people," says Waldo. "Tauber says that if we let him play third base, I can name my own terms."

"Not fucking third base again. The whole team is playing third base by now."

"Well, it's different, anyway. We'll call ourselves The Hampton Hot Corners." They retreat into softball, and I decide to step outside the conversation for a moment. Billy's presence indicates that Nikki is not up for grabs tonight. At the same time, I can see that this fatuous male-bonding is getting on her nerves. Billy is incurably boyish, which can be downright repulsive to women and may be destroying his marriage. But here is Waldo outchildishing Billy.

All anyone has to do to win Nikki is to *stop talking softball*.

Can't they see that? My two novelists here, my interpreters of the human heart—do I have to teach them everything? I look at Nikki and her lowered eyes burn a hole in my coat. Look, Oglethorpe, you want Waldo's book, you want Billy to be happy—his career seems as uncomprehendingly tragic as any I know—but I just can't help myself. I start talking seriously to Nikki. The prize is mine, when can I collect it? I ask casually if she ever comes into the city. Dentists, gynecologists, things like that. They're much better in New York. So are the yoga classes for that matter. I look at the guys to see if they're getting mad: a fellow is not supposed to pull out of the club like this. If male facetiousness is the order of the day, everyone's supposed to join in.

One signal from them and I'll give up Nikki for the evening. But I don't get one. They are both discussing not softball, but the local Democratic candidate for Bay Constable, which is worse than softball, and don't even notice me and Nikki.

As I say, I can't help it, it's my nature. Taking candy from a baby, taking women from an author. I have some scores to settle. Perhaps Nikki has too. At any rate, we flirt with a vengeance.

7

BEFORE I leave that evening, with a possible lunch date in my hot little paw, Waldo whips out a fat manila envelope that he has inexplicably brought along with him.

"Here it *is,*" he whispers, as if it were a hot shipment of cocaine. Did Tauber hand it back to him at the station? Is that why he has it? I remember no such transaction over the gleaming snow.

No, he had brought it here just for me. Further, my scenario advises me, he has let me have Nikki without a contest, as part of the deal. You can always find another woman.

On impulse I decide to drive back to New York that very night, even at the risk of getting to work on time. It's still early, but the team of Mavis and Waldo has unstrung me and right now I want a big city to hide in.

You wonder why I resent writers, eh? I should like to pause here and insert into the record a story I wrote in my twenties, which characteristically was not published. Among other things, it helps to explain why I chose to give the name Waldo to my character in *this* book.

THE FINGERS OF A PUBLISHER

At the dinner in his honor, Waldo Chesney made a mess of himself, as usual. Watching Waldo eat was the worst part of Arthur's job—stand-

ing by for the dismal procession down the shirt front and the licking
of rubbery lips. Arthur did not lick, but bit his own lip at the far end
of the long table: it was simple agony for him—and would continue to
be, even when the last stick of celery had fallen silent. Waldo was like
an open wound.

After defacing a particularly endless dinner, Waldo Chesney, gent,
rose a few inches to speak: "The trouble with literary dinners," he
started out. Arthur groaned. "The salmon, stale . . . the wine, disas-
trous." Everyone tittered, at Waldo's wicked wit; no one but Arthur
knew that it wasn't the least bit wit, but a quite serious account of his
dinner. Nothing entered Waldo's stomach by inadvertence; he would
discuss each mouthful far into the night. (It wasn't wit, was it? Arthur
asked himself anxiously.)

The candles in front of Waldo sweated down slowly, and the great
man rumbled on in a self-absorbed trance, but the moment of general
impatience never came. Arthur strained for the whisper of a yawn.
But nobody, from the glowing librarians on the fringe to the distinguished Englishman on Waldo's right was even fractionally bored.

Arthur's eyes hurt, and he swung them gently inward: a more sensitive and appropriate soul awaited him. Thin, as a matter of principle, grave, ethereal, fiery but pure: a melancholy list, all the wrong
things as it turned out. Waldo had none of them, and there he was at
the head of the table. Still, it was better to be sensitive, so Arthur
supposed. Better than nothing.

He would most likely never have met Waldo at all, if it hadn't been
for a tawdry device called Cynthia Withers. The two men orbited
separately from their first days at the University, Arthur around Art,
Waldo around the dining room table—no, that wasn't quite fair, he
thought: Waldo also liked money, fox-hunting and Society. He came
to Freshman classes in a pink hunting coat, and would doubtless have
remained a distant figure of fun forever if it hadn't been for Cynthia,
and then, the other one, whatshername.

Cynthia wrote poetry in tight pants (Cynthia, not the poetry) and
dirty fingernails, which seemed quite poignant now, at this spruce
gathering. Together she and Arthur used to sit on the library steps
and, oh, sneer at the Average Student, and slowly this blossomed into
earnest affection. Cynthia was just beginning to turn yellow in the
Faversham yearbook. "Cynthia of the earthy lyrics and the conspic-

uous integrity," it said underneath. That sort of girl. But he couldn't really make a joke of Cynthia now. The women who scuffled for Waldo these days had left her some way behind: but it started with Cynthia.

At first Arthur used to smirk no end under his compulsory beanie at the way she railed against Waldo from their perch on the steps. He was a fat, pompous, oafishly prosperous fellow, more like a cartoon from *Krokodil* than a Faversham man. Arthur had never dreamed back in Youngstown that such stereotypes really existed. And, ironically, it was Cynthia who helped him to see the fun of it.

All the same, as the stones got colder with the coming winter, he became tired of Waldo. He became tired of the Average Student. He wanted to talk about his work.

"What are you working on these days?" he asked her, as prelude to winter.

"Oh the same thing, *you* know, the cantos. Look, here he comes."

He began to wonder whether her aesthetic was not rather negative, compared with his own. He sort of hoped it was, in a way.

But it was getting to be a nuisance about Waldo. "Look, he's silly, I know he's silly." "Yes, isn't he?" "But he's not *that* silly." "I think he is." He began nagging her about it, and she turned her integrity on him all of a sudden and told him to go away. He didn't, of course: he just squatted down next to her tight pants and fretted. Freshman winter came in and everyone went indoors, and suddenly she stopped making fun of Waldo.

It took Arthur a few weeks to get onto the reason. She had met Waldo somehow and was going out with him on the sly.

Around Christmastime, Arthur spied them together for the first time in the Faversham taproom, and was shocked frozen. He glared at them, he supposed. Cynthia smiled. Waldo paid no attention. Life went on.

The wise thing, he knew, was to abandon both of them then and there, and hurl himself into his work, with new reserves of wistfulness. But it gnawed at his literary conscience. Waldo was the enemy, with his cloth cap, his red suspenders and his pig-bristle hair. Cynthia, negative aesthetic and all, stood for something publicly— sensibility, the examined life. By going around with Waldo she was blurring issues hopelessly.

He raged about this through the holidays, aggravating himself with the hope that it was all a mistake. Perhaps she was just gathering copy for something. She had been certainly writing more lately for the *Faversham Funster*, as well as *Preview III*, and becoming a kind of literary lioness to boot. People said that her poems were perceptive; and they said that her images were fresh and her insights pregnant. She was elected to meet Mary Tubshaw, the English novelist. All this could hardly co-exist with a deep interest in Waldo.

Come January, and Arthur went back to seeing Cynthia on Tuesdays, and Saturdays; but he trembled to ask her about Waldo and postponed it indefinitely. It was like a bad dream. In real life, Chesney was probably watching stag-movies at the fraternity house all winter long. Spring, and they were out on the steps again, pale and scruffy from hibernation; and Waldo was shooting again in his Spring outfit, and waving at Cynthia with little fat fingers.

"There goes your friend," said Arthur tentatively. "In his nice Spring coat."

"Yes," said Cynthia.

"He certainly wears funny clothes."

Cynthia shrugged—clothes were so utterly unimportant, weren't they?

Arthur was stung in the values. "You used to think he was pretty funny," he said.

"Yes, I did."

"Has he changed or something?"

She shook her head. Arthur's antennae groped through his turtle-neck sweater, but felt nothing. Cynthia was not coming through to him.

He made a final, despairing lunge. "He looks insensitive," he said.

"He isn't really," said Cynthia, not unkindly.

That was the end of Cynthia, but it wasn't the end of Waldo. Arthur soon found a new girl, Margot Squid, who wrote "prismatic sketches" (yearbook) for *Wunderbar* and *Preview III*. Cynthia's verse went into satisfying decline. Her perceptions coarsened delightfully—and Waldo bought himself a new sports car, to round out the first year at Faversham.

Meanwhile, Arthur was having some trouble with his own work. It lay in incoherent drifts across his floor, and halfway up the closet. He couldn't get it into shape, and when he finally sent a chunk of it over to *Preview III*, it came back with a bewildered note.

Margot could afford to be sympathetic. She was already going from strength to strength with her own rather slick stuff, and was, ran the talk, already being groomed to meet Mary Tubshaw on the English novelist's next go-round. Out of politeness, she asked Arthur for occasional opinions, and he was inclined to be waspish with them.

"Margot, look, it's a nice little story. There's nothing wrong with that, is there?"

"But can't you see what I'm trying to say with it? I'm trying to say that, for these two people, I mean for people like these two, love—"

"Yes, I saw that, it was right there on the first page. But really, Margot, love—"

It was a sour wrangle, right through sophomore autumn. He was getting pretty damn tired of girl-writers who aimed their superficialities at the English Department and scored with mechanical efficiency. It wasn't really writing at all. He felt he ought to tell Margot about this. And the next thing he knew, she had turned up in Waldo's sports car.

He began to think it might be a practical joke of some kind, and the next time he saw Waldo, he bounded down the steps to tax him about it.

From close up (he realized he had never seen him close up) Waldo proved to be disconcertingly featureless. There didn't seem to be any *approach* to him.

"I'm Arthur Spears," said Arthur.

"I never said you weren't," said Waldo, holding out his hand. It didn't feel as if it had any fingers at all. Arthur was curiously unmanned by this. After a minute of silence Waldo offered him a lift. Arthur scrambled vaguely into the M.G., hoping that once they were seated in profile, something would come to him.

They shot off and Waldo said, "Glorious day isn't it," and then, incredibly, with the wind scratching at their faces, "Are you interested in the market at all, Spears?" It was pointless to go on. Arthur selected a corner and asked to be excused. Did he look as if he was interested in the market? For God's sake. Waldo scooted away in a swirl of red scarf.

"What do you talk about with Chesney?" he stormed at Margot the next time he saw her. That was bad enough. He didn't want to say anything about the hands that felt like cold hot-water bottles.

"Oh, I don't know," she said. "We drive around in his car."

"Is that all you do?"

"Well we eat dinner sometimes. He buys wonderful dinners. And," she paused shyly, "we go beagling sometimes."

"He must be pretty rich," said Arthur. "Somehow I didn't think that you would care for that sort of thing. I mean, you're an artist."

She smiled. "Not much of one I thought. Anyway, there's more to him than that."

He was getting a sickly premonition about Margot. "What more to him? Fast cars and dinners and money, and what more besides that?"

Margot yawned, looking very much as Cynthia had looked the last time they talked about Waldo. He seemed to be missing the point again. "Maybe that's all," she said at last, with a small smile. "Just fast cars and dinners and money."

Arthur gave up on literary women for a while after that (it seemed to be the only way of getting rid of Waldo) and went back sadly to piling up manuscript.

Margot was no more serious about writing than Cynthia had been; he had at least been vouchsafed an insight into women writers. They were too easily deflected. Margot would soon loss her touch, thin out, give up; he would endure.

He glanced wretchedly over at Margot, who was this very evening sitting a few places down the table from Waldo. She hadn't thinned out at all—and neither (he gave a silent shriek) had Waldo. In the candlelight, one suddenly realized that Waldo had never had any bones at all. He was just a comic balloon. Funny that no one else had spotted it. Margot laughed and laughed until Arthur's head ached. Margot's mouth had gotten very big since the last time.

"Arthur's a writer," Margot had said the last, and only, time, he sat with them at the Faversham taproom.

"Oh yes," said Waldo. "He looks like a writer, doesn't he?"

Margot giggled. "What do you mean, he looks like a writer?"

"Well, his hair and his fingers," said Waldo vaguely. "Isn't that how you tell writers? What are you working on right now, Spears?"

"He's writing about his boyhood in Ohio," said Margot. "How he used to go down to the station and watch the trains come in—"

"Oh, Margot!" said Arthur. When she put it like that— .

"Well, I bet it's very interesting," said Waldo. "Writing down all your experiences." Margot was laughing cruelly, incomprehensibly. "But what are you going to work at seriously, Spears? I mean, for money."

"Write," Arthur croaked a bit self-consciously. "If I can. It seems to me the only thing worth doing. What's so funny about that, Margot?"

"Good luck to you," said Waldo. "You certainly look as if you'll make a fine writer." He paused. "It doesn't sound much like a profession, though, does it?"

Arthur began to quiver. "I know what you're going to say, Chesney. You're going to say you'd like to write yourself, if you had the time, because so many interesting things have happened to you. And you've always felt you had a flair—"

"Well, as a matter of fact—"

Arthur strode peevishly out of their lives, or so he hoped. At the door, he fancied he heard not one, but two, kinds of laughter. He whipped around: Margot seemed to be wiping beer off Waldo's sleeve. You might say he was laughing. Or you might not. It was hard to tell.

The next few years were spent by Arthur in the usual abrasive vigil: long, cold trips down five flights of stairs to peer into the mailbox and tug the manuscript out again; baked beans and canned peaches and slowly shredding pajamas; and finally modest recovery in a publishing house. Maybe someday he would whip the Ohio boyhood into shape and give it another whirl. It didn't seem so terribly urgent anymore. So many boyhoods were strewn across his desk.

And among them at last, Waldo's boyhood in Connecticut. Arthur jumped when he saw it, thwacking his knee against the desk. Waldo had finally written down his experiences. He tore at the wrapping with incredulous glee. It was an offbeat form of vengeance, sickly sweet in the mouth. What happened next was too dreadful to remember. The vengeance began to curdle almost immediately, turning to another, older flavor. The effort to sneer proved exhausting; by page twelve he was in genuine distress. No point in exhuming his then-thoughts now. He took the manuscript weakly upstairs, and Waldo was on his way.

And now as Waldo Chesney's editor he had to endure these dinners. Which Waldo insisted he attend, as his favorite editor. The people here who had met Waldo backwards, book-foremost, so to say, were already laughing and clapping. The flatulent speech was wheezing, bubbling, to a finish; and even Margot, who should have known better, seemed to be amused by it. Arthur tapped his fingers (the graceful fingers of a publisher) into his palm. Was his own sensitive boyhood a hoax of some kind? And the damned trains? He sighed at the impossible thought, stood up and shook himself gently.

Waldo was already on his way over, hacking bluntly through a covey of admirers. "Spears," he said loudly. Amazing how brutal a face without features could seem; there was still no approach to it, just a smooth slide of flesh. All that beagling hadn't done him a bit of good. "Have you been seeing any ballgames lately, Spears?"

There could be no doubt at all that Waldo was laughing.

What is so poignant about this story, if that isn't too strong a word, is that it has everything backward. *I* was meant to be Waldo Chesney.

Although I was not precisely a florid mountebank in a hunting coat, I could not convince myself I looked like a writer either. In the years (ten to twelve?) when such impressions are formed, I decided I looked like a corporation lawyer. And however artfully I raise and lower the sideburns and lay in fresh mustaches, that's still what I see.

The short story was clearly one last kick at fate. I didn't *have* to look like a writer, I tell you, in order to be one. Hah! The hell I didn't. Already publishing had its little piggy eye on me, and in a couple of years, its trotters as well.

When I succumbed to my own literary invisibility I wasn't even allowed to start out at the top of publishing, which is the least one can ask of such a profession, but had to do time cleaning up lesser men's messes, correcting their grammar and punctuation—and even this, not creatively, but according to some loathsome rule book.

Thus was forged a hatred of writers that survives all my fleeting crushes. Every now and then I would be allowed to hop off my high stool and meet one of these godlike yahoos in the vestibule and I would want to scream "illiterate baboon! fouler of the temple!" But they wouldn't let me. Instead, these strutting popinjays were supposed to be treated with deference, the worst possible thing for most of them.

Worse, it seemed that my own future was tied to the tail of one or more of these people. Just to get out of the cottonfields of editing, I had to acquire an author of my own. So, like an organ-grinder looking for monkeys, I went back to my Columbia yearbook; and found the original "narrator" of my short story, the loser of losers, who turned out to be twice the writer I was, and the progenitor of my career. "Arthur Spears" was my first star.

Imagine then the enraged tremors of my pudgy publisher's-hands as I rip off the brown paper around Waldo Spinks's novel and find it—well, what?

At first, I found it ridiculous. It was all about a place called Sammy's in Middle Hampton, Long Island, and he had gotten every single one of us wrong. His Ferris Fender, for instance, is a mincing Southern belle. His Billy van Dyne is impotent, which keeps him from literary greatness. And his Cecily Woodruff smokes cigars and is an accomplished thumb-wrestler. Whatever is most obvious about us, and whatever can possibly be misunderstood, is made our central characteristic. I mention this because the fellow playing me is a heartless predator who lives in a mansion—which is superficially true—and sucks up to writers in exact order of importance. There is not one word about my Presbyterian soul.

The Waldo figure, on the other hand, is a very complex chap indeed. Women are forever saying "I don't understand you. I wonder if anyone understands you?" and he throws them a half smile or, in extreme cases, a lopsided grin.

His agenda as the novel begins includes bringing Woodruff to womanhood (I imagine a crashing cadenza as she finally decides to give up cigars), lending heart to weaklings like Fender and van Dyne and—this is where his complexity comes in—humping Nikki van Dyne on the side. In a sense, he is doing this for Billy because she will certainly leave the poor fellow for dead if somebody doesn't cool her off at regular intervals. And who better than a disinterested friend with a devotion to literature?

"He needs you," murmurs Waldo from the next pillow. "Someday Jasper will write a book that will make it all worthwhile."

Trash? Of course. But I'm already at page 100 and turning fast. I want to see how the Billy figure makes out. Right now, it looks bad. In spite of Waldo's best efforts, our Bill is suicidally depressed. He stares at his typewriter. "You bitch," he snarls. "After all I've put into you, the love, the heart's blood—what have you given me?" He starts to fling it across the room, realizes he can't afford the repairs, grins ruefully. "OK, honey, we'll give you one more chance."

In fact, mass suttee seems a promising conclusion for the whole ensemble. Ferris Fender is riding high at the moment, but there is something hysterical about it. He, like everyone else in the book, is drinking heavily, and he is also dressing like Vivien Leigh more than is good for him. Waldo nurses him through these bouts as best he can. "You're a *man*, Percy. Never forget that." (The Southern author flutters his lashes helplessly. "I'll bet you say that to all the girls.") But inwardly, Waldo too is troubled. Why is he trying to save all these people anyway? His mind flashes back to a bird in a trap. Little Waldo, aged eight and already a hell of a man, is trying to extricate the bird, but the latter flaps her wings and frightens him off. He is the one thing that can save her, and she is preventing it with all her force. Isn't that just like life?

At last, in desperation, little Waldo lunges at the bird and pins both wings in a Herculean grip and yanks. With a sickening tear, the bird comes loose, leaving her foot in the trap. The wings go berserk, driving Waldo's hands away, and she hobbles in a frantic circle, looking for the foot (not for her galoshes as you might suppose). Waldo runs into the house and returns with his father's shotgun. Aiming sadly and carefully (at that range, you don't really have to aim at all), he blows the bird's head off. The wings flap twice more and are still. Waldo starts to become complex then and there.

Of course, one doesn't really become complex overnight, even if one is Waldo. He also throws in his old dependable, the Korean War, which leads me to think he may be getting scared, returning to the scene of his only critical success. Since this is the first sequence to snap my attention, I make a note to have him cut it, before I realize it's none of my business.

I haven't taken the damn book, and I don't want to take it. For one thing, it obliterates my own fictional efforts so far, since big authors drive off small ones in this particular jungle, and there certainly aren't two books in this stringy little cast. And for another, it's kind of lousy.

And yet, and yet. Here I am at page 220, and it's way past my bedtime. The retarded sonofabitch has something I don't have, they all do. All those posturing pigs have a secret. It doesn't show under a microscope, otherwise I'd have it myself. I know more about fiction than any of them, yet I can't keep you up past your bedtime, can I? Look at you, fast asleep already.

Oh Lord, why doesn't the pain go away? If I could repress Waldo's book, believe me I would. But somebody's going to publish it. And no one can do a better job than I can.

I'm a professional, which means that when the bell rings, I perform heart surgery on Adolf Hitler, and I defend Charlie Manson. It also means that I make a bid for Waldo.

What does that decision do to this thing here, my own little novel? Scrap it, I guess. What the hell, it was nothing. One last spasm of the old ambition, like Waldo's bird wings, stronger in death than a boy's hands, but not much future.

I surrender, Waldo. My terms are modest. I have already extracted pages 53 to 55, in which one Lucy Gelder is salaciously inventoried. Full-breasted, passionate, too much woman for her husband. *That's* what I'll take in exchange. And I'm having lunch with her next Thursday.

8

I HAVE another motive for wanting Nikki. It seems the character Waldo has based on me, a smoothie named Otis MacIntyre, strikes out a lot with women. He brings these sad little girls out from New York for weekends, there is never a bright moment, and they are never seen again. This is put down to his inadequacy, not theirs.

My man Otis's problem deep down is that his profession has made him superficially charming, just enough to sign up authors but not enough to form attachments he can't always get out of, like bad contracts. And this has affected his whole life. Thus that horny tigress, Lucy Gelder, waits for him to become more interesting, but nothing happens. Like some minor heavenly body, he shines but cannot come closer. His light is impressive (Waldo gives me that much) but unvarying, and finally boring. Cecily Woodruff is also terribly disappointed. She hoped Otis would make a woman of her, but he's only made an author. As for Ferris Fender, he is beside himself, because Otis shines impartially on men and women alike and, yes, Ferris has slept with him. After which, things are exactly the same between them. One cannot even turn off the light when it's over. I am equally charming after as before.

What is this perverse claptrap, and why has Waldo given it to me to publish? Is he trying to insult me? As the plot goes on, we find the malignant publisher gradually destroying all the writers on the island, like elm blight, while Waldo tries to keep them alive. Otis envies their talent and their beating hearts; he wants everyone as dead as he is. I don't have to take this.

"What made you think it was you?" I can already hear the real Waldo. They all say that. "Why, this guy has *nothing* in common with you. It's fiction, man."

As if *you* could write fiction, Waldo. The kicker is, of course, that if I can see myself in the villain, well that's really too bad. So I must, like all the characters in a roman à clef, strain *not* to see myself, to praise, if possible, the person based on me as a particular triumph of the imagination. It's only fair; I'm sure Waldo would do the same for me.

As you will see, I am still noodling along here. Because I do have in front of me the great equalizer, a novel of my own. Maybe I *won't* give it up—it makes *such* a darling weapon, if I can just pull it out of the stone. With it, I can turn the tables on Waldo, narrowing my vengeance to a fine point—if I only can learn the skill, the secret. Maybe I can get Waldo to write it out for me, in his porcine prose. At least, I can learn from him.

I have just finished his novel at dawn, and am slightly sick. It isn't easy coming off such a personal kick in the head. Not that any of it is new to me. I pride myself on my self-knowledge, and I have been telling myself these things for years: that I hate writers and have a cold heart. But it's all in fun when I only tell myself. In print, it takes on a horror that I can't shake.

I decide to call the office and cancel all my appointments. But good grief, if I cancel all my appointments, where will I be? Today of all days, I need company in maddened drafts. Need it but can't face it. Have you ever appeared in a novel?

Look, Waldo is a jerk, right? and his novel is trash. Talk of self-knowledge. His picture of himself is the joke of the century. He has never helped anybody. He is about as amorous as a walrus. And he takes no interest in other people, except to undermine Billy van Dyne and make jokes about Woodruff's sex. This novel, when published, will savagely wound more people than the fictional Waldo could save in a lifetime.

What a man. As for me, well goddammit I do love Cecily and

Ferris, and I do get books out of them, which is the only real way to keep writers alive. All writers are at the point of death, until a new book arrests it. But why am I even arguing with this numbskull of a book? and why am I trembling?

Because I have to call Waldo. He is too important to keep waiting. And since he is a friend, I have to call him and not just his agent.

It is only 8 a.m., and if I know my Waldo, he won't be up for hours. He has to sleep off his poker game. Bereft in my pajamas and dressing gown, I make some coffee to get my nerves really jumping. "Jolly good show, Waldo," I rehearse. "Capital effort." Oh to be English at such times.

The thing is, if I turn him down, it will be clear that I recognize myself in the book. The best possible cover is to publish it. But this is also the deepest possible humiliation: to assist in my own degradation. The publishing world will think me a good sport, but Waldo will consider me his victim, his bathtub toy.

And then there is my Fall list to consider, a porous document so far with plenty of room for Waldo. Jack Vines has just taken his novel back for repairs for the third straight season. He is gun-shy from his last exposure to the critics and he can't face the battlefield again. I should spend more time on the Cape, building up Jack.

What tawdry considerations. Yet you should see some of the other editors I know. Some more coffee, please. There's still one nerve in my elbow that hasn't started twitching.

I've got to do something. Which in New York means I have to phone someone. I carefully insert my shaky finger into the hole and jam it round and round. Hours later, I have done all ten digits. Nine rings, ten . . . a sleepy voice, "Wha' the fuck?" And then, "Get off my phone, you interfering bastard."

"Waldo? Did I wake you?"

Sounds of confusion, of a man trying to pull himself together. "Who's that? Jerry?"

"No, it's Jonathan."

"I meant Jonathan. How are you, Jonathan?"

"Listen, Waldo, I hate to call this early, but I just finished your book and I'm so excited by it I couldn't wait to tell you."

"You are?" "I think it's your best ever," etc. The deed is done. The rest of the conversation follows prehistoric guidelines. His vanity runs over like egg yolk. I mop it up cheerfully.

"What did you think of the editor character?" he says at last, the bully surfacing for the first time.

"Well, I thought you were a bit hard on him," I say jocosely. "Thank God none of us is really like that. At least I sincerely hope not. But kidding aside, Waldo, I think MacIntyre is a classic villain, almost Shakespearean. Please God, I never meet him." Thank God, please God. Nice God.

"You won't," says Waldo, flicking me lightly with his whip.

Mildred Struthers gets to her office early, like a good little agent, but when I call her at 8:45, Waldo has already talked to her.

"I think it's just terrific," she says. "I've always felt Waldo would be a great writer if he only had a great editor."

Come off it, Millie, I thought. Don't bull the bull. Waldo could be made a little bit better, but if you tried to make him great, he'd combust, and the whole effect would be ruined. "I really like the book, Millie. But I don't know how well I can sell it. Whoever does know?"

"He's got a great track record."

"He has, huh?" I knew his last book had not earned out its advance, and the question was meant to convey just a puff of this knowledge. We'd get down to the real grunt-and-groan later. "He told me Jerry Tauber couldn't meet his price."

Silence. Millie and I are friends, a very treacherous thing in this business. We've worked together too much for either of our authors' good. "Well, his price is not exactly fixed. I mean it's not engraved in stone. I'm sure he'd sacrifice at least a bit of it to go with you. You know how he admires you." Another pause. "The fact is, Jerry couldn't stand the book. For personal reasons."

"Oh? And what were they?"

"You know the horrible editor whatshisname? He thought it was based on him."

I have to laugh lightly at that one. Until the tears run down my pajamas, in fact.

"In the other version, the guy had a Jewish name and Jerry thought the whole thing was anti-Semitic. Are you all right?"

No, I'm not. I'm delirious. I have just agreed to publish my first anti-Presbyterian book. "Just a coughing fit. Call you later."

So Waldo had one version for Tauber and another all ready for me. The sadistic prick. OK Jerry, we're in this together. Publishers of the world, unite. Together we shall bring Waldo to book. I won't say that Jerry is the editor of this very novel you're reading and I won't say that he isn't, but let's pretend. In fact let's pretend that a whole paragraph has been omitted at his request describing his own charms. I had painted him warts and all (he actually has warts, otherwise I wouldn't mention them), but he felt this weakened the narrative.

He is in fact a handsome outgoing fellow, and he has given me some insights into his former author that more than pay for this empty piece of flattery. Jerry, you're a goddamn prince.

9

TAUBER believes this next bit stretches credibility, but that's because he's never been a Presbyterian. The pact I've made with myself, and cosigned with the Devil, states that now I've taken Waldo, I can publish Billy too and sleep with his wife. Tauber says I should at least try this equation out on some other Presbyterians, but I know what I know.

It is also necessary to take away the taste of Otis MacIntyre. If I can get the girl, it will knock a chip off the almighty Waldo character. It is the first step toward total vengeance.

Negotiations for Waldo prove pathetically easy. His so-called price is a joke. He was one of the first of the million-dollar authors, but his sales have slumped so far short of his advances that anyone can have him now for a song. The only stipulation is that I lie about the price—or at least that I do not deny any rumors I hear about it. Waldo will float these himself. "Believed to be well up in six-figure country." When this happens, I must do my best to calm my partner, who stirs uneasily in his doze when he hears rumors, any rumors.

Waldo is actually so far down in five-figure country that I wonder if I've overrated the book. Perhaps because the materials are familiar, perhaps because the awfulness of Otis MacIntyre made it my Christian duty to overrate . . . Well, what's done is done. Once you've bought a book, you are condemned to enthusiasm.

The pleasant part of that motley Tuesday morning was

phoning Billy van Dyne. "I've decided to make it a two-ring ceremony, Billy. I'm sorry I took so long to decide but you're that kind of author, Bill. You foment slowly in the mind," etc. Standard burble from the other end. I lay the phone on my desk and skim the morning mail. I can't listen to all the crap that comes in over the wires. I'm a busy man. When the burble stops I retrieve the phone and say gently, "We feel that way too, Billy."

Billy's price is no problem at all. He has no price. Nikki runs a small real estate office and that's how they live. So I pay him scale and his agent accepts without a murmur. His novel, you will be relieved to hear, is *not* set in the Hamptons and does not contain a brutish publisher. Instead it is set in Paris and contains a brutish art dealer, who lets young artists starve while he sits on their work, and waits for it to ripen. Sort of like a publisher, in fact.

But Billy really is good. The fellow understands greed incredibly well for an outsider. The story doesn't matter; the author is interested in essences, and their verbal equivalents. He can seem as brilliantly opaque and elusive as Joyce but—I don't know what the trouble is: he doesn't live in Trieste, he doesn't have an eyepatch, something is missing with Billy. But this book should be published. By somebody.

All in all, this threatens to be quite a weekend. Unless Waldo is embarrassed now that I know his price, he will be lunging about like an old football player, snapping wet towels, and pouring champagne over coach's head (in this case mine). The kidding at Jimmy's will be ferocious and interminable. And I'll have to wear my funny hat with the two of them until dawn.

Ah well, a publisher's duties. But first the pleasures, namely lunch with Nikki van Dyne.

For one nice thing, she isn't an author. Authors can be hell to have lunch with. They know that *I* can't shoot the afternoon by drinking too much, but they can and do. And watching these guys disintegrate while the clock slowly turns can be torture. One of them, who shall be nameless, says he never drinks any other time, but when he sees a publisher he feels he has to. Young writers, this guy explains, never get to eat in good restaurants, so when they do they make the most of it. Their eyes run down the price column first, because getting something expensive out of a publisher tastes good in itself.

But today will be different. How you become amorous over club soda I don't know, but Nikki must have figured a way by now. I, for a change, have a scotch on the rocks, being still a little shy with women, after all my efforts.

"Isn't it wonderful about Billy?" she begins warmly. "You were so kind."

"What do you mean, kind? I wasn't doing him any favors. He's a fine writer." I will not be Otis. I will be warm and wonderful.

"Do you really think so?" she says. "I thought you were doing it out of charity." She lowers her eyes, and without warning, the boom. "Because otherwise you would pay him properly, like other writers."

What's this, what's this? It's a hell of a way to start a tryst. How can I be warm and wonderful now? Authors' wives are, of course, the greediest creatures in nature. But this is so unjust I could cry. "I don't control these things, Nikki, the market does. Billy hasn't made his breakthrough yet. But I'm confident—"

"I don't see how he's ever going to make a breakthrough if he has to starve to death."

"Come on, Nikki. He isn't starving."

"He is, for self-esteem. I can't tell you how hurt he was by your offer. He even threatened to quit writing for good."

This is incredible. My good deed has turned to ashes. She stabs at me with her finger. "He needed you to show some faith in him. Now he says he can't even look you in the eye."

Piss on him. I don't *want* him to look me in the eye. I've had a lot more thrilling experiences than that. What does he take me for anyway, a greedy art dealer? Will these writers never stop picking on me?

She orders a cottage cheese salad before I've finished my drink and bolts it down. The seduction is not going too well, I surmise. "I've got an appointment at two o'clock," she announces, "at my gynecologist's." I feel like handing her the check.

But instead I say, "Well I'm sorry, Nikki. But we're not a rich house. And it's a good contract in other respects. I struck out some clauses myself to make sure Billy gets his money the minute the book takes off. But I didn't come here to talk about money."

In this case, why did I come here? She has turned off the sex like a stingy housekeeper saving electricity, and it's hard to believe it was ever there. Must be a biological trick, to ward off undesirables from the next swamp. At this point, a thought too horrible to contemplate taps lightly on my left temple. Was she vamping me earlier in order to get her husband published? In that case, *Gott in Himmel*, I could have had her easier if I *hadn't* accepted the book.

So what does she do now—go back to Waldo? This is unbearable. Waldo's novel is coming true: the loveless publisher losing out, the Waldo figure triumphing with laughable ease. I find myself saying, incredibly, "Well, nothing's been signed yet. I'll take another look at the contract, and maybe we can sweeten the pot a little. And of course there will be other books."

"I'll tell Billy," she says coolly. "He will be pleased."

She wipes her mouth. Obviously I can't expect her to melt in my arms over this vaporous offer. But perhaps it can reopen the bidding. The Waldo figure would not have to stoop to these tricks. But I must have this woman now, or Otis MacIntyre's wounds will bleed forever.

She gradually loosens a bit, smiles a bit, has a dessert, though she really shouldn't. She knows why I asked her to lunch, all right, and she must give me something. The conversation is subflirtatious, but brisk. Will there be a next time? It's going to be hard to think of a good reason.

"It's nice to see you away from Jimmy's," she says. "It's nice to see *anyone* away from Jimmy's."

"I don't know, you meet a lot of authors there. Did you hear about Waldo?"

"Did I ever? Didn't everyone in the three mile limit hear about Waldo? He tied one on two nights ago, and as far as I know, it's still on. The only thought that is perfectly clear in his head is that he is the greatest writer in America." Is she glad about this? Impossible to say. "Jimmy ought to thank you. You've brought him a lot of business, Jon. I only hope you know what you're doing."

Amen to that. "Well, he's brought me a lot of business too. Tell me, is Billy tying one on too?"

"Yes, but a mean one. He tells everyone you insulted him. Waldo just smiles. You obviously didn't insult *him*."

Ah, writers. Is it too late to take up zookeeping instead? "I hope he forgives me by Saturday. Otherwise I'm not showing my face in Jimmy's."

"I'll let you know about that." It's time to go.

She kisses me surprisingly on the mouth. Her lips are soft, but her left eye says dollars and her right says no-sale. Soon someone else will be staring into those precious entrails, opening the dewy lips and inserting a finger, or whatever those medical cads do. I, for my part, must return to my office where those two hulking manuscripts await me like prison wardens, or leg irons. I have saved a lot of money on Waldo (that's what I mean about agents and publishers. I was prepared to go higher than Mildred realized) and I can easily spare another thousand for Billy. Would that do it?

Like some colorless bank teller in a French movie, starting to plan his first embezzlement, I shift money from the left column to the right: for the sake of a girl I took for granted only this morning. Rereading pages 53 to 55 of Waldo's ham-handed prose, I realize that circumstance has made Nikki an obsession.

"Breasts like hills, melons . . ." When Waldo does breasts, he gives you the full run of the fruit and vegetable stand, plus surrounding topography. But where the hell are the pomegranates and alabaster thighs?

Yet even swathed to the chin in clichés, his Nikki character works, she appeals. And I wonder if Waldo isn't, in some mad act of defiance, trying to prove he can make *any* words work for him? But I am too in thrall to the paper version of Nikki to worry about Waldo right now. Much more snow will fall before

I get another chance to find out if the real one is as rich with promise as she seems, or as totally empty of it as she also seems. But then, I have that problem with most women.

I do not increase Billy's advance right now. I have too much professional pride for that. As I say, in real life nothing much happens, although everything is considered. Actually, I join a charm school, take dance lessons, buy a uke. And wait chuckling behind the arras.

10

THE snow begins to fall in real earnest that afternoon, pale, grim, implacable. And the cold damp sky tells me it will not stop until it's good and ready to. By tomorrow the highways will be like end-to-end skating rinks under wet fur. It is entirely possible I won't be able to get into my house. The sea winds take their pleasure in tossing snow at my door all night until it is jammed solid. A sane man would take a hint and stay in New York. But I must get out this weekend. I am curious about something, I don't know what. It is the crescendo of winter, complete with full orchestra, crashing cymbals, the conductor beside himself with excitement. To be fair, I have this feeling many times, and nothing has ever come of it. But I'd hate to miss the time it does.

I won't bore you with my harrowing trip or my dexterous use of back roads. As I've told my first novelists a thousand times, snow is just snow. Gritting my teeth over the miracle of the snowflake, I finally got to Jimmy's at two in the morning.

The place was quite dead. Jimmy was polishing glasses, and talking to a couple of locals who know no season—guys who just put on more flannel shirts and take them off again to mark the passing of time.

"Where is everybody?"

"They were here a while ago. Billy was stiff as a board. Waldo was throwing out challenges to Norman Mailer."

"Lucky Mailer didn't hear them."

"I don't know what you've done to those guys, Jonathan. But if they don't make it home tonight, I'm holding you responsible."

Death by publication. It's happened before, I suspect. "How was Billy? Was he still sore?"

"You mean in his lucid moments? Hell no. He was happy as a clam. I think he was challenging Edith Wharton."

Jimmy, it goes without saying, is a writer himself, and someday he'll come scratching on my windowpane, and with just one more trifling sellout on my part, I'll never have to pay for a drink again.

In fact, now that he's got me alone, he's beginning to get that I've-got-a-manuscript look already. What with Billy and Waldo, I must seem like the money tree this week. In a moment, Jimmy will be telling me about *Thoughts of a Bartender* again, that unique mixture of prose and verse, of nature ramblings and earthy chitchat and celebrity gossip. I start to back away. "My house is under snow," I say.

"Yeah? I was just going to say"—I am five feet from the door, freedom is so close—"I finally think my book is ready for you to look at."

I am trapped on a snowy night by a mad bartender. Shoulders droop. "Is that so, Jimmy?"

"Yeah, you know, I'd just like a reading."

"Wouldn't you rather have an outside opinion? It's so hard to judge a friend's work. . . ." I let it go. Billy and Waldo are living proof that being my friend doesn't hurt a bit.

"Look Jimmy," I temporize wildly, "I love this place, you know that. As an innkeeper, you're *at least* a genius. But suppose by chance I don't go for your stuff? Will it ever be the same in here for me?"

"Sure it will. I'm a professional."

"They're the worst, Jimmy. Believe me, they never forgive anything."

Jimmy, so help me, starts to pout: no easy job under a big red beard. He thinks *he* would be different, *he* wouldn't get mad—and here he's getting mad already, before I've even looked at his damn stuff.

I needed another problem like this to complete my set. It's 2:30 a.m. on a cold morning, and I'm making a bad recovery from snow blindness. Ahead of me lies a wall of more snow that probably won't let me into my own house. Behind that, when I've shoveled till dawn, irreparably twisting my spine, there'll undoubtedly be cracked pipes and heavy flooding. The ice floes in my basement will make it the ideal place for freezing wild game. The roof—please let's not forget the roof. It reacts badly to all weather conditions, including mild sunshine. My self-pity is already a collector's item.

And now this wild-eyed fanatic wants me to read his junk on the spot. His green eyes with the seaweed base wheedle and threaten. If I'm not too good for Waldo and Billy, I'm surely not too good for old Jimmy, am I?

Taking those two was an even worse mistake than I'd feared. It had alerted every manuscript-bearing mammal in the area, reminding them who I was and what I could do for them. Jimmy was only the first. By tomorrow they'd be gathered quietly on my lawn like Disney animals.

"That glass is pretty shiny by now," I said. Jimmy had been polishing it for five minutes. Could his writing possibly be any good? The line on bartenders is pretty discouraging. They seem to have the wrong idea about writing altogether. For one thing they assume their readers are drunk. They picture a circle of eager merry fellows, ever ready for a good roar, instead of the pinched-up little people in apartments, worried sick about their regularity, who comprise the actual reading public. And writing bartenders think that *all* anecdotes are funny.

The line on big red-bearded men is bad too. Jimmy undoubtedly has a way with words, which will be a problem. He will have a tempestuous Celtic soul, although under his trappings I'm convinced he is an Armenian war-criminal. Or rather he is, like many real Celts, a hard-eyed operator with rather less soul than a good computer. On account of his red beard and all, he will feel obliged to carry on anyway, especially about the sea. I really dread the parts about the sea.

Anyway it is not the poet who is looking at me now but the operator, and he is telling me silently that if I don't read him, I shall start losing points right now. My welcome will be a little less warm, I won't get that table immediately on a crowded night—it's not much he can do to me, but a malignant inn-keeper can make you feel like a loveless child.

"You want to put it in writing that you won't get sore?"

"Absolutely. Here." He writes it on a cocktail napkin. "Guaranteed not to get sore. Jimmy Bresnahan." I have the napkin still. But I doubt if it holds up in a court of law.

Of course he'll get sore, but since he's sore already, I have nothing to lose. Besides, it's my job. I can't refuse to serve an author unless he's drunk and disorderly. Talking of which—while Jimmy is in the backroom endlessly scraping his manuscript together, the door slams open and in flails Waldo.

Oh no, not now, our Hemingway, our Big Fellow. Am I to be spared nothing tonight? I brace my tired soul for an hour of egotistic blather. But Waldo only says, "Fucking car stuck in a drift."

So it's to be a bad hour all right, but there'll be no blather, because Waldo has drunk himself speechless. I bundle him into my car and drive him home. "Where you taking me? I wanna pick up car," he says. But I'm damned if I'm going to lurch around in the snow with Waldo, propping him up against various trees, only to watch him drive off into another drift. So I ignore him.

"This is my home, right here," he announces loudly. Since we've been parked in front of it for several minutes, this doesn't altogether surprise me.

"You OK?"

"Perfelly OK. You want a drink or something?" He peers at this guy who has brought him home. Does he know me from someplace? My three heads should give him a clue, but there are so many of those these days. He gives up gracefully.

I teach him slowly how his car door handle works and push him out gently. He flattens briefly against his front door and then opens it somehow and flies on through it like a large package delivered by the Mafia. Inside an unearthly howl greets him. His giant dog Thor will have to take care of him the rest of the way.

My new author. He doesn't even recognize his own benefactor and the proximate cause of his drunkenness. There should be some kind of overtime for this. But when I get home something nicer than that awaits me. My driveway has recently been swept clean, and only a few stray late night flakes remain. So in this scurvy week, I have bought me at least one friend.

The next day, and I mention it without rancor, is my birthday. This day, if there's nothing better to do, I usually dedicate to hating my family. They, both the Oglethorpes and the Mac-Spaddens, dedicated *me* to business, as one might christen a battleship the *Jolly Gross National Product*. They did not confuse my mind with love. Birthdays were a God-given opportunity to reflect on another wasted year. Yet here is their annual telegram, wishing me auld lang syne and many prosperous years on this my fortieth birthday. Their greatest wish was always to get out of my way, and I suppose there are worse ambitions. When I read all those books by authors still puling and growing colicky over their childhoods, I realize there are worse things than coldness.

At least, I hope so. My own son Alan goes to Andover, and I certainly keep out of his way, too. Yet it would be nice to hear from him. He'll drop in this summer no doubt, and I suppose we'll again give each other more space than two human beings strictly require. Yet when I try being loving, he looks, well, sympathetic, as if I were playing the piano for the first time or singing out of tune. Nice try, Dad. You should have taken it up younger.

I got all this from Waldo's book, so it must be so. His paragraph on my son "Angus" is especially corrosive, which is interesting, since he's never met my son. I'd always thought of Alan as a nice, friendly fellow, but it seems I'm transmitting my coldness to him, and who am I to argue with my own author?

As you can see, working on this particular novel is somewhat dislocating. Already I am seeing myself through Waldo's eyes, and obeying his commands like a circus dog. I have even retouched what I've written about myself, to make it slightly worse. The weekend with Mavis wasn't that bad, I'll swear it. Yet now it seems as described here.

And what about Tauber? How did he see *himself* in the Otis person? Are editors as susceptible as mediums? I can picture Jerry taking young girls out and being immediately bored by them. Doesn't everybody? It's the malady of the times. And I can see him nursing his authors as I do, just to squeeze books out of them: visiting them in the drunk tank with the Fall catalog under his arm, smuggling contracts into the sanitarium. Again, we all do that. But, aside from the important fact that Tauber hasn't got half my charm, how did Waldo manage to change Jerry's Jewish characteristics into my Scottish ones in the course of five minutes on a railroad platform?

I asked Jerry about that just before I left town, and he said he did get Waldo to change the Jewish name a month before, but the stereotype remained the same, and unmistakably Jewish. There are ethnic mysteries here I don't begin to fathom.

I am bolstering my ego for the evening by working on my own book. Unlike real writers, I go at blinding speed, unaware of any difficulties, unshaken by malaise of the spirit. In fact, it seems ridiculously easy, and I marvel that people get paid for it.

Obviously I don't understand the craft at all. It doesn't even seem especially lonely, yet all writers insist that it is. Do they think that regular people work in great chattering gangs? Here at least one can summon a character and cuff him about playfully. E.g., Waldo again.

His voice when he calls the next morning sounds better than he deserves. I can almost smell the Bloody Marys he's been bracing himself with—the tang of tabasco and the musk of tomato. The poor bastard has an iron constitution, which will be the death of him. *Requiescat* American letters, hic! "Thanks for the lift. I knew it was you all along," he says. Then he does a funny thing. He invites me to dinner. At Jimmy's to be sure, but from Waldo that's a magnanimous offer. I'm all aglow about it.

Now who swept my drive last night? It couldn't have been Waldo, that's for sure. Otis MacIntyre's cold heart skips a beat. I have *two* friends out here—one for sweeping, one for eating.

11

"HAPPY BIRTHDAY, dear *Otis*." I could hear Waldo's voice peel away from the others. "Happy birthday to you."

They're all there at the Round Table grinning like children in the firelight. Archie and Cecily and even Ferris. The great detective must now explain why they're here.

Jimmy comes out of the kitchen with a cake as big as the Ritz. One candle, and a little black figure with a silver crown. Jonathan Rex. "Speech."

"No, please. Somebody else speak and I'll correct it."

"I'd like to propose a toast to everybody's favorite editor," says Waldo. "Now you may not think that's much of a title, and it isn't. In fact, it stinks. But Jonathan is much more than an editor. He can also change tires and babysit."

"And drive his authors home," I say.

Waldo furrows. "He does that too?"

Horseplay in short. Affectionate kidding, except that every joke is intended to kill. Huge fun. Billy van Dyne gets up and I reach for my blowgun. He drinks. "To the thriftiest editor this side of Aberdeen."

Ouch. "Who gets his authors at lawn sales," I murmur weakly. This game is unfair. They can insult me, but I can't insult them. I am their servant, their fool. Perhaps Ferris here will change the tone.

"I'd like to drink," he says slowly, "to a man who has never——

once—allowed literary taste to interfere with his judgment." Ferris smiles angelically. "To a man who makes no nasty distinctions between good writers and bad, but publishes *all* of them willy-nilly. Just tell me this, my good friends. When a bad writer is really down on his luck, *you* know, when he's drinkin' too much and gettin' his fingers caught in the typewriter keys and the dog's chewin' on his manuscript and he doesn't even notice—who does he turn to? And when he writes a truly stomach-turning piece of trash, who takes him in and calls him the new Faulkner?"

"You should know," says Waldo, smiling with odd admiration.

"Damn right I should," says Ferris vaguely, and decides to let it go at that. After all, he is a gentleman.

Cecily Woodruff, you'll help? "At least," she says, "Jonathan doesn't discriminate *against* good writers. Everyone at this table knows that. Each of us knows that, although the rest of his list is disgraceful, there is *one* exception."

"Shall we have a closed ballot on who that is?" says I. "I'm proud of all of you, but thank God you don't have to publish each other. The book industry would shrivel and die."

In roasting me, they have set fire to each other. It's as if my Fall catalog had turned on itself with a snarl. Any more of this fun and I'll choke to death. Fortunately, the monomaniac Munson gives me a breather.

"Frankly I don't know what this guy does for a living and I don't care. I had him figured for the vice squad, you know, dropping his pants in the men's room to entrap state senators, but I guess it's worse than that, huh? Never mind.

"None of that stuff matters now, any more than Spinks's shitty book or van Dyne's adolescent posturings matter. You're all Other Hampton Friendlies now, and from now on you will be judged solely by your performance on the ballfield. Otherwise, I know that you're all grownups, and I respect that. So long as you give me a hundred percent on the diamond, what you do in your lousy boardrooms is your own affair."

Munson has interviewed one baseball manager too many, his mind is practically gone.

"What about me?" Fender asks Munson. "I'm not a Friendly."

"Are you sure? I loved your last book."

"That's different. Where do I play?"

The conversation blessedly splinters. The poison will come now in smaller doses. I talk to Cecily, but I'm watching Nikki. She is animated again, and she smiled as she raised her glass to me just now. But for the moment, she is mainly Billy's. A newly accepted novelist deserves at least that. She catches my eye, and kisses him right on some baseball statistic. Maybe it's Jimmy's that turns her on, and no one in particular.

Why don't I just give up? Because the kiss looked so temporary. She did it *because* I was looking at her. It was aimed more at me than at Billy, who in turn paid it no mind. He returns the kiss, squeezes her hand, keeps talking.

Waldo is watching, too. He wants to win as much as I do, the greedy bastard. Americans are so competitive. He receives the same signal: not tonight, honey. But he keeps looking, and so do I.

"I'd like to propose a toast," says Nikki. "To my husband the writer. I'm very proud of him." Billy absentmindedly raises his glass. "Not you, you klutz," she says. "Even a writer isn't supposed to drink to himself." You can't give up on a case like that.

It is enough for now that Waldo is not scoring either. He presumably returns the sentiment. So we both take a raincheck on Nikki and I try to sort out what Cecily is saying to me.

Consulting my answering service, I find the phrase. "In short, I think I've found what I'm looking for," followed by an eager silence.

"Boy or a girl?" I say.

"Boy, thank goodness."

"Somebody I know?"

"Yes."

"Somebody in this room?"

"I can't say."

"Does he talk good male dialogue? That should limit the entries."

"I think he does. But I'm not an editor."

"You're just my only good writer, right?"

She smiles and her eyes brim with happiness. When a writer finds love, it is more than usually thrilling, because often as not it means the end of a writer's block. Cecily has found a new character to explore and scavenge. There is no love like unto that.

Could it possibly be one of *my* writers? What is this incestuous madness? It means she will be putting him in a novel, while two of us are putting *her* in a novel. It's like the end of the world with nobody left but us novelists. I'm going crazy. There are other people outside of Jimmy's, I swear it.

I look around. Well, there are the usual out-of-towners, staring back at us as if we were under glass. Watch the writers eat. Watch them cut each other up. And there are the men in the flannel shirts, and there is Jimmy, our ringmaster, who'd rather be under glass himself.

In Waldo's book, Cecily is a lesbian, which should leave him out of this particular running. On the other hand, in the same book he also brings her to full womanhood. This sexless blob brings *everyone* to womanhood, including Ferris Fender.

Talking of which, the majestic Southerner seems, incredibly, to be still talking baseball. "Well, I did play a little back home, and I have to admit I hit the ball a ton. But that's for little boys."

"Don't knock little boys," says the brutal Waldo, but Ferris affects not to hear.

"Played the outfield and threw the ball a mile."

"That's great. It makes a nice change from third basemen."

"Didn't say I was playing for you."

"Didn't ask you to. Say, I especially liked the part in your book where the kid plays taps at dawn for the enemy regiment."

"So you actually read the sonofabitch?"

"Twice."

"Right field would suit me nicely."

All this time the champagne is whizzing by like speeded-up film, and the crowd is beginning to bubble. Waldo simply wants to talk about his own greatness, which is easy enough to cope with, but Billy wants to talk about his book, which I'm having trouble remembering. "That scene on the Quai d'Orsay, for instance."

"Yes, I think so."

"What do you mean by that?"

"I didn't get the question."

Anyone but an author would just give up. But Billy pretends this is a rational exchange. "The scene with M. Maggot, the blackmailing critic. Wasn't it wonderful?"

"Wonderful."

"Doesn't it say everything there is to say about critics?"

"Everything."

Each of these knee jerks he takes as if they came from the heart. "So you thought that about critics? I did too," he says owlishly. As if *I'd* written it, and he was agreeing.

"Definitely." The champagne flies by again like a bird.

"The question I ask myself is, could anyone else in America have written that scene?"

"I strongly doubt it."

"Fitzgerald? Maupassant? *Waldo* here?" He whispers the last name loudly.

"Waldo's a different kind of writer," I whisper back.

"You can say *that* again," Billy says in his natural voice.

Nikki is paying attention now, squeezing his hand for emphasis. He looks at her uncertainly, and she smiles sweetly. The message is in the hand, you fool.

"If no one else could have written that particular scene"—he stops, Nikki squeezes again—"how come," and he lowers his voice once more, "you're paying *him* so much."

"Because I'm *better* than you are!" shouts Waldo, who has heard every word. "No offense, Billy. The fact is that I'm better than anybody. Isn't that right, Jonathan?"

"In a way," I say miserably.

"And what in-the-name-of-sweet-Jesus is that way?" booms Fender.

"Yes, I'd really like to know," chimes Cecily.

"Ask Jonathan," says Waldo slyly. "He's the one who said it."

I don't want to be forty, ever again. Why can't I join a nice, civilized tribe where they simply skin you alive and roast you on a spit and leave it at that.

The eerie thing is that each of the contestants is still smiling. There is some code at work here, an understanding that once the kidding stops we won't be able to talk at all, but will fall to clubbing each other.

"You're not thinking enough about baseball," mutters Archie. "The team is suffering."

"I'm waiting for Jonathan to tell me in what precise way I am the greatest."

"Bullshit artist?" says Billy.

"Windbag. Gasworks. Oral windbreaker," suggests Fender.

I look at Cecily—it's her turn. She blushes and is silent. Oh no! Waldo is smiling—same old smile I guess, but it looks like the shiteating smirk of the old Marine. What made his war writing so strong, you'll recall, is that he admitted enjoying the whole thing. To his horror, he orgasmed in combat. He gibbered as he shot his first gook, and laughed like a mad baby when he sank his bayonet into slopehead flesh. This is the case against war, he seemed to say. Me! No one else.

Or rather, of course, his fictional self. Nobody really believed Waldo had done those things. A big, rawboned, genial guy, always kidding, but never really cruel. And lumberingly sensitive between times. The boy and the bird episode is a fair sample. He can do a lot with that one basic smile—which is why they designed the recruiting posters that way, I guess. Right now, it is telling his editor that his novel is the plain truth or soon will be. He *is* bringing Cecily Woodruff to womanhood. He *is* going to get Nikki too, if he hasn't already. And if all that is true, Otis MacIntyre must be true too, no?

Otis writhes like a Korean impaled on a bayonet. "What am I the greatest at, Jon?" Waldo asks gently.

Sadist. Pigsticker. Unacceptable. "You are undoubtedly"—pause—"the greatest *researcher* of your generation."

12

WALDO led the laughter, some of which sounded confused. The joke was on him and he loved it. "Well I guess researcher is better than no writer at all," he says, stepping down from his pedestal next to Hemingway. "Billy here is the real writer, and I'll finance him as long as I can, with my research."

The laughter is *very* confused now. Nobody knows what the hell he's talking about. Ferris has wandered back to green fields, with a bumper crop of white crosses, and is right now jotting down the Confederate body count one more time; Cecily is glowing inwardly—novelists don't want to share their love with *anybody*, even the poor schnook at the receiving end (the public will hear about it before he does); Billy has wandered over to the bar to talk with the real people. Only charlatans consort with other writers after midnight.

The worst is over, I trust. We've laid out our grooves for the night; all we have to do is chug safely along them to beddybyes. "A tragedy, a real national tragedy," I murmur to Ferris. "We're all really high on the book" to Waldo. "Batter up" to Archie. And "?" to Nikki. And around again.

But what's this? Voices raised at the bar? It's like voices raised at the Wailing Wall. It is no mean feat on a Saturday night to make such an attention-grabbing sound. The normal noise at Jimmy's is at once so loud and so irregular that only another species, say a moose or a quail, has a chance against it.

This is not exactly a moose, but a local plumber, and he seems to be talking to our Billy in a loud cracked voice. Plumber, repair thyself, I think severely. Why is our bar always so full of plumbers anyway? Maybe I only *think* they're plumbers. And why is this one talking so loud? It makes no sense at all. Somebody turn him off.

In fact, he seems to be almost at fight's edge. This is next to unheard of at Jimmy's, which is not a fighting bar. Jimmy is too big, and his patrons are too snobbish. The locals who come in here tend to fancy themselves. In their small way, they remind me of French collaborators in World War II, hobnobbing with the invaders and making a fast franc off them. In here, the writers can nourish the illusion that they're locally popular, and this has to be paid for in nylons and cigarettes.

As you can tell, I am too bogged down in philosophy to take in much at first. It is the Scottish vice, I can't help it. Where others fall to revelry, the Scots fall to arguing. We don't even do it very well, according to my steel-cornering father, we just do a lot of it.

So I'm still working on the meaning of meaning when the blow lands on Billy's thorax. Plumbers know these delicate spots in the human piping. If one takes the throat to be the drain of the body . . . hey, what is this? Waldo has bounded over and is talking to Billy and holding off the plumber. "I can't help it," Billy is saying tearfully. "It *is* more important."

I notice that Waldo has left his napkin on the table and the napkin has fresh writing on it. Very thoughtful of him, because it brings me right up to date. "B: you can't possibly compare what you do with what I do. P: You're a fag. B: Writing is the noblest activity given to man. Why, I'd rather be a *bad* writer than a good whatever you do. P: You're a *fag*." Fortunately, I know Waldo's shorthand by now. The creative sonofabitch has simply transcribed the whole conversation. I always wondered where he got his ideas.

I glom my little group for reactions. Ferris looks lazily amused, as if he finds fighting restful. The word "fag" keeps spitting in our direction, and this amuses him even more. "Maybe we got us a re-cruit," he whispers. "Never knew a guy uses that word so much isn't at least interested." Archie Munson is barely even amused, he's seen so much of this sort of thing in Sportsworld, and he just wants to keep talking. Simmons, our house plebeian, is glad to oblige him. He has come over expressly to detach himself from the bar people.

Cecily is outraged. "Make them stop, Jonathan. They remind me of my ex-husband." A good enough reason for me. Still she watches—she has never written a fight scene before. Maybe she can use it. Nikki watches too, like a fan at the Garden; her lips are parted, her eyes bright. She is sexually sparking, I want her right now.

I also want a better seat. A publisher has a right to know. So I amble over to hear what's going on. Jimmy, it turns out, has left already, so Waldo is still holding off the plumber, whose arms are wheeling and flapping as he shouts. Necessarily, his thoughts are simple; in such a situation, it's a triumph to think at all.

"You're *all* fags," he says. "Good-for-nothing fags. Coming to the door in your pajamas at ten in the morning. Living in big houses by yourselves or with your boyfriends. Despising us working guys, thinking we're simpleminded."

Well— now that you mention it . . .

"You people have no idea how you're hated in this community. Believe me, we know what you do all day. And everyone you see on the street knows it too," he adds darkly.

The guy would obviously rather talk than fight, because Waldo is not guarding him closely. Although his right hand is braced against the plumber's chest, Waldo's head is half turned to Billy, with whom he is trying vainly to reason.

"I'm sorry, I won't apologize. It's the truth, and you know it. Writers *are* more important," says Billy.

Good liberal Oglethorpe, who has not spoken yet, sees his chance to leap in with a good deed. "I'm sorry, sir. My friend seems to have insulted you. I'd like you to know right now that I completely disagree with him. I believe that plumbing is, well, a wonderful calling. And I think that a good plumber has more value any day than a . . ."

I stop. The cruel little plumber's eyes in the shapeless red face have narrowed to slits. "*You!* You're the worst of them!" he screams hysterically. "Who said anything about plumbing? I'm your goddamn postman!"

I don't know if Waldo's grip slackened or whether anger had lent the man strength, but the plumber's arms burst loose like the bird's wings in Waldo's novel. My God, he's going to hit one of us. Which of us does he resent the most on his rounds? Is he going to hit one of my authors?

In the event, he hits Oglethorpe here, a jawbreaker on the right followed by a tap on the left to even it off. My head snaps and my cheekbones cave in. My last thought is, he hits awfully hard for a postman.

When I come to, a cop is leaning over me. They are still dredging the bars for doctors it seems. "Don't move your jaw," says the cop, as if it was evidence. My friends' faces dance in the light. Ferris, Cecily, Nikki, faces thrusting with concern. They'd all hit me at once, I can tell. That's why I feel so rotten. "I'm all right," I start to say, and my face falls in again. I can't talk at all.

The town has left its calling card.

I later learned what happened while I was out.

It seems that Waldo (my hero) pinioned the pseudopostman, who seethed like a lobster. He wanted to take out one more fag, if not the whole festering colony, while he was up.

"Let him go." The command could have come from General Lee himself, and Waldo dropped his hands like an enlisted man.

The postman capered free and faced the void for a gleeful moment. Ferris stepped forward, one two three, and almost contemplatively popped him one. A haymaker from the floor, from the past. The postman began to gyrate, like a dancer who's lost his partner. Still spinning, he approached the glass door slowly, cyclonically. Ferris had put him in orbit, and was already sitting down. Jimmy chose that moment to walk in the door and catch him—and they both flew through the glass door together. All of which complicated my case that it was all a conspiracy against me.

This is a writers' account, Billy's, Waldo's, Cecily's (Ferris leaves it to history). I have omitted the grosser additions: hurtling bodies, broken bottles, bites administered by Cecily (Waldo's touch). I do believe that Archie Munson said, "What a swing. I've got to have him on my team. I mean, the postman." Otherwise, I'll never know for sure what happened. By the time I got back, new glass had been put in the door, my blood was mopped up, and the snow had gone. In fact, it was summer.

A
Mad Dance
to the
Changing
Seasons

13

"I WAS talking to Bill de Kooning."("How is Bill?")The first sounds of summer come fluting across the Merryweathers' patio. "I hear that Roofman sold a painting for half a million." Good old Roofman. We may not know about art but we know what it costs.

When abstract expressionism first hit our little backwater, people did try to talk about it aesthetically. But this is hard to do with abstract painting for more than a few minutes. The phrases, even when used right, sound almost as funny as wine criticism. And who uses them right anymore? As the artists get old and die, so do the people who can talk about them. It's much safer these days just to discuss the money.

And why am I talking to myself? Because somebody has to talk intelligently around here. I actually quite enjoy conversations about painting, but the few practitioners left out here talk like ballplayers ("I had the real good curve and the real good fastball") while their admirers nod and sigh at the wisdom of it all. When there is no real painter present, as today, we resort to our Stock Exchange ways. This is just one of my latest, and least felicitous, attempts to keep out of Jimmy's, with its overtones of playpen and slaughterhouse. I will not go back to that rancid locker room. But I'd forgotten how dull culture can be in the wrong hands. It is almost as bad as talking about softball, and just the wrong thing for a guy trying to give up arrogance.

* * *

If it is possible to slam a whole house shut, that's what I did to my country seat as soon as I could after last winter's unpleasantness; and from there set forth with wired jaw and a sparkling new dental bridge to prove that there is more to my life than writers, especially these writers.

It wasn't easy since I still had to deal with their books. For a vicious moment, I thought of letting them out in the world unedited, so the public could see them for what they really are—an author in the nude is not a pretty sight. But it seemed too cruel—even to Waldo Spinks, who, while I was still in the hospital, sent me a brand-new scene he'd written, in which the local grocer unloads one on my surrogate, MacIntyre, after the latter has asked for truffles sneeringly. What a clumsy reworking, what a . . . "Only kidding, old man," added Waldo on the flip side of the page. "Hurry up and get well now." A jolt like electricity had already run along my jaw and around my mouth before I got to the "only kidding" part.

I received a flurry of hearty, bracing little notes. Archie Munson thought the whole evening had been a triumph of teamwork, which I guess it was at that, if the game was "get the publisher, and then get the postman." The two natural enemies. I had already had a dream about that very thing, at the sly urging of sodium pentothal, the day they wired my jaw. In my delirium it was revealed to me in eye-aching color that I had been set up all the way. While I was still lying on the floor I distinctly heard the group talking about how well it had gone. It seems that first they had hired an ex-boxer and stuntman to play my alleged postman (come to think of it, I *swear* I'd never seen the guy before). Then Billy in an agony of vengeance over his advance, had staged his preposterous (and uncharacteristic) scene at the bar. Waldo had recorded the conversation between him and the postman in just such a manner as to guarantee my bellying up to join them, so that I could protect my author like a mother hen. Clearly one tap on the snoot and Billy would have flown into a million pieces. And there would go my $1,000 investment. The scene then shifts to Waldo holding off the alleged postman with laughable ease until I've talked myself into perfect position. And then pop, splat, the fist starts to wheel, the pain is already there waiting for it, and I am awake and drenched in sweat.

Claptrap of course. But a sodium pentothal dream has its own authority; for a man who's just been drinking, it is stronger than real evidence. I still don't like to think about it, because the dream plays back obligingly and in full every time it is tripped. Fender, thank God, was not in on the joke—or was he? His facetious note doesn't help. "And, pray tell, what an itty bitty Yankee publisher was doing in a brawl like that . . . just kidding, old buddy, get well real soon, do you hear?" He and Waldo had obviously colluded on their notes; the lightning streaks around my jaw again and flicks my molars.

They'll leave me alone eventually. But to be on the safe side, I checked myself out of Nether Hampton Hospital prematurely before they could land on me in person; closed the house with stealthy venom—tiptoe and bang—and asked for a leave of absence in almost the same breath. My last mementoes were Nikki's two cents' worth and Cecily's.

Nikki's note was kind of funny, as if she'd completely forgotten what game she was playing with me. At first she chastised Billy for starting a fight which I, poor dear, somehow wound up finishing. But then she praised him for sticking up for his principles. And then she praised me for standing by him. And so on, round and round.

Nikki without her immediate sexual allure simply flounders. She hasn't given up hoping for that extra advance, but she has no idea what the magic word is, so she tries them all. If ever a woman needed her body with her at all times, it is Nikki. Her tentative presence on the page only diminishes her memory. Of course, if she walked in right now . . . never mind. Anyway, Billy van Dyne's bonus hasn't got a chance in hell.

Cecily disappointed me. She was just as repulsively playful as the others, as if it had all been a wonderful party, too bad about your hangover. She particularly gushed over Fender's manly form as he propelled the postman through the glass door—as if she didn't know that stuntmen are paid well to make such punches look good. OK, OK, I know he wasn't really a stuntman; but all I can see now is this ream of writers standing round my fallen body grinning hideously and voraciously. There is no feeling in these people except wanton curiosity and a lust for things to happen—any things.

The bastards have dined on me for the last time (could Cecily and Fender really be an item? I thought they both loved *me*). They can look elsewhere for their carrion. I shall edit henceforth with forceps and rubber gloves, and leave the real dirty work to my assistants, like other famous editors. As a gentleman publisher, I shall see my clients in person as seldom as a Park Avenue doctor.

But I was obliged to admit that it wasn't *just* the writers' fault: a better man would not have wound up on the floor at Jimmy's. Somehow I had let real life get away from me. Thus perish all barflies, I suppose, although I don't even like to drink that much. (Could that be the problem? Some people can't stand being watched at their favorite sin by a non-participant. Maybe the crowd at Jimmy's hated me for my sipping.)

It's hard for someone of my stock to write about his soul, so I'll keep what follows to a parsimonious Scotch minimum. I blush to say it, but I set out then and there to improve myself in a modest Presbyterian way, like a Glasgow schoolboy: no chest-beating or underwater therapy, but simply trying to be a little kinder and more attentive, and even attempting at least once in a while to think of something higher than who's screwing whom (which can prove drainingly difficult for someone working in an office.)

Kindness, it turns out, is not as easy as it looks. My son Alan just seems perplexed by it when I visit him at school to give him the keys to a new Corvette which he is just old enough to drive. What kind of conscience money is this? He has never forgiven me for divorcing his mother. So everything I do for him has to be construed as a pay-off. Seeing him today feels like returning to a boarded-over house that you used to live in when you were young. Nice place, once upon a time.

"You shouldn't have done it, Dad," he says, staring at the

keys; I had long ago asked him to call me Jonathan but he pre-
fers Dad. It has a nice bite to it.

We stand in the school hallway. Will that be all? he seems to
say. Irrationally, I feel as if I ought to keep giving him things
just to justify my taking up his time.

"How about a drink?" "You know I don't." Christ I'm rusty
at being attentive.

Then again there may be cases where it's simply too late: a
bitter thought to add to my collection. Alan seems to be studying me, with a face that has always struck me as preternaturally
old, wise, and craggy, though others say he's just a regular,
good-looking kid, and he appears to relent. He will show me
around the boarded-up house just this once. A Corvette surely
deserves that much.

We go to a coffee shop, and I ask about his studies. Naturally
the courses he is taking have slipped my mind completely, but
he talks as if it doesn't matter. "I really get a boot out of French."
French? "That Montaigne is fantastic." "He certainly is."

I am relieved in a crushed sort of way to find that he is just as
vague about my work as I am about his. This is no sin in his
eyes, either way. I've left his home, his company, taking all
responsibility, his and mine, with me. He is as free now as a
miser in Aberdeen; he expects nothing, gives nothing.

It seems inane to say "Son, I'm trying to improve myself,"
but I have to confess to someone.

"Alan, do you notice something funny about my jaw and the
way I'm talking?"

"Yes." Ah, these garrulous Scotchmen.

"I got punched. By a postman." I feel like "show and tell."
Now *you* tell me something silly.

"How'd you manage that?"

It wasn't easy. "It doesn't matter. The point is, it was just
part of a sloppy pattern of things. My life had become kind of
incoherent. And I've decided to change it."

Good for you. He doesn't say it, but he gives a small nod.
You left my mother, you see. There are no other sins. Of course
if I wanted to do something about that one . . .

89

God knows, I would right now on the spot if I could. But I have left between Ann and me such a brightly lit trail of petty adultery and embarrassment as no one can ever walk back over. It didn't seem like such a big deal at the time—adultery was her word. I thought it had pretty much gone out of use for people like us. In those days I had valued candor, and when I took other women to restaurants and parties, I thought why demean them by hiding them? Why, I even introduced one or two to little Alan. What in sweet Hell did I think I was doing? "You can do it too, Ann," I'd said airily. "I won't mind." And if she didn't *want* to do it, that wasn't my fault.

As it turned out, my not minding what *she* did wounded her much more than anything I did myself. Or so she said in her "which of us leaves?" note.

Alan looks at me almost tenderly. I'd really like to help you, but you see how hopeless it all is, don't you, Dad? He has of course read all my thoughts, which saves time. Our understanding of each other has weathered every horror, even the loss of love. We would have made wonderful friends.

It is considerate of him, having read my mind so far, not to dash the Corvette keys in my face. But as he swings them gently in his fingers, I am reminded of some old Scottish caretaker clanking a huge chain of rusty black keys. "Time's aboot oop, mistair." The boarded-up house of Alan's soul is to be reopened now only by the gift of a yacht or a townhouse. Oh unfair, unfair. Well at least my son has the honor not to invent some class he has to go to. He just shakes my hand politely, a move I hadn't expected. "Thanks again for the car, Dad. I really appreciate it." We'll save the Montaigne for another time.

It breaks my heart to think that the Oglethorpe men can muster no more of a scene than that. *Give* me something, Alan. It's too late, Mr. Scrooge.

But I soon find that predestination lurks not only in the prehistoric features of my son, but in the facts themselves. When I try being nice around the office, my colleagues think my "accident" has weakened me beyond repair. "That must have been quite a knock you took," says Sly Sam Welman, the moment after I agree that someone else might be right about something .

Alarm and contempt war in his piggy face. "Some accident, huh?" I am already under enough fire for signing up all the writers in my own neighborhood ("it must save a lot of legwork . . . finding all the nation's talent within walking distance") without admitting that all these writers have witnessed me in a meaningless punch-out. Hence my "accident"—a mugging that I hastily invented for office use and which I have tried to keep as vague as possible. "It was dark, I barely saw the guy."

Just try keeping something vague in New York. "Did they catch him? How'd he get away in such a small town? Anybody see him?" No, only the four gabbiest novelists in America. "Did he take anything, was he black?" What about cops, newspaper coverage, insurance? They take turns working you over with these questions until the culprit cracks. They pretend to feel concern, but what they really want is to have something on you, the New York edge.

Anyway, my accident soon moved into quotation marks as an unsolved crime, probably shameful. If I had known how *much* story they would want of me, I'd have thought of at least a couple of details that held together. As it is . . .

Ah well, I can still be kind even to these pricks. The talk turns to Waldo Spinks and his manuscript, and Sam says unexpectedly, "You know, I'm still not sure about it. A guy who writes as badly as that better have a pretty good engine to run his crap up the track. And I get a feeling his engine's just about burned out."

They look at me eagerly, as the well-known scourge of these meetings. But the timing is bad. My mind isn't on it. "I don't know. Maybe I made a mistake."

This wakes even our senior partner, Prescott Williams, who doesn't actually hear the words so long as everyone sounds happy. It is as if the old man feels a chill; his hands seem to reach for an invisible shawl. "Are you sure you didn't come back too soon, Jonathan?" he quavers.

You may be right is bad enough; *I may be wrong* bespeaks total disintegration. Even Jane the secretary stiffens, like an animal scenting fear. If I get any kinder, I'll end up in the stockroom— the repository of kindness in business America. Absurdly I feel like apologizing for being so nice. Instead I growl weakly, "But I don't happen to think so."

"Thank God for that, Jon. *Some*body better believe in that book the way she's budgeted."

Another note for young writers: villains do not gloat or even barely conceal their delight, they just look concerned. That expression that says "are you sure you're all right?" can bring a healthy man out in running sores. *Better than you on your best day you flatulent ferret*, my face replies politely.

That, of course, is the nub of the problem. What's the point of acting kind if you're not a kind man? Does character follow behavior? Does it really want to?

Anyway, my bristling countenance appears to hold them at bay for now. Old Prescott sinks back as if his shawl has been magically wrapped around his shoulders. The only one of his senses he has left tells him that everything's okay again. I make a note that Waldo has once again been the cause of my discomfiture. I have danced to his tune.

Obviously, working on his book is bad for me. I have absorbed his character MacIntyre so completely that I am actually acting out fresh scenes for him. The trouble is that after my ringing affirmation of faith in him at this meeting, I can't very well palm him off on somebody else. I am the only soul in the place who seems to want him at all.

As I shut the door on the sedate nineteenth-century boardroom, I can swear I hear a burst of maniacal laughter. I have indeed come back too soon.

I don't know, maybe you have to take up decency early, like the violin. My attempts to apply it in the lower depths meet with a different but equally unsatisfactory fate. Without my thin-lipped intolerance to hold them together, my various assistants start gratefully falling apart. Letters are mistyped three times in a row. My false smile lights up my jaw like a row of Watusi firebrands. "Give it one more try Janie, OK? and do try to get it right this time, huh?" The sheer sweetness squirts poison into my gut. I feel a pinprick of pain someplace in my right middle—ulcer country, as I recall. "There's a good girl." Stab. "I'm afraid this blurb doesn't quite make it, Freddy." Ouch. I'm on fire. "Get this fucking garbage out of here!" Peace settles like a sunset. It's the only way.

So now, I at least know the real ending of Dickens's Christmas Carol. Either Bob Cratchit turns into a slob overnight and spills ink over everything, while Scrooge breaks out in boils; or else Cratchit interprets his master's good nature as senile decay and brutally muscles him out of the business, by getting him to sign a stock transfer in the guise of a gift certificate for Tiny Tim. Scrooge ends his days in a workshop, vainly trying to be kind and becoming an all-round pest. Cratchit and Son prospers until . . .

A Scrooge cannot change his spots, he can only offer them up to God. There are still a couple of things I can do, though. The first is to stop whoring around like some burlesque clown with a salami in his pants. I can make at least this part of my life serious—which rules out Nikki van Dyne, regrettably. My intentions are so pure, I can barely whisper them to myself without blushing (to students: there is no such thing as blushing. It's an optical illusion, like the curve ball). All I can report here as elsewhere is what happened, and add that I did it, in a roundabout way, to win back Alan's respect. Fat chance, I understand, but a pilgrim needs his grail, even if it's made out of thistledown.

Unfortunately, the women I've dated in the past expect roughly the same routine as before, so just to discuss weighty matters I have to hang up my clothes and get into bed. (This reminds me bizarrely of my mother, who made the same condition before reading me fairy stories.)

Some of these women have made it conclusively clear that they don't want marriage, or anything like marriage. "I didn't leave Waterloo, Iowa, just to lock myself in with one guy. New York is *variety*. It isn't anything else." Well, I am hardly the one to show these ladies around Fidelity and Seriousness. In fact, they are more serious than me already, because what they're doing is an adventure for them, it takes an act of will, and it often shows in their highstrung faces and voices. They are a mile from being slatterns. I am an inch. "Look, I like to do things my own way, OK?" they say. "If I want to play rock music at four in the morning, ain't nobody going to stop me, man." That will be all, Jenkins.

These bachelor girls have walled themselves in very carefully behind their decor and their crotchets. "What guy would put up with me?" they announce from the battlements. "Look, I simply have to take Poochie wherever I go—parties, restaurants, planes, trains. If they don't want him, I don't want them." "Listen, I have to leave the TV on all night to keep my cat company. If someone doesn't like it, tough." There's a Yankee determination in all this—no one's going to get them back on the farm, by God—which I have to admire, but which chews up "serious" men for breakfast, let alone half-fledged serious men.

"Why don't we just sit and talk?" I say to Mavis II, another composite.

"Aren't you feeling well, Jon?" says she.

"No, I feel fine. It's just that a man likes to talk sometimes." And fish gotta fly. Oh, my aching jaw!

"So, what would you like to talk about, Jon?"

Smut, mostly. "Oh, you know. Commitment. Sharing. Caring," I babble.

We look at each other in bottomless embarrassment.

Mavis III, on the other hand, just laughs. "You're just not the type," she says. Mavis IV adds "You're always a lot of fun except tonight." "Commitment sounds so like an institution, doesn't it?" chimes in an English agent, Mavis Chumley the Innumerable. "You're very, *very* New York, you know."

One night, I return shrunken from positively my last Mavis. You can't change, Jon—you're fun, you'll always be fun (fun obviously being a technical term, as in "he is fun like a rabbit"), forever and ever and ever. You can't be anything else but fun. The merciless God of Scotland will see to it.

My heart is heavy and bleeding with fun as I return to my apartment, only to spot a corner of manila envelope peeping out from under my door. I know what it is immediately. Only an ex-Marine could have smuggled an envelope into this high security building. Waldo has just added another chapter to his hellish manuscript. It is entitled "Otis MacIntyre Finds God," or "What I did for Lent," and it contains word for word everything that you've just read.

It doesn't, of course. It is actually a short story written by the Building Superintendent's backward son, and it isn't even about me. But that's beside the point. In some sense, the deed has been done, just by being imagined.

I sit down and with trembling hands (N.B. to students: hands *do* tremble. A lot.) begin to read the kid's droppings just to make sure that, in the late-raging March of this year of Hell, at least my heat will not get turned off.

The winter finally releases its precious burden of manuscript and it is time to prune. My own editor (you have to be tacky or desperate to publish yourself) has persuaded me to cut my dark night of the soul to the bone. Naturally, I obey, if only to be a good example. So you will find no hint here of my conversion to Zen that winter or my harrowing trip to Tibet.

"Editors are just no good at introspection," says my man Tauber (the same), who thinks he's doing me a favor just by publishing a colleague and who has paid me a laughably small advance. *He's* no good at introspection, is what he means. I get a pleasant tingle from having an editor of my own to feel superior to.

Spring has taken its sweet time about getting here, but it's a little beauty and I feel an irresistible tug to drive past those white clapboard shops that say "boats repaired" and "fishing tackle and bait." I want to mill around vegetable stands with women in baggy pants. I even want to repair my roof. In gleaming sunshine.

After you've slammed a house shut, you feel a bit sheepish about opening it. "Sorry dear, I guess I lost my temper." The old thing has weathered the winter OK—better than OK in fact. I couldn't have left that fresh vase of daffodils, for instance. It seems my mystery sympathizer has struck again.

An anonymous friend is almost as unnerving as a faceless

enemy, and I wish he or she would quit. After eliminating the usual suspects, I settle on that damn postman again, for peace of mind. That time he swept my drive was for *his* convenience. And this is his idea of a peace offering. Ah, who can read the heart of a postman?

The trouble with him is that, despite all that hullabaloo, I've completely forgotten—again—what the bastard looked like. They seem to have put a new guy on my beat, little shrimp of a man who couldn't hurt a van Dyne, while my nemesis prowls at large. So if I go to Jimmy's I'll have to smile at everybody, which is out of the question. Besides, I'm not going to Jimmy's.

This brings us almost back to the patio, where I am "doing" the arts. I am determined this summer to sample every aspect of the Hamptons. Every politician who has ever deigned to drop in on us and take our money has affirmed that we are the most intelligent, sophisticated people in America. And I want to live up to that trust, by God.

So for now I give Jimmy's such a wide berth that half the time I'm practically in the woods skirting the village. If anyone from Ye Olde Softball Inn spots me, I make a hideous face and scurry away. Well, not quite. I have only gone back to my old ways. I was never cut out to be a barfly. From now on, I tell you, I shall be one of those fashionable editors who dines with everybody except his authors. Or if I must have them over, I shall surround and smother them in beautiful people, socialites, distinguished foreigners, investment bankers, whatever it takes to make them feel totally insignificant. I shall never again take on more than one scribbler at a time, and I'll always sit facing the door.

It is what Waldo would have wanted MacIntyre to do.

Summer

14

[Note from the ass Tauber: Don't you have to get yourself off the patio? You can't just change the subject, can you?]

I'VE noticed a new development out here—new to me, anyway. Movie people. They can be hard to spot at first, but they have one tail-marking in common that gives them away every time: they are all jarringly inconspicuous. Nobody has to try that hard *not* to look Hollywood. Nobody has to be seen with *that* few starlets.

Anyway, if you catch someone wading out to his knees to talk to the bay constable, or chatting with the haulseiners as they come in with the day's catch, it just might be one of them furtively soaking up atmosphere. But mostly they don't do *anything* special except work on their camouflage, like sailors painting their boats.

However—birdwatchers note—one movie person frequently leads to another. Follow them home to their nests, and you may flush out a whole covey. And then, if you make *absolutely no fuss* over them—act, in fact, as if you hadn't quite caught their names—they may invite you to stay and share their food and their simple customs.

Well, not quite. Once safely inside, the food offer turns out to be Lucullan and their line of work becomes faintly discernible. Huddled together like early Christians, they talk about movies.

So, making my apologies, I leave the damn patio just like that, striding off through the dapples and kissing the arts good-bye for now, along with the dusty fossils who stand guard over them. I am having dinner tonight with Marty Hearthstone the director, and I must go home now and jump on my clothes until they look authentic enough.

The reader may wonder at some point how I seem to have so much time out here. My colleagues wonder too, especially in the summer. It can't just be to be near my authors, can it? As I set out for my five-day weekends, I can always be seen trundling manuscripts through the hall and dumping them into a large suitcase (which Sam Welman claims I later drop down the elevator shaft. Droll fellow). "I work better out there," I announce to anyone who'll listen. "Fewer distractions." But of course I have to deliver books eventually, even in this sleepy little firm. So I talked about art books a bit with the Merryweathers, which always boils down to memoirs of Jackson Pollock, and tonight I shall talk about—what *do* you talk about with film people?

Well, with the Hearthstones you talk about arts and letters, letters and arts. Marty and Celia are so cultivated that they glow like stained glass. My previous writers seem like farm-hands in comparison. Have I read the latest Ladislas Svago? It seems he's the most underrated of the current Bulgarians. As we spin from one arcane name to another, I can only hang on grimly. Yes I've heard of them, of course. But I couldn't make five zlotys out of publishing the lot of them. And I don't read books for fun.

"It's so hard to find good properties these days," laments Marty, "you can't overlook anything."

I would have thought you *could* overlook Terence Bagshaw, the Irish minimalist, for instance, but Hearthstone thinks otherwise. In such sensitive hands, it's a wonder that the industry ever makes any bad movies at all. Yet among his own credits, which I mugged up on this afternoon, can be found such titles as *Flash Meets the Apeman* and *Space Orgy*—no doubt based on the original Czechoslovak, but still . . .

It seems that Marty used to teach modern literature at Sarah Lawrence, while Celia taught Art History, both happy as clams in their baggy tweeds. Then one summer, Marty was asked to be a technical adviser on some Romanian satire or other, which Columbia had bought and now couldn't make head or tail of. Was this stuff supposed to be funny? they asked. Marty had to explain that Romanian humor was not quite like other people's humor, but that from a Bucharest point of view, yes, this was quite a rib-tickler.

I won't say that he proceeded to turn it into a Doris Day comedy, but he did enough tinkering to make it filmable, and in the process learned the business. Being indispensable on just one piece of inscrutable junk had made him the Ruler of the Queen's Navy. The Romanian author's howls of dismay got lost in translation, and Marty was on his way.

So the Hearthstones have every right to be in the Hamptons, by God. I imagine Marty telling his Romanian story like a tour guide to anyone who walks through the door.

"Celia still teaches, don't you, dear?"

"Three times a week, the UCLA adult extension department. That's what's so nice about Art History, you can take it with you wherever you go. Like knitting."

Knitting? What was like knitting? My mind has wandered to the paintings and is pricing—as we highbrows will—de Kooning and Pollock, and of course, the Gottlieb, Motherwell, Kline: just right for out here. There must be money in this film business. Since there is no obvious music for out here, except maybe *The Three Little Fishes* or that childhood classic "The Potato Song (I've got my eye on you)"—obviously not quite the thing—they have settled for a simple singalong with John Cage.

Not that the Hearthstones are pretentious, far from it. They are nerve-rackingly unpretentious. For instance, "And what about you, Jon? Read any major motion pictures lately?"

"Nothing from the Hungarian," I kid heavily, Romanianly.

"No? Pity." He returns my wet doughnut of a joke in kind. "We may have to make do with American just this once. No, seriously, Jon, have you seen anything that looks like screen material?"

"Are you kidding? Everything I see *is* screen material, or thinks it is. Scene One of your average manuscript—'The hero with his long John Travolta face strode toward the (fill in your favorite color)-haired beauty in the half-light. "Who is it you remind me of?" he breathed hotly.'"

"Well, who?" says Marty.

"Oh, Jane Fonda, Vanessa Redgrave, Garbo, whoever's available. No, as a matter of fact, most of the crypto-screenplay stuff winds up in our garbage can, otherwise known as [name of rival publisher deleted]. We like to do books that *can't* be made into films." I seem to be talking in a nervous rush, as if this was a story conference and I had three minutes to impress him. It must be an atmosphere these people carry with them.

"There's no such animal as a book that can't be filmed."

"I'll send you our list, and you'll see. No, we at Williams and Oglethorpe think that the only justification for the Novel is for it to do what *only* it can do. (Sorry about that, Marty. Sentences about 'the Novel' should be drowned in infancy.)" (Yes, you *can* speak in parentheses.)

"I think I'll take you up on that, Jon. What *is* on your Fall list?"

I rattle off some names. Of course, he's heard of all of them. The guy must be either a snob or a nut. When he nods thoughtfully over Billy van Dyne, I just give up. "I liked his last one," he says. "It had possibilities."

"You can still buy it, if you hurry. Anyway, that's about it. Oh, and the new Waldo Spinks," I say casually, as if trying to slip it by him.

"*Waldo Spinks?* He's got a new one?"

"Yeah, the mixture as before."

"God how I admire that man."

"You *do?*" My Hollywood man of letters is unraveling before my eyes.

Marty raves on for a bit—"major talent, raw power," the

usual—and I let it wash over me like stale dishwater. But why had I tried to hide Waldo? Didn't I want him to have a movie sale?

Well, it depended on who played my part, of course.

"Is it true he lives out here?" Marty has finished unpacking his clichés and is moving in the general direction of Deal.

No, he lives someplace in the woods with his pet grizzly and his mongoose, Micky. I don't want these elegant people to meet Waldo, movie or no movie. He's the kind of guy who'd bring them a rubber Camembert as a house gift. These people are too fine to meet writers like Waldo.

"Yeah, he's a year-rounder," who also eats with his mouth open.

"I'd love to meet him."

"OK, I'll see what I can arrange. He can be pretty hard to get hold of" except during the hours when Jimmy's is open. Otherwise you have go round to the back.

"Have you got his number? I'll call him."

"I think it's better if I take care of it," I say quickly. Waldo sometimes does funny voices on the phone, his Mafia hit-man being a special favorite. Anyway, if there's no stopping this science fiction meeting I might as well be in charge of it. Waldo needs his tamer. On his own, he's likely to turn up, at best, drunk and playful.

It sounds, does it not, as if there are no other people in this room. I forgot to put them in, but they're there all right, and now the conversation turns general. And forgettable, like the stuff they put in boxes to keep the contents from rattling. I am quietly planning in my own mind how to keep Waldo from rattling too—the perfect setting, time of day or phase of the moon when he turns into a human—when my ears pick up a truly horrible sound. "Do you know what we need around here? A good softball game."

"What about that, Jon?" My host rubs it in. "Do you know any players out here?"

I am trapped as if an assegai has just ripped through my chest and nailed me to my chair. This has gone way beyond Waldo; now they're calling in the whole menagerie.

"I'll see what I can arrange," I say smoothly. Howling with pain simply isn't done on a first date.

I hope that this whole crazy thing will fade in the next few days. Waldo, softball and all, the dingiest side of Hampton life. Have these people no shooting schedules? What I hadn't reckoned on was the can-do nature of movie directors. The very next day, I get a call from our willowy ex-literature teacher, to say "I'm planning another dinner party for Friday and I asked your friend Waldo to come along. Would you care to join us?"

"Just tell me—did he sound funny on the phone?"

"I didn't actually get him. I got his Chinese manservant. But the guy said it was OK, that he did all Mr. Spinks's planning for him. So, you coming?"

I look at my wrists, too pale and lovely to slash. "Sure, that'd be great." Waldo's manservant claims at least seven nationalities that I know of. Since no one has ever seen the inside of Waldo's house, except maybe some bar girls, we'll never know.

Film people, it seems, go to parties on time, so they can gag down one whole white wine spritzer before the screening. In my ignorance, I blunder in on Eastern time and get the feeling it's already too late, everyone's made his arrangements, the groups are all set. In each clump of guests someone is talking nonstop. You could wait all day for an introduction, and still not get one. I edge toward the bar trying not to look like the new kid in school.

"Hi there, Jonny!" Waldo is already ensconced as King of the Castle next to Marty Hearthstone on a sofa built for two. He is wearing a necktie, which I would have thought beyond his abilities, and looking every inch the stockbroker.

"I'm glad you're up and about, Jon. We miss you at Jimmy's."

"Busy."

"Of course, always. How's the old jaw?"

"Old jaw's fine." It clenches on me and I sound like a dying Sioux.

"You know, Jon here took a terrible whack in the jaw. What was it, a mugging?" He smiles, I smile. Marty isn't listening. It's our joke.

In fact, Marty seems impatient to get back to his conversation with Waldo, who shoots me a "do you mind, old boy?" look. Well, I can't just stand there hovering. The tide begins to swirl me away into the mindless underbelly of the party. The next glimpse I get is of several big names bowing respectfully over Waldo and shaking his paw. Everybody admires my author more than I do.

Celia sees me drifting and comes over to help like a Salvation Army wagon. We talk about how wonderful it is out here and what a wonderful change it is from out there. Looking around, I can't imagine what the difference could be, unless they make the Perrier some other way on the West Coast. Anyway, while Celia rattles on about values and traditions, I have plenty of time to seethe. Waldo has taken over my new kingdom just like that. Any moment he will be introducing *me* to *them*. The bully has kicked over my sand castle one more time.

"Come here a minute will you, Jonny." He summons me over by the name I hate. Hearthstone's face is like an open cash register. A publisher is a nice little acquisition, a cute trinket for a producer's vest pocket, but a big-name author is a castle on the Rhine. I can see it already. Waldo will spend the rest of the summer telling people what Marty Hearthstone said last night, and Marty will return the compliment. Waldo will become a regular here. On my rare visits, I will find him slumped in an armchair. They will be planning a trip to Pamplona.

"What is it, Waldo?" I come panting to his side.

"Marty here has been talking about getting up a softball game, and I told him that you are the very heart of the softball movement out here, its conscience, if you will."

"Waldo is too modest. He could be describing himself."

Hearthstone has no time for persiflage, he is way over budget already. "Can you get together a team to play against anyone I can scrape up? They shouldn't be too good, but they shouldn't be ridiculous either." Right sir. You want a cute little blonde who does Tragedy.

Before I can click my heels and wheel away, Waldo interjects, "We're having our first practice tomorrow. We tried to get hold of you."

"Funny, the service didn't pick it up."

"Oh? Anyway, we were hoping you'd be in shape to work out. We're really counting on you, with your depth of experience and savvy."

Listen Hearthstone, just *listen* to this crap. Your favorite living writer is a facetious moron.

"So can you get your people together?" Marty says to me.

"We'll have to see how they shape up. They may astound me by being too good, but at the moment, calling them people at all . . ."

"Sure we can get them together," pipes Waldo. "The main thing about this game is to have a few laughs, right, Marty?" Marty smiles palely. "And I can practically guarantee you *that* with these stiffs. If worst comes to worst, we can just mix up the sides, right?"

Marty nods. Anything you say, you Major Talent you.

"To tell the truth," say I, "I'd really thought of hanging them up this year, what with the jaw . . ."

"That'd be too bad," says Waldo briskly. "Let's see then, who else can be our conscience this summer?"

Marty looks utterly indifferent. Just deliver the bodies, OK?—not too hot, not too cold.

"Well." I can suddenly see all the doors of summer locking on me, and the windows barred. "I guess I could try one practice session and see how it goes."

"That would be *great*," says Waldo hollowly. "Eleven o'clock, the old Cumquat Park. Bring your own glove."

Will that be all, sir? "Oh, one other thing, Waldo." I linger for the sake of lingering. "I don't think we should mention this project to the other guys until we see whether they can play the game or not."

"Why is that?" he asks absently, as if I've already left.

"Can you imagine a bunch of writers and would-be's practicing to play a bunch of producers and directors? They'd trip all over their feet."

"It's up to you," says Waldo, cementing my position of dogsbody, the guy who calls ahead to rent the field and who counts the balls and bats afterwards. Isn't that what an editor does, MacIntyre?

That *will* be all. Marty is not quite as rude as I'm painting him, and he smiles politely, but the moment I back away, he and Waldo are at it again like newlyweds. I feel spiritually as if I next proceed to walk backwards all the way to the front door and into my car, and drive backwards all the way home.

My resolution to stay out of Jimmy's (for the game *is* Jimmy's) has lasted exactly three weeks.

15

THE unassuming ponk of a softball, the howl of van Dyne
as it hits his hands, the curse of the first baseman as he
heads for the bushes. The season is open. Fielders
scurry about as if they don't know where the hostess wants
them to sit: two at third and none at second? That can't be
right. They both rush to second, but it's OK because Nikki the
incumbent baserunner is still glued to first awaiting instructions
as the batter wallops into her, sending her down in a pretty
heap. (I lust briefly, impersonally. I can do no more.)

A ball appears from nowhere and everyone is tagged out at
once, with Monique still writhing in her purple jumpsuit. Since
the first baseman is by now buried in flora one has to question
the pedigree of this felicitous ball, which turns out to be gray
and lopsided, more a sack than a ball, and suspiciously like the
one we used in practice. Waldo, the pitcher of the moment, has
left the mound already to get something out of his car, probably
yet another ball. Ho ho ho. I strain to laugh at my author and
his little joke, but my jaw still hurts.

Everyone else laughs. This early in the season, incompetence
is still funny. Later it will be our prison, our high security
funny farm. I straighten up stiffly behind the plate, and take off
my mask, which feels like a surgical appliance. Obviously my
account will be jaundiced. *Nothing* seems funny to me today.
However, in a pure spirit of anthropology, I would have to say
that these people meet all the criteria for "having fun" estab-

lished among the Hopi Indians and the pygmies of Hoboken. Monique is still rolling around seductively while her hairy assailant, some photographer from *Newsweek*, affects to dust her off. I get what small pleasure I can from the darting patches of winter-white female buttock around the field which seem to have just been taken out of mothballs. The slit in the catcher's mask is not unlike a window ledge, and peering at the batter-persons as they take their dainty lunges at the ball would normally give me a small boy's pleasure; but as soon as I try to leer, my jaw cracks and I am punished. Look at it this way, Oglethorpe: thousands of years of oppression have made batter-persons swing like that.

I assume that only the feebleminded will expect the fun to keep up week after week; there's only so much to be had in any sport that isn't played underwater. But right now we're just trying to establish a good spirit, which will carry over right into the wheezing heart of the season. The survivors will then show the rest of the world that winning isn't everything, week after dreary week. But I will be long gone, as soon as we've had our game with the Hollywood Stars and nailed Waldo's film sale. And I don't care *who* plays me in the movie, I tell you.

Please God, Waldo will not be our full-time pitcher. A few hours of staring at this child-man, waiting for him inevitably to toss in a grapefruit or exploding beanbag one day, would be too much like real life. I should mention that all is even worse between me and Waldo right now than I've admitted. Partly to stall him while I got on with my rebirth last winter, I requested a fair number of rewrites, all of them justified, but few of them strictly necessary. Waldo is like a necktie made out of gravy— one more stain doesn't make much difference. Waldo, as you might suppose, is an author who practically bellows to the waves that no one tells *him* how to write, by golly. But he is also an old pro hanging by his thumbs, so he made the changes in his primitive fashion. But with each one, he made the Otis MacIntyre character slightly nastier and more recognizably me. How much of this can you take, he seemed to say as our thumbs locked. What price your perfection?

"Waldo," I wrote back, "don't you think you're overdoing it a bit? You already have a perfect villain, why not leave him alone? It doesn't add much to your Iago character to have him picking his nose." In other words, what price your malice? You want to ruin a good book just for my sake? I plead silently.

I can picture Waldo chewing his thumb over this with the zest of some great mastiff. Perhaps the little bastard is right, thinks he. Waldo wouldn't be so dementedly out to get me if he didn't know that I have this one tiny edge on him. His first novel had been edited mercilessly, first novelists have no choice, and of course it turned out to be his one big success. Since then, he has been blundering around in the long grass, trumpeting ever more wildly—and the critics tell him he has lost his raw power. His raw power, indeed. The name of his raw power was then Jerry Tauber, a skinny fellow raised in a library, and is now Otis MacIntyre a.k.a. me.

This aspect of literature quite rightly maddens a half-formed genius like Waldo; simply the fact that squinty-eyed defectives like me and Tauber should know a secret that he can't seem to learn, a secret that turns on his juice and makes him, to some extent, *our* monster. So well do I understand his rage (and even see its value—the MacIntyre passages bite deeper than anything else he's done) that I grit my new side teeth and decide to take it like a publisher. But please, not in the troubled pitcher-catcher relationship.

Our last rewrite conversation went roughly as follows. Waldo calls in to say, "You know, I'm beginning to dig this Otis guy. You sure it wouldn't be all right if I have him stick his finger up his ass now and then? I mean, only when it's artistically justified."

"Yeah, you can do it then."

"I'm also wondering about the son, Angus. Maybe he's too nice. After the way his old man has treated him, he should have a mean streak himself, don't you think?"

For once in my life, I hang up on him. Holding my kid as hostage is too much, and Waldo knows it. If you bite him in the leg, he is wonderfully perceptive. The rewriting ended in a one-hundred-move draw, quite a bloodbath for such a quiet sport, and his manuscript is safely out of his hands for now.

Anyway, I can't have this guy a mere forty-five feet away from me on the mound armed with any kind of missile at all. He has already tried one surprise, a smoky sizzling fastball that easily split my hands apart and squirted up my chest to tap the wired-up chin. "Sorry, old man. It got away." Does this sound too bad to be true? Perhaps. My villain has to keep pace with his villain, my Iago with his Iago.

And so we leave Waldo with his finger halfway up his ass, and check out some other old favorites. Cecily Woodruff is loping around short center field, and I really mean loping. Her strides are as long and lovely as DiMaggio's and her arm is nothing like the wet noodle she has painted. On one play she spears a line drive and doubles the runner off first—or would have if the first baseman were anywhere to be found. She scowls and turns her back smartly. Somebody better be there next time. In right, Fender is statuesque of course. If he could, he would obviously prefer to play it on horseback. Nothing happens in right field anyway. He is free to create himself.

Van Dyne is playing good defense at second—which is to say, he rarely gets hit by the ball. Archie Munson at short soldiers on professionally through the chaos, making normal plays that come to nothing because of missing basemen. He reminds me of Buster Keaton in a rainstorm. Pete Simmons's left field is, let's call it, understated, and that's about it. I had expected better from our house prole, but maybe he's holding back for that reason. There are also some nondescript hangers-on from Jimmy's, including one of our hard-drinking painters, red-faced and muscular and totally silent, and a few smooth-looking chaps alleged to be with the media, any medium will do.

Some summer bunnies have already taken off and gone to the beach. And in fact a whining beach group has already begun to form at the fringes, although it is a cool day. The whiners seem mainly to have come from some kind of secretarial pool, which the guys grabbed at hastily on Friday. And now they want their beach. They will be frosty, unrewarding bunnies if they don't get their beach. So the media guys, who look like Californians to begin with, trickle away. Nobody knows for sure who they are except Waldo, who presumably brings them in by the bus-

load. No *Women's Wear* second-string reviewer in Bangkok is beneath Waldo's attention when he has a book in the works.

The pickup game dies of evaporation, but not before Ferris
has parked one in the adjacent tennis court and trotted regally
round the bases and into the dugout, carrying his bat all the
way like General Lee's sword. Does he do that all the time?
Talented but difficult. Billy is treating himself for blisters,
mainly by squeezing them and yelling. Cecily lopes further and
further as the field thins, until she is covering both sidelines at
once. Other players leave one at a time, as if this was the safest
way to escape. Each of the rest of us is down to his own private
reason for staying.

Pete Simmons looks questioning: you intellectual guys want
to go on, right? Otherwise, I can drop it right now. Archie is
pitching now. He at least knows what he wants, so he leads the
flabby masses without being asked to. Since we are down to our
hard core of winter now, we find ourselves taking batting practice, or rather we find Waldo taking it. He hits a screaming line
drive and another and runs out to the mound again. Finally I
am allowed a grudging cut and the result feels promising, but it
takes off like an old pillow. Waldo has substituted the fetid
practice ball just for me. Oh well, if it gives him pleasure, I,
with my sickly understanding of authors' needs, forgive the
prick.

I believe the whole season might have ended then and there,
in a final burst of bored incomprehension, and saved us all
much grief, except for Madman Munson and Spinks. I think
Waldo at that moment just wants to have as many media people
see him at play, and sense that other dimension of his, as he can
cram in. Waterskiing would have served just as well. But Munson's insanity is more specific and scary. He wants to drag us all
into his old world of baseball where he is King, not to mention
young and alive again.

His tactics are not uninteresting. To begin with, he herds the
remnant, the beloved disciples, straight into Jimmy's, our
shrine, our Cooperstown, where he persuades us that we have
had a good time. It is clear that a leader of his caliber could as
easily convince us that we had a rotten time. We don't know

what kind of time we've had. This is the mystery of softball. Also the secret of Munson's sportswriting career. (He was known as a rooter.)

"You were great out there, Cecily. I don't care who we play around here. You're on the team. Billy, your hands are now battle-hard, tournament-tough. Use them with discretion, my boy."

He works us over one by one. It seems *I* was the real surprise—a genuine pro back there. The catcher is the heart and balls of the team and that was little me. My nausea at being back in Jimmy's abates slightly. I know it is bullshit, but is there any American anywhere who really minds being called a good ballplayer, never mind by whom? So with mad, grateful eyes, we all gulp down our praise. Even Ferris the Proud, who has mysteriously decided to hang out with us, seems faintly pleased. "The way you carried your bat—what bravura! It reminded me of Pickett's charge," says Munson. Cecily and Ferris glance appraisingly at each other. "Johnny Reb comes to Park Avenue" say her eyes. "A Northern belle at Bull Run" say his. The air is moist with book titles. After a while, the warmth of winter reenters our air-conditioned bones. We *did* have fun today, all the fun we said we were going to have.

Once Archie has us all purring steadily, he launches into his second ploy, first heard around old stone fires and illustrated on cave walls in France. He begins attacking the outsiders, the Summer People. "They're really not like the rest of us," he says. "To begin with, just being out here is a fad for them, so everything they do is simply a fad spinning off of another fad. I can see it already: 'this summer's place to be is definitely the softball game at Jimmy's where such communications biggies as Waldo Spinks and Billy van Dyne frolic their weekends away. You can't afford *not* to be seen there.'" And so our game, lovingly nurtured during the unfashionable chilblain season, will be casually destroyed.

Everyone murmurs his horror, except me, with my dreaded message from the Coast. It goes without saying that we all abhor publicity. "We've got to keep it out of the news," says Waldo, winking at me. I can almost see him scurrying to a telex office as soon as the coast has cleared. This doesn't seem like the time to bring up our film people who will undoubtedly insist on total privacy, and not get it, as is their way. Meanwhile, it's interesting to see someone like Billy van Dyne deciding with glinting eyes whether to accept publicity or not. It is nice just to be close enough to the Great Beast to be asked. And of course, if a story does appear, Billy and the rest of us can vie with each other in feats of outrage over the breach of confidence.

Munson's third child psychology ploy is the most despicable of all, namely keeping us busy. He has arranged a game just two weeks away with another tavern, so we'd better look lively. Practice tomorrow? Why the hell not? "The guys we're playing said they'd whip our asses," murmurs Munson. But instead of snarling defiance as we should, Nikki squeaks with apprehension, "Do you think they will?"

"Just a figure of speech, my love," says Waldo. "You have nothing to fear, personally."

It is a relief to find out that we've enjoyed ourselves so much. Otherwise our dawn session the next day wouldn't make much sense. Even with Archie chattering as he slaps ground balls at us, the battle with the sandman is grim. This time Arch has the cunning to call it off early. Otherwise at least one among us might have woken from his trance. "Just a little tuneup," breezes Archie, as if we are seasoned concert masters and not the same old dog act.

My jaw, which has felt up to now like my whole body, suddenly has to move over and make room. Everything hurts today. My thighs as I stoop behind the plate burn my calves like a hot stove, snapping me back to attention. Munson notices of course. Any displeasure on our part will destroy his precious game a lot faster than the Summer People ever could. "Why not just shag a few in the outfield, Jon? Get the kinks out." He runs back and grabs the mitt himself and hunkers down enthusiastically, pounding and hollering.

I've seen kids do this, as the sluggish majority begins to look bored at pickup games, but never a grownup. Archie at this stage clearly cannot face the blank Summer without his game.

He'll do anything—chauffeur us individually, do our laundry, babysit—to keep us interested. It becomes a point of honor for us not to drive him to these degrading extremes. So we hustle our asses off for him. And begin, against nature, to improve.

Not enough to take on the Tall Men from the Coast just yet. These have grown in my mind to superb specimens, swimming pool tough and massaged to a fine edge. They don't *look* superb, of course, but we must have our little superstitions. They probably think that everyone in the Eastern print racket is a towering intellect. We, for our part, endow them all with bodies.

"What do you say, Wald?" I whisper as we trot professionally off the field. "Another week before we break it to them?"

Waldo and I are, bear in mind, the best of friends, and are doomed to talk like this forever. "Whatever you say, Jonny. It's all the same to me." He wants to be casual, but suddenly can't. "I don't know, though. Marty is getting kind of impatient."

"After *three days?*"

"Well maybe not quite yet. But he will. You know these guys, they have tight schedules."

We both know what he's talking about. We stroll toward our cars with his arm around my shoulder. Enmity would be less taxing than this. "Has he seen it yet?"

"Hey wait a minute, Wald. We're still cleaning up the manuscript."

"And why is *that* taking so fucking long?"

"Because we took turns beating the shit out of it, remember? You don't want Marty to see it in this condition. They like things squeaky out there, and your manuscript looks like an outhouse. An outhouse of genius, to be sure . . ."

"Give it back to me, Jon, right away! I'll clean it myself, with S.O.S. pads if necessary."

"You promise not to rewrite the whole thing?"

"Only the parts about Otis MacIntyre, old buddy. He comes through a bit bland in the present version."

I don't even feel it, and neither does he. After enough torture, neither party is fully present. "OK, the minute she's ready, I'll announce our guys fit to play. And then God help us all."

"Yeah, but I'd like to keep in, you know, touch with Hearthstone in the meanwhile."

"And what makes you think softball keeps people in good?"

"I didn't say 'in good.'"

"I know what you said. Games are unpredictable, Waldo. As many enemies come crawling out of the ruins as friends."

"I can control it."

"You can, huh?"

"Look, he wants his fucking game. These Hollywood guys have minds like fleas. He doesn't get what he wants, he suddenly decides he doesn't like it out here. So he rents a million-dollar hovel in Bar Harbor, and if they won't play with him there, he's off to Japan or someplace."

Off your knees, Waldo. I shall pay for this sickening display of abasement.

"I really want that fucking sale," he says.

Well, that's clear. He wouldn't be calling Marty Hearthstone a fleabrain quite so soon if he wasn't desperate.

"I understand that, Waldo. I want that sale too." I feel like an atheist hearing confessions. "But it doesn't do to seem over-anxious."

We have reached his car and are resting our backsides on the hood. He squints at me a moment and seems to snap out of his trance, and straight into another one. "You think I don't know that, little buddy? Jesus. 'It doesn't *do* to seem overanxious.' That's a good one, Otis. I love that 'doesn't *do*' part. It's got a lot of polish." He has never actually called me Otis before, except when singing.

He gets into his car, leering. "All right, Waldo," I shout round at the closed window, "*you* tell your ass-kissing pal Marty when *your* lousy team is ready." The car starts up and Waldo almost sends his old friend flying off the hood, as he drives away waving and smiling. My last words would have been meaningless even if he'd heard them.

Because he doesn't know I'm writing a book too, and that I've given him the epicene name of Waldo in place of his manly real one. So, this is the first time I've actually called Waldo "Waldo," if you follow me. When he finally sees the name in print, he might turn *really* mean. A happy thought strikes me apropos of that. His Otis character is fixed now, stuck in amber in all his petty vileness, but I can still make my Waldo worse.

It is no strain to smile and wave back as his car leaves the parking lot. I feel more than ever like Iago saying "safe home" to his boss in a modern version of my favorite play.

16

THERE'S more to life out here than softball though I wouldn't dream of telling Munson that. There is also croquet, tennis, and its little friend badminton, not to mention golfing, sailing, and various things you do with horses. And there is fundraising.

The very next Saturday I am slated for an afternoon at the Padgetts' where all the above sports and more have been known to go on at once. The Padgetts' estate has the makings of a great sports complex for inner-city malcontents, i.e., just about everybody I know. But most of the time it simply sits idle in the sunshine, patting its green stomach. In fact I've sometimes thought of placing a sign WASTED ACRES at the entrance, right between DANGEROUS DOG and WE SHOOT TO KILL.

The Padgetts' lawn rolls right up to the house and the house rolls out to the sea. The only sound you hear is the distant, always distant, clip of the lawn mower and whatever it is a roller sounds like as it smoothes the way for Chip Padgett's passing shots.

The Padgetts are among the cream of the Summer People. When they open up each year with their Memorial Day Benefit, it's like the opening of Parliament: you feel the Queen should pound on the door with her mace. And when they close things out with their Labor Day fund raiser, that's it. The Bentleys and Rollses pull out silently, leaving us to our Tobacco Road realities.

Yet the Padgetts are also hyperactive in liberal causes, which is what makes me think of inner-city kids. (The rich must choose up sides about things like this, giving 10 percent, or a tithe, of their team to the left.) The Padgetts have had their own money for so long that they no longer connect it with their ideals. In fact I'm not sure they even *know* whether they can give it away by this time, or exactly where it is right now. But they are indefatigable about raising the stuff from other people.

Piggy Padgett can hardly conceive of a party that isn't a fund-raiser. One day it's politics, another it's the Arts or Saving Our Water-Table: just so long as it raises funds most anything seems to do, although she may make an exception for weddings and very small breakfasts. So street arabs like me get frequent opportunities to thread our way between signs saying KEEP OFF and DO NOT TOUCH to view one of the stateliest homes out here, of which Jimmy's with its Tiffany lamps might be called the fun-house mirror version.

Today's beneficiary is the latest Lochinvar to try "with your he'p" to rescue and transform the Democratic Party in the next presidential election. He looks like a shifty-eyed cad to me, but Piggy Padgett, who never recognizes me on normal occasions, presses my arm intimately and assures me that Bo Chapman here has wonderful, well-nigh saintly, ideals and more integrity than a man strictly needs. "He is something completely new in our politics." Oh, no, not that again. "And he isn't afraid to be unpopular."

Against my will, my mind drifts back salaciously to the bright infield grass and the bouncing ball as Piggy waxes vague about Bo Chapman's ideals. It seems that he believes in a break for the little guy, for one thing (I think of Billy van Dyne's fielding) and world peace (not with Waldo around) and nuclear sanity (except for the Confederacy, eh Ferris?). "Oh, he says it all so much better than I do. And by the way, he's terrific on the Middle East."

"You mean he favors a weak Israel?"

"What?" She is now total vagueness, as the human body is almost total water. "I don't think I heard you." She decides to let me go anyway, just on the off-chance that she did hear me and has a criminal lunatic on her hands. In fact, I could have chased her with any one of thirty such remarks: a new idea has to walk a narrow line with Piggy Padgett.

Yet in a while Bo Chapman will be assuring Piggy and the little piglets that they are the most politically sophisticated people in the whole wide world. I try to immerse myself in the beauties of the house, which are really much too good for politics, before the flesh-peddling begins; but everything seems to be roped off, and everywhere I turn in the visitors' compound I hear another Voice reverberating like sounds in a cave. *He's really spoken up to the Moral Majority . . . thinks a woman's right to choose is sacred . . . believes that talking is better than fighting.*

"What Southerner ever thought that?" I mutter to the last of my Voices. "The man's an obvious charlatan."

"What? Eh?" You can't interrupt the Voices. They must proceed with their chant, their plainsong, until Bo Chapman, that seething cauldron of originality, silences them with his New Vision of America.

Well, at least I've gotten away from Waldo, who has never had an ideal in his life except making it a better world for Waldo. Only kidding, of course, about getting away from Waldo, which is about as easy as escaping from Alcatraz this particular summer. I spot him at last in a window seat chatting with our host Chip Padgett. If his new book was out yet, he'd undoubtedly have his own little bookstand here, with something like "Cambodian War Relief" written above it.

The clichés from behind press me ineluctably in his direction, the only quiet dell in the room. At least it will be fun to hear Waldo talking about, oh, the War on Poverty or the real causes of crime (which Waldo secretly believes to be obvious: "crime is so goddamn appealing"). But, then I see him making a small flicking motion with his forearm, and I understand with horror that the sonofabitch is demonstrating his backhand dropshot, and that the subject is tennis.

"Jonathan. It's good to see you, old boy." He is wearing a white sportshirt with an alligator on it, under a blue blazer. Where did he steal that?

"Yeah, it's been hours."

"Chip? Do you know my friend, Jonathan Oglethorpe?"

Chip, concentrate. Heel and concentrate, for Christsake. "Pleased to meet you, Mr. . . . Er," he says at last, shaking my hand firmly. Meeting me at a thousand fundraisers clearly doesn't constitute *meeting* me; he must stumble through these things like a blind man.

"Chip has invited me over to play tennis on Tuesday," says Waldo. "You want to help me warm up tomorrow? I'm kind of rusty."

Tauber advises me that there is no need to write down my thoughts at this particular point, if it's going to upset me too much. *Didn't you know, Jon old boy, that any real novelist can master a crowd like this in five minutes?* says Waldo's face. I want to say something rude right back about his tennis, about how he usually plays it with a stick and a tin can, etc. But his candid, preppy expression unmans me.

"Waldo's new book is wonderful," I say to Padgett, jumping on the bandwagon instead of flinging my corpse in front of it.

"Book?" says Padgett. This man here writes books?

Oh, well. Bo Chapman is about to speak from the palatial staircase, sparing me further foolishness from any other quarter. Behind me, Waldo and Chip continue to mumble, and it dawns on me at long last that Chip is a political imbecile who needs company at these events. It's just that Waldo has grasped this instantly.

Chapman, it turns out, is a lot less dumb than his supporters, and his task will be to keep this from showing. "I don't have to tell *you* people what the problems facing America are," he says. In fact, most of them would have their work cut out locating New Jersey on a map, but let it pass.

Politics has always been a headache for me, because they remind me of home. My own family were upstate Republicans, who found that the Grand Old Party makes a very snug fit with atrophied Calvinism. People are what they are. You can spend a ton of money trying to improve them, but at the end you are merely exhausted and out of pocket, while humanity just sits there blinking like some great dumb brute. My father Fergus was and is himself quite a generous man, and my mother Alice even more so. But their bleak, unwavering picture of humanity as a distended pig sitting around in its own slops always gave the lie to their kindnesses. According to their lights, their gifts did no one any good, except possibly themselves. "Give till it hurts." The old slogan suited Fergus perfectly, because the pain was the point, the only constructive thing about giving.

When it came time for the wearisome rituals of my own teen-age revolt, I was faced with a problem. My parents didn't seem to care one way or the other. I have a vision of Alice practically running upstairs and packing my bags for me the day I suggested moving out at sixteen, and of Fergus saying humorously "what kept you so long? I was gone by fourteen myself." Alice did in fact say things about wrapping up warmly and eating properly, as if she were reading me the Miranda Act. Fergus said, "Be sure to keep up with your studies. And son, always have a plan."

It wasn't really that quick or that cold, but it *was* over before I could get up a head of steam. In fact, I wasn't dead sure who had uprisen against whom around here. Fergus shook my hand enthusiastically and mother pecked my cheek and they both stood on the porch and watched me go. My move wasn't that epochal. I went to New York with a friend and wound up at Columbia. It wasn't exactly shipping out under Captain Flint.

Anyway my parents' determination not to stand in my way amounted to a fetish. So when I told Fergus I was voting Democrat, I wasn't surprised when he said, "Well there's plenty of time. *I* used to admire Eugene Debs once upon a time." But even if I didn't come round to Coolidge again as I got older, it was no business of theirs. It wasn't a life or death matter like personal achievement. Now *that* might have been something for them to worry about.

But probably not much and not yet. For a few months, I did pronounce myself dead set against worldly success and even had some heavy sessions with the Catholic chaplain (surely *that* would get their goat? No. Father had once had that inclination himself). I gobbled up the great mystics like candy, being, as you will note, given to such spasms, but I didn't even bother to tell Father about it, because I'm sure he would have said, "Ah yes, I used to be quite a fan of St. John of the Cross." He kept close to me in his own way.

So when I became a campus radical, writing fiery stuff for the *Spectator*, I didn't even have to ask what he thought; it was obviously the best move I could make in my particular circumstances. "I owe my own business success entirely to a close reading of Karl Marx," he wrote at that time. "What an economist!" As it happened, I did believe hotly in the Left, and could have argued his arm off about it, but he would just have let me have the arm. *You can't go through any phase well if you don't believe in it at the time*, he would have said. I guess one leaves home when one *always* knows what they're going to say next.

To my mother, these were just men's games, as bracing as a cold shower or a sprint at dawn, but of no point in themselves. She was the ultimate keeper of the flame. I think she found her husband a bit cynical at times, if not downright agnostic, but his actions were more or less upright, so it didn't matter what he thought. He was a good man.

Sara MacSpadden Oglethorpe was the true believer, the family theologian, the Keeper of the Book, and it was her negative spiritual genius that I had to rebel against if I was going to get anywhere, the rest was tactics. So I tried being a fop, a campus character, a blithe spirit. Thank God, I never told her I was a writer: that was my secret, my private escape plan, because she like my father was waiting at the end of every tunnel. She knew my capering meant no more than her own quite surprising friendliness did. Predestination makes no exceptions for loved ones anyway, and I sometimes had the bloodcurdling—and I'm sure quite unfair—feeling that if *I* was damned, she'd say "God's will be done" and send off some more fruitless money for famine relief.

So out went the fop and finally out went the politics too (it was all right, I still had my writing!). Halfway through my radical phase, I felt a magnetic pull. The undertow of my parents' early training started to suck at my little rowboat and all my energetic little heaves in the other direction went for naught. Radicalism might be loads of fun, but it didn't match the world I knew in my bones. So I climbed down gingerly from early Maoism or wherever I'd perched, until my toe found the liberal rung, and there I rested. It was a good place to be, because everybody else was there too. You don't even have to ask.

At the Padgetts', for instance, it is assumed one is liberal. People start talking liberal to you as soon as you walk through the door. In the other mansions on Frog Lane, the situation may be completely reversed. I don't know, because we don't meet those people. Luckily for everybody, they voluntarily lock themselves up in country clubs for months on end so they won't get in people's hair.

As long as I keep my trap shut with the Padgetts and their infinite equivalents, my liberalism remains untarnished. I don't even have to nod, or grunt enthusiastically. And since nine-tenths of my authors and colleagues are in the same boat, I'm content to leave it at that. It must be a bit like working in the Politburo; there may not be another Communist in the joint. No one will ever know.

Right now I feel as if I am standing in Red Square applauding every cliché that marches past: noble old things, some of them—it's a pleasure to give them a hand at their age. Why am I here at all, you ask? Because it's where the money is, and one must see *some* rich people some of the time, if one is to feel one has truly lived out here.

"Don't you think that if we just talked to the Russians and never stopped, and wouldn't let *them* stop, that the world would be, er, a safer place?" So says Piggy Padgett in the question period, and why not? This policy has worked wonders for her.

Bo Chapman leans across the banister with great sincerity. "You've certainly given me something to think about, ma'am."

You know the rest. Everyone agrees that indeed Bo Chapman is a fresh new face and a bold new voice. He presses all the flesh he can lay hands on, including my own crawling variety. "Nice speech, governor. Thought-provoking." "Thank you so much. I need your support. You and all the people like you."

If he makes *three* wishes like that he'll end up with a sausage at the end of his nose. His handshake is firm, though. First baseman? I banish the thought. I disengage my own flesh swiftly. It's a sin to waste this good man's time, although he obviously doesn't feel the same about mine. I shimmy out past a radiant Piggy who has just encountered her Messiah of the Year. *And* given him something to think about, too. Bliss.

I notice that the window seat is empty. Perhaps the tennis talk got too hot, and Waldo and host decided they must do it *now*. I hope wanly that Waldo will prove a duffer and then somehow with the same breath that he won't. I have discovered my very own commandment. Thou shalt not publish thy enemy's goods.

Then back over the acres to my car, with the lawn no doubt being rolled up behind me for dry cleaning. In a short while, the film people will be flapping about town looking for interesting restaurants, of which we have none. I will pick up Mavis V (a groupie, this time) and drag her by the hair to Jimmy's—to which I have utterly capitulated—where, who knows, the talk may eventually turn to softball.

To soften the pain, I have invited Mavis V *solely* because she has a good glove.

It turns out that Jimmy's, on a summer Saturday night, is not quite as I'd remembered it. For one thing, the place is packed. Honest, middle-class folk who have come to the Hamptons by mistake occupy our usual tables with their sullen children, holding down our chairs like bags of cement; the bar is lined with singles of every sex, all plying their ferocious business and clogging the aisle between Jimmy's food and Jimmy's drink. I peer through the fugg for a friendly face, but there's no one in sight. Even the summer waiters don't recognize me; even Jimmy wouldn't recognize me if he could help it. "It looks like a long wait, Jon," says he. "Maybe I should take another look at your manuscript," I murmur jocosely. "Excuse me." He is already moving away, his eyes on the horizon. I swore I would never come back to this place, and it turns out I'm the only one of us here.

Jimmy's has to cater to all the little needs of our summer community, not just those of a few dependable old soaks. So the bartenders are constantly surly from making ridiculous pink drinks. The waiters are half-mad from taking plates back to the kitchen, because the customers didn't understand the menu. Huge voracious families that have apparently never been in restaurants before leave without tipping. Right now, I'm staring down at an ancient couple who are lingering over their coffee. They have that settled look and will obviously still be here when I leave. They wouldn't be in Jimmy's at all if they had any place to go.

It's obviously a disgrace for a regular to be caught here on a Saturday night. I think ruefully of those regal dinners I was *not* going to invite my authors to. Everyone I know is at a regal dinner right this minute, even Archie Munson, even Pete Simmons. And I can't get a table at Jimmy's.

"Do you mind standing back, Jon," says Jimmy. "You're blocking the drink orders." *Aren't you ashamed to be here? If you leave right now, I won't tell them I've seen you.* He turns his back as if he is counting to ten. On Saturday nights, Jimmy is all business, and the barroom bard from Bantry is nowhere to be found.

I do most devoutly think of leaving, but even this wouldn't be easy by now, as ever more wildly inappropriate people come barreling in on all sides, forming a tight, heaving corset around us. I look at Mavis for clues. What does she think of her evening on the town with Mr. Masterful, eh? She actually appears to be standing and staring as patiently as a cow, or a right fielder. "Wanna go?" I whisper. Mavis, glove-woman, shrugs. "Where to?" I don't know; maybe we can go outside and play catch.

The old couple experience a spasm of energy, and stand up just like that. I am convinced that Jimmy will give their table to the first punk rocker and her pimp that he runs into before he gets round to us—but no, he isn't that far gone. "I've got one for you, Jon. Thanks for waiting."

So we say farewell to the zoo in front of the bar, and as I swing out into the feeding zone I notice the biggest table in the joint—our table of winter, our hot-stove league stove—standing empty. Usually one or other of us will have parked there until the crowd accretes around him, but it seems that this will not do in Summer: our crowd must accrete before it gets here, or it's no deal. Suddenly the table looks like King Arthur's own no. 1. I can just see it surrounded by jolly fellows, with rosy faces and beakers of grog, defying the winter and the outside world, while Jimmy feeds the flames like Vulcan. But in reality it is as bare as an operating table tonight. I gaze at it, I trust questioningly (I don't really know how this look goes, so must take it on faith), and Jimmy says, "It's reserved for another party."

Reserved? *Another party?* Jimmy has never used such a phrase in his life. His soul must have been removed for the season and replaced by an air hostess. I hunker down glumly at a table built for one-and-a-half and gird myself for conversation with Mavis the Glove.

We are just mopping this up along with our dessert when, what ho, in flap the movie people, like a flight of Canadian geese. By whatever mysterious code they use, honking or rolling their eyes, they have decided this is *the* place to be after the regal dinner. And they are, of course, the other party that has commandeered our table like so many Visigoths ransacking a temple.

Hearthstone, a natural leader, turns round as if to count heads. The whole pack is there. I will not name their names just to sell books, I'm not that kind of author. Suffice it to say that you've probably heard of all of them. And tailing along like an organ-grinder's monkey—but need I say it?—Waldo, practically in jodhpurs and riding crop by now, plunks himself down with the directing greats and two major stars and three French hens, and starts talking about antiques, I'll bet.

At some point he sees me and beckons me over. Oh, no. There are some things even I won't do. If I can't get a table myself, I certainly won't take one from you and your new patrons. Besides I'm having too much fun with Mavis. We sit for a minute or so in miserable silence and then she perks up for the first time. "Isn't that _____?" she says, referring to one of the world famous actors. "And if so, why isn't he with _____?" These are deep questions. "God, I'd give *any*thing to meet him," she whinnies.

Anything is a very decent offer, but not tonight, toots. An Oglethorpe dies on his feet, not on his knees. Just then, by chance, Pete Simmons shows up and asks if he can sit with us. Even the question bores me unutterably. You simply do not spend a Saturday night with Simmons. "That's OK, Pete. You can have the whole table. We were just going over to sit with Waldo."

Well, there had to be a first Oglethorpe to do it. I feel like Toulouse-Lautrec as I stump over to the star table and introduce Mavis all round. Please, honey, now don't ask for autographs, OK?

This time Hearthstone seems positively eager to see me. He must want that ballgame awfully badly. I start to line up my excuses in a pretty row, but hark! "Waldo has been telling me more about his new book. It sounds wonderful."

"It is," croaks Jonathan the Dwarf.

"I'd love to read it."

"What about it, Jon," says Waldo airily.

"That shouldn't be too impossible. Have you talked to your agent about it?"

All this prattle is quite unnecessary, as all three of us know. Waldo has bent Hearthstone out of shape to get him to this point. He will now bring him the manuscript in his teeth, if necessary.

I somehow sense that what Hearthstone wants from me now is enthusiasm, something to get his own burner lit. For all his literary folderol, he doesn't know he's excited unless you tell him he's excited. So I must perform the task of his staff, of his flunkies, and warm up the master.

Or am I being unduly sensitive tonight? Editors do this kind of thing as a matter of course. Well, here goes. "Not since . . . raw power . . . but tender, too . . . and literary values, oh my yes, literary values to burn . . . and of course, a *real* love story." I parody myself in atonement. What I probably said was something low key like "we're tremendously high on the book at Williams and Oglethorpe," uttered in the dead man's drawl of the aging preppy.

Hearthstone looks at me with fierce intensity. Come on baby, give it to me, excite me. I am cold. Light my fire. Two box-office flops have snuffed out even his confidence for now. "I'll get you a copy," I say, "and meanwhile, what about that softball game?" I say desperately. Anything, even that, to change the subject.

Marty goes blank for a moment. What softball game? God, I've heard about these guys' tiny attention spans, but this is sub-luna moth. He stares at me as if I were nuts. Why is this guy always talking to me about softball?

"Oh that," he says. "I guess we'll just have to postpone the game for a few weeks. I hope you don't mind. I've got some business to do on the other coast. As a matter of fact I'd love to take Waldo's book on the plane with me."

"I'll get you a manuscript."

"I have one right here," pipes the mischievous Waldo.

They all leave soon after that, as if the evening's movie were over and they had to go home and pound themselves with cold cream. All that remains now is for me to convince Mavis V that _____ has nothing on me hunkwise; or failing that, that if she says the right words, I may turn into him during the night.

Anyway, it's a relief about the softball game. I feel like a kid let out of school early on Friday. Monday is a million years away. I bounce over to Jimmy, who stands stooped over his accounts, looking haggard and joyless. A slap on the back would just about cave him in, so I settle for a species of pat. "How's it going, Jimbo? Land-office business, eh?" Sallow eyes look up from the once mighty Celtic boy-o. "Believe me, Jon," he says without smiling, "I hate this every bit as much as you do."

Thus endeth another Saturday. Mavis V says she doesn't do it on first dates. Not with character actors anyway. This in its way is a relief too. I must be getting old. So I fling into my immaculate white nightgown, adjust the tassle on my cap, and reach for my goose quill. The rest is history.

17

WELL, there isn't *much* more to life out here than soft-ball, I'll grant Archie Munson that. We have just had our last lamentable practice before our first outside game and the group mood has changed even faster than I expected. At first, the good players had snarled sort of abstractly as the bad players continued maddeningly and methodically to goof up. They would curse the sky, shake their fists at the grass, or try to copy Archie Munson's rueful grin.

But by the fourth session all pretense of civility is gone. Oh, they still look away to say "fucking asshole," but they glare straight at the guilty party as they growl "goddammit." Munson alone among the Competents acts as if everything is coming along just splendidly. "Good throw, Nikki . . . well, almost good throw. Try to bend that elbow just a little bit, dear." Among the Disasters, Nikki van Dyne is the most sublimely unconscious (she thinks everyone plays like that), which may be why she bursts into tears when Cecily Woodruff calls her a paraplegic twat.

"I thought we were supposed to be having fun," she wails, and sinks to the ground in her usual luscious heap.

"You have fun at this game by doing it right," snaps Cecily, turning on her heel.

Woodruff is probably our most remorseless Competent. She tears off the field in a rage after every woebegone inning, and refuses to talk to the culprits. I thought she was going to dash the can from Nikki's hand when the pretty thing offered her a peacemaking soda.

Even the men are getting a little apprehensive about Cecily. Billy van Dyne flinches when he drops the ball, as if he fears immediate retribution from short center field. And at the end of this ghastly session, Munson stands beside her, with his head bent nervously, as she pours more spleen into his ear. "Those people next week will make complete fools out of us." The rest of the players edge closer, like children listening on the staircase. "We've got to play our best people, Archie, and you know it." Archie's mutter is hard to pick up, but Cecily's roar is not. "*Fuck* the spirit of the game," and *she* begins to cry. "Does that mean," says an unidentified feminist from NBC, "that you want to throw out all the women?" "If they're no good, yes," sniffs Cecily. "Leaving only you?" "If I'm good enough, yes."

It had to happen. It was a year when men and women should have conducted all their activities separately behind chain-fences. You couldn't even play charades without some version of this argument arising. "Why do you have to *win* everything, George?" and so on.

Cecily is not to be deflected by some pusillanimous sister. Drying her eyes like a brave soldier, she says, "It's an insult to women to play us if we're no good. It means we don't belong in real games at all!"

I hope that she will now tail off into argument 58, or whatever the number is, and we'll all get bored and go home. I almost offer to say Cecily's lines for her, so she can get an early start. But Cecily is not tailing off into anything. She strides up to Archie who has tried to slip away unnoticed. "Well, is that it, Arch? Are we going to field all our turkeys and have our collective behinds whipped, or do we play a little ball?"

Munson nods miserably. "It's the game we talked about all winter."

"Well it's not my game. Here." She yanks off her cap and hands it to him, apparently thinks twice about yanking off her T-shirt as well, and stalks off. Ferris Fender, who's been standing by motionless, trots up and puts his arm round her. She shakes it off and walks on alone. He falls back as if stung, his

worst fears and expectations realized. I have to wonder at times
if this game is worth it.

The only good thing about this last session is that Waldo
doesn't show up. As with any marriage, I need some time away
from him; and God knows what sort of shambles he'd have
made of that last act.

I go off with Archie to have a beer. There is no sense of the
team bubbling around us as there was on the first day, but more
of refugees struggling out of a bombed city to rebuild their shattered lives.

Munson it seems is a divided man. "I'd like a good team as
much as anyone," he says over his first beer. "But you guys are
my *friends* . . . hey, I didn't mean you, Jon. I mean you *are* my
friend, but . . ." His mind has come completely unraveled.

"Yes, yes, I understand. You'd play me even if I was your
mortal enemy." (Actually, I am the most marginal of marginals,
both as a player and as a friend.)

"But I can't hack it without Woodruff, that's for sure," he
says. "We'd barely make respectability even *with* her."

"Want me to call her?"

"Would you mind?"

"Sure, after she cools off. In a year or two. No, I'll call sometime during the week. She's really a very nice woman."

"Sure. I mean, I'll bet that's so."

"And besides, I owe you one. I won't be here myself."

"*You* won't? Jesus Christ. No *catcher?*"

"Sales conference," I say, using the basic publishing excuse.
Nobody knows when we actually hold the buggers, so you can
use the alibi all year—our version of the splitting headache.

"If I could do it, I'd hand in my uniform to *me* right now,"
says Archie, and his Adam's apple registers his beer intake like
a maddened grain elevator.

Oh, you child of whim. Why did I say that about a sales
conference? Because I couldn't think of a broken ankle fast
enough. I don't want to be in that game, or any other until we
play the Hearthstone mob. After last night in Jimmy's, and
after the night before that—months ago to be sure, but not
as my jaw counts—I'm not certain my self-respect is up for

another pummeling. And chasing Waldo's maliciously wild pitches to the backstop all afternoon might just prove the last straw for the Clown Prince of publishing.

No, it isn't just that. In my heart, I don't want to see any of it: Nikki landing on her prat, waiting endlessly for any some-one's approval, while Billy turns grave pirouettes around a ball that nests patiently at his feet. The van Dynes. That's it. There are other shadowy hangers-on from Jimmy's who could be scraped off like the barnacles they are. But dropping the van Dynes would be cutting out our heart.

Munson sits for so long with his head in his hands that I ask, "Awake, Archie?"

He nods slightly, not wanting to shake the image. Behind his fingers, I imagine, dance the same flames I saw last night, the dreams of winter. In his case, though, he sees old ballplayers round the big table, and Gibson girls and sly old managers with side-whiskers, all flushed by the fire—but above all he sees friends. This scene has sustained him through the bad months, and he is being asked to scuttle it by next Saturday latest. He unwebs his fingers just long enough to say, "Crazy huh? You know I really thought we could do it."

I count off two days before calling Cecily from the city. This gives me plenty of time to work out ingenious compromises, or failing that, pleas for understanding from the Queequeg team on Saturday. Maybe they'd agree to some trade-offs—a sex kit-ten for a sex kitten, a guy who throws like his grandmother to cancel out Billy van Dyne, and so on. It would be hard to achieve a lineup *quite* like ours, but maybe they could arrive at one that comes in no more than ten runs ahead.

But when I get through to Cecily, she isn't buying any of it. "I hate the beastly game," she answers. "I wish I'd never heard of the damn thing." She doesn't like, says she, acting the way she did on Sunday. The game seems to bring out a horrible side of her, a compulsive driven hag of a side that she wasn't aware of, and now wants, with my *kind* permission, to forget. Her voice suggests that I planned the whole thing to humiliate her.

"Hear anything from Ferris?" I say casually.

"He won't return my calls."

So that's it. I look down sadly at my hypothetical lineup. "Look, Cecily. Is there any conceivable change Archie could make that might get you back?"

She pauses a heartening split second. "Oh, what's the use of asking that? Archie is totally wedded to his Campfire Girls concept of baseball. *I* don't want to spoil anybody's fun."

The next word here, logically, is "good-bye" but she doesn't say it. There is some point that still has to be nailed down.

"Look, Jon. If changes *were* made, they'd have to be blamed on me, wouldn't they? As if the whole game is being played just for my sake. And I couldn't play my best in an atmosphere of hostility."

The hell you couldn't, baby. "Cecily, I'll tell you something. Maybe more people agree with you about this than you know."

"Oh yes? Well let *them* make the changes. Let *them* take the blame."

How about a plot to assassinate Archie Munson as a token of good faith?

"Anyway," she says, "what's the use of talking? As I say, I hate the beastly game and it's already ruined quite enough of my summer and good-bye." Bang!

So I guess she will not be with our little group on Saturday after all. At least I have done my duty by Archie. Right now, heretic to softball that I am, I am much more concerned about Cecily and Ferris. Their affair, if that's what it was, always seemed too good to be true: two authors under the same roof would have cut down my walking almost to nothing. I call Ferris and get his guarded answering machine. Clearly he is taking no chances on Cecily's voice slipping through. As soon as I start to speak, he is right there on the spot.

"How you doing, Jon, old boy? And what can I do for you today?"

I stuff a little padding into the conversation before I get to the gist. "How's with you and Cecily, by the way?"

"Cecily who? I don't know any Cecily."

"Don't get coy with me, Beauregard. You know who I mean."

"She wasn't anything special to me."

"I warned you, Beau."

"Well, it would have been a terrible mistake. You saw her at the ballfield."

"Yeah, I saw her. I thought she behaved like a regular guy."

Ferris chuckled surprisingly. "Funny you should bring that up, coz usually that was true about her. I ain't kidding myself about what I liked in her, I haven't changed so much. But that wasn't like a guy at the ballfield, that was a spitting, hissing cat. And you know how I feel about cats."

I nod into the phone.

"Hell, it was like my mother, and I already have one of those."

"You're full of dark, twisted, Southern passions, Beau."

"You said a mouthful, Ebenezer. Now to talk of sunnier matters, where's the game on Saturday, our place or theirs?"

"You mean you still want to play?"

"And pray why not? I've taken quite a fancy to the old pastime. Besides, I want to be near you, old buddy." Back to his dead, roguish ways.

"I won't be there on Saturday."

"I'm crushed."

"And Cecily won't be there."

He laughed. "She will be missed."

"And you're playing at their place, thank your stars. None of your friends will see you. The team's meeting at Jimmy's at thirteen hours Saturday for last minute instructions, like which end of the bat to hold."

"Sounds like my kind of game," he says and hangs up.

What do you do with yourself when you're supposed to be at a sales conference? Well you get out of town for one thing. My harmless little social lie had euchred me out of a lovely weekend in the country and incidentally out of my own story for a while.

I moped around the office for two featureless days, thinking about what I was missing. I couldn't even phone anyone about it, because I had told Archie (God knows why) that the meetings were in Baltimore, and I don't know how to sound as if I'm in Baltimore.

On Monday around 7 a.m. I was awakened a little by the phone ringing and all the way by a woman's tears. "Jon, are you there? It's me, Nikki." More sobs. So at last she's capitulated. Do I still want her? On the whole, yes. "Jon, you won't believe this—I've been cut from the squad."

Oh my. "You mean from the first team, don't you?"

"No. That's what they did to Billy. He gets to play in the late innings when the game is safe. But Archie said that in my case, he'd love to keep me around, but he couldn't promise me any more action at all. Can't you *do* something?"

Is this the favor that will unlock her heart? "I'll talk to Arch," I say vaguely. "What was the score by the way?"

"*I* don't know. I guess it was big."

"Didn't anyone have a good game?"

"*I don't know.* I just know that Archie cut me."

You might gather from this that her head is not, as they say, all the way into the game. I ask her what *she* did that was so bad and she can't even remember that. "But the whole team lost. How can they pick on one person? And why does it have to be a woman?" Her desperation can be gauged by the fact that she is usually about as feminist as Shirley Temple.

"How does Billy feel about this?"

"The same way I do. He's talking about dropping out too, in protest."

"That should bring them to their senses."

"What?"

"Nothing. I'll talk to Arch."

The rout must have been apocalyptic for old Archie to do a thing like that. I crave his side of the story, but Nikki wants to pick at the scab a little longer. "He took me out in the third inning. He disgraced me in front of the whole team. My friends." And so on. All that remains in that pretty head is her own humiliation, stripped clean of details. The other players, the game, the point of the game are all gone, if they were never ever there. "They clapped when I left." I'll bet they did. "And Waldo tried his best to comfort me." That I'll believe, although it's too ugly to think about.

She finally is all wrung out, and hangs up. I dial Munson quickly before she has any further thoughts for me, and he gives me the rest of the story. It turns out that the score was 35–2 after seven innings. "I scored a run and Jack Melon of *Newsday* popped one out of there. Fender hit some majestic flies and that was about it for us." By then both teams decided that an edge had been established. So what about Nikki? "The other team was *laughing* at her," said Archie. "I had to take her out, for her sake."

"What was the score at that point?"

"Twenty-three to nothing and one out in their half of the third. And this was while they were still weak from laughing."

"So you weren't that great without her either?"

"That's right," he said tersely.

"And how do you feel about the spirit of the game now?"

"I thought Cecily put that rather nicely, don't you? I've invited her back by the way, and she's considering."

"And does the bloodletting stop here?"

"No. I cut about half the squad, just to make Nikki feel better."

"Funny she didn't mention anything about feeling better."

"Look," he said pleadingly. "I couldn't get the other guys to put some gals in *their* lineup to balance things. They said women don't play softball in Queequeg. 'Ugh!' And I'm fucked if I'm going to ask every team on the Island the same question. Anyway, I'm keeping Billy around for sentimental reasons. If Woodruff plays right in back of him, the carnage may not be too great. Hey, and I want you out there too. Your backup was that fat little guy Stuart, you know? From *House Beautiful*? Well he practically runs and hides behind the backstop whenever he sees the ball coming."

"Did Waldo behave himself?"

"Like a fucking angel of mercy. He grooved every pitch."

"He won't do that if I'm back there."

"What do you mean?"

"I'll talk to him," I say cryptically. Of course, Waldo will try to tear off my jockstrap with every pitch.

"So anyway," wraps up Munson, in a voice I barely recognize, "from now on we play to win, right Jon? As long as I live I hope never to have such an experience as that again. Next week, we play Cove Hollow at home. Be there, Jon, for pity's sake."

Well, it was Archie's dream in the first place, so I guess he can do what he likes with it.

When the team assembles next Saturday, it is a whole new creation. Woodruff is back to be sure, glaring embarrassed defiance at me, but all the hangers-on from Jimmy's are gone, even Pete Simmons, who I guess a critic would have to call a flat character. It takes some purge to get rid of such a totally adequate nonentity.

Next winter he will sit with us again as we talk about *next* summer, and so on forever. The new blood consists mostly of anonymous young smoothies, barely out of the cellophane: I don't know them and it seems I never will, because they don't talk. You can bet right now that they won't congregate with us after the game, but will stroll off with their arms around their personalized designer cuties, who are already sitting in our humble grandstand in their dark glasses and utterly perfect shorts. Some of the smoothies will in turn be replaced in the weeks to come by even sleeker models, as Munson fine-tunes his war machine.

Twenty minutes to game time, and Billy sits alone in the dugout like a typhus carrier. I say "hello" and he mumbles, Waldo says "hi" and he mumbles. After a while, he stands up as if suffocated and goes over and joins Nikki in the grandstand, where they sit in grim silence surrounded by indifferent lovelies. It is like inserting a Grant Wood couple into *Playboy*. Mavis V is sitting there too, glove and all, more debris from the Munson massacres. Perhaps she will console herself with a Hunk.

Archie, our little Napoleon, now conducts fielding practice with big-league crispness. He seems to have the proxies now on *all* our old dreams and enthusiasms. When an infielder bobbles the ball, Archie slaps him another one immediately, harder than the first. "Way to go, way to hustle," he says, to step up the tempo. Throws begin to slap into mitts. I am startled to see one fizzing toward me like a firebomb from the general direction of first base: naturally it spins out and away and I have to lumber after it, feeling, that most certain sign of middle age, grossly put-upon.

"Hey Jon," says Munson on the next play. He bunts one, and I just stand and stare at it in disbelief.

"Come on, Oglethorpe, gun it down to second."

I turn slowly and look at him. "Archie, for Christsake," I say. He stares back. We are at an impasse. What is our Napoleon to do with me—have me fielding bunts for half an hour? or will he just strip me of my chest protector and hand it to a smoothie? He seems to snap awake. "I guess not, huh?" He sheepishly retrieves the ball himself and smacks it to third. "Way to go, way to hustle."

After that, as an older settler, I am left in peace. The ball continues to whip around faster than ever, but as far as I'm concerned it is like kids playing on the beach: nobody wants to disturb grandpa. With any luck, I'll be sitting in the stands with the lovelies before long, telling them the old stories.

Munson abruptly announces that he is taking *himself* out of the lineup today. This is surely meant to be a hint to the fogies, the gnarled veterans of winter. "I want to see some of the *young* talent out there." He points at a random smoothie. "Dale here covers twice as much ground as I do at my age."

I am willing to rip off my equipment on the spot and call it a season, but Munson signals me back. "Not you, Jon." This is one sacrilege he will not commit. "We need you to handle Waldo," he explains. "You know, talk to him, like you said."

Although he talks age, Munson actually seems younger than he has all year. It is as if he has been forced up to now to disguise himself as a lovable retired sportswriter, but here we have the real Munson at last, a lifelong competitor, a legendary hard-nose, who in his prime never hesitated to lampoon the gorillas who play pro sports, or take away their base hits when he was keeping score, even though he knew he'd be interviewing them minutes later. "You're holding me up to ridicule," Munson remembers one grunt saying to him in prizefighter English as he lifted Archie three feet off the ground by his lapels. "Well now we're even," said Munson calmly from on high.

So now he's back in the world of men and happy as a kid in a sandbox. His only problem will be how to be masterful with the smoothies (and with Cecily who gobbles up mastery) and just one of the boys with Waldo, Fender, and me. Not that Fender seems to care. He just stands out there in right thinking his great thoughts. But Waldo—how will Waldo react to this new regime? He is not ready for fascism. Today's the day he will undoubtedly throw the grapefruit *for sure*, and Munson will have sobbing hysterics on the bench, his identity splintered irrevocably.

As we take the field, Waldo flings an arm around me, a gesture I find menacingly ambiguous, and says, "OK, my man. What shall we show them today? A little dipsy-do?"

Just show them a softball, hold the fruit and vegetables, OK? "Dipsy-do would be just fine, Bobo," I say, as we return to our corners.

Waldo's dipsy-do turns out to be mother's milk to the first three hitters, who whale line drives to left and score two runs before the last lovely has crossed her legs. "Talk to him," Munson hollers to me. "What about?" I say. "Anything special?"

This is a bit flippant for the new Munson. I certainly don't want to hold him up to ridicule, so I pad out to the mound and say, "Waldo, you're throwing too many strikes."

"Isn't that what you're supposed to do in this game?" he says, all innocence.

"Not in slow pitch, I guess. Look—the umpire is standing in back of you, right?" (today's arbiter is a big craven fellow who's forgotten his home-plate mask). "You know he can't tell high from low out there, only side from side. So throw a few in their eyes and see what happens."

As it turns out, the first baseball thought of my life is also my best. The hitters seem completely mesmerized by the high pitches, reaching all the way up on their toes to get them, so we don't even need the umpire to bail us out. The result is a trio of long, elegant fly balls that must please them as much as they please us, if my own reaction is anything to go by. (I'd give my whole Fall catalog to hit just one of those beauties.) The first fly scores a run, their third, and the other two are hauled in harmlessly after spirited chases.

"Attaboy, Waldo—let those baby-boomers out there do the work for you while you work on your next novel," I say between innings, and Waldo nods, mighty pleased with himself and his brand-new pitch.

That sets the pattern for the next few innings. Last week's outfielders might have been hammered into the ground by so many fly balls, if they'd gotten close enough. But today Woodruff and the smoothies spear everything left of second, and nothing goes to right anyway, where Ferris keeps his dignified counsel. Right field is a fine and private place for old Gen'l Fender: a man can survey the battlefield from there without committing his forces. Cecily darts glances at him, but she'd do better with a bust of Stonewall Jackson—that is, until the eighth inning, when he runs all the way over to snag the third out in front of her, and keeps racing off the field and plunks down next to me.

"Why d'you do that?" I ask.

"Because I felt like catching one," he said, as if that was the sole principle that determined who caught what in baseball.

I realized to my surprise that I was actually enjoying myself. There's a tingle to competition, which is magnified behind the plate. The ball seems to head straight for your eyes, but at the last second a bat snakes viciously in front of them and sends the ball soaring. We have about seven innings of this at which point Waldo removes himself to the outfield, and my happiness ceases.

It is while I am still in my euphoric period that I ask Munson how all those other players felt about being cut last week, and he says that some of them actually seemed relieved. "Your new girlfriend went so far as to call it a silly old game." Apparently they seemed bored and embarrassed at losing so badly; they wanted to go to the beach instead. Only Simmons exploded. Yes Simmons the inarticulate, Simmons the man without characteristics.

"Yeah. Matter of fact, he was quite eloquent about it. He said he'd really *believed* in the spirit of the game. What a sap he'd been, huh? he said. All winter he'd been excited by our plans for it—can you imagine old Pete excited by anything?—and he'd really been looking forward to it, and that he would never listen to a bunch of fucking intellectuals and their fucking daydreams again as long as he lived."

Funny how they call us "writers" when they like us and "intellectuals" when they don't.

"Can't you reinstate him?"

"Are you kidding? I can't even reinstate myself with the regulars at Jimmy's. Every time I go in there, he's sitting at the bar with a bunch of locals, as if he's finally discovered his station in life. Jimmy tells me he's even talking about moving out West."

"Shit, Archie. That's the worst yet."

"Yeah, it's bad"—he seems shaken by the memory for a moment—"very bad." Then he brightens. "I really think we can win this one, don't you?"

So Simmons was the turning point, eh? After that Archie can only keep going in this direction, Utopia Parkway. "Sure we can win it, Skip," I say, "if we all give it one hundred and ten percent out there and play like there's no tomorrow and pick each other up like we've been doing all season and . . ." but he isn't listening. He is clenched in with his fate. "Dwight," he says abruptly to a guy on the bench, a magnificent specimen of baseballhood, "I'd like you to pitch the last two innings. Waldo, you spell Ferris in right." Fender shrugs, stands up, leaves without a word. Munson, you old charmer.

"Hey, Waldo's doing OK," I whisper.

"They'll get to him," Archie whispers. "They've been swinging at bad pitches, that's all. They've got to wise up sometime."

"You know too much about baseball, Archie."

At this point we are tied at three. My own contribution, outside of my unappreciated brainstorm, has been slight indeed.

My theory of hitting is the other side of the coin of my pitching theory, and it has served me tolerably well in practice. I simply hack down on the ball with all my might, keep it on the ground somehow, and hope for the best. But this technique turns out to require someone like Nikki van Dyne or Billy at the other end. The lads from Cove Hollow are, by contrast, regular carpet sweepers with rifle arms and I begin to measure my achievements by the number of feet I am thrown out by. (In my third at bat, distance from the plate would have been the appropriate measurement.)

But we're tied despite me, and we have a young hotdog out there who can impart amazing spin to a slow pitch, and the sun has come out from behind the cloud of Simmons. (If he thinks Munson is an intellectual, maybe it *is* time he moved on.) Well all right. "Come on now, pitch it in. No hitter, no hitter," I holler. The real hitter looks around incredulously, as if to say "Is that coming from *you?*" I guess I'm not the type.

Hey, I can catch this guy in a rocking chair. But then maybe that's not such a great idea. Maybe he could be hit from one too. That's a nice pitch he's got there, but he should try another one sometime. Their guys are fooled at first by the change of style and they swing way over the ball. They don't breed them for brains in Cove Hollow. Two away. Say I don't remember investing Munson with these sweeping powers. Have to ask him about that. Crack, a single to left. No sweat. On the other hand, nobody else offered to rent the field or schedule the games either, and I guess if another team agrees, in good faith, to play you, they expect a reasonable game. We simply couldn't march out our Beggars Army for them week after blushing week.

OK, Archie, we don't need to have our little chat after all. I just had it for you.

Whack, and they're off and running. The guy at first seems a million miles away, and I watch dreamily as he rounds second without breaking stride. And then, Jesus, he's hurtling straight at me, knees up and cleats digging and nostrils snorting. What the fuck do I do with him? Step out of the way and holler something cheerful to the team?

My program is indeed roughly along those lines until I spot the ball streaking over his shoulder and heading for my midriff. I am trapped inside my duty. I'll be just as dead if I catch the ball as if I drop it, so I catch it, and a split second later the guy slams into me, knocking my mask twenty feet away and the ball God knows where. Uncle. I don't want to get up. Ever again. But I do. The other runner is straining off third, assessing my confusion. Munson is trying to point at the ball through the wire screen, and all our guys are racing in on me, yelling in different languages—Urdu and Hungarian for the most part. *Please*, fellows, one at a time. I circle the area like a guy looking for his rubbers. A roar tells me that the runner has broken from third.

Ah, *there* you are, you little rascal. I pick up the damn ball and dive head first for the damn plate and lay the damn tag on his ankle, only to watch the ball squirt loose once again. With a tiny flick of the foot, the runner has dislodged the little mother one more time. I sit there a moment. There's no hurry now. All the runners are gone. Finally the pitcher picks me up and says, "Nice try. I should have backed you up."

I can't see how, the backstop being only ten feet or so in back of the plate, but it's a pretty sentiment. And at least he didn't call me "pops" or "granddad." I gather when I get back to the bench that I have not disgraced myself totally. "It's happened to some of the best catchers in the world," says Munson, proceeding to list all of them. "Hey you stood your ground," says Waldo. Any virtue in me seems to astonish Waldo unutterably.

Archie offers to take me out of the game, but I'm feeling brave now and insist on finishing. I'm OK as long as those two guys don't come round again. I have to bat that inning, and I work my usual understated magic, and find to my surprise that I hurt too much to run.

Catching after that turns out to be sheer agony. The stooping and the straightening tug at every little unit of pain, until I'm alight all over. That first bastard must have just about broken my ass in two. Oh well, it's a nice change from my aching jaw which, by the way, is much better thank you.

We get them out in the eighth, and add a run in our half, then it's their half and—oh let's get it over with, we find ourselves with the score still 5–4, two outs, the bases loaded, and me due. (Did you ever wonder with those schoolboy stories how the hero always seemed to be involved in *every* situation? Well, there's nothing to it.) I look around desperately for a pinch hitter. Everybody looks around for a pinch hitter. Archie has already used himself, and is now perched on third base, from whence he scans the stands for a lovely with hitting potential. All the noncombatants have left already. Such is the grip of the game on the smoothies that they bolt the moment they find themselves not playing. So it's a lovely or nothing.

Munson makes the most of it, pretending now that I am exactly the guy he wants in a situation like this. "Attaboy, Jon baby. Wait for your pitch. Only takes one to hit . . ." he falls to babbling. He knows and *I* know and even the dimmest lovelies know what's going to happen. I vary my routine slightly by uppercutting the ball. The pitcher, of all people, plucks it from the air like an insignificant detail, and the ordeal is over.

There is heavy disappointment in the air. Even the most detached sportsman exudes a little of it. But Munson at least knows the right words. "I'm sorry about that Archie," I say to him. "Forget it," he snaps. "Never apologize in baseball. I'm only sore at the creeps who left early. Christ, after that knock I'm amazed you could even pick up a bat." He is of course massaging his own morale too. "And hey, man—five to four. That's an improvement, wouldn't you say?"

"So, you want to have a beer and celebrate?" I say.

"Not today, Jon." Munson drains out. "The truth is, I don't feel too comfortable in Jimmy's these days."

Munson, everybody's Nice Guy. A leper in his own bar. The Game claims another victim. Archie slumps off, no doubt muttering "five to four, five to four, only five to four" all the way home. I believe I've read someplace that 5–4 is the average score of every recorded game of baseball ever played. So we have dragged ourselves all this bloody way through mud and slime just to reach the average. And at that there is practically no one left from the old regiment to plant our flag on it.

So now it's off to the Plimsoll gallery to bathe my bruises in

culture and try to forget bats and balls and the other impedi-
menta of childhood, and also to see if I can still fool people with
my imitations of a grownup. But as I stroll around the gallery
all I can see in the paintings are the pounding hooves and flaring
nostrils of those baserunners, eternally thundering towards me,
turning back at the last minute and starting over. I might as well
be in church for all the good this is doing me.

Pounding an imaginary mitt in my mind, I return to my
lodging where Mrs. Hudson is *not* awaiting me with mulled
wine and porridge, and seek the last and scurviest of escapes—
writing—which, as you see, I'm still doing.

18

TIME, I guess, to look in on some of my other patients. During the next few days, I visit a couple of my cookbook writers out here, whose names would stun you, but since they don't play at softball or fundraising, they have no business in this book. However, I do allow each of them to warm my ice-cold spirits on successive nights and I jot down the recipes they use, to their manifest annoyance. It is an editor's privilege.

Although you may think I'm not the type, I had a grandmother once who believed that no novel was a real novel unless it had some food in it, so here goes just a crumb. Among our scrawny ranks at Williams & O. I have become cookbook editor by default, and have developed a formidable but purely literary knowledge of the subject. Like one of those Las Vegas oddsmakers who has never actually seen a football game, my understanding of how the sport is played on paper is incomparable, and I am often tempted to write to hopeful authors as follows: "You call these things *recipes?* Why, my cat makes a better bouillabaisse," etc. But I have a subterranean fear that they will all come to my house and demand to be fed and I will be found out. My mother, as opposed to granny, stressed that I shouldn't make a god of my stomach and I believe laid a Scottish curse on me. Because recipes flatly refuse to work for me, and my table groans eternally with failed pretensions. I am a *château général* of cookery.

Nevertheless I am determined to try out one of my author's dill-poached salmon the very next night. Fortunately the van Dynes are coming over, and good cooking is usually wasted on saloon guys—none more so than Billy, who deploys meals wonderfully as fictional devices, but has never actually noticed one. So I have nothing to lose but some good salmon.

Usually I would have some other guests over anyway to buffer Billy and release Nikki for some soulful eye-contact, at which she is simply incomparable; nothing else about her detracts from that. Artistry is artistry.

But not tonight. I fancy the van Dynes to be so steeped in rage and gloom that no dinner party can stand up to them. And I imagine myself nodding and shaking my head like some half-witted doll, and murmuring "I know, it's awful" every five minutes. Or "isn't it the way?" or "who would have thought?"

Well—they don't look too bad getting out of the car. At least they don't fall on their knees and rend their garments. That's a good sign, I think. And their walk up the drive looks OK. Kind of straight, one leg at a time, no complications. So far, so good. I guess I have to let them in now. Their faces are actually just a few inches from mine, and if they look up they'll find me staring back like a goldfish.

"Ah, there you are!" I cry as I open the door.

"Jonathan! How the hell are you?" Billy pumps my arm like a mad thing.

"Give us a kiss," says Nikki, and for once doesn't turn her cheek. Delicious. But, really, what the hell is this?

Whatever it is, it's probably luckier not to talk about it. "You're looking well. You're *both* looking well," I say firmly.

"And why the hell shouldn't we?"

"*I* don't know. No special reason."

"We feel *great*," says Nikki, and hugs me again. Surely this is one of the great recoveries from disappointment of all time, an inspiration to all of us.

But how long can they keep it up? How soon before the rage comes slithering and howling out of its lair? Maybe the magic will hold as long as nobody says the word "softball," the witch's curse *du jour*.

"I'm really puzzled why you shouldn't expect us to seem well," pursues the cumbersome Billy. The question is so inane that he obviously wants me to ask *why* they aren't mad at the softball game. Such is the fellow's deftness.

"I *didn't* expect you *not* to look well"—I try.

"Oh, Jonathan's probably thinking about the silly old softball game," says Nikki, unable to wait another minute.

"Ha!" Billy gives a loud chuckle, almost too large to be true. "*That* crock of shit!"

I nod and shake my head. Is this the beginning? Is the beast finally coming out?

"Oh, it's all so childish," says Nikki. "We're both just happy we're out of it."

"That fuckhead Munson is completely infantile," adds Billy. "It's pitiful."

"I know, it's awful." I am trying to find my rhythm.

"But we've decided not even to think about it," says Nikki. "Imagine—two grownup adults breaking their hearts over a silly old ballgame."

Well, it happens all the time, in fact. But what I can't quite understand is why this particular decision, simply not to think about the game, has put them in such delirious high spirits.

"Munsonism everywhere," growls Billy.

"Billy, you promised!" says Nikki.

"I must say," chimes in Old Father Oglethorpe, "that you're both being very adult about this. And you're absolutely right about the game and its place on the scale of things. An artist like you . . ."

"So why do *you* stay with it," says Billy sharply. He is obviously having trouble with his cure.

I ponder a moment. Is this a seal of the confessional matter? Not too likely, considering the other mouth involved. "The truth is," I say, "we have this one game planned later with some Hollywood guys, and I thought it might help focus them on Waldo's book—and on yours too, of course. We *must* have you back in the lineup by then, Munson or no Munson. Every opportunity counts."

This extraordinary couple proceeds to laugh like hyenas.

Is this hysteria? And is that the answer to softball?

"You're talking about Marty Hearthstone and those guys, right?"

"Yeah. I didn't suppose you'd even heard of them. I mean, you're a serious writer." I shuffle through the sentence like some old railroad porter. "You know, movies are still in the fetal stage."

"That's too bad," laughs Billy.

"Huh?" Yes, huh.

"Well, not only have I heard of Marty, but I had dinner with him while he was out here last, and he took my book to the Coast with him and to make a fascinating story short, he wants to take out an option on it."

"Just a teensy one," dimples Nikki. So *that's* where her frigid wiles have gone all summer. Marty Hearthstone!

"Why that's *great*," say I. "That calls for champagne. Chug down that swill you've got and we'll hit the Dom Perignon."

As I load up the ice bucket, I start ever so slowly to think. Does Hearthstone give options out like party favors, to thank people for a lovely summer? I should call Waldo right away and see if he's got his.

Waldo! Mother of God—if Waldo has one I wouldn't have to call him about it. Shit, this could be calamitous.

I stick my head back in the living room. "Did you tell Waldo about it yet?"

"You bet. I made sure he was the first to know, the competitive sonofabitch."

"How'd he take it?"

"Ah, you know Waldo. He practically patted my head and said, '*There's* a nice little novelist. Down, boy.'"

"He didn't get sore?"

"Nah. He said he was working on a *real* deal with Hearthstone, and some of the other guys, and for real money, and it might take a little longer."

I step back into the kitchen and fetch the champagne and, with trembling hands, pop it and pour it and raise a glass. "To the movies, be they ever so fetal."

"To the movies" echoes the serious novelist and his now forever unattainable wife, who looks as if she is already sitting beside a pool.

I don't know why, but I'd feel better if Waldo had gotten sore.

One bottle follows another, and there goes the last of my date-bait. Dom Perignon, bought with my heart's blood, wasted on these savages. Oh well. Nikki continues to simper divinely, but the firewater takes Billy the other way. "That arrogant prick," he growls apropos of nothing.

"You mean Munson?"

"No, I mean Waldo. Real deal, indeed! with great big money! Who the hell does he think he's kidding? He's got no deal and he knows it. And don't think I haven't told him so. Loud and often."

The worm simply won't stop turning. It is a desecration to serve even my poached salmon and dill to this man.

"Look honey, you've got yours, isn't that enough?" His live-in keeper pleads anxiously.

"Yeah, Nik. I feel great, I really do." Pause. "That know-it-all cocksucker." The school bully is going to get his lumps if it takes all night. I always figured there was some, but I never knew how much, resentment lurking beneath the festive friendship of Billy and Waldo. Billy has the good nature of the absent-minded, but it strikes me now that he may have noticed Waldo's sadistic attentions to Nikki over the winter. This would explain their respective positions in the conversation. With her expansive world view, Nikki instinctively assumes that all quarrels are basically about her.

I would like to warn Billy for my part that Waldo's the kind of guy who would pay a million in printer's alterations to get even with a fancied slight, let alone a movie deal, in that plague spot he calls his novel. The Billy character in the novel is bad enough as it is, without any further provocation. I can't tell Billy that—can I?

I give up the idea of saying that Waldo's a deeply sensitive guy underneath, and try a more plausible tack. "I wouldn't gloat too much if I were you, Billy. You know our Waldo. If he gets sore, he's likely to bombard you with calls from the Nobel

Prize Committee and the French Academy and so on until you slowly go mad and have to disconnect your phone."

"That's true," coos Nikki.

"Yeah? Well two can play at that game," he says vaguely. He takes another slug of Dom Perignon as if he were a dockworker and it was a Budweiser. (Does he really believe, even in this afflated state, that he can beat Waldo at the art of making crazy phone calls? This man, who has never done an imitation accent in his life, and who cannot even tell a lie without giggling, actually thinks that two can play at that game? He wants to go one on one with the Father of Lies himself?)

Perhaps the folly seeps through even to Billy, because he trails off with "anyway, it's just kidding, is what I'm doing with Waldo and he can take a kidding as well as anyone"—about his *writing?* "And besides, he's shoveled a lot worse stuff at me in his day. This is the first time I've had an edge, and I'm not giving it up just for the sake of my telephone."

"I'd still go easy. It's only a movie."

I know while it's passing through my mouth that this is not quite the right thing to say. Billy stares at me with a glazed incomprehension that will turn to anger as soon as it dries. It is no use reminding him that a year ago he despised movies himself, almost as much as a professional film critic: that was a fluffier, more absorbent Billy. Now in his drunken confusion, he could suddenly turn on me with the strength of ten in defense of "Cinema," and *nobody* would get to eat. Nikki looks nervous. I am toying with the only prize Billy has ever won, and telling him it's made of shit. "I better take a look at the dinner," I say, hightailing it to the kitchen before I can wreak any more damage. Is it too late to change the menu to scrambled eggs?

I have done everything in my power to head off this crazed man. The least I can do now is put away the Montrachet and give him the Bulgarian Riesling-type.

If you want to know what the rest of the evening was like you can run the last few pages backward, except that Billy does not return to his car one leg at a time, but in a kind of one-two, two-one routine to correct for listing. Prior to that he has been through another euphoric phase and another black one, the sexual tension has mounted and Nikki has praised the food. I must say that the latter is miraculously and heartbreakingly good.

As they totter down the drive, with Billy apparently determined to shove Nikki against each hedge in turn, I watch from my goldfish bowl and reflect that Billy as much as Waldo is *my* character too, and that I am free to immortalize the sheer wetness of his soul right now. What I still cannot do, even on paper, is bed his wife Nikki. Because I'm not sure by now, even on paper, whether I want to anymore.

"Who shall I tell Mr. Spinks is calling?"

"Fuck off, Waldo. What kind of a cockeyed sentence is that anyway? You need an editor."

"I'll tell the master that it sounds like a rather rude tradesperson."

Jeeves shuffles off to be replaced by Squire Spinks. Theater in most of its forms bores me, so I identify myself immediately to end the charade, but I'm not to be let off that lightly. "Oh hi Jon. May I ask—*why* were you rude to Roderick just now?"

"I'm anti-English."

"Well you made him cry—up to now he thought all Americans were so nice," and so on.

I shut my eyes and wait. "So what can I do for you today?" he says at last.

"I had dinner with Billy last night."

"You mean the famous screenwriter?"

"Yeah. I hope that doesn't bother you?"

"Me? Bothered by Billy? You're kidding, of course."

"Well, he says he's been teasing you a bit."

"Has he? The dear fellow."

"Glad you feel that way."

"Listen, Jon, any little crumb that comes Billy's way is fine with me. You and I know just what a movie option is worth. I used to paper the wall with them once upon a time."

"Well, that's right," I say casually. "By the way, hear anything from Hearthstone yourself?"

"Yeah. A postcard of the Brown Derby. Says he'll be back before Labor Day and we must have that game. And listen—when we really talk, me and Marty, we won't be talking option. At least *I* won't."

To my surprise, I am touched for a second. He must get awfully tired putting on his show day after day. "Yeah, I wouldn't settle for an option if I were you," say I, not absolutely sure why I'm saying it—is it right to encourage his delusions? I don't know, but it seems *safer*.

"But it's wonderful for Billy," he says.

"Indeed and it is." I suddenly sound to myself like an Irish tenant farmer. *And isn't it lovely for Billy, me boys, ain't it just darling for Billy? Faith and bedad.*

"So is that it for today, Jon? I have this tennis appointment at the Padgetts'."

"Then tally ho. And break a leg."

I don't know, he still sounds dangerous to me. But then Waldo, like Richard Nixon, believes deeply in Madman Theory: once you've convinced the other guy that you're a trigger-happy nut you can go on about your business. At least Waldo hasn't asked when he gets his galleys back, so he isn't planning to tinker with his imaginary version of Billy just yet. So by his standards, the situation seems fairly stable.

Tauber says I ought to say something about the beaches around now. People will expect it, he says. Next he'll be wanting me to do the golf courses as well. Yes, I believe we have beaches out here, but I don't go to them myself. The suntan oil doesn't exist that can keep me from turning a dull scarlet, with molten shoulder blades to top it off. I don't really swim that well because I always catch fire en route to the water, and my idea of a picnic is a table set with gleaming napery and fine silverware high above the ants and broken glass, and this I'm told is hard to arrange on a beach.

My friends think I'm crazy to live in a resort town with this particular attitude, but I think my attitude is just about right. The beaches leach away most of our bubbleheads, leaving my beloved potato and strawberry fields in peace. The flat vistas out here remind me of Russian novels, and I won't have these clowns blundering into my *Anna Karenina*.

Even inland we have our troubles, though. In July and August, each of our noble hamlets turns into a cross between a brawling seaport and a suburb on the way down, with bored day-trippers gazing like cows into shop windows while unidentified rowdies roam the sidewalks in bands, shoving and gouging aimlessly. They have no idea what they are doing here, there are no tourist attractions and nothing for children to do, so they fall into their primitive ways, gazing or gouging as the case may be. In the evenings, the cream of them will wind up in Jimmy's.

The only good thing about them is that they take some heat off us year-round Summer People (as we are known around here). After a pack of them has ravaged a store, complaining, bringing things back, and hogging the counter as the hard-won beachhead it is, the harassed merchant may even smile at us lepers of winter and call us by name. Not so long ago they had thought we were the worst thing that could happen to them, but Christ! "I can't wait till it's over" they start confiding to you as early as June. "Me too" you sigh sympathetically. Of course when it *is* over you will go back to being a leper, as if nothing had happened; but better to be a leper in a civilized setting than a summer weekender in Hell.

Naturally we seek refuge in each other's company: even in this year of strain, nobody understands us like us. So I was taken completely off guard by Ferris Fender, who was my next stop on the house tour. I have just delivered one of my bittersweet spiels like the above (I make them up between houses) and Ferris gives me one of his slow, appraising looks and says, "No wonder people punch you around so much."

"What do you mean by that, Ferris? That's the way *everybody* talks about the Hamptons. I mean, that's the way it's done, there isn't any other way," I babble ingratiatingly.

"Is that a fact," he says softly. "You know, I never knew that. Everybody, huh?"

Southern irony, slow and heavy as a hammer against a spike.

I fold, before it really gets going. Ferris relents in his own peculiar way.

"Well, Jonny, one thing you'll never be—and thank God for small mercies, I guess—is a writer. 'Tourists and locals,' indeed. Do you know that out of any ten people you see walking along the street, one will have more guts than you, one'll have known more sorrow, and one'll have more brains—how many does that make? And, of course, an equal number will have even less. Be they tourist or be they local."

What the hell's gotten into him today? "So you believe in statistics at least?" I say.

"Bet your sweet ass. Ever read a book about combat? In any war, anytime, yea many heroes, yea many cowards." Nice of him to acknowledge the existence of more than one war at least.

"This mechanical cynicism of yours and 'everybody's,' shit, how it wears a man down. You ever actually meet one of these tourists you're so smart about? Well I have. And you know that at the least every one of them has come farther to see us than anyone's ever gone to see them. And what do they find? A bunch of sniggering New Yorkers and some out-of-shape merchants who can't wait for them to get out of here because serving them would be too much like work. Don't hardly see why anybody ever bothers to go anywhere these days."

"I think I'm going to cry."

"Ah skip it, Jon. The woods are full of writers, but how often does one find a dandy little publisher like you? Treasure your uniqueness, old son. At least you know what you are. Too many of you guys have delusions of creation."

I clutch guiltily at the secret of my manuscript, pressing it to my bosom. "So who's a real writer around here?" I ask quickly.

"Well, Waldo's got the makings, I reckon. I've always kind of admired his stuff." Waldo? Ferris? I've never even thought of these two in the same connection. They glide past each other constantly without friction, like two giant fish who eat different things. "Yeah, I'll bet ol' Waldo's met more tourists *and* locals than the rest of us put together. You should be happy to have him on your list."

"Oh I am, I am."

"And that's quite enough of that," he says before I can get to Cecily. "It's bad luck to talk about writing. So how's your summer been, Jon? I mean in general."

Me? I don't have Summers. I *watch* people's summers. However, I guess I'd better try to act normal. "Well—kind of hectic, I guess. What with the damned softball game and everything."

"And pray, what's wrong with the softball game?"

"You mean you're not mad at it?"

"Hell no. I'm enriched."

"Jesus, congratulations. You mean you're not going to quit because Archie took you out of the game?"

"Why should I? A leader's entitled to make his own mistakes." Oh my—Munson reminds him of Briggs at Shiloh or Longstreet at Gettysburg or some such. Of course, that would be his angle. The replacement of the romantic amateurs who began the war by less glamorous professionals—why the game is but a shadow of the one Great Tragedy. Ferris can get there from anywhere.

There is a manly silence as Fender refills our glasses. I use the time to meditate on how frequently young novelists tend to refill their characters' glasses. By now if they were in charge of us, we'd probably have put away about six apiece. Impossible. We'd be spitting booze as we talked.

"Tell me, Jon. You know anything about a guy called Hearthstone?"

Don't tell me. He wants you to work on the remake of *Gone With the Wind*. "Sure, he's a movie-making culture vulture."

Ferris stares at me a second. Am I being glib again? "He seems to be a pretty well-read guy," I add. "I mean he does the reading himself. No help of any kind."

I'm afraid Ferris, in another spasm of perversity, is about to start telling me that movie people are really the salt of the earth, but he just says, "He wants to meet me."

Be sure he brings a contract. Hey, wouldn't that be neat? We'll build a *cordon sanitaire* around Waldo. *Everyone* out here gets an option except Waldo. I'll even pretend to have one myself.

"He says he's a Civil War buff."

"I wouldn't put it past him."

"I wouldn't put it past anybody. You know, the moment an American baby can lisp he says he's a Civil War buff. But is there any *point* in meeting this guy?"

A strange author, this one. "Well, he makes movies, you see. *Movies*. Out of *books*."

"Not out of mine he doesn't."

"What?!" (I've always wanted to say that.)

"He'd tried to set them all in Acapulco. I know his kind."

"I'm sure he wouldn't do that. He's really quite cultivated."

"Yeah? He makes films doesn't he? then he's a purple-ringed asshole." *Not* the salt of the earth I gather. "Look, he'll, whoever he is, put the guns in the wrong place, he'll use the wrong kinds of horses, he'll get the battles in the wrong order just to oblige the love interest. How can I get it through your thick Yankee skull that Vicksburg is not the land of Oz, you can't mess with it."

You don't have to get it through *my* skull. I wouldn't dream of messing with Vicksburg. "But, listen—supposing Hearthstone made *you* technical adviser, and agreed to all your demands?"

"Fuck off, Jon. You're talking like one of them. Even if they did just what you say, and they never have yet, the cameramen won't know what it looked like, the actors won't know what it felt like, and you can't even *get* the smells." Not much point my dallying on about Mathew Brady's great photographs and how illuminating they can be. So I say, "Well, in that case, I don't see any pressing reason for you gentlemen to meet. But you will meet him eventually, anyhow. On the softball field. Hearthstone has challenged our guys to a game."

"He has, huh? Well I trust we shall beat their little neon asses to a fine powder. In fact, I shall be there personally to supervise the operation."

Yes suh!

Now let me tell you something else about drinking. *Two* of Fender's are worth a dozen of Sam Spade's or Philip Marlowe's. "What did you put in this one, Colonel," I ask, "and why?"

"I want to get you drunk and out of here in a hurry. I've got a big date."

"Huh?"

"With muh typewriter," he says in a sultry voice, indicating that it is time for little publishers to get off the track and let *The Spirit of Antietam* come howling through. "Get out there and mingle, boy," is his last benediction.

I shamble out determined to snap at the first innocent soul who mentions locals or Summer People or any category of person whatever without simultaneously paying warm tribute to their personal courage and honor and I forget what else—it'll come to me. We'll see who's a writer around here, by God.

When I come to about a minute later, the tawdriness of Fender's game appalls me. He has of course never met a tourist in his life; and if he did, he would most likely charge at him with his musket. I don't know what he thinks of the locals, because he's too regal to talk about it, but I assume he lumps them in with the rest of us joyless, juiceless Northerners. "Why do you live up here at all?" I've asked him a hundred times, and two answers stick in my mind. "They flog little boys like me down there," and "I can't write about the South in the South. It all seems too obvious." Take your choice, but I think he likes us.

One thing my authors seem to have in common is an insatiable urge to tease me. No wonder Ferris admires Waldo so. Fender's suggestion that the best writers are really the ones who rush down to the boats and introduce themselves is worthy of Spinks at his prankish worst. In fact it could almost be an imitation. (Do my writers see too much of each other? Must remind myself to keep them apart.) At any rate, I can just imagine some twit armed to the teeth with notebook and camera and Fender's advice, stopping these tired, careworn people who work the boats to ask them what they're really like, and coming back with his typewriter draped round his shoulders. Fender hates raw material himself. How could I forget that? Talking one time about various famous exchanges of wit among legendary people, he startled me by saying that, of course, none of those things had ever gotten said. "Truth is nothing has ever been said unless it was written down first. Anything worth hearing was written down by somebody. That's nature's way."

One other thing I notice about the conversation is that Fender doesn't sound quite as Southern as he used to. Is it just that I don't hear it anymore, or has he been up here too long? I make a note in my head to hire a speech coach and tear it up in my head and continue on my way.

I also cancel my plans to mingle, in order to go home and read manuscripts, where all the interest in the world lies waiting. I am loath to see Cecily today, partly because I'm beginning to feel like a commuter branch line with my punctual stops at the same old stations, but also because I vaguely fear rocking the boat. I'm not sure what boat—the softball boat, the love boat, the sanity boat, all the ships at sea. Cecily seems to be balanced ever so delicately on a pane of glass, and she knows it.

But not tonight. For a change she bursts in on me, to demand to know how I can live in this goddamn monk's cell. "Get some paintings, get some flowers, get some fucking *something*."

"That's pretty earthy talk, Cissy. You've been hanging out with the wrong elements."

"Fucking right I have. Hey listen, you don't happen to know a guy named Hearthstone do you?"

"And who am *I* not to know a guy named Hearthstone?" I flare up indignantly.

"Well, it seems he simply loves my work. Says he's read every word I've written." That's funny, Cecily's name drew a blank when I showed Marty our publishing list. (He must read awfully fast for an asshole, purple-ringed or otherwise.) "He says they'd make wonderful movies."

"That's a dastardly slur."

"Oh Jon, drop your boring old mask. Give it away to some deserving prune. Aren't you really excited?"

Without my mask? Frankly no. Without my mask, I'm not even mildly interested. Hearthstone's endless flirtations are getting on my nerves, and I don't really care to see my authors jump through any more hoops for him. So I put on my mask anyway, like the old catcher I am and say, "That's wonderful Cecily. I mean just great."

I've got to hand it to Hearthstone in a way. He has brought a fairytale spell to Sleepy Hollow. With the merest sprinkle of tinsel he has caused Cecily completely to forget about the pane of glass beneath her feet; indeed, she is capering over it right now. Ah the movies! I only hope she stops capering before she runs into Ferris, the last honest writer.

"Marty tells me—oh by the way, we had supper last night, just the three of us, and his wife loves my stuff too—that he's getting together a softball team to challenge us soon. How should I play?"

"What do you mean, how should you play?"

"You know—should I play tough or should I play feminine? Which way sells books?"

"Cecily, I don't believe this," and I really don't. This is the Cecily of the thousand stormy scenes, and the ruthless pursuit of excellence? The spittle still drips and burns on Munson's cheek from her integrity. But, as I say, my authors are great kidders.

"Come on Jon, don't be a baby. This is *serious*. I would kill for a Hearthstone movie. Have you ever seen his work?"

I shake my head wearily. I'm beginning to believe I have never met anybody or seen anything anywhere. I am a blind old monk blundering about the busy marketplace.

"Well take my word. They're sensitive. They're just right for me."

"Cecily," I croak like a Victorian aunt, "this just isn't like you. This sounds, I don't know, so mean and hard and un-scrupulous." You hussy!

"Jonathan, what's come over you? Have you turned into one of those wimpy gentlemen publishers? How do you think people sweat out novels and fill bookshelves without exactly those qualities you just mentioned? Also, next to gout and childbirth, I believe that a bad review is the worst pain known to man, and I've had a shelf-full of those too. So what do you expect, a fucking namby-pamby? Some pissant Girl Scout?"

She sounds so earnest as she reels off this tough talk that I feel a flash of chauvinist sympathy. The little dear! But when I look I see precisely what frightened Ferris that day—the Medusa herself.

"It's not as if I'm selling my body—that's a discussion for another time. But betraying my baseball talents, for pity's sake! did anyone even know I had them two months ago? can you find them in any reference books?"

I am still, and incurably, aghast. Is this a man-woman difference? I know there's no such thing anymore, but to me dumping a game seems infinitely more dishonorable than selling my body. (OK, I grant that we are valuing slightly different articles here.) So I run quickly through my male authors, not excluding the cookbook boys and one aging ecologist, and decide to my dismay that there probably isn't one of them who wouldn't see it Cecily's way, with the towering exception of Ferris, who is the Great Exception anyway. Even in my sheltered life, I have seen junior executives flub easy putts and flagrantly mis-hit tennis balls to grease up the boss. In fact probably the only thing they *won't* do is play like girls, as Woodruff is proposing— and what do I even know about that these days?

"Look Cecily." I temporize: if I stay on my moral high-horse I'm a dead duck, so long as Cecily's on the warpath. "The truth is I don't think it matters a rat's ass how you play, so you might as well have a good time. They're buying a book, not a center fielder. Or if you really believe that ridiculous myth about male vanity, have yourself a sick headache and sit it out. That can't hurt you." I find myself giving the strangest advice at times.

The thought of Cecily trying to play feminine is just more than I can stomach today. I pray to my cold Scottish gods for help: they never speak back because the porridge would fly out of their mouths, but they do strike people down occasionally. It might help.

Cecily furrows and purses the relevant features, and finally says, "I'll ask somebody else."

She rises to leave. "Hey, don't spread this around," I bleat.

"All right," she says, though she obviously can't see why not.

"So whose advice are you going to ask?" Her hand has

reached the door handle, I've got to talk fast, sweetheart. "Not Ferris for God's sake!" I cry.

She glares at me malignantly. We haven't reached the state of giddy freedom where we can talk about Ferris.

"I thought I'd have a chat with Waldo," she says, and is gone.

A joke? I fervently hope so. All the same I feel a small sting of jealousy quite separate from the swarm of stings that hit me like one saturation bomb whenever I think of Waldo's other spiritual takeovers around here. Not Cecily, he can't have Cecily.

I dismiss the thought then, and dismiss it still.

19

WHERE was I the night before St. Crispin's Day? At Jimmy's, of course, like all God-fearing souls. Archie's Army prepared to do battle with the wild men from the Holly Wood by getting crocked the old way.

I couldn't have assembled that particular mob by now. The van Dynes were not talking to Munson, who'd stopped coming here anyway. Cecily and Ferris hadn't exchanged a word since the Day of Wrath. They played the outfield together in icy, brilliant silence (Cecily had packed it in with the melting glances). Waldo's vast social connections had taken him way beyond our little cracked set, and I wouldn't have known how to round up the smoothies because I still didn't know their names or particulars, if any. Besides, I imagined them all stashed safely away in milk bars and health food stores by seven o'clock at night.

But Marty could and did round them up in a twinkling and could make us all behave ourselves too. Nobody wanted to act like a jerk in front of Hearthstone. He had even exercised his *droit du seigneur* by reserving our own old table for us, and leading us back to it like sheep to Dreamland.

But first, a glimpse of a great director's methods. "I must meet your captain, what did you say his name was?" he asked me that morning.

"Archie Munson. Look, he's not talking to Billy who's not talking to . . . I'm afraid this is kind of complicated."

The line was silent. I'm a busy man, it said. I felt like a kid with an inadequate excuse. "What's his number? I'll call him myself."

"What do you need Archie for?" I chaffered. "You can't make a movie out of old sports columns."

The Boss laughed genially. "I told you I can make a movie out of anything."

So why do you always make them out of . . . oh, never mind.

"And Billy? He's coming tonight, isn't he?"

"Billy was dropped from the team."

"Say, you guys must be really serious. Dropping people yet. I'll have to call an extra practice this afternoon."

"Look, even without Billy, we're barely medioc . . ."

"Anyway, we've got to have Billy." He wrapped it up for me. What did he say he was? *football coach* at Sarah Lawrence? "This is basically a writers' game," he said, "the artists versus the sellouts, you might say." We both made certain to laugh at this. It would have been awful if only one of us laughed.

"OK, I'll see what I can do," I said.

"Never mind, I'll take care of it."

The fuck you will, I muttered inwardly. Pride thus satisfied, I hung up the phone, and left it all to Hearthstone. It was no worse than drowning.

In fact, I still have the drowsy feeling that nothing can go wrong now. In the hands of this two-bit director we will proceed to have a perfectly average pregame party and a B-movie, middle-American game. "Unpretentious . . . quietly charming . . . you could do a lot worse," agree the critics.

My feeling is confirmed when I see Hearthstone and Waldo chatting on Jimmy's barstools before the adequate festivities commence. Waldo reminds me right now of a performing bear in a Russian circus: his barstool could turn at any moment into a bicycle which he will then proceed to ride round and round the saloon. He nods at Marty and smiles and nods some more. He is perfectly tame. Marty could put his head in his mouth if he felt like it, although to be on the safe side, Hearthstone probably gives him a light crack and a flick of the contract every now and then.

They stand up and shake hands. See how easy it is? Marty is looking intense, with that rapture he only gets in the presence of Art. Waldo is smiling seraphically. All he needs is an ice cream cone to make life complete. Saints be praised. Our most dangerous weapon has just been defused at the last moment.

Hearthstone carries his *gemütlichkeit* over to our table like a portable aura. The smoothies materialize at a twitch of his wand—*our* smoothies mind you, but his wand. Meanwhile among us earth-people, the ones who don't talk to each other still don't, but they don't need to under the guidance of our Guest Conductor. For instance:

"Archie—I used to love your sports columns," says Marty. "Good old-fashioned American sportswriting. One of our vanishing glories. Tell me, why did you ever quit?"

"Book," mumbles Arch.

"Hey, that should be *great*. I can't wait," etc.

Archie, our very own Svengali, is instantly mesmerized by his own medicine. All he will need is a touchup on the way out. ("I really wish you'd get back to those columns. We *need* you.") With that our fearless leader will dissolve into a baby who's just had a good burp.

What's annoying is that I've been burping these guys for years without any result at all. Of course, I've *seen* Archie's book, all seventy-five booze-stained, soul-weary pages of it. It hasn't grown in a year now, because it has nowhere to grow to and no one to take it there. Archie is still a youngish man by normal standards, but as a writer he is very very old.

Anyway, Hearthstone works the table according to its needs, until a peaceful eupepsia settles over all. Marty reminds me of someone on hands and knees pulling out every dangerous cord in the room. Then he leaves, and the smoothies leave with him, dancing ghostly attendance on their new hero, the Lord God of Film. I understand that in Hearthstone's racket, it is a mark of failure ever to have more than an hour to spare. But I must admit, he's given us quality time.

"We'll whip your asses tomorrow" are his sprightly last words.

"We'll whip yours too" we pipe back dutifully. He gives a

special little earnest wave to Waldo, and is off on his rounds, while the smoothies repair to their Nautilus equipment.

In this becalmed state, the old hard core of us drinks and chats the night away, while still scrupulously observing our taboos: Billy talks to Ferris, I talk to Cecily, Waldo talks to Nikki and Archie talks to himself. He hasn't heard praise in a long time, and he wants to run it around in his mouth forever. As I twinkle-toe off to the men's room, I look back and see the group just as they were in January. The cracks in the plaster don't show from here, so long as everyone looks in the right direction.

Where were you during the next twenty minutes, Oglethorpe? Why I'm not sure, officer. Went to the bar to get some cigarettes. Must have talked to Jimmy longer than I thought. He sees Labor Day in sight and is returning cautiously to his old self. I massage his recovery vigorously. "Here's to autumn," I say, and mean it wholeheartedly. Because for us year-rounders, autumn is our season, with all its stillness and gravity. It is a serious, grownup season; summer is more like a plague of gypsy moths that gets worse every year. I am, you will observe, relatively mellowed out for the moment.

Oh no. Not tonight. Not that. I turn around to look at our table, and sure enough Billy is at it again, glaring at Waldo to beat the band. "What do you keep grinning about?" he shouts. Among Billy's uncoordinations is a total lack of vocal control, so he may not even be angry. "You've been grinning all night, you smug bastard."

I guess he is angry.

"I don't know," grins Waldo. "Maybe I'm just a naturally happy man."

"I suppose you cut some kind of fancy deal with Hearthstone just now?"

"I didn't say that."

"Well what if he did?" says Nikki. "Shouldn't we all be celebrating? Why must writers always be so *envious?*" She suddenly looks as if she's going to cry, as well she might, having just stubbed her pretty toe against an iron law of nature.

Billy glares at her and Waldo both, and I see that what's on his mind may have little to do with Waldo's movie rights. Still, he is temporarily speechless, this is a very good time to leave him alone. He cannot score many points attacking Waldo's success.

Unfortunately, our leader chooses this moment to step down from the clouds and make a little peace around here. "Ah look, Billy old friend," Munson says in a placating voice, careful not to rouse him, "we've already got this great feeling going for the game tomorrow. Let's not spoil it, huh, fella?"

"The game!" Billy bellows, "the fucking game!" Wrong thing to bring up. We will now be raked mercilessly for our childishness, our infantilism and our all-round refusal to grow up, at which point Billy will stomp out, missing the last trick step as usual. Any good mood we had will have faded as if it was never there. It should be against the law to serve this man firewater.

But what's this, what's this? Billy has turned his baleful gaze, not on Munson, where it richly belongs, but on Cecily of all people. "You"—he points—"you're the one. You're the one who spoiled it for everyone"—his pointing becomes a demented jab. "We had a pretty good game going there for a while." When was that? I must have blinked. "But you, you virago . . ."

"Every brat has his day," mutters Ferris, and if I were Billy, I would have a care right now. Ferris has begun to stalk him.

"What did I do?" chimes in Cecily, as confused as anyone by this crisscrossing of feuds.

Billy gnaws on his thumb knuckle as if biting through a gag. He might have stopped right there, he is not a natural savage, but the lady here has asked him a question; Cecily has unwittingly kept the ball in play.

"You," he says—and whatever is eating him bites sheer through the protective thumb and through five thousand years of civilization. "*You* had my wife kicked off the team—because she's a real woman"—he tries to put an arm around Nikki, but she slips it, gazing at him fascinated—"a warm, wonderful woman, the kind dikes always hate. As for you, Miss Woodruff, and what *you* are . . ."—Ferris is rising slowly—"I wouldn't care to say."

Billy seems surprised to see Ferris's hairy chest in his eye. It must be like a blur on his lens. They'd been talking amicably just a moment ago. What sort of scene is this? Waldo reaches out a hand to intervene and find out at the same time, and we all sort of shuffle about, but there is no need for us.

"Little Billy," says Ferris softly, although when Billy tries to stand up, he isn't really so little; it's just that Ferris is so close that Billy can't quite straighten his legs. "Dear little Billy. We all love you—*you* know that. But you've been saying naughty things tonight, real naughty. In fact, you've been a bad little Billy, haven't you? And when you get home, I'm just sure that your beautiful wife is going to give you the spanking of your life." He pauses and says *real* slow, "on-her-way-out-for-the-evening."

Jesus, what is this? Billy stands back a step as if to get a better look and Ferris leans into him even further, trapping him someplace between his chair and the embarrassment of trying to throw a punch on his back. Nothing in Billy's career has remotely prepared him for this. Only a few Big Game hunters have been there.

"Now is there anything you would like to call *me*, Billy, before you go—real soon?" Ferris croons. "My sweet Billy?"

"Give me room," cries Billy, and Ferris steps back as he might for a lady. There is only one thing to do, and Waldo and I know it. We both grab Billy before he can either look as if he's fighting or look as if he's not. This allows him to glare noncommittally at Ferris, as we drag him a few discreet paces back. But Ferris has already turned away.

"I guess I'll make my goodnights," he says. "I have an appointment with a masterpiece. If I don't write it, it just won't get writ."

"You were wonderful Ferris," breathes Cecily, still glowing with panic.

"Thanks ma'am." He kisses her hand as coolly as a bureaucrat franking stamps. "But I'd do the same for any lady."

And with a "bye all" to the rest of us, he strides off to meet his destiny. No Johnny Reb ever disposed of a Yankee sentry more smoothly; the people at the next table don't even look around as he leaves.

There's no point holding on to Billy any longer. But when we let go of him, he seems quite lost. There is no plausible part for him in this scene. Even leaving it will be clumsy, but it's the best he can possibly do.

"Guess I'll be on my way," he says as if he had just dropped by for a moment. "Coming, Nikki?"

She looks, incredibly, questioningly at Waldo. He nods briskly, kindly, and she stands up. At this stage she doesn't know quite what to do about Woodruff, so she gives us all one of those inane little itsy-bitsy finger waves and exits with her he-man.

That leaves just four of us. I move closer to Cecily and put my arm around her just to comfort. She is still shaking from anger and fright. "By the way, Waldo," I say, "I don't want to start something, but why *are* you grinning?"

"You'll find out," he said. "I wouldn't want to spoil it for you, man." He stands, stretches lazily, and says, "That was quite a party, huh? Old Ferris looked mighty good in there. Billy really *bought* that Southern shit, do you realize? What a talent." Now he decides to imitate Nikki's finger wave. "Well, my bachelor couch awaits. Gotta be up for the big one tomorrow."

What's so big about it now? I wonder. All the contracts are signed and the pigs have gone to rest. Waldo looks benignly at me and Cecily as if blessing our union, and says, "C'mon, Arch, you too. Brainworkers need even more sleep than us strong-back guys." Archie wakes up and says "right." Brainworkers. Columns. He's going to have a wonderful night's sleep tonight.

"Break a leg," I say to Arch and Waldo.

"Whose?" says Waldo merrily, and is gone.

Cecily leans against me and her lips brush my ear. She looks at me with a cozy expression, and gives me a little hug within my larger vague one. "It's just you and me, babe," she says. We laugh. At this point simple friendship seems a pearl beyond price.

"Have you decided how to play it tomorrow?" I ask.

"Waldo advises me to play my balls off."

"Well that would give Billy two less things to worry about," say I—a tired businessman's type of joke, very big with bar girls.

She smiles. "Just you and me, babe," she repeats, and we sit just like that, in peace, until Jimmy's closes.

Thus ends, for me at least, the Night before Crispin's.

20

THE French pavilions gleamed in the sunshine, and the English flags flapped defiantly in the breeze, but it isn't like that at all at our place. The outfield fence is as shabby as an old boarding house and the signs saying "Joe's Pizza" and "Sinkwitch's Funerals" are almost indecipherable, dim reminders of Springtime when the paint was fresh.

The only difference today is, so help me, a movie camera. All our protests about publicity die unborn in our throats. Nobody even asked us. "That's disgraceful," I say to Munson. "I agree," he says absently. We stalk over to the camera, hands deep in our windbreakers, like real baseball men. "Who told you you can come in here?" "Watch it Mac." The snout of the camera wheels around and almost clocks me. "Get *down*, you asshole," the guy hollers. There is no question about who belongs here, and who doesn't. Munson wanders off, too preoccupied to fight.

There follows a courtly exchange about who the fuck is he to give me orders, topped by an "OK, it's your skull, buddy." Without deigning to look at me, a mere subject, a photo opportunity at best, he hands me various scraps of paper, a permit to use the park, releases from all of Hearthstone's players, etc. "Well you'll never get *me* to sign one of those things," I shout. "I don't remember asking you," he retorts. "Say—" snaps Mr. Bones. "What charm school did you go to anyway, Jack?" "Same one as you, only twenty years later," says he. "Sure has gone to hell, ain't it?" I mumble—but he's already had quite enough of me. He has a job to do and just to emphasize this he swivels his giant toy around so that it tickles my nose.

"Well, you can't take *my* picture anyway," I pout.

After a long pause, he realizes I'm still there. "OK, we'll shoot around you," he says and peers once more into his monster, waiting for me to shove off.

"Look, does talking give you any special trouble?" I'm too sore by now to let go. "I can get you lessons."

"Look mister, and this is for the last time. I don't know how to break this to you, old buddy, but I didn't come here to take your picture in the first place. OK, understood, *capisce?*"

Just then Hearthstone ambles up and drapes a Hollywood arm around me. "I see you've already met Freddy."

"Yeah. He's quite a guy."

"One of the best. Hey Freddy, how about taking a picture of me with my friend Jonathan here?"

"He doesn't want his picture taken," comes the muffled voice.

"What's that?" Hearthstone looks at me in wonderment. "I don't understand."

Oh what the hell, it's just a picture and it'll give so much pleasure. "Forget it," I say, and I let Freddy have his beastly way with me.

This incident turns out to be prophetic. As I look back on it, it might be the start of an old Movietone News reel in which a giant camera sets the tone for what follows. "I am the boss" announces the lens. "I am the eyes and ears of the world. No one goeth on the screen except through me."

When the Hearthstone Kops, as Marty roguishly calls them, finally show up, they are not at all what I expected, not at all the cream of the executive suite, or the pride of the sauna. Two of them seem to be acrobats, and they start out by turning cartwheels for the camera, until a clown in baggy pants chases them away, only to blow kisses at the same camera and wind up giving it a wet smack.

"Nice of Marty to lay on a pregame show, huh?" says Waldo lazily.

"Do you think that's it?" I ask hopefully, but even as I speak the merry-andrews continue their tumbling and prancing all the way onto the field where they commence to practice. At first they do it without a ball at all, and then with a series of beach balls, Wiffle balls, and Frisbees. Ah what Waldo could do if he only had a prop department.

"This is great, isn't it?" burbles that great man. Waldo still seems high from last night. Otherwise the thought of so much comic competition might have rendered him peevish by now.

As our presumed liaison man with the Martians, I trudge back to Hearthstone again. "Is this your *team?*" I ask, and he nods. "Don't worry. They're pretty good ballplayers."

"Yeah, but I'm afraid our team may look kind of, how you say, lackluster in contrast."

He gives me the industry-famous blank stare. What do you mean, your team? It dawns on me for the first time that he gives no more of a shit for our team than the warmhearted cameraman does. They didn't come here to shoot us.

"Don't worry," he says. "My guys will settle down eventually. And your fellows will have a good time, too, I promise. How often do they get to play against real stuntmen?"

"We came to play ball," I growl.

"Great. So did we. And listen—we'll whip your ass." He grins and holds out his hand.

"Not if I see yours first," I say and turn my back.

I don't know: all the bullshit of summer suddenly backs up on me and I start to steam like a manhole cover. Indeed, I have to be just about insane with rage to act against my own interests like that, and even now I am tempted to turn and grin, and go along, seething, with the fun. But I brace my neck against it. Our miserable little winter game has long since been degraded and abused like an old trollop, but even so we didn't come this far to be set up, without warning, as straight men in a Hollywood sideshow.

"Let's get 'em gang," I rasp to our dugout.

"If you say so," says Waldo, smiling.

"Definitely," says Munson, vaguely resuming the reins in his reborn hands. But he doesn't really want to get anybody. He, too, is floating. The indispensable sportswriter, oh my goodness. Fender is another matter. "I seen too many good men crawl to that prick's whims lately," he mutters, and I see that he is ready to play ball.

Gazing along the bench, I see no other allies in this. The smoothies are chuckling and shaking their heads with delight— the first time I've seen any one of them so much as smile—and even Cecily looks faintly amused. If I try to explain my annoyance, nobody would understand.

"Why didn't he *tell* us?" I whisper to Ferris.

"Haven't you figured that one? You're on Candid Camera, boy," he says. "Hey, and you know why the guys prolly showed up so late? The bastard must be paying them scale!"

Thus it is that two hearts full of hate and seven starstruck members of the general public take the field to be entertained (Waldo our number ten, is, as always, the wild card). "Remember how you're going to play, Cecily?" I say, patting her rump.

"Absolutely boss. Soft and feminine, right?" She takes one look at me. "I'm kidding, of course." But she can't help smiling.

Through my catcher's mask, my disguise, I look over at Hearthstone. He is nodding slightly, pleased with the way things are going, but not too pleased. I believe I could still forgive the mother if he beamed with self-satisfaction: but no, this is just one day's shooting among many. We are nothing but an *auteur*'s footnote.

I also note that Billy and Nikki are nowhere to be seen. Whether or not Nikki gave the lad that spanking last night, she must surely have said enough to keep his embarrassment aflame for weeks to come. Too bad in a way—this is just their kind of game. A really rotten team would be the only way to frustrate these sharpies; the van Dynes alone are funnier than all the stuntmen in the world. But by sedulous self-improvement, we have actually honed ourselves into the perfect victims, the brave bulls of Nether Hampton.

As if to round out my alienation, I also note that the stands are packed to bursting with people I've never seen before, who are already laughing in disciplined waves like a studio audience. Our little band of explorers has blundered through the jungle and onto a movie set.

I guess what follows is technically funny. Fielders falling down under pop flies only to leap up and catch them behind their backs; baserunners doing the splits. Their clown whoops along beside *our* baserunners, sliding with, and finally hugging, them until they look as chalky as he does. I am sick with loathing in a sea of mirth.

Unfortunately, this does not improve my game. Indeed determination only makes one more vulnerable. When Ferris Fender busts one out of the park, the clown capers alongside that noble figure as he rounds the bases, mocking Ferris's dignity with every mincing step. As Bobo the Fool crosses the plate, shaking his fist triumphantly and hopping up and down, Ferris scoops him up casually by the armpits and carries him over to the enemy dugout. "Anyone want to pay for this?" he says, dumping the clown at Hearthstone's feet. It is our one good moment, but everyone roars anyway. It proves that we have a sense of fun, too, in our simple way, and it somehow renews their license to humiliate us to the legal limit in the sacred name of humor.

The more sensible of our smoothies simply break up with mirth every chance they get. It's the only thing to do with insult comedians: keep howling until they go away. Waldo seems to take an inscrutable middle position out on the mound. Since I have come to respect Waldo as a social tactician, I study him closely. He obviously sees that there is no point trying to out-comedy these guys, so, after a first playful balloon pitch hurled up to the sky (which the batter first spits at and then catches in his mouth), he settles down to his work as if it were another day at the office. He smiles slightly at the funny stuff, but never cracks up. Instead he tends to stand with his arms crossed, tolerantly waiting it out like a professor. Kids are so cute when they're this age, aren't they? When a batter tries to engage him in the horseplay by catching a pitch in his bare hand and running it out to the mound, Waldo motions for him to put it on the ground, then picks it up and tosses a strike before the guy can get back. All very businesslike, just funny enough, and after that they give up on Waldo.

It is impossible to describe such a game: the scorecard would look like a Jackson Pollock painting. Yet the score itself remains reasonably close. The Hearthstone Kops are, as expected, wonderful ballplayers, but they delight in foiling their own efforts, stealing bases backward, playing leapfrog in rundowns and what not, the whole venerable repertoire of antics that a diamond can accommodate. It seems like a century ago that we started to have a "fun" game—and just couldn't do it. It finally took professionals to show us.

After two outs in the sixth inning, Hearthstone trots across the field and looks in on us. "Hope you boys are having a good time. Aren't they wonderful?" If he really cared what kind of time we were having, he would see that my face is an Aztec mask of hate and that Fender's is a poem in dreamy violence. Even Cecily is frowning. Only the enigmatic Waldo is still smiling politely. That must be some deal they've cooked up. "Glad you guys are such good sports about it" says the impervious Hearthstone. "I think this is what village softball is really all about, don't you?"

"Absolutely!" says Waldo firmly.

"But enough is enough, don't you agree? So we thought we'd play the last three innings straight, if that's OK with you guys, and I'm making a few changes in the lineup." He hands me a card, which I pass on to Munson—Hearthstone seems to have forgotten our famous sportswriter's existence—but not before noticing that Marty's own name is on the list.

He gives Waldo that earnest worshipful look and gives him a wistful punch in the arm. You're the greatest. At just that moment, and before we can even take the field, the camera's twin, which has been lurking in right field, wheels up smack in front of us. Hearthstone nods approval at it and trots off. And Cecily explodes.

"What the fuck are you doing in our dugout? We're trying to play some baseball around here."

"Is that so?" says the operator of this one. "You could have fooled me, lady."

"Why you little pissant"—Cecily leaps up, bent on slaughter. But before she can dismantle either the man or the camera, Waldo stands up and says, "OK, don't worry about it," and

reaches into his hip pocket and hands me a little square envelope of the kind you stick on birthday presents, and he heads
for the field. I glance down at my billet-doux. The envelope has
been quite fussily inscribed, obviously not in the last five minutes, and it says right under my name "not to be opened until
the end of the inning."

What the —? Well busy, busy. On with my mask and off to
my chores. The first batter is a portly producer whom I've seen
around, and I can only say that his swing reminds me of mine.
If there are any more at home like him, we can still win this
thing—whatever this "thing" is.

But he is just the banjo act, the tummler, that opens the
show. Marty Hearthstone is due next, and I am suddenly aware
of cameras boring into my skull as they zoom in on the master.
Marty taps his shoes with his bat, knocking dirt out of his imaginary spikes, and assumes a slightly comic stance, waggling his
bat and looking ferocious. "C'mon. Show me something,
busher," he hollers at Waldo, who gives a friendly nod and
wheels.

I have seen the films, but they don't even come close. Waldo's
first pitch is a rising fastball which rips off Marty's shirt buttons
and leaves scorch marks across his chest. Or so I imagine. The
ball hits my mitt like a cannonball and actually embeds itself
there; it is too fast to drop.

"Hey," I shout with what's suddenly left of my breath, "what
are you doing? This is meant to be slow pitch."

"Take your base, take your base," chirps a solicitous
smoothie.

"Sorry, it slipped," says Waldo.

Marty stands in shock for a moment, then his demeanor
changes. For the first time all afternoon, he is paying attention.
"That's all right," he says, "you don't get a free base in slow
pitch." He digs in again and his stance now is not at all comical,
but coiled, feral. His camouflage flakes away and he actually
looks like a guy who could make movies. "Is that the best you
can do, Kid?" The words are hardly out of his mouth when the
pitch arrives. His teeth seem to rattle around for a moment, he

is flung back almost into my lap. And there he lies, motionless at my feet, like a gift from the Mob.

The film shows Waldo strolling calmly off the field at that point, picking up the ball, which had ricocheted weirdly back, like a keepsake and heading toward his car. But I doubt if anyone but the camera sees it at the time. I myself am reaching ineptly for Marty's pulse, and so it seems is everybody else. The least practical people somehow manage to get there first, forming an impregnable barrier against anyone who might possibly know what he is doing. Seconds are lost while the closest thing to a doctor in the house claws his way in, only to announce that someone should call an ambulance.

Well, at least he's alive, I think frantically—not having let myself think death before. People scurry for their cars, while our medical expert does whatever it is you do in the way of amateur resuscitation. I have clawed my way *out* by now to make way for the latest sightseers. Ferris and Cecily are still standing on the rim of the outfield, and I explain what little I know of the situation. "Jesus," says Cecily. "We didn't mean anything like this." "Where's Waldo?" says Ferris with faraway eyes. And then, "Never mind."

In my dreams, I will forever hear a car pulling out long before the others with a mocking squeal, but I don't at the time. Instead, I go back into the crowd, which seems larger and more unruly by the minute, to look for him. "Waldo?" I call forlornly. And at the same time I reach in my pocket for his note.

It turns out to be simplicity itself. "The sonofabitch turned down my book. See you in the funny papers. Love, Waldo."

Autumn

21

SOMEBODY should have played taps as we straggled out of the park that day for the last time, like dead leaves gusting. The ambulance shouldered impatiently in and out of the crowd, removing our centerpiece, our point, and we followed it out like some sort of Hindu funeral cortege, kicking up infield dust and muttering.

A smoothie came over to me matching strides. "You know what I think the problem is, Jonathan? Lack of communication. Why I'll bet you don't even know my name."

I looked at him dazed. "Maybe that's best for now," I said.

It wasn't a fall day, but it might as well have been. Summer had been shot down by a fastball. Softball was dead around here too; nobody would ever mention it again.

Probably everybody mourned something different. Munson came by and draped an arm over my shoulder; for him it was the Game. For me it was that fucking book, another pustulating dream of winter. I never wanted to see the bloody thing again, or have anything to do with it. For somebody, many people perhaps, it might even have been the man who was hit.

So we shuffled along in our many-colored griefs. Cecily walked alongside Fender—not intentionally, it seemed, not looking at him—repeating at intervals "we didn't mean *that*." Ferris looked grim. In his world, you could trust things to turn out badly, but not meanly, not shabbily. For myself, I could still see a perplexed-looking Hearthstone lying at my feet. I don't know if he really looked perplexed, but now he does, and I hear him saying "why me? what did I do wrong? we were having such a grand time, weren't we?" Poor sonofabitch. He just got in with a bad crowd.

I would be asked afterwards why we didn't all go hunt for Waldo and the missing ball, but that was only after a few people had seen the film. At the time, nobody thought about the damned ball—why should they? who knows what happens to old softballs? And, in Hearthstone's camp, which was legion, a novelist like Waldo didn't even exist on a scale of celebrity, and they had barely registered what he looked like. To them, he was just part of our gang; we had all done it, it was a group crime.

As a sort of unofficial host I felt I should get on over to the hospital to apologize to someone. But Hearthstone had already been whisked into intensive care, and his Hollywood friends had already gathered in the lobby like Apache warriors and they glared at me as if I'd crossed enemy lines. The felling of their hero was a team effort all right—by us the public, us the critics, us the envy-ridden losers in life, and the sooner I got back to my People the better.

"How is he?" I asked.

They looked at each other. Was I entitled to this information? "Critical." "Extremely critical." The worse they could make it, the better they liked it. The words came like darts from a pygmy's blowgun.

I retreated, but realized I didn't want to go home either. There was something wrong with my house now. It was poisoned by the day's events. Don't ask me to explain this. I just wanted the place cleaned and if possible repainted before I went back to it.

At Jimmy's the afternoon crowd was bigger than usual, and buzzing with horror and curiosity. What do *you* know? they seemed to buzz at every new arrival. Ferris and Cecily sat at a corner table not talking, as if they had fetched up together by accident. I had this strange feeling that both of them had gone their separate ways, but kept winding up at the same place. At some point they would each decide independently to leave, and, quite by chance, they would walk out together. There was nothing between them now except a dazzling series of coincidences.

Can an affair endure on such terms? Maybe a very old marriage can. Maybe that's what everyone here will settle for by now. Safety. No more excitement. "I still can't believe it," says Cecily for the one hundredth time as if she were telling her beads. "It might be a good idea not to talk about it just yet," says Fender. He looks at me instructively: you and I *know*, don't we, old buddy? Nobody else does. It's just that *I* know about Waldo, and *you* felt the ball.

The ball. Well what *about* the ball? Yes, I can still feel the thing splintering and numbing my palm—one hell of a pitch all right, all right. Still, the ball felt normal enough when I threw it back, lighter than a shotput at least, and I never got to feel it again. Fender continues to stare: well, maybe you know about something else then. Whatever it is you know, keep it as a souvenir. The world doesn't need it. Waldo's note, of course, is still sitting snug in my pocket. I have more souvenirs than I can use.

I need now to argue with Fender's silence. Why the fuck should I cover for that monster? He just tried to kill a man. In cold blood. He planned it all day. Shit Ferris! Well maybe that's not quite the way to start a rational discussion.

"I'm sorry, Ferris—I happen to feel like talking."

"Well you go right ahead," he says.

I am naturally stumped by this, so I turn to Cecily for help. But she just shakes her head. She doesn't even know anything, and she isn't talking either. "Do you guys have some kind of union or something?" I snarl at Ferris.

"You're the one who wants to talk," he says, "not me."

Stasis. I am suddenly lonelier than the man in the Pequod Lighthouse. Won't somebody take me in? Couldn't we all just make separate decisions to leave, and wind up in the same bed?

No, of course not. I'm only "one of them" when the sun shines. So they just sit there patiently waiting for me to shut up or go away. I need company desperately. But there *is* no company. Billy van Dyne would either howl "get the bastard," or else he would invoke union rules too, and pull down his own

STORE CLOSED sign. In either case, Nikki would whimper tone-lessly, and I would go mad.

If, on the other hand, I call my city friends for an outside opinion, they will chirp "but of course . . . you've got to . . . you have no choice."

I stand up from the table, feeling like some ancient trapper pulling on his snowshoes and leaving an empty cabin on a cold and windy night. I will have to argue this one with myself. No help, no prompting from anyone.

It is in fact still warm daylight when I get out, but I keep walking until that is straightened out, into darkness and beyond, hoping just to reach the edge of the planet and slip away. Meanwhile, my desire to settle scores with Waldo, or someone like Waldo, is so overwhelming that it makes my head pound. It isn't enough for the Waldos of this world to win gracefully, they have to celebrate their lifelong victory over you every single day. On paper and in real life, Waldo has taken every chance he can drum up to crow to the world that he is alive and I am dead, that he is a man and I am a soul-less, ball-less, scheming little toady. It is my job, of course, as editor, to flatter him and humor him while he is doing this.

But goddammit, Jonathan, you can't turn in a man just because of that, just because he's hurt your little feelings. If you do, you'll be everything he says you are, a worm, a traitor, a dead man. Dammit, you've got to choose sides on this.

—For your information, I'm not turning him in "just because of that." In case you missed it, something happened out there today. Waldo tried to kill a man.

(There ensues some confused blather about whether you can kill a man intentionally by throwing underhand at him from forty-five feet and how do I know there was anything wrong with the ball anyway. It didn't break my hand the time I caught it, it only feels like that. Look, I'm not accusing him of anything, just making the facts available what facts just a note he entrusted you with yeah he put himself at your mercy all right—just the time for a little weasel like you to pounce, what do you mean at my mercy he tied my hands with that note he knows more about weasels than you ever will, he knows that his

character Otis would be thinking these very thoughts I'm thinking right now Christ he's not God end of tape.)

—I repeat, for the last time, you've got to choose sides, Jonathan. Although Waldo may be a crumby blackhearted villain of
a friend, he is still a friend, which those glitzheads from Hollywood will never be. You think *he's* been playing with you? Jesus
that guy Hearthstone has been conducting Roman games over
you and your friends all summer long. This afternoon was the
really big event, the one where the slaves get to dance on hot
coals. Then just for a wrap-up, and to prove who's boss, he
practically dares you to hit him like a cheeky kid (see how tame
these guys are?). Come on, admit it. You wanted him to get hit
yourself. For one precious minute your heart leaped up. . . .

—No it did not. I was sickened. Look, sure I might have
wanted him to get hit. But I don't *know* about violence, I might
wish it on someone without knowing what I was saying, like a
kid at the movies. I just didn't know how godawful the conse-
quences are.

—Well violence is kind of like having your jaw broken by a
postman, while you're being knocked down by a baserunner.

—Oh, like *that*. Funny, I never connected it. Now where
was I? Waldo does know about violence. He's really been there,
he's stepped over the bodies. And he walked off that diamond
not even looking at the guy he'd hit to see if he's alive or dead.

—What good would looking have done? OK, so violence
turns your pretty stomach. That does you great credit. But
maybe it doesn't make you the best judge of that world [more
angry garble here] but I still say that if anyone was begging for
it, fairly pleading for exactly what he got, it was Hearthstone
this afternoon.

—Well maybe Hearthstone didn't see it that way. In fact, no
sane person would see it that way. Marty simply thought he
was putting on a dandy entertainment for the folks out here.
And he did. Maybe he was a little insensitive, but that isn't
grounds for cracking a man's skull.

—That all depends. It could be pretty good grounds. Anyway you can't turn in your own author! It's unprecedented.

—Well, *Waldo* is unprecedented.

My ravings have brought me finally to the beach where I sit perched on a dune staring at the sea, and trying to scramble my thoughts away from Waldo. For instance. Good old sea—keeps coming at you, sneaky fast. Looks friendly from here, but don't mess with it. Biggest killer in history, next to whatshisname. Living out here is like sleeping next to a lion's cage. Listen to that growl. The sea is always ready for the next meal. I don't know, maybe I'll step into the cage one night, and find out what it feels like. Have you considered taking your temperature lately, Jonathan? I touch my forehead and it feels red hot. How can you *feel* red? never mind—you can, you can. In fact, my head must look like a torch for weary beachcombers to comb by. Or weary softball pitchers.

Weary. That's it. You've got it, my boy. Time to go home now. Got to face the old house sometime. The sun is coming up and it's the hour for little publishers to be in bed. Tired little publishers, perplexed little publishers. I drag my feet through the sand and then along various forms of sidewalks trying to pretend that they're sand too, anything to feel sleepy. But when I reach the house, I am as awake as I ever was. This is the cage, right in here. I sling open the door and a voice calls from the kitchen, "How's it shaking, Otis?"

"You bastard," I scream. He is sitting at the table whittling idly at the linoleum. "What the hell are you doing here?" I am not ready for this. Just let me walk around the block for another twelve hours or so.

"Time hangs heavy, my man," he says.

"You realize, I'm going to have to turn you in," I squeak.

"Yes," he says, "that's probably your best move. Considering."

"Considering *what?*"

"Never mind. The thing is, though, you'll have to wait a while. It seems that nobody's even looking for me yet."

"How do you know that?"

"I been listening to the news on your kitchen radio. Great reception by the way. And all it said was stuff like 'Marty Hearthstone, the movie-great, was felled this afternoon by an errant pitch.' Isn't that nice? He wasn't even a 'movie-good' this morning. Now he's great. How little it takes."

"Well, it's just a matter of time before they start looking."

"Maybe so. I liked that part about the errant pitch, though. Hey, and Jon, you look all in, man. You've got to watch those late nights, fella. You already caught a great game today, yesterday, whatever the hell it was. Isn't that enough for you? You're only human, Oglethorpe."

"And what do *you* propose to do with yourself?"

"Oh, I'll just wait around here until they come and get me, I guess. Don't worry, I'll wake you for that one. I'll want you as a witness, to see that there's no, you know, police brutality."

"Waldo, this is a naked power play on your part."

He looks slightly pained. "Jonathan, what on earth do you mean by that?"

"I haven't the faintest idea." I am suddenly so tired that I have only two choices. I can sleep right here with my head on the table, which means doing it in *his* presence, which in turn is like sleeping with all the lights on—or I can totter off to bed.

I scarcely notice as I wriggle feebly, amoebishly, against the sheets that these stiff unyielding clods of cotton are already warm from someone else's body. The bastard has even slept in my bed.

Call it sleep, indeed. As soon as I shut my eyes the softballs start flying. And when I open them, I am in a barred cell, with a gorilla just outside, alternately clanking his keys and chewing on them. No, that's the dream, and it's the best I can do. When I truly wake up, the gorilla is sitting right there on my bed offering me a cup of tea.

"Good morning," I say noncommittally.

"Good evening, you mean," says Waldo. "It's six o'clock, chum. I wish *I* could sleep like that. I'm sorry—I didn't know whether you took sugar." Waldo as nursemaid is the most grotesque transformation yet.

"What's happening what's going on what'd I miss?" I ask calmly.

"Not a thing. The great manhunt has not materialized yet. In fact, the whole story has been dropped from the national news. Maybe they're setting up this dragnet behind a smokescreen of silence, do you reckon? Anyway I don't even know how our movie-great is doing."

"So," I say very patiently, "why don't you just go home now and *leave me alone.*"

"*However.* There was one item on a local station about some film of the game that someone has just seen. You remember those vultures with the cameras? Well it seems they caught something in their beaks."

"Did they say what?"

"Nope. Just something."

"Any ideas yourself?"

He yawns and stretches. "Yeah, you might say so. Everyone has ideas, don't they? All God's chillun, to name one."

"Christ, Waldo," I blurt—a prisoner has *some* rights, "why in hell did you do it?"

He stands up slowly and pours himself another drink. I assume it is another. I don't know how many it is other *to.* "Good scotch," he mutters. "I gotta say it, you always travel first class with Oglethorpe." He takes so long over it, that I figure he's waiting for my question to go away. But when he returns from the bar his face has clouded strangely, as if he has just stepped into deep shadow, and he says, "Why did I do it, huh?" He sits down and taps his glass on the table almost hard enough to shatter it. "Why did I do it indeed, indeed," he says dreamily. And then, violently, "Christ, I wish I knew."

Then nothing for a while. He acts as if that about wraps it up as far as he's concerned. He takes a sip of my liquor, goes to my window, and pulls down my blind. Sits once again at my table.

"So? That's all?"

You really need more? He pulls at his nose, as if making a painful decision. "I guess I never told you about my injury, did I, Jon? It's not something I talk about much—not because I'm noble, God knows, but because, you know, it puts you at a disadvantage if people know your weaknesses. Anyway this injury makes me act crazy sometimes, and that's all she wrote."

"For pete's sake, what is this so-called injury, Waldo?"

"Well, if you must know, it's a plate in my head, courtesy of the North Korean forces and the nearest MASH team. I guess it must press on the old brain now and then, and scramble things a bit. And out comes vengeance baby. Somebody's hurting me *right this minute*, and somebody's going to pay for it. It could be mortar fire or it could be a dripping faucet. But somebody's going to get it."

"Jesus, Waldo, I had no idea."

"I guess you thought I was just naturally crazy, huh? Well, you know, it's not a bad idea to let people think that. If you act crazy all the time, people may miss the real thing when it comes along. It's like gaily colored camouflage."

It would simplify things if Waldo would stop crapping around for just one minute. "Gaily colored camouflage"—how madly gay. "Are you sure the plate isn't pressing on your brain right now?"

"No, as a matter of fact. I'm not the least bit sure. We'll just have to wait and see, won't we?" he laughs unexpectedly and I echo him nervously. If he's trying to scare me, he's doing a bangup job.

"Not to change the subject," he says, "but do you know what I was doing when you were out last night, and then again *really* out all day? I was reading your manuscript."

You sonofabitch. Plate in the head or no plate. "And who gave you permission to do that?" I say stiffly.

"Ah come off it, Jon. *You're* a writer. Next thing you'll be telling me you don't read other people's mail. Hey—I let you read my book, didn't I?"

Yeah, that was another rotten trick.

"Anyway, it's pretty good stuff, some of it. I'm not sure you should let this cat Waldo run away with the novel like that—I mean he's a great *great* invention but fair's fair—and could it be that you're just a tiny bit rough on your guy Oglethorpe? Nobody can be *that* constipated. But what the hell, it's your book, and I really enjoyed it."

Just my luck. My first critic, and he has to have a plate in his head. Waldo gets up now and prowls his own cafe, and I think, well, poor bastard, he's entitled. No wonder he never stayed married. He might strangle the first kid who crossed him. If teasing my book eases the pressure, be my guest. Waldo looks over from the bar with a mute appeal I've never seen before.

"Hey, Jonno, *we're running out of scotch*," he says. "You should *think* about things like that! Get your head out of the clouds, you old author you. Here we are on a Sunday night and all the stores are shut."

"Sonofabitch! As I recall they have great scotch over at the van Dynes'," I say, "and Ferris serves a very tasty bourbon."

"Nah." He holds up another bottle of something. "I guess we can make do."

"Waldo. For Christ sweet sake. *Why did you come here?* If there's going to be trouble, Ferris will protect you with his life. *I* won't. I'll hand you in the first chance I get. Believe me, it's better for you that way. Maybe they can help you with that plate. Anyway, it's what I'm going to do. In fact, I'll even show them that note you wrote."

"Yeah. I want to be here when you do that. I want to see it with my own eyes."

"Why me, Waldo?" I almost sob. "Just tell me, why me?"

"Because I like you, old buddy. And because you took my crappy book when no one else in the world would touch it. And now I discover that you have a major talent yourself. You know I've been doing some thinking about that. I'm not so happy with my own little effort now that I've read yours. And now that I also know you a little better through your work, I think my novel is unforgivably cruel and hurtful. So maybe just as soon as I get home I'll consign the damn thing to the flames and we'll forget the whole thing."

"But there goes our Spring list."

I say it before I have time to think. And he begins to cackle before I've finished the sentence. Oh God. *And this is Hell nor are we out of it.*

"Where did you say you got that plate?" I snarl.

"It was Pork Chop Hill."

"Funny, I never knew you were at Pork Chop. You never mentioned it in *The Thirty-ninth Parallel*."

"Well, sometimes a man doesn't like to talk about the things that really happened to him, you know?" He looks at me quizzically. He knows and I know that this particular man has never talked about anything else. Oh, well. He shrugs good-naturedly.

"So you won't buy the plate, huh? Well what would you say if I told you the doctor gives me only six months to live?"

He returns still cackling to the bar where he commences to deplete my vodka.

I tell him that I don't know about *him*, but I have some reading to do—and I march off to my study, which isn't much of a march because the study adjoins the living room. "That's all right," he says. "I'll find something." And for a while I hear him banging about restlessly, above the hum of the radio. I strain to hear but it sounds like endless baseball scores. I imagine that each of them conceals some horrible story.

I have no intention of being manhandled again by that saturnine maniac, so I concentrate grimly on some highly touted first novel or other. Unfortunately, the thought hits me simultaneously that I have to eat and I have to pee, and that I can't do either without slinking back through the living room. In a pinch I guess I could relieve myself out the window, but I can imagine the cops choosing that very moment to flash their lights in search of Waldo and catch me instead hanging out in the ultimate, Chaucerian embarrassment. So to hell with it. I seem to have trapped myself in my own study.

If the highly touted first novelist knew the circumstances in which his little darling was being read, he would have had every reason to holler. I get a vague sense that this manuscript is too polished. If the author is this polished at twenty-three, the cat is really gonna *shine* when he's forty. This is unfair, I know. I am still thinking about the wild man outside, banging about like John Milton on the first day of his blindness, not conceding a thing. Say what you will about Waldo, he has a touch of greatness about him, unlike this here slick little veteran of too many creative writing classes, unfair.

At long last things seem to be quieting down out there. The radio continues to buzz but otherwise it's good country silence. I don't know how much longer I can read like this with my legs crossed, but I decide to hold on for a few more minutes to be on the safe side.

And then the wall phone in the kitchen starts to ring and I figure I'd better get to it before Waldo does. I burst out of the room with my bladder bursting along with me. Already I am imagining Waldo on the phone. "Yes, officer, Mr. Oglethorpe has been acting quite strangely all day. In fact he just ran out of here muttering something about some killer softball he'd substituted in the game yesterday. . . ." But the room is empty. Waldo is nowhere to be seen. Or felt. Especially felt.

I just make it to the phone, and the dam bursts. I wet my pants at first reluctantly, and then with childish abandon— they're my pants and I'll do what I like with them. "No officer, I haven't seen him since the game. Right, I'll let you know. No trouble at all." As I stand there in my infantile puddle winding down pleasantries with the gendarmes, I reach idly for Waldo's note, only to find that it's gone. Wait a minute, no it isn't. It seems to have found its way somehow from my hip pocket to the windowsill right next to the phone. I tear it open with one hand and squint. The wording seems to have changed slightly. "Thanks for the hospitality, old buddy," it reads this time. "I knew you'd come through for me, but I just thought I'd make it a little easier for you. Your admirer and fan, W."

Well, of course. The sonofabitch had had all day to rifle my pants and all night to run up this latest edition of Games Waldos Play. In serious sticky confusion by now, as if waiting for someone to change my diaper, I am assailed by a totally perverse squall of rage. "Why," I howl at the window pane, "in the name of God didn't you trust me, Waldo?"

22

THE hounds seem to have assembled in front of Lord Trumpington's manor (you know the place, of course), all of them moiling and yapping and anxious to get going. Among them, the horses wheel like sheepdogs, appearing to keep order but in fact as restless as anyone. A couple of stray notes emerge from a fat man in a red coat, who is testing his horn. Thus, the orchestra tunes up and the actors mill about in the wings, waiting for Lord Trumpington to raise the curtain.

As his Lordship steers his majestic nag through the melee, he seems to be holding up a piece of white cloth. His face is as lined and world-weary as a Scotland Yard inspector's, and when he speaks it is with a tired authority that expects no back-talk, from you or the day or God himself. Right now, he seems to be addressing the hounds. "Remember this object well, gentlemen," he says, brandishing the cloth. "It will lead you to your next meal." He holds it down for them to sniff, like a bishop extending his ring to be kissed. "I promise you, you shall dine well today, gentlemen."

He stiffens and the horn really lets it out and they're off, leaving me alone in the driveway. My God, I remember that piece of cloth: it's part of Waldo's T-shirt! Somewhere out there my author must already be ducking and darting and stumbling. . . .

* * *

What seems to have happened here is that I had taken a couple of Nembutals, which at this very moment are floating roguishly on a sea of coffee and vodka. For a fleeting instant, it dawns on me that I might conceivably be dreaming, because somehow I seem to be running along with the pack. But I haven't enough brain left to pursue the thought and besides, we are moving too fast now, skimming over hedges and waterways and clambering up ravines. Trumpington whirls by, purple-faced and coattails flying. Tally-ho! Everyone seems to be tooting and barking and neighing at once—a man can hardly hear himself think around here. So I decide to peel off from the din. It is suddenly imperative that I find Waldo before the others do and warn him.

I find him instantly, of course, and he says good-naturedly, "And what am I supposed to do with your warning, old buddy?" He is resting for a moment under a waterfall. Now where have I seen that before? Are you *sure* this isn't a dream? Well, no time to find out now. Waldo looks like a suffering saint, a sacrificial lamb behind the cascading water. "Here, you're hurt," I say crisply, for his shirt is indeed torn and bloody from brambles. "Got to get rid of the blood. Got to destroy the evidence." I rip at the shirt impatiently. If we can simply get rid of the damn thing, we're in the clear. The hounds'll wind up eating T-shirt for lunch.

But the saint's vestment seems to be glued to his blessed carcass with blood and sweat, and as I tug, I begin to hear the hounds baying at both ends of the waterfall at once. Waldo looks at me sadly, almost sweetly, and just like that starts to walk away. What the hell is this? I look down at myself and see that, my God, *I* am now wearing the shirt. Christ, get me out of here. I force myself (as I sometimes do in real life as well) to believe that this *must* be a dream, and grudgingly the vision begins to lift and thin. Waldo is last seen strolling among the dogs, patting their heads and pointing at me, but the baying grows fainter, the picture flickers, and I am awake on my sofa, with a cushion in my mouth. Naturally enough.

So what time is it anyway? Clock seems to say seven—but

seven what? Looks kind of like a morning. Can't tell what day of the week it looks like yet. Well never mind. First things first. Coffee, eggs, daylight. I start to bustle about as if to emphasize the normality of everything. But my hands beat a tattoo with the coffee cup and my jaw locks on a piece of toast like a dog that won't let go. My dreams tend to turn playful as they leave, and that last sequence has just about shaken me to pieces.

As I am still pulling at these pieces, trying to get them back together, the phone rings. My God—the investigation. The phone is stalking me with angry black noises, coming straight for me. Five, six. Don't touch that phone, Jonathan. It's a trap. Seven, eight rings. Waldo is behind this somehow. *I have nothing to add, inspector. Yes, I'd be delighted to take a lie-detector test.* Eleven, twelve. OK, you win.

"Hello, Dad," the phone says improbably.

"Who the hell are *you?*" I shout.

"Dad? Are you all right, Dad? It's Alan."

"Oh thank God. Bless you, Alan."

"Has something happened, Dad?"

"Yes, no, not really. I had a bad dream."

I feel like a little boy. A grateful little boy. "I didn't mean to wake you, Dad. I just wanted to ask if I could drive out sometime soon and show you my new car. The one you gave me."

Yes. Right now. This instant.

"Did you hear about Mom, Dad?" he chats on. Nothing could be further from a bad dream. "She's getting married next month. To a state-of-the-art creep, if you want my opinion."

"Why that's wonderful."

"What?"

"I don't know." That you think he's a creep, of course. Get with it, Alan.

"Anyway I'd really like to see you, you know, when it's convenient, when there aren't any exams and stuff to worry about, OK?"

"Roger. How soon can you make it?"

"Well school starts in three weeks. So I thought . . ."

"What's wrong with today?"

He pauses, little realizing that a man's sanity is in the balance, then he drawls maddeningly, "No, I don't think I could make it today. You see I'm at Gladdy's place. . . ."

"*Gladdy?*"

"Yes, she's this girl. This girl I *met*. Hey would you mind if I brought her out? I was thinking about weekend after next."

"Fine." Name your terms.

"Of course we'll sleep in separate rooms," he said carefully, out of respect for the old adulterer's feelings.

"Whatever you say."

And so on. Plans. Warm good-byes. So he thinks the guy is a creep, huh? Well, well, well. I have regained my prize.

It's probably a good thing kids don't know their powers. My son has just crowned me King of the Universe. And I must say, he picked a swell day for it. I sit now calmly waiting for the phone to ring and the investigation to continue. I shall take part in it now all right, shielding my author with fiendish dexterity. OK, now calm down, Jonathan. He only said the guy was a jerk, hey hey.

Anyway, nothing happens. More eggs, more coffee, but no action, no manhunt. Finally I ring the police station, but nobody seems to know what I'm talking about. "Waldo who? Never heard of the guy. Yeah? News to me. You looking for this fellow or what?"

"Never mind." I hang up. Manhunts are not what they used to be.

The day, when I look into it further, turns out, as so many days do, to be a Monday. But not just your ordinary Monday. Oh, no. It is the quintessential Monday, the Monday to end all Mondays (if only we'd signed the right treaty). It is Labor Day.

Labor Day is a day of embarkment out here. Pickups and trailers weave slowly out of town, in a demented conga line, lugging masts and oars and hunks of sail back to where they came from. To the untrained eye, it looks like one of the worst naval defeats in history.

I realize later that there must have been some hallucination in all this: there were probably just a couple of cars like that and I made up the rest. It was what I wanted to see, and I really wasn't taking in much of anything as I stood by the highway like a parade crowd of one, relishing the fresh air and the empty clarity of the mind.

Indoors all my summer friends—including the world's finest gardening writer, who will be nameless—are packing up grimly. I don't want to go indoors today, I don't want to poke about in attics and exchange gossip. It's more a day to savor, in fact, a day for filling one's lungs with our reclaimed paradise.

So I reach for my trusty Buick, and point it against the refugee hordes and go zipping by them on the empty side of the highway, and then along the deserted northwest shore where our own navy bobs imperturbably in its nest of marinas. If push comes to shove next year, we'll blow the buggers out of the water.

It is strangely silent along here, as if the whole place had been abandoned, not just five minutes ago but aeons and aeons, with just a few caretakers left to molder in their shanties while the trillionth layer of paint peels and cracks. And then suddenly a genial roar goes up in the middle distance and then another. What is this? Have all the inhabitants gathered in one place for some primitive Labor Day ritual of their own?

Well, just about. When I get there, I see a huge banner that says HAVE THEY GONE YET? Beyond that, a large (for the off-season) crowd sits in a circle, watching a clam-shucking contest. What this means is that the seven fastest shuckers in the East End, all bearing fierce names like "Captain Clam" and "The Red Hand" and "Zorro" on their T-shirts, simply shuck to beat the band. Each of them has his own private judge or guardian angel who hovers beside him and peers at his clams to see that they are well and truly shucked, with no shrapnel adhering to the juicy flesh, and the results are then passed around for us the audience to gobble, while we swill mugs of beer provided by the tavern in back of us. There is not a movie producer to be seen.

As the contestants grunt and their hands fly, the announcer seems to get funnier and funnier. At least the crowd finds him so. They must know all the foibles of the principals, of which foibles there seem to be an astonishing number. This is patently the real thing, but I wish I understood a word of it.

Well it's a lovely day, anyway. The white sails in the marina flap their edges now and then like a dude shooting his cuffs, and the sky is a calmer blue than the purples of August. I feed myself, gorge myself on the scene. This is what I want. I'll get to know these people somehow. Everyone thinks locals are cold and stolid, but once I get into their club I'll know better.

The show winds down eventually and people head for their cars, their faces stolid again, as if sobering up for the winter. I will clearly not get to know them today. As I trail along with them, the sense of communion evaporates completely and it dawns on me that I'd better be back in my office by Wednesday at the very latest, or heads will roll.

I don't want to visit my friends that evening because, frankly, I'm afraid of running into Waldo hiding in some closet or other. But I do phone them, ever alert for funny voices, only to find that Ferris is out, and Cecily is bored. "No, I haven't seen him. Should I have? . . . Why on earth should the cops call me? Look Jon, I have a friend here, if you don't mind." The preposterously irrelevant Billy van Dyne says that Nikki is very upset and that he can't talk to me now.

What is it? What have I done wrong? Never mind. The Presbyterian God, one Laird McTavish, knows, and he's put out a call on me. I don't even bother to pack, but climb into my car and head for the city, flinging myself in among the last refugees, who at least have the grace to know when they're not wanted.

I switch on the car radio just for the sake of the noise, and that's all I get for the first half hour as we pass crackling under antique overhead lines. Crackle is perfectly OK with me, but eventually it evolves into some kind of all-night news, and it's then, when I've given up expecting anything at all, that I get the next bulletin.

"A spokesman from Nether Hampton Hospital announced

tonight that world-famous producer Marty Hearthstone has just come off the critical list, subsequent to a softball 'beaning' sustained by the producer yesterday afternoon," etc. *Yesterday?* What the hell does he mean yesterday?

That was all the news for that night, though I was doomed to hear the exact same message three more times as we lurched and hiccoughed toward New York. So! no corpus delicti, no case, it never happened. Now let's concentrate on that old mental health, eh, fellow? Just about then an infernal racket breaks out, shredding my new resolve. It seems that we have at last reached the honking area where all the cars converge on the Midtown Tunnel and begin to shriek like animals, before entering Manhattan two by two.

There is something about the city that jerks the nervous system around immediately. Right now, it is like stepping onto a busy street after a horror movie. The clash and thrust of taxis clears one's mind of everything else, as a good battlefield should; and by the next morning I wonder if I haven't been taking things a wee bit too seriously.

There are several more sparse bulletins over the next few days, so I decide to pick up a cheap radio and listen for them, I'm not quite sure why, while jousting absentmindedly with Sam Welman. Thank God, it's easy: his office politics are so banal, he must have got them out of some book. The Gospel according to Sam, read every year at the end of the Summer Solstice, goes like this: that while I, Jonathan Oglethorpe Superstar, am off pleasuring (pleasuring!) myself in the Hamptons, *he*, unsung dark horse of publishing, is holding the firm together virtually between his teeth. "Don't you know, Sam," I tell him languidly, "that any publishing house that hasn't got at least one superstar in the Hamptons is in bad, bad trouble?" Quick, hand me another epee. This is *too* easy. I feel like fighting someone else at the same time.

"OK Jon, it sounds kind of quaint at that, like Franz Josef visiting the spas in 1914. Any emperor who doesn't visit the spas is in bad, bad . . ." he drones on, bad bad, Baden Baden "trouble." After tangling with Waldo, this guy is a kitten. "But are you quite sure modern publishing still works that way,

Jon?" he whinnies. "And does it really take a whole summer to woo Waldo Spinks?"

Yeah, a whole lot depends on that one doesn't it? That's why we have this radio on, you see. I turn it up louder, so I won't have to hear about how Harry Creepstitch at Goniff Books is much too busy making money to waste time at the beach, and Sam for his part doesn't have to hear again how no self-respecting author would be caught dead signing with Goniff, busy little Creepstitch or no, and so on, parry, thrust, my rapier against his shovel, all the live afternoon long. I feel full of the breezes of summer today and can blow this paleface away any time I want to.

If you've ever tried to follow a *mildly* important news story you know the feeling that comes along next. For two days it seems that Marty Hearthstone has slept well, taken nourishment, talked briefly to friends. At any moment I expect a report on his bowel movements—and would treasure it. Anything to keep the story alive.

"You expecting news or something?" asks the perceptive Welman. Well I won't really know until I hear it. All I do know is that somebody somewhere has been studying film for several days now and each time it runs, Waldo presumably disappears with the ball. Hearthstone's "people" are preeminently men of celluloid anyway and would easily pick up a softball being palmed on screen where they might miss, say, a lady fainting at the next table in real life. So all it takes now is for Marty to unleash them and we will all be flooded with movie fan deductions based on early Hitchcock and *The Shadow*. However, Marty seems content for now to rest comfortably, absorb his nourishment, and talk quietly.

God knows it takes a lot to bore station WLOG, but I guess enough hospital food is enough even for them, and by Thursday it sounds as though Marty has lost his place in the lineup to a controversial cornerstone in Bed-Stuyvesant, and I am happy enough to comply with countless requests to "turn that fucking thing off." Listening to local news for three days has already shattered my health, and by late afternoon I am wondering slyly whether I can get away with a long weekend. I've got to face the haunted house sometime, and right now seems good. Up here on the sunny twenty-second floor I can forget for whole seconds at a time what's so haunted about it.

I compromise with a fake lunch date on Friday. No one expects you to come back from Friday lunch, if you're of any importance at all, and if Welman brings it up he will be stamped forever as the small potatoes God intended him to be.

Friday morning turns out to be much too lovely for publishing. However, the Devil finds work for idle hands, so I decide at least to read the morning newspapers at my desk (you can always do this, so long as you remember to frown and clip things occasionally).

But even as I am sitting there a-frowning and a-clipping I come across the following item in the Miss Chatterbox column, datelined "Hot from the Hamptons," to wit and to clip. "Rumors that the errant pitch which felled film producer Marty Hearthstone on Sunday afternoon may not have been so errant after all [deep breath] were firmly scotched today by none other than my old friend Marty himself. Marty has said, and I quote, 'I have always had the highest respect for Waldo Spinks (a novelist who apparently threw the pitch) both as an artist and as a man, and I cannot find it in my heart to picture such a man stooping to anything so small-minded.'" (Sonofabitch has never met any writers at all!) "'In fact,' continued Big-Hearted Marty, 'I had been talking all summer long with my good friend "Waldo" about actually making a movie together. I'm tremendously excited about his upcoming book *The Hamptons Are Killing Me*, and I still believe it has excellent screen possibilities.'" (Hey, that's really wonderful of him, I really misjudged the guy, and other gee-whiz thoughts on my part.) "Well, I guess film conquers all," rattles on Miss Chatterbox, who is known for the sting in her tail. "I myself don't know if I could be quite so noble or forgiving as that if my ears were still ringing after four days, and if I faced the possibility of permanently impaired hearing. Marty's friends are pressing him to bring charges and they hint at compelling new evidence, but Marty says that as far as he is concerned, the case is closed. 'I want no part in taking a major American writer to court. And besides,' he chuckled, 'I had a bat in my hands, didn't I?' And so this remarkable man seems to stand just a little bit taller after this seamy episode, wherever that leaves Mr. Spinks, who I'm told is considered a has-been in literary circles. Incidentally, Marty's friends doubt strongly that the film will ever be made."

Literary circles! I can just imagine the ones that Miss Chatterbox moves in. "Who da hell is dis bum Spinks? What kinda pickshus he make?" grunt, and out. Hey, do you think we can sue over that "has-been" crack? Yeah, sure, and watch Miss Chatterbox's expert witnesses kick off the Fall Season by sneering at Waldo's writing day after merciless day in court—just the blurbs we need right now for a rousing sendoff in the Spring. And under oath yet.

I feel confused, but this is good news isn't it? Damn right it is. Miss Chatterbox's poisonous buzzings have unsettled me slightly, but they are all outside on the window screen. My first instinct is to call Marty Hearthstone and congratulate him on his sheer wonderfulness. I must admit those friends of his bother me, though. If they keep rolling that film often enough to a man with ringing ears and a splitting skull, anything can happen. My mind goes back to last winter and the night of the postman and what a film of that would have done to my head, and I think, Jesus, this man needs encouragement right *now*.

But already Marty turns out to be completely inaccessible, even his agent's agent is unlisted: like some famous statesman who has once made the ghastly mistake of mixing with the public, Marty has said his good-byes to the human race. From now on, he will exist purely as a report and an unconfirmed rumor. No doubt his fingernails have already grown ten inches in anticipation.

At any rate, there is no reasoning with the man right now, no way of creeping through that electric mesh of friends. My only hope is that Miss Chatterbox's snap canonization of him in print this morning will make it impossible for him to revoke his decision not to sue, friends or no friends. And now let's get out of here before I even think my next thought. "My duty as a citizen"—I'm not listening, Hearthstone—"and my responsibility

to the society as a whole compels me to re- . . . ." I'm on my way,
buddy.

"Going somewhere?" says Welman, our beloved watchdog of
the elevator bank.

"No, just tearing around the place having fun. You know
me."

"No kidding, where you going? You just got here."

"It's a little thing called lunch. Publishers do it all the time."

The elevator grabs me and squirrels me away, before Sam
can trot out his list of publishers who *never* eat lunch. I imagine
him returning to his desk now, glumly, to chew on an old bone.
Publishing without the lunches would be unthinkable.

I thought everyone had left the Hamptons last weekend, but
it seems they were only fooling. Although it's only 12:30 or so,
here they are all again, sneaking back. Maybe they forgot something, a bowsprit or a mizzenmast. September can be cruel that
way. After two hours of bumper-to-bumper indignity, I slink
off and find me a hot dog stand for my sumptuous publisher's
lunch and decide to take the leisurely, graceful, coast road the
rest of the way—only to find that they've all followed me over.

Well, I thought you'd like to hear something about the traffic
out here. The upshot is that I don't get home until late afternoon. The radio converts back gradually from news—which I
listen to with either polite curiosity or feverish anxiety, I'm not
sure: anyway, nothing happens—to honest, local crackle and I
feel hungry as hell, so I must be in the Hamptons. I look in at
Jimmy's, our first base of choice, only to find the bar lined with
surly strangers. OK—I know that all strangers in bars look
surly, but what are they doing here at all? It seems, saints pre-
serve us, as if Jimmy has instituted a "happy hour," and the
peasants are already in full slurp. Maybe Jim is trying to tamper
with the demographics of his joint. We literary types have put a
curse on everything. In fact, I half expect to be greeted with
cries of "unclean, unclean" from the yokels, but Jimmy tending
bar simply says, "Hi Jon. Seen anybody?"

I pedal on home, feeling like Joan Fontaine returning to Man-
derley, and sure enough my little saltbox does seem a teeny bit

haunted. As I enter the hallway I feel as if I've stepped into a closet full of dirty clothes. Has somebody been in here lately? A Japanese wrestling team perhaps? I advance cautiously into the empty room with my forearm slightly up and out, guarding against God knows what. If someone says boo, I shall probably scream with terror. As it is, there is only another letter, perched primly on the sofa, so I settle for a violent start.

Yeah, it's another of Waldo's. He is turning into one of your classic mid-Victorian correspondents. I open it calmly, in the manner of a raccoon, and when I piece the shreds together, it says "Hi old friend, I called your office and they said you were on your way out here [so much for my fake-lunch ploy]. I wonder if you'd mind too much dropping over to my place, where you will find your next clue. Oh, and I miss you dreadfully. Your pal Waldo. P.S. Don't worry about Thor, he's been prepared for your visit."

If Waldo would ever stop crapping around, I'd know whether I was scared or not. But in a haunted house, everything takes on a little spin, and I definitely don't want to go to his place. For one thing, I don't give a damn how well Thor has been prepared or what changes have occurred in his black animal heart. Thor is the main reason for the strange fact that I have never been inside Waldo's house—that and a ravening lack of invitations. Waldo claims that Thor is a dog but I would have bet puma, and it seems strange now to be walking up to Waldo's door just a few minutes later without being deafened and spiritually diminished by the creature's unearthly howls.

Waldo's door is unlocked. But mother of God, this must be the wrong place, we must have come on the wrong night dear. I thought *my* place smelled stale, but this is the real bottom of the basket, down among the old jockstraps and sweatsocks. Doesn't the guy ever open a window around here? Hard to tell, since they all seem to be covered by black blinds. But even in the dark, I can tell the room is a pigsty. "Waldo," I howl, as I bark my shin on a wedge of something. "Waldo, are you there?"

No answer. Shit, man. He must have stepped out for a bag of squirrel shit or other delicacy to make my welcome truly memorable. What the hell does he need Thor for with a setup like this? I totter off toward what looks like a window blind, only to find that the sonofabitch is glued on with Major's cement. Is this Waldo's idea of looking inconspicuous? By now I have completely lost touch with the front door, but in my researches I do come across a light switch, and as I turn it on, I hear a voice, the Voice.

"Jon, is that you? Why don't you pull up a chair, if you can find one, and take a load off. I'm sorry I couldn't wait for you any longer, so I put this message on tape—very 'movie' of me, don't you think? To hell with papyrus from now on. One thing that really brought me into the twentieth century this summer was this gizmo that Hearthstone gave me for my birthday. Wasn't that cute of him? You can trigger it with anything from a light switch to a door handle to a loud fart, whatever you've got. If it isn't working today, fuck it. You will, of course, proceed to the next clue anyway, following the trail of burnt manuscript that starts at your feet. Yes, the manuscript is you know what."

There it is indeed, a brown crinkly ribbon of scorched paper winding towards the next room. The poor, crazy sonofabitch has taken the trouble to strew a path for me out of his own mutilated novel.

"Never mind, the book wasn't worth shit to begin with. Even you could write a better one. What a laugh that was, when I learned that. No, strike that one—kidding is what you do when you run out of talent."

"Waldo, where the fuck *are* you? Are you back there, watching all this and cackling?"

"You'll be wanting to know something about the odor, I suppose. It wasn't always like this, I can tell you. Only since the staff began to move out last spring. Around the time I got my princely advance from you, as a matter of fact. Since then I've been rather pigging it, as my English butler used to say. Old Wiggins dropped in recently and was close to tears when he saw that a great man of letters, as he insists on calling me, was living like this (Wiggins, of course, is not one of your leading critics). He offered to come back to work for practically nothing, but not for *ab*solutely nothing, which was what I was offering. The poor chap still looked like death as he left, though he brightened slightly when I told him I had film 'prospects.'"

"Please sit still, Jonathan." Naturally I had been prowling around trying to find where the voice was coming from, so as to demystify it, and, above all, to prove it had no ears. The air as I moved, or spooned my way, through it seemed even fouler than it had to be, as if Waldo was making a statement with it. "I don't know why, but I feel like talking today. Very relaxed indeed. But I won't take up too much more of your time, Jon. Before you leave, you might be amused by my little closet of disguises—the blue blazer, the ascot, the 'whites' and the 'pinks' too—and of course the ironing board that makes it all possible. You know, things like the wooing of the Padgetts—and by the way, don't ever try to put the touch on a patron of the arts. So—what dya think, Jon, would I have been better off in rags? Jesus God, does *every*body have to be a salesman? How many ways can I say this? I needed the fucking money." Pause, as if he's checking a grocery list, leading me to wonder how I could ever have assumed that he was richer than Billy, or anyone else in the world. Fame is everything in this game, I guess.

"Well, that's about all I can think of for today. I would hate anyone to think I ever gave a rat's ass about that bastard's opinion of my work. My book may not be great, but it's plenty good enough for his shitmill. The thing is that you just don't hold up a piece of red meat in front of a hungry dog unless you plan to feed him. Right?" Pause again. That's it? Come on, Waldo, how many stinking rooms do I have to go through to get the whole story?

"Oh, one more thing, Jon. Our relationship would be hopelessly violated if I said something nice to you at this point. But that doesn't cover stuff I may happen to say behind your back, and maybe you'll find something in the next room—well just, something. However, before you go into that room, I strongly suggest you get some help. And listen, Father Pat—one *other* last thing. I don't want anyone thinking I turned into a nice guy at the last minute. I just wish I could have taken the sonofabitch with me." Click. Jesus Christ.

I don't know how long I sat there. My mental picture of the

next room was suddenly too horrible to enter, help or no help. Yet I couldn't just leave now. The smell seemed to get worse, and yes, there might have been some dead dog in there at that. Thor's body, I tried to reason, would still be fresh—Jesus, what a thing to say. *I can't stay here by myself and think such thoughts.*

I get up quickly and start scavenging for a phone, which I finally find hidden under a pile of boxes. Ferris is who I'll call. *He'll* go in there all right, and he'll say the right things to me, and I'll be OK. Then we'll call the cops.

I start dialing the good old number, feeling comforted already, only to realize that the phone is dead. Waldo has had it disconnected or, more likely, has cut the lines himself. With a saber. I gaze at the front door. All I really have to do is open it and holler, but before I can do it I am interrupted. "Jesus, Jon, that's the kind of pissant thing that Otis MacIntyre would do." I can still hear the voice, or think I can. "Try to show a little class for once in your life."

"Waldo, you bastard!" And I think, in my fever, Jesus Christ he's composed one more Otis MacIntyre scene for me to appear in and I'm acting just like Otis for him. This whole thing is just another of his lousy hoaxes, like the plate in the head and the six months to live, and Waldo is off someplace watching and pissing himself. Yeah, Hearthstone probably gave him a set of cameras too. For Father's Day. And you can probably even buy those foul smells someplace. *Soldier of Fortune* magazine no doubt carries a full line of them.

It is only by thinking like that, by *forcing* myself to think like that, that I am able to negotiate the frail ashen path through the squalor to the next room. At first I don't see him in there. Great. The power of positive thinking is better than I supposed. But of course he's there, plainly visible through the open bathroom door, perched placidly in the tub with his arm around Thor. He is wearing a baseball uniform, and his belly is ripped neatly across. I will later learn that his, by now crimson, shirt bears the legend *American Samurai.*

Waldo's face seems almost benign. "You see? This isn't so terrible is it?" Under his encouraging gaze, but only under it, I find myself able to perform the few humble tasks he obviously wants done. Even in death, a real take-charge guy, as he might say. He has laid out some items on his bedside table for my inspection. I hesitate to turn on the gooseneck lamp, for fear of setting off another speech. But it's OK this time.

The first and most obvious relic is the softball, which sits under a plastic bell of the kind you usually use to cover cheese. On the jar is pasted a label marked Exhibit A, under which is scrawled "I won't have that sonofabitch *forgiving* me." Next to it is a schoolkid's exercise book, of a kind I thought I was the only grownup still to use. It is, appropriately enough, inscribed to me, and on the first page it says "You'd be amazed how much an old hack can know about writing," followed by a detailed list of editorial suggestions on my own novel. One glance tells me the man was no primitive; one glance was *meant* to tell me that.

Christ, what a way to spend your last days. While I have been idling away the week in my office, Waldo has been sitting here in the stink preparing his final effects. I glance over the suggestions, just long enough to note that they are quite tough and serious and that he has, had, oh God yes that's right, had a great memory for stuff he'd recently read; I have the rest of my life to study the notes more carefully. But the night and day he spent at my place seem a little different now. Especially when I think about that exercise book. *My* exercise book.

Ever since that Sunday, he must have been walled up here in his blacked-out house, eating God knows what—no law on earth says that I have to look in his icebox—and exchanging thoughtful last words with Thor.

No—he must have gone out at least once to procure this next item. It is his will, and it was notarized just yesterday by a local odd-jobs lawyer, the kind who wouldn't know who Waldo was, or who anyone else was either.

Before dipping into it, I decide to do something about that softball. If I fling it out the back door and into the woods, I will achieve the double benefit of clearing my author's name and obtaining some fresh air before I suffocate in the hot fugg. I glance over at Waldo and murmur "You may have to accept Hearthstone's forgiveness after all, old man. After all, what do *you* care, wherever you are?" I cross myself atavistically, not

sure whether it goes left to right or the other way. Then I raise
the bell solemnly and reach for the ball, and heft it and toss it
idly in the air a couple of times, before it dawns on me that
there might quite possibly be absolutely nothing wrong with
the thing. It feels like a regular softball to me, and certainly not
the cannonball of memory. "What are you grinning about in
there?" I suddenly shout. "Still enjoying your little joke?"

I've got to get out of here. Waldo seems to have set off yet
another stink bomb to round out the merriment. To hell with
his reputation. If some damn fool wants to waste an afternoon
analyzing a perfectly normal softball, be my guest. But first,
the will, the will. What jokes does *that* contain, I wonder? what
compendium of deathbed, or rather deathtub, humor have we
here? I wipe some slickum off my forehead, and find that my
hands are also running sweat, so badly in fact that I can't even
open the will without drenching it. So I wrap a handkerchief
round my right fist, feeling more bizarre than ever as I start to
read.

After the usual opening palaver I suddenly come across this:
"To my best friend, Jonathan Oglethorpe"—*what?*—"who believed in me when there was nothing left to believe in. . . . I
once told Jonathan that I was dying of cancer, when I was only
dying of loss of talent." Come on Waldo, what's the gag this
time? The man has set me up once too often to con me with this
stuff. Best friend indeed. Waldo's sincerity is like a hurricane
warning. There is in fact not one thing about us that comes
under the rubric of best friend. And what's with this tragic,
broken man routine? There is absolutely nothing tragic and
broken about this clown. Dead, maybe, but that's positively all.

"Level with me, Waldo. Did you write this crap?" I beseech
him, and find my voice is quavering. I am alone in here with
this document.

"Jonathan is a true man of letters in a world of trash, etc., etc.
I'm afraid I haven't got much to leave Mr. Oglethorpe but he's
more than welcome to all of it. My house in Nether Hampton is
only rented, and I owe back alimony, but maybe my books will
be worth something someday. In any event, I hereby appoint
Mr. Oglethorpe my full executor, literary and otherwise, to do

whatever he can for the books and to receive any royalties that may accrue."

Against my will, and against every fiber of my judgment I am moved. I know that it's like being handed a share in an old miniature golf course, but what a gesture! "To my former wives I leave nothing." That's what you think, old bean. Do you really think those royalties are going to end up with me while those dames are around? Come on. You're too innocent to live. Excuse me.

I pause and wipe my eyes. Sweat, tears, who cares. Waldo is welcome to whatever *I've* got, too. However, I can't help thinking with the next breath of what a *scene* Waldo has left us with, in the close air and the half light and with me at once the best actor and the best audience, guaranteed to attend and performing to measure. Lost his talent, my foot. For one mad fleeting moment I can still summon the belief that he has actually planted a wax dummy in the tub, as phony as the softball, and is out there laughing. But no, dead is dead. A corpse has a certain quiet conviction about it, not to be mistaken for anything else, except in the movies.

So come on, let's get this thing over with and vamoose from this morgue. I pick up the will again; there can't be much more to it from such a drastically intestate sort of guy as Waldo. However he was never one to surrender a stage lightly and he is still in full flight. Right now he seems to be going on about me again, and my ineffable virtues, as if he were playing for time. "We had the kind of kidding relationship you only have with a brother"—you don't put twaddle like that in *wills*, do you? Well, I guess you pay your dime and you write what you like.

I rub my eyes again, causing them to sting with unidentified moisture. The perfect audience, indeed: laughing, crying, is there anything else I can do for you, Sir? In this peculiar state I don't quite take in the next paragraph at first. "In light of this friendship and of other lesser friendships, and to prevent any posthumous distress or misunderstanding, I hereby insist, with all the power still at my command, that all traceable copies of my latest manuscript, provisionally entitled, etc., shall be incinerated, and that in no circumstances shall this manuscript *ever be published.* I look to my executor to carry out this instruction to the fullest of his abilities."

So he wants that, does he? I think airily. Well, we'll just see about that. Imagine for a moment, a soldier listening to the whistle of an enemy shell and thinking, gee that's interesting, just a second before it lands on him. Well, that's me. Now *this* (I shut the will and hold it up dramatically) is the exhibit that ought to be thrown into the woods, and *voilà*—it goes out of existence, and on with the dance. I hate to destroy such a lovely tribute to myself, but it would be infinitely better than destroying a whole book. So, thanks for a tender last moment, brother Waldo, and for your undying thoughtfulness, but you didn't quite get the point did you, in that last paragraph? *I* didn't mind if my feelings were hurt, bless me no. I just needed the damn book, and you wouldn't want me to lose that now, would you, brother dearest?

It is just beginning to hit. *I needed the fucking money.* I can still hear Waldo's words sounding over mine. The book, the money, sonofabitch. The only thing worth having about Waldo is that damn manuscript, and he knew it, and it's "How do you like it now, gentlemen?" as Hemingway would say. Of course Waldo's lawyer has a copy of the will, and it must be on file someplace as well, and shit what I've been through to land that sucker. No wonder the bastard is smiling at me. Why for two cents I'd like to . . .

I don't precisely know what I do next. When I come to, there is a breeze, still smelly but a definite breeze, on my face and a cop is leaning over me solicitously—surely I have been here before? "Are you all right?" he asks. "How did you *breathe* in here?" The lights are on and the windows are open and more cops are milling about in the bathroom. "What are *you* doing here?" I ask foolishly. "The guy next door heard you screaming. Either you or your buddy in the bathroom." He winks and pats my shoulder. "Hey, don't *worry* about it. That guy's been stiff a long time from the looks of him, so it wasn't *him* screaming for sure."

Well that's that. I look down at my hand and see that the will is still clutched there safe and sound. In fact, I seem to be delivering it myself, like the faithful doggy I was obviously meant to be. "Hey, don't start that up again," says the cop. "It's all over now."

Hysteria can take some funny bounces, I tell you, and before you know it I am grinning up at the cop and shaking his hand vigorously. "You said a mouthful, partner. Oh, and while you're standing"—I hand him the will grandly—"I thought this might amuse you."

I am still giggling foolishly as they take me away for questioning, or the funny farm, or whatever they think best. "By the way," I manage to blurt, "what was I screaming anyway?" My keeper turns on the glove compartment light and examines his notebook carefully. "Mr. Spinks's neighbor, the Reverend Rodney Forsythe [oh no!] says that it *sounded* like," and he frowns in perplexity, "the Devil is dead, long live the Devil"? "I'll drink to that," I cry weakly, and collapse in angry giggles.

23

I F IT wasn't the funny farm, it was the next best thing: it was my own house. Before I can turn back or scamper off into the woods, the police doctor who is along for the ride hands me two gigantic pills, and says "don't worry, you won't dream tonight," and in no time I am sprawled in my own haunted bed, sleeping as soundly as if I were at the office.

The doc was right: there was nothing left to dream about anyway. I'd done all that. I awoke around noon to a sinister absence of phones ringing, and dogs barking. By the time I put in some calls of my own, it seemed that the people who take care of everything had already taken care of everything. There would be a short local funeral tomorrow afternoon. So soon? Yes it's all been arranged. Flowers can be sent to . . . After wringing from the furry tongues of the funeral people the precious further information that they believed there might be a memorial service in New York at an unnamed date, I gave up.

Next I called the police: after all, I was the executor, wasn't I? So I had a right to execute something, didn't I? Well, maybe I had the right, but no one I talked to seemed to have anything on hand for me to practice my skills on today.

"Have they performed an autopsy yet?" I asked.

"I wouldn't know, Mac."

"Well who *does* know."

"Nobody in this office, that's for sure."

"What about the *next* office," I say, as to a child.

"There ain't no next office."

Then we gotta build one, eh, Groucho? A cop with a totally blank mind can really stonewall you. What I would like to find now are the good police fairies who took such spiffy care of me last night; but you never get to see people like that twice.

"Look, just tell me one thing. Am I a suspect?"

"In reference to what?"

"The death of Waldo Spinks."

He spared me this time: He didn't say Waldo who? Instead he shuffled some papers, like one of those radio sound effects— nobody in his right mind would give this bum *real* papers, and he said, "No, you're not a suspect."

"The name is Oglethorpe, by the way," I prompted.

"Hi there! Well anyway, you're not a suspect."

"Does that mean I can leave town anytime I like?" I say sarcastically.

"Yeah. Absolutely. You can go anywhere you like in the whole wide world. Isn't that grand? So, hey, why don't you start on your wonderful adventures right now by getting your ass off my goddamn phone?"

"Thank you for your courtesy, offi . . ." Buzz.

I feel like a kid myself now, chasing firetrucks all day. Ending up on a stoop someplace sobbing. For the hundredth time I ask myself, where exactly do I belong in this town, what hinge have I got on it? I'm damned if I'm going to call up my fellow untouchables, and sit around with them irrelevantly bathing our wounds. Anyhow, they've already turned me down in their own different ways and made it clear I don't even make it as an outsider. In fact, I sometimes wonder if Nether Hampton is *quite* the perfect setting for me.

I deposit my last spiritual dime and call up the editor of the local paper and am positively elated to get a busy signal. *Now* we're getting somewhere. Now that I know where someone actually is today, I decide to go visit.

Godfrey Lester is not, from what I hear, a promising inter-view. He is in fact a craggy, impartial Bonnacker who considers all us *auslanders* equally loathsome and expendable. Waldo, for instance, he probably considers a simple case of good riddance, and maybe even an example to the rest of us on various exciting ways to leave town.

In this holy cause, Lester might even suspend his usual rule of pretending we simply don't exist. All summer long the area residents go through their paces in his paper as if there were no one else in sight. It makes for a charming idyll, and in fact his paper, *The Hampton Crab*, is probably the best late-Victorian reading around. But I wonder whether he will actually *see* me when I turn up at his office or whether he'll walk clean through me. The way things are going I'll understand perfectly.

However, he's a print guy and as such the closest thing to a colleague I've got left in this town. So, here goes nothing.

Well—he's craggy all right, but the rest turns out to be just more Oglethorpe magic: it seems I'd completely invented that mean streak of his. "My God," he says, standing up quickly to put a sheltering arm around me, "you've been through a hell of a time, Mr. Oglethorpe. A *hell* of a time."

So somebody noticed, I think dazedly.

"Here, have a chair, let me get you something." I feel positively expectant. At least, he doesn't advise me to put my feet up, but hurries on. "I don't suppose you want to think about any of it just yet, let alone talk about it, right? Well, don't worry about me. *I'm* not going to pry. In fact," he confides, "I'm planning to play the whole thing pretty far down."

"You're *what?*"

"Yes. This isn't a tabloid, Mr. Oglethorpe," he said, with a hint of his imaginary tartness. "I'll run it as I see fit."

Lester let go of me, as if he'd suddenly run out of warmth, and strode to the window. Some people, don't ask me why, seem to like looking out the window when they make pronouncements. And I must say that, framed between a couple of ancient maps and with his hand resting on a sextant, his mere back looked more powerful than anything in Power City. "Waldo Spinks was a pretty good man by my lights, Mr. Oglethorpe. In fact, I used to think of him as almost one of us. You know, he used to come around here a lot and chat with the staff—none of the other New York writers ever did that. And he would talk to me with genuine concern about the plight of the bay fishermen, whom he also seemed to know personally, and about the whole history of the town. If all you New York guys did that, it would . . . well, never mind. Anyway, I think Waldo Spinks deserves a quiet death, don't you?"

"Well yes, I'm sure he does. But you may be the only guy around who'll let him have one. What about the rest of the nation's press?"

"What about it? Have you seen any TV crews poking around lately, or guys waving notebooks? Maybe Waldo isn't that famous anymore."

Maybe. Maybe most writers aren't. We need the delusion in our business, that's all.

"Anyway a lot of people around here feel the way I do," he says firmly, and I suddenly get a picture of a drawbridge being pulled up, with cops and doctors hauling away energetically at the ropes. No wonder I got the runaround this morning; they thought I was a reporter.

"What about murder," I almost whisper. "Has that been dismissed?"

"Yes," he says quickly. And then, more guardedly, "I *think* I can say that."

He gives me that look I've seen on so many, otherwise quite different, faces: whose side are you on anyway, Oglethorpe?

"Well, it stands to reason, doesn't-it-may-I-call-you-Jonathan? That incredibly complicated drama simply could not have been rigged up around him by somebody else. I'm told by Ferris Fender—you know him? the Southern writer? Well, I talked to him about it this morning. He's a good man too, for a New York writer"—we both smile weakly at the generic pleasantry—"and he said, this thing has Waldo's signature all over it. The detail work, he said. Other people might think up stuff like that, but only a dedicated artist would have the divine madness, as Ferris called it, to make it *real*." He paused. "Well, that's what he said."

"That's funny. You know Waldo was exactly the opposite in his"—my God, Jonathan, what are you saying now? You're

talking faster than you can think—"his novels," I end
uncertainly.

My tongue has tripped and sprawled over a sad truth. Almost all of Waldo's talent, by the end, had gone into his practical jokes. So why had it been so important for him to go on
being a writer anyway? He had plenty left as a man. Just for
one thing, it took a hell of an athlete to throw that pitch, and as
for acting—well, none of it counted as far as he was concerned.
It was writer or nothing.

"Anyway," I say, "that's absolutely right about his signature
and nobody else's. But in that case"—I think and say slowly
this time—"what makes you so sure he wanted a peaceful death
after all? He put on a show, he signed it himself—so why
shouldn't the world see it?"

"Well Ferris—you *do* know him, right?—says that he thinks
it was more of a *private* show. The rest of the world might
misunderstand the whole affair. They might even think that
Waldo was crazy."

Waldo, crazy? What a laugh. Of course he was crazy.

"Ferris also says"—hey, what's with 'Ferris says' around
here? Doesn't anyone else get to say any more?—"that a really
big news story might raise other complications."

"Ferris isn't God," I mutter, but he may be right in spite of
that oversight. Where *is* that damn softball, anyway, the real
one, the killer ball of thread and lead?

"Whatever the so-called complications may be," I say stub-
bornly, "Waldo obviously wanted the whole bloody thing
played out."

Lester gave me another kind of look, to save both of us any
further time: this one, which I'd never seen before, said clear as
day, "*We*'ll decide how people die around here." I read a little
further. "In our view, you see, Summer People cause quite
enough nuisance as it is. A winter full of publicity for their
antics is all we need to turn next summer and all summers
thereafter into a living hell. Yes, *we* decide about things like
that, *not* Waldo, and certainly not *you*."

There doesn't seem much point in arguing with that. It had
been his position from the beginning, and he had only thrown

in all that guff of Ferris's to cover up the obscene sight of a journalist burying a story.

The flaw in my character almost piped up "well we'll just see if you can do that; we'll see if you can cordon off your precious town from the whole rest of the world." Well, damn it, Waldo's wishes had *some* rights didn't they? And if I, his executor, didn't start executing right now, when the hell would I start, and what difference would it make?

And then I realized that Lester hadn't actually said anything in minutes; I was just arguing with my own wild thoughts again. Waldo, you dog—you've dropped me in it for the last time. Here I am flaring at the local editor over nothing. And I'm still not sure if I owe you anything at all.

"Well it was nice meeting you, er, Godfrey," I say quickly. "You must be a busy man."

"It's been a pleasure," he says, putting his arm around me again, as if we have finally clinched a very difficult deal. And steering me to the door in this fashion, he says, "I know this seems a funny time to bring it up, but after you've had a good rest, and you surely need one, would you consider writing a regular column for *The Crab*? Don't laugh. I'm serious about this. I'd love to have a column from a 'year-round summer person,' if you'll pardon the expression." No way, buster. If I can't be "one of us" like Waldo, I won't play at all. "Of course you understand, Jonathan, that we couldn't pay you very much—it would really be more a token than a fee. But we'd leave your stuff completely alone. In fact, we'd even leave your commas alone, and we don't do that for just anybody. Well, think about it, Jonathan. It might be fun."

So saying, he released me gently into the sunshine, leaving me to wonder what palsied brain-damaged deadbeat had ever wandered into this office *without* being offered a column.

For the rest of the day, I resume my lonely radio listening, but the local station merely repeats on the hour that the author Waldo Spinks died in his home in Nether Hampton last night, and the Connecticut stations don't bother to mention it at all.

To be beneath the attention of radio news—there's glory for you at the end of the long struggle.

The next day's *New York Times* ran a medium-size obit, complete with youthful photo in khakis. As far as the *Times* was concerned, Waldo had written only one book, *The Thirty-ninth Parallel*, which had "created a flurry of interest." Come *on*, *Times*. Couldn't it at least have been "excitement!"? I still have books to sell. The obit also listed three wives and four children, so Waldo's boasts had not been so far off the mark after all. As I read the numbers again, I pictured Waldo restlessly discarding one life after another, as he strove to get it all back, the golden thimble, until he came to the gaudy end of the line last night.

Incidentally, the *Times* agreed with our local radio station that Waldo just died.

Miss Chatterbox dropped the subject like a live grenade and donated her whole Sunday column to a rather frantic description of some "Save the Mosquitoes" benefit or other, as if she planned to devote the balance of her life to good works. Did she know something? I doubt it. The death of unknowns is just too horrible to contemplate in her world.

And so it happened. Waldo just died. Later that day some guy from Waldo's hometown in Oklahoma would call up eagerly to say "it was raining and nobody came, right?" "No," I was happy to reply, "it was sunny and the funeral was well attended." All failures don't get buried in the rain.

Waldo did indeed have friends around here, from the Padgetts on down, and they all showed up, buzzing with "what happened, whad he die of?" "Heart attack" seemed to be favored by the first wave of know-it-alls, but I wondered if this might not simply be the official line as handed down by Godfrey Lester, because a moment later I heard a bay fisherman, of all people, confide "he told me he only had three months to live." (In a Spinksian sense, that was almost the truth.) And as more people shuffled in, it became clearer that Waldo, in his usual way, had prepared today's audience all too thoroughly. As I listened further, I also learned that "he told *me* there was this curse on all the males in his family. At age forty-seven, zingo! over and out." "The way *I* heard it was that this tropical

fungus, one in a million, had lodged in a very delicate place."
And this was just among the fishermen.

Thus Waldo's spirit seemed to dance among us in the sunshine, defying us to mourn. Although I had seen the corpse
myself, I didn't dare pull a long face with Waldo dancing out
there. Instead, I tried to picture some crazy, and incredibly
harmful, religion forming around the legend of the Living
Waldo. "Go to hell," I muttered to his shade, "and for God's
sake stay there, like a good fellow." If I couldn't look sad, I
could at least look angry.

Nikki van Dyne, I noticed, had no trouble mourning at all. It
figured. She was the type who could cry buckets at strangers'
funerals, and even had to stifle a sob over *Times* wedding an-
nouncements. Billy looked as though he didn't know whether
to laugh or cry—another of the strange faces of grief. Stunned
puzzlement seemed popular among the gallery, as at some ma-
cabre magic act. At any moment, a puff of sulfur would reveal
our host descending into Hell. "Are you all right?" asked Cecily.

She had been watching me intently, and I realized that I had
grown so used to my hysteria that I didn't know it showed
anymore. "You poor dear," she said, touching my arm. "I hear
you've been through a perfectly unspeakable time," and she began to cry over *me*, not over some silly old corpse. That was her
way and today, at least, I loved her for it. But was there *anyone*
out there who had not as yet heard the whole top-secret story of
Waldo's death? It would be a shame for someone to miss out.

I'm pretty sure I do not shout these last words, although who
can tell these days? I do know that I whispered sharply to
Cecily, "Who *told* you that?" "Ferris." Naturally. "And who
told Ferris?" "I don't know," she said. "I think he had a boy-
friend once who went on to become a cop."

Of course. I'd forgotten that this was the Hamptons. "You
know," she said, "I'll never forgive Waldo for playing those infantile games on you. He certainly *had* lost his talent, if he was
down to that."

"It was just man-play," I said. "You don't understand."

Cecily didn't get mad, but squeezed my arm in sweet
uncomprehension.

Meanwhile, the main feature was proceeding, and I strove to block out all thoughts of Waldo and coffins and graveyards. Just remind me to give this place a wide berth on Halloween, I thought. The preacher, who blessedly seemed to know nothing at all about the deceased, seemed to be saying that we would all meet together in the next world, atheists, Christians, and Jews alike. It took even more swallowing to hear Waldo described as a child of God, in Whose company he, Waldo, would now proceed to spend eternity. "Watch out, God!" I almost shrieked, but Cecily squeezed my arm like a tourniquet.

The man of God ceased his babbling eventually, and Waldo was lowered and covered, and a few more words were said. Ferris called Waldo the only thing the latter ever wanted to hear—a great writer: "Whatever he may have been in the rest of his life," Ferris went on "—and all I really know about that is that he made a mighty fine friend—at least in his chosen calling, in this strange, monastic vocation of ours, Waldo Spinks came very close to being a saint. In fact, it would not, to my mind, be going much too far to call the man a martyr to his craft."

"Yes, it would," Cecily whispered surprisingly. "*Much* too far."

Ferris returned to his post (wherever he stood was a post), some distance away from us. I had wondered at his comparative aloofness today. It had seemed safe to assume that Waldo's death, which he seemed to know more about than I did, would have mended our mysterious differences. After all, I did *not* turn Waldo in to the cops (never mind how close I came), and I did not talk to anyone about the guilty softball either. As for Waldo's crazy will, you could read it a hundred different ways, interpreting me as anything from a prince to Waldo's last whipping boy, but there was nothing in there to be *aloof* about.

So I scampered on over, in a dignified sort of a way, expecting at the least to be told once again what a ghastly time I'd been through, and maybe get a pat on the head as well for not fainting sooner. But Ferris still seemed curiously formal, as if we'd never been introduced before, and—could this be possible?—he even seemed slightly shifty-eyed. After a moment of this, he muttered "the softball is safe" which a passerby might have construed to be the goofiest message ever delivered anywhere. Otherwise, he continued stiff—although somehow *shabbily* so. Something must have happened to Ferris in the last few days that had knocked some of the starch out of him, too.

As I turn to go (Ferris, I know, hates to be seen at less than his best), he says gruffly, "I'll talk to you later, Jon. I have something to tell you."

That's all. I guess I will now simply have to await his pleasure for any further word on that. The crowd is slowly beginning to disperse and congeal again into little knots, and I feel, as I so often do after a session with Ferris, as if I am wandering around a battleground at the close of day—only there are so many mourners and only one corpse to speak of—except that this time, I am lugging with me a large prickly question mark like a thorn bush. What on earth does Ferris plan to tell me? Is he going to open new doors on this nightmare? If so, I'm not going through them—for him or anyone. But as I look back at Ferris now, still rigid at his post, but more desolate than tragic, I suddenly get a disturbing vision of him, too. For the very first time I can actually imagine him on the losing side in that war of his.

On my ragpicking rounds, I veer swiftly over to the van Dynes for light relief, and also because they seem to be on the brink of leaving, and so help me Nikki mumbles through her tears and her veil. "I'll talk to you later. There's something I think you ought to know."

So now I have a tiny question mark (made of fur) to go with my big one. Back to Cecily then, to find out immediately if she too wants to tell me something later, but she says "only that you're a nice man." As if the van Dynes had been a plug holding the rest of us in, the people now start pouring out and I notice how lovely the cemetery looks without them. It is a famous cemetery, and people put their names down for it years in advance to get into it (how sad to be turned down at the last minute).

But in the autumn shadows the place suddenly feels bitter cold, and I want nothing more than to make my own broken-field run through the tombstones and huddle with Cecily around a fire, preferably the big one at Jimmy's. Only it will still be last year when I get there, and some wise person will be saying thoughtfully "nah, I think a softball team is probably a lousy idea. Nothing but trouble ever came of those things." Did somebody actually say that? In the roar of flames, I can almost hear it. But it is instantly drowned out by surges of drunken gabble—those surges that reign autocratically and absolutely and no questions asked (or heard), over every saloon in the land. Only this time, I swear *I'll* listen.

"It was an interesting year," says Cecily out of nowhere. "I wouldn't have missed it."

As I run various other interesting years through my mind—the Sack of Rome, the Fire of London, those were pretty interesting—a figure steps cautiously from the farthest shadows, and begins to thread its way toward the grave, toting a funeral wreath of red and white roses. You're not supposed to do that just now, are you? Put the flowers on? I rack my mind for funeral lore, but the shadow seems to move in a dream of his own, far beyond protocol; he kneels next to the grave and lays his wreath just above where you might figure Waldo's heart to be if it was anywhere, lingers there a moment, as if in prayer, and then walks slowly towards us, suddenly the only people left in the pretty meadow of death.

"I'll never understand it," says Marty Hearthstone, as he notices us for the first time, "not as long as I live," and he just keeps walking until he reaches, I guess, the nearest limousine.

We have the place to ourselves now. If we were kids we could run and hide behind the stones and make sinister, little kid noises. But as big brave adults, we simply clasp hands to form a lifeline, and approach the grave ourselves. I have nothing further to say to Waldo, we've both said our piece, but I'm curious about the wreath. There is indeed a card on it with a few more words, clearly intended for the dead man's eyes only. "Dear Waldo, I'm so sorry. I had no idea." It was signed "Your lifelong admirer Marty Hearthstone."

Cecily watches my hand closely—paper is so beautifully easy to crush. "You *should* have had an idea, you sleazy bastard," I burst out, "if you're going to go around killing people, you ought to have an idea about them from time to time. And now you, you come in here with your fucking perfect little gesture. . . ."

Cecily shakes her head, and she doesn't have to say why. I am just wrong, that's all. Miserably, foully wrong. Even at the height of the ass-kissing, none of us, including Waldo, ever had any real respect for Hearthstone, beyond the respect vultures must feel for extra-fat visitors. And now that he's gone and done this modest decent thing, with nary a camera in sight, nor even a gossip writer, I am still reviling him like a guttersnipe. And we thought *he* was the barbarian.

"The thing is," said Cecily, "that *none* of us ever had any idea about Waldo. Did you know that he lived like that? Did you know that he was broke?"

"Never. I never saw his house, partly because of that animal, and partly because it was always being renovated. He would say that the spackle was giving him perfect hell right now. Shit like that. And as for broke—I'll swear I never saw him miss a round at Jimmy's. All the money he had must have gone straight into his bar bill."

"And his car."

"And his suit. Maybe he was right. Maybe he should have gone around in rags and a begging bowl. Then maybe even Hearthstone would have noticed something."

"You really think so?" laughed Cecily. "I hear rags are considered very bad luck in Hollywood. Anyway, darling, to cut a dull story short, if none of us could understand Waldo, what chance did Hearthstone, a man from another planet, have?"

There was only one important word in that speech, of course. Her declaration was as simple and straightforward as herself (except curiously, when she was writing. Acting is permitted when one writes). As for twisty old me, I have no such outlet, and all I can do is kiss her passionately—a much more *interesting* kiss than I'd expected, but then, she was right, it was an interesting year.

24

WELL, stone me with Mrs. Murphy's britches, we're having a wake. Jimmy has decided to turn Waldo into an Irishman for the occasion and has festooned his place with green crêpe and clusters of green balloons on the ceiling that look like grapes.

"Every man is entitled to be an Irishman on the day of his funeral," intones Jimmy, which sounds to me like the right day for it (Oglethorpes have been known to wake up in a sweat thinking they've turned Irish during the night).

In Waldo's case Irish is as likely to be true as anything else one might say about him. In life the man had claimed several different ancestries to match his passing moods, including Choctaw which, for some reason, I believed utterly. The Spinks were actually very, very Western stock, and if there were any more at home like Waldo, they probably sampled everything that was going out there.

Wakes don't really work with Americans. Today a few of Jimmy's customers try desperately to sing, but only Jimmy himself puts anything into it. Far too many of them mutter "it's just what he would have wanted." If somebody has to want it, it might as well be the corpse. Mourning is mourning is lousy to most of the world, except for the mad Celtic fringe to which I grudgingly belong. Normal citizens will never understand the savage, murderous glee of the grieving Celt.

As my ear leans this way and that, I make another small discovery, namely, that it is possible for quite a large number of reasonably loose-lipped people to be in on a secret without the secret going one inch further. Jimmy knows, and I think Archie Munson knows, but within a few feet of them folks are still speculating about the cause of death. So this is what a social circle means—an iron band from which nothing escapes. Waldo's secret is perfectly safe with about twenty close friends.

Does he *want* it safe? That, I realize, is a question I now have years to think about. Meanwhile, the ambiguous celebration sputters on, as tentative as Fall weather, and it seems only decent to lend it a hand. So I sidle over to the bar and attempt to help Jimmy out with "The Wearing of the Green." Irish songs are all about their own defeats and humiliations, so I don't mind singing them at all at all.

From this vantage point, I am granted a bartender's view of the room. In one corner, Nikki seems to be keeping her face red and wretched by sheer force of will. A small vial of poison suddenly bursts in my spleen, the peevish eruption of unresolved feelings about her; all that that narcissistic bitch really wants, I tell myself as if settling the question, is her own piece of the day. With her ever-ready tears and her piddling scraps of information she hopes to insert herself into the drama of Waldo's death.

Well, she can keep her damn information and stuff it. She'll get no attention from me. Unfortunately, she chooses that very moment to turn her great melting eyes on me—eyes that would once have brought me crawling through hot sand to her side—and I turn my head too quickly away, only to bang it like a gong against Ferris's. Doesn't he also want a piece of funeral to take home like wedding cake? Right now, he looks more as if he wants to get rid of something; his head nods once again, missing mine narrowly, towards a corner table which the gloomy revelers have overlooked so far.

We hunker down at it, and I say immediately, "Is it about Waldo? Did I do something wrong?"

"*You?*" he says with apparent surprise. "No, you were just fine. As I knew you would be, of course. No it's nothing like that." He fell silent, and then he said, "I'll get to Waldo in a minute," and more silence.

And then, at last, with a supplicating hand on mine and in a drawling, tortured voice, "I don't know how to tell you this, Jon, old buddy. The timing on this thing is absolutely damnable. But the long and the short of it is, and not to mince words, is that, oh fuck, I'm changing publishers."

"You're *what?*" What happens next is that he hangs his head, and I try not to laugh like a loon. "Is that all?" I cry merrily.

"Why, I consider it just about the biggest betrayal of a friend that I've ever committed, or even thought of committing. Yes, *that's* all, I reckon. And the thing is, I'm doing it for *money,*" he whispers, and seems to fall back in shock.

"Well, I hope you make a bundle," I say breezily but he is too wretched to pick it up.

"So here I've been the whole summer long, talking a great game about the evils of selling out and whatnot, and now here I've gone and done it myself. I'll promise you one thing at least though, Jonathan, on my word as a former gentleman: I shall never, ever again use the word 'honor' so long as I live."

He looks at me in a kind of agony for which there is no absolution. I for my part am having my work cut out trying to hide my relief. The truth is that Ferris, after a flamboyant start, has settled into being your average marginal, low-budget author for quite a while now. As such I'd be happy to publish him forever, of course: he dresses up a list, and I relish our little talks, and it beats publishing books about basketball. But if somebody actually thinks that Ferris is worth big bucks, well go for it, baby.

By now, he is in full confessional spate, and not to be headed off. "You see I met this chawming young man—no, chawm had nothing to do with it, not much anyway. And it seems that this kid has just started up his own perfectly *huge* Southern publishing imprint, and he claims to have more funds at his disposal than a country preacher and . . ."

"It sounds like a match made in Heaven," I say quickly, because I've never heard him talk like this before, and I don't want to now. "And, incidentally," I add, "I hope that charm had *plenty* to do with it."

Again, he ignores me as if I am just some old man mumbling in Latin behind a screen. "The thing is that Stanton, that's his name, really knows his South, and he could be of real help to me on that."

I wouldn't try it if I were you, Stanton, I mutter to myself.

"Well now, face it, Jonathan, you're a great, great editor, I've always said so, the best in the business. But when it comes to the South, really all you know about it is what you read in my books, right? Why we could *both* be leading each other pretty badly astray by now."

He manages a weak smile and I answer with a brave little one, doing my damnedest to look heartbroken, for his sake. His distress up to now has been nothing compared with the kind he'll feel if he suspects that I don't really mind losing him anyway. To betray a friend and find that the friend doesn't care— hand me my sword, sergeant.

You can only keep this kind of thing up for split seconds, so this time I put *my* hand over *his* as if we were choosing up sides, and say in a warm little voice, "Let's talk about Waldo."

"You mean you're not sore?" he says surfacing briefly from his trance.

"I'd like to kill you," I say jovially, "but what good would it do?" Back to Waldo, indeed. "Come on Ferris, it happens all the time in publishing. Believe me—there are a million broken hearts on the Great Inky Way. Don't *worry* about it. Nobody's that noble."

Wrong thing to say to Ferris. Nobody, eh? We'll see about that. But before he can change his mind about switching publishers, I add, "Look, the kid has promised you huge printings, right?"

"Right. Absolutely enormous."

"And unparalleled access to your own best audience, right down there among your own people?"

"Yup. Unparalleled."

"And beautiful bindings and stock and all?"

"The works. The moon."

"Then I'm coming with you," I say with my incomparable light laugh. "Now let's talk about Waldo."

For a moment I think I've got him, but then he sinks back. "Yes, I think I'd better move on down there for a spell myself. Been up North too long. Tasting kind of flat these days. I need some of that old Southern jism again, just to keep my stuff from sounding artificial."

If your stuff ever stops sounding artificial, you won't sell any copies at all, think I. But out loud, I say, "I hear the old place has changed a piece."

"Yeah? So they tell me. But not if you know where to look. What I have in mind is . . ."

By now, even *she* comes as a welcome change. Nikki has snake-hipped her way across to me and is looking down at me imploringly over her magnificent breasts, still after all this as regal and somehow above the battle as ever. "I *have* to talk to you, Jon. You're the only one I *can* talk to."

Can't you see that Father is busy? But then again—as I wrench my head back to Ferris, I find that he is droning on about the Piedmont and the Delta, and little day trips to the battlefields. It's a mighty big region, once a man gets started on it, so Nikki's breasts, I mean Nikki, it is. Ferris merely says "huh" as we leave the table.

The two of us go off in search of another clearing, which finally turns out to be the parking lot itself. On our way, I wonder what trifle *this* creature is going to hurl at me. Is Billy planning to leave me too? Am I to be bereft of *all* my low-selling authors?

"It's Waldo," she says, hiding her face against my chest, and no doubt drenching it. I suddenly seem to be backed up against a car, so it seems to be important to keep on talking.

"Yes? What about Waldo?"

"It's what he *did*," she says.

This extraction could take a while if we maintain this clip, and my mind drifts back, don't ask me why, to some old playground where little Alan is describing the latest indignity inflicted on him by an unjust world. "And you mean to tell me," I say, "that you did absolutely *nothing* to annoy Butch?" and he rends his diapers, or whatever he's up to by then and says, "Nothing Dad, I swear. I was just playing with my truck and he came over and he hit me." Meanwhile Butch is no doubt off someplace telling some other parent, "Geez, Mom, I warned him over and over that if he called me Fatso just one more time, he was really going to get it. So what does he do? He says, 'Hey, how'd you like my truck, Fatso? You think they make trucks big enough to fit *you*, Fatso?'" Snivel, snivel. There is no such thing as a guilty kid.

I have this same feeling about Nikki right now, from the moment she starts framing her words: kids with their backs to the wall tend to talk haltingly, because every single syllable has to help clear them, while nailing the other guy good. It is how Man first learned to think. But it seems that Nikki's charges right now are a little more serious than my memories.

"He—he tried to rape me."

"Tried?"

Silence, and then, "He, he—he had a knife."

"I see."

So he raped her. With or without a knife, he raped her. A guy who could almost kill a man with a softball, never mind what kind of softball, shouldn't have too much trouble with Nikki. The thing that surprises me is why he had to do it at all. Or is this just the playground version I'm getting?

"When did this happen, Nik?" I edge along the car hood for breathing space, which is the last thing I ever thought I'd want from her.

"Right after the game, I guess. Billy hadn't come home yet, I remember that, and Waldo just came storming in and shouted 'you're next!' Some saint, huh?"

"Was that all he said?"

"Well, I guess he said, 'You're next, you gorgeous slut!' or something like that."

"And why do you suppose he called you that?" I was still halfway in the past and I almost called her "Alan."

"I-don't-know. But I tell you, it was just awful. You see, he had this knife and . . ."

Spare me, oh Lord, the details. "Surely he must have said something else, being Waldo and all," I say quickly.

"Well, he said I'd been luring him on all year, which I swear isn't true, and that he'd had quite enough grief this summer without being turned down now by a two-bit, frigid, cock . . ."

". . . teaser," I finish for her out of delicacy.

"That's right. And then he just came at me . . ."

"What did *you* say?" I continue to stall. "And by the way, would you like to sit down someplace?"

We stagger blindly, in close formation, over to my car and I bundle her in somehow or other.

"Well, I told him that I loved my husband, and that that was that, and he simply said, 'Bullshit.' Then he said he'd been watching me making eyes at other guys all year long, especially at *you*, Jonathan—crazy huh?—and I said I was just being friendly, and he said, 'Bullshit' again."

Well that seemed like fair comment on Waldo's part. "D'he say anything else at all?"

"Well, and he said, 'If you're going to make eyes like that at people it doesn't *matter* whether you fuck them or not. You've already humiliated your husband—who, by the way, is worth at least two of your ladyship—to the core of the poor bastard's being. After that you might as *well* fuck them, and get *some*thing positive out of it.' I tell you, he was talking like a madman." It all comes out in a flood exactly the way it went in, like a baby throwing up his dinner.

"Waldo must have been over at your place for quite a while," I say judiciously. "When did Billy finally get home?" There is an awful lot of sheer police inspector in every American blood-stream by now. (At least I don't call her "ma'am.")

"He talked fast, like spitting bullets in fact, and I guess he didn't say much more. 'My only complaint,' he did say, 'your *High*ness, is that I don't much care to be used as a bit player in Billy's ongoing degradation and then thrown away like an old condom. So, my little dumpling—I've come to collect.' And then he . . ."

"So what was keeping Billy all this time?" *Get* there, Billy. Haul some ass.

"Does it really matter what was keeping Billy?" No. "I guess we'd agreed to meet at Jimmy's sometime after the game. Billy didn't know when that was, of course, because he'd gone to the

Nature Conservancy to forget the whole thing. But I'm really so glad he didn't just walk in on us anyway. I mean, what could he have done? with Waldo's knife and everything. And it would have been so awful for him, so *truly* humiliating."

"So you *did* do it."

She looked at me without answering and said, "Of course, I haven't told Billy anything about this, and you mustn't either, but it's all left him pretty confused."

Suddenly she seems talked out. There doesn't appear to be much point in filling me in on any more corroborating details concerning the putative rape—the flashing blade, the anesthesia. I do wonder about how Waldo got hold of that knife on the way back from the game, but no doubt it was part of the death kit he always kept in his car. It doesn't matter anymore. Nothing can ever be proved about the rape one way or the other, so why go on? Naturally, I have my own biased notions. I believe, from appearances, that she and Waldo *were* having it on at some stage, and that later, and probably at the worst possible moment, she blankly refused him. I don't know, maybe she saw his house one day. Or maybe she'd heard about the movie deal that never was, and decided that one loser in her life was enough. Stupid people can be awfully hard to figure.

And then it comes to me with a dread of recognition that it's all quite true—nobody ever believes a woman's account of rape. In my case, skepticism is weirdly sharpened by my own failure to score with this same woman. A redneck sheriff could hardly have reacted more delicately.

"You know, he could be very rough," she murmured sleepily. I almost put an arm round her to console her vaguely, and realize I would probably touch breast and forget what I was doing. Yes, still.

So maybe that was it too.

Whatever it was, Nikki had driven another nail into Waldo's rickety confidence. Writers, of all people, have to score one way or the other; even publishers rather prefer it. But, as I think about it now, what struck me most about Waldo when I found him at my place the next day was not his lack of confidence but his serene elation and sense of triumph. His twin acts of vengeance, his Saturday doubleheader of sex and violence, had put him right back on his toes.

Time to go now. And as if to remind us, a flashlight suddenly thrusts its way through the open car window. "Are you in there, Nikki?" Ohmygod, it's Billy, probably checking out *all* the cars tonight.

Like a pair of guilty teenagers, we tumble out to face the music. "Why, hello there, Billy," I say casually as the torch beam skewers me; he swings the light sharply onto Nikki and then back to me as if deciding which of us to hit first. Well, he can't hurt as much as a postman, I bet.

Finally, he steps forward, nods briefly at me and puts his arm around Nikki and leads her quietly away. Scenes from a marriage? or just Billy retreating from life in confusion one more time? Who knows? I'm just glad the van Dynes are gone before I can blurt out the immortal teenage words, "Hey, we didn't *do* anything, mister."

I return through the parking-light shadows to the tavern which now rings with the sound of honest, drunken laughter— nothing "wake" about it anymore. Archie Munson has reclaimed our old group table and perches there like one of those toy birds who dips his beak into anything you put in front of it. Earlier in the evening Archie had seemed on the verge of despair but right now he looks as if he might suggest a new softball game at any moment, "only this time we'll do it right, guys." Important to keep him singing at all costs. Ferris, sitting next to him, appears, incredibly, to be tapping his foot. It must have taken an ocean of bourbon to reduce Ferris to this.

I mention these two, because I have seldom seen either one of them *appear* drunk before. Clearly it is an important thing to do tonight. As usual no two people are probably drinking for the same reasons. The changing of the seasons is a private matter out here. But whatever your spirit makes of it, you drink to it— to make it feel better, to make it go away. "This round is on Jimmy's," says our waitress again and yet again, as if our chieftain were atoning to us for the profits of Summer. He had sinned grievously with the Summer People. But when Jimmy forgets, *everybody* forgets.

"What you boys been up to since I went away?" Begorrah, Cormac Burke, our wandering Irishman, has returned from covering the Troubles.

"Pretty much the same as you have, I expect."

It's refreshing to gaze once more upon a man who is completely innocent of softball. Whatever terrors Cormac has seen lately could not have stained his soul in quite the same way.

I tell him briefly of our little internecine squabbles, friend against friend, culminating in our subjugation by wealthy outsiders, and he says, "Why that's *exactly* the same as what I've been up to."

Would he have made a difference if he'd stayed? His outsize personality, as big as a size ten hat, would have made him more than a match for Waldo. And I also find that working reporters have a slight edge in sanity over housebound writers: they don't see those shadows dancing on the wall of the cave. But the Game might have taken care of that.

Where the hell is Cecily? I want her here right now, beside me: not out of mad desire, but because this is where she belongs. Whatever it was I was waiting for to happen between us has struck just like that, smoothly and sharply, in the few hours since we kissed this afternoon at the graveyard, yes, the graveyard. I had actually been counting on months and months for Cecily and me to circle each other sleepily, patiently—our winters are long out here, especially this coming one, and you have to do *some*thing. But suddenly, there doesn't seem so much time for anything.

All this while, I realize that Ferris has been talking to me, and the subject sounds at long last like Waldo, but just now I can't be bothered. I have spotted Cecily through the smoke and fumes, she is gazing at me steadily, and she looks for the first time as if she is actually old enough to be in here.

How did that happen? The first time I saw her at Jimmy's, not so very long ago, I thought that all she needed was a lollipop and a hockey stick to complete the ensemble. And then when we played that phantom game of pitch and toss back in that winter—even Humbert Humbert would have drawn the line at such a lover. And yet here she is, one softball season later. . . .

"Is that right?" I say politely to Ferris.

"Damn right that's right" the Great Man insists vehemently, "and not only that . . ." He is going round and round, so I can step in anytime.

On the face of it, the softball game seemed the least likely place for anyone to grow up in—Archie was practically sucking his thumb by the end of it, Billy was pouting like a child, even Ferris had unraveled slightly; no one had gained. If Cecily really had grown up, she must have done it on the side.

"Next thing I knew, Waldo had . . ." it occurs to me that all Cecily has done on the side is hang out with Ferris. That couldn't have made much difference, could it? From where I sat, their affair, if you could call it that, had seemed well up to our highest standards of foot-stamping, hair-pulling infantilism. But perhaps, through all the sulks and the pets, she may have gleaned something from the Colonel that she couldn't have gotten from anyone else—some notion, beyond sex, of what else a man wants from a woman, and some other notion of what a bright woman can get out of a man who doesn't *quite* like women. A demanding regimen for our schoolgirl—no wonder she found the year "interesting."

No sequence of Oglethorpe thoughts would be complete without one trashy one, to wit, could a mature Cecily Woodruff still turn out the "wide-eyed on Park Avenue" type novels that did so genuinely well for us at Williams and Oglethorpe? I have refrained so far from rating Cecily commercially but she might fairly be defined as the stakes winner that pays for my Nether Hampton stable. So, if I really am down to my last author . . .

This is such a sickening drop from my previous lofty thoughts about her, that for a moment I can't look at her. Up to this moment, I had fervently hoped that the wretched Otis MacIntyre had simply died with his creator Waldo, peacefully, of course, and in his sleep. I wouldn't want to hurt him. But here he is back in full caper, rattling his cashbox and screaming for his ducats. If Otis has his way, he and I will soon end up doing to Cecily what Willy the rat did to Colette: first we'll marry her (Otis can be best man), and then we'll lock her in the attic and *make* her write bestsellers. Otis assures me that there's nothing to it. All we have to do is dress her up in pigtails and pinafores and line the shelves with Nancy Drew books and all that nasty maturity will melt away in no time, like the bad dream that it usually is.

I look at her finally to avoid looking at myself—and once again I am taken off guard. I know that smoke can play funny tricks, but I could swear our Cecily is actually looking *sultry*. As if to confirm this, she proceeds to raise an eyebrow at me worthy of Shanghai Lil, and there's only one thing to do about that. I nod.

It could have been a deal at a Moroccan flesh market. Because without more ado, my prize begins walking gracefully, sinuously, straight towards me. Ferris must have taught her a *hell* of a lot (or can we concede the new walk to softball?). There is no chair, so she shares mine as if we were the last couple left in a game of musical chairs, which perhaps we are, and I feel a magic in her hip that seems to bind us like steel. No Mavis ever had a magic hip. And together, we tune in on Ferris, the all-night show. Right now, he seems to be muttering to no one in particular like a bum on a bench setting the record straight, once and for all, to the empty air.

Just to get his attention, I break in with a question that has puzzled me for a while. "Hey, Ferris, something I never could quite figure. You always used to despise writers who write from experience and nothing but experience. And yet here you have this great respect for Waldo. How come?"

"Are you kidding?" He snaps to alertly. "Waldo faked his stuff just as much as I fake mine, if not more so."

"What do you mean you fake yours?" I say sharply. I mean, *I* know he fakes his, but *he's* not supposed to.

"Sure I do. How much of that gracious old South do you suppose a kid like me could pick up on a hardscrabble farm in East Texas? Why we didn't even have it in the library where I came from. I'll tell you, Jon, when I got to New York, I kissed the sidewalk with joy—and do you know what I tasted while I was down there on my knees? I tasted Gold!"

Thank God, I enjoy being laughed at. Otherwise I'd be convulsing pretty badly by now. "C'mon Jon"—he won't let up—

"you don't really think a *real* Southern gentleman would carry on the way I do, do you?"

"I don't know, I never met one."

"Well, believe me, if he did he'd be laughed all the way from Little Rock to the Hamptons—where, of course, he'd make a fortune. Anyhow, bless your innocence, my son, and hang on to it for dear life. It's your most valuable possession; it makes you the perfect reader."

The perfect sap, the perfect reader. Same guy? Jesus. But is it even conceivable that he really is telling me the truth this time, and that I have been fooled all along by a professional Southerner, a con man straight out of Mark Twain—although what other kind did I expect in the Hamptons, pray tell? The more I think about it, the more his act seems to crumble and dissolve in a smirk, just like Waldo's. Ferris puts out a consoling hand as if to assure me that there *is* work for the mentally defective. "Don't worry, Jon. There's a real dream in here somewhere." He taps his breast nobly. "It's not all fake, believe me, buddyro."

Stop *playing* with me. *All* of you. Waldo, Ferris, whoever you are. Put me down this instant. I swear, the teasing among writers must be rougher and more brutal than any locker room the law allows.

"Anyway, to get back to Waldo." Ferris is suddenly all business again. "You ever read that Korean War book of his? Yes, of course you have. Well you may not remember it, but I happened to be in that war too, and where he got his version *I'll* never know. The other guys called it *Waldo in Wonderland* when it came out, although I thought *Through the Looking Glass* was even closer."

"But it all rang so true."

"That's *it*," he says slapping my knee boozily. "You've *got* it, you little publisher you. Why the hell do you think Waldo ran out of gas so early in life? He could have written realistic novels forever, God knows he was smart enough, but he *despised* that stuff; he thought it wasn't worth writing at all if you were down to that."

"I guess you haven't seen his latest."

Silly me. "Sure I have."

"Well, didn't you notice some real people in it?"

"Nope. But he was thrilled that *you* did."

"He *talked* to you about it? . . . about me and it?" I jabber.

"Yeah, he especially loved your response to the character MacIntyre. He called it his greatest triumph. The way he figured it was that if he treated you enough like MacIntyre in real life, you might just begin to think you *were* MacIntyre and maybe, *just* maybe, you might begin to act like him too.

"You see, he was still trying to write total fantasies that rang absolutely true, and it was getting harder every year, and he was getting desperate, as indeed we know. So it's my belief that he took to creating scenes just to see what would happen."

"Bullshit," I say uncertainly.

"Well yes, I thought so too. Stuff like that just doesn't happen, does it? I'm just trying to convey what was on his mind as he fought for life. 'Have you any idea how much energy it takes to create a whole world of your own?' he would ask me, as if he'd forgotten what line of work I was in myself. I remember telling him one time 'whole worlds are too much for me, daddy. I only do regions,' and he said 'oh Christ yes—I'm sorry Ferris.' He really respected other writers, you know," he rambles.

"Even Billy?" I whisper.

"Even Billy," he hollers for the world to hear, though it doesn't matter in that shrieking fun-house of a bar. No one could hear his roars except Cecily and me. "Waldo could never understand how so much talent as Billy's ever fetched up in such a miserable container. Unlike some authors, you didn't have to write like Waldo to get his attention."

Mention of Billy has turned my mind into safer and, by good chance, more salacious channels. So I change the subject—Ferris won't mind. "When did you last see Waldo anyway?" I ask.

"Why, I believe he came straight over from your place and stayed a couple of nights at mine."

"And how'd he seem?"

"As a matter of fact, I never saw him sassier or more at peace. He said he'd just done three important things. I guess I don't have to tell you what the first one was. The second was that he'd gone on from there and given Lucy a good, you know, diddling. . . ."

"What?" Lucy was Nikki's name in the novel.

"Yeah, he said it was just what Lucy needed and that her husband Jasper, not to mention the rest of mankind, would live to thank him someday. As you recall, the Lucy in his book wouldn't even, you know, with her husband." Ferris hates talking smut in front of the ladies.

"I see. The book."

"And Waldo said that, number three, he'd finally made a man out of Otis—but that if he hadn't, well, fuck it. It'd been fun trying. It's strange, he talked as if he'd just come from his typewriter, and not from a round of visiting. It was a creative day for him, one of his best. He was exciting to be around."

"Who's Otis? Who *are* all these people?" asked Cecily, with exasperation.

Ferris chuckled. "Ask Otis here sometime. He'll tell you all about them. Anyway, the one place he struck out on his crazy holiday-weekend rounds was at Penelope Purbright's, and he wasn't even so sure about that. It seems that while he was beating on her door, she emptied a hot kettle smack dab over his head, and when he looked up, scalded, to see what the Sam Hill was going on, he swore he could see a breech-loading musket in the upstairs window. Penelope wouldn't have done that a year ago, he said."

"The heck she wouldn't," says Cecily. "I'd have done it the first day I met him, if I'd had the angle." This is probably not true, but it's prettily put. "And did the old charmer say what his plans were for me if I let him in?" she continues.

"He said he just wanted to say 'good-bye.'"

"What the hell for?" I bark. Don't tell me that Cecily was also in one of Waldo's famous scenes? Did he perhaps make a woman of her in his spare time? "Listen," I cheep like a referee's whistle, "there's just one thing wrong with this whole farrago. The book is already written, remember?"

"Oh, *that* book. You mean the one he actually wrote? *I* was talking about the sequel he was planning. Fancy him not telling

you about that. Yeah, it was going to take the gang right
through the next summer, and maybe a little beyond."

"Where is it, for Christsake? I thought you guys hardly knew
each other," I add irrelevantly. It is just that I am getting that
old feeling that the whole world takes place behind my back.

"I don't *know* where it is. I don't even know whether it exists.
The cops found a couple of notebooks which were practically
empty. Maybe he buried it in the yard."

"Great. Not only do we have Waldo's ghost to contend with,
but now this Flying Dutchman of a manuscript."

"So it looks as though the world has been spared one more
lousy book in that execrable prose," says Cecily briskly, as if
she's had just about enough of this Waldo crap, and I feel wildly
comforted that at least one person around here had stayed outside the great man's zone of enchantment. (I brush aside, now
and forever, the possibility that she had ever for one minute
strayed inside.) It was bad enough hearing just now that Waldo
had gloated like Lucifer over his last mad acts, but then, that
Ferris had found him "exciting to be around" in that state—it
froze the blood. So Cecily seems by contrast like some talis-
man, like a whole gorgeous font of Holy Water in fact, with
which I'd like to sprinkle both of them, and everyone else in
the bar.

Metaphors don't just happen. I suddenly realize that it is
men's room time for me, and then some—and a wonderfully
jolly scene the men's room turns out to be with everyone acting
as if taking a piss was the funniest single thing he'd ever done in
his life. I would have liked to splash in there forever with the
lads, absolving my sins in acid rain. But the court is still in
session outside and I must hear Ferris out.

"Talking of manuscripts," I say breezily on my return.
"What did Waldo think of my novel? Did he mention it?"

"Oh yes indeed, he mentioned it the very day before he—
you know." Ferris suddenly looks around cautiously. It is hard
to believe that we could talk so long at a crowded table without
being overheard, and in fact we haven't. Cormac Burke, two
chairs to my right, and four times as many sheets to the wind,

has miraculously heard it all through the din. I guess Jimmy's to him is no worse than an average city room.

"You been listening," says Ferris sharply.

"Sure have. Grand stuff, I tell you. Frankly, I couldn't put it down."

"What the hell did I say anyway?" says Ferris blankly.

"Right now, I'm not too sure, old man. Have to work it out in the morning. But I tell you it was *grand.*"

You'll notice that the moment I mention my novel, the meeting breaks up like a busted crap game. Buy that man Burke another drink, and let's get out of here. Fortunately, Cormac's face is already beginning to weave slightly. I know the guy is a super journalist, which means that he can sing, drink his brains out, and listen at the same time, but did we really say enough to interest him, in this condition? I too will have to wait till tomorrow to find out what we said, from my rickety playback machine.

"I guess Waldo was kind of depressed at the end, huh?" says Cormac.

"Yes, that's it. A wee bit depressed. You know, what with being sick and, er, this and that," I say breezily.

"Boy, it certainly sounds a hell of a lot more complicated than that," says Cormac, fading fast, now that his concentration is no longer at full stretch. I signal the waitress to fill him up, and to bring me the check for all of us. (I trust my authors will let me pay.) So Cormac's memory joins Waldo's phantom manuscript among the swords of Damocles that hang over the case like a display in a hardware store.

"Anybody use a nightcap?" says the indefatigable Ferris. "I think I got a couple at my place that might fit."

"Damn right" I say. I don't care if this takes all night. Welman can run the office without me for one day, can't he? Cecily frowns at me mightily. She *hates* this story, and maybe she thinks it's bad for me to hang around it too long. But I have no choice.

"You want to go on home and I'll meet you there?" At our ages you don't have to fence, thank God.

"No, that's all right." She puts a protective arm through mine. "I just love those great Southern storytellers."

The crowd as we push through it is either numb or last-ditch obstreperous—in either case, nothing to worry about, until it hits the road in a body; the spirit of the evening has moved on (taking Waldo with it I vainly hope), but the guests don't know it. In those days the mothers of America had not yet been aroused, and anyone who could crawl, paddle, or knee-walk to his machine was allowed to drive home unchallenged, except by the odd tree, ditch, or other car, so it seemed a good move for us three to beat the gathering chaos out of the parking lot.

And then there was this: any time you can't lay your hands on an old English country house, with whiskey and cold lobster waiting for you by the fireplace, Ferris's Confederate Gothic is the best atmosphere I know for discussing dark doings. So Ferris drives off to prepare the feast (bourbon and more bourbon) and Cecily and I follow along more slowly, to enjoy the simple pleasure of being alone in a car together, on entirely new terms.

25

ERRIS'S house, as we pull up to it, looks slightly wrong. It is brighter than it's supposed to be, and in fact it looks almost like a normal house. The invisible Spanish moss is gone, and could that possibly be a FOR SALE sign in the window? Something white, anyway.

Ferris greets us at the door with woozily elaborate courtesy.

"Yawl sit down over heah while I fix yawl a posset," he says smiling, now that the game is over.

Cecily takes my hand and leads us to the sofa. A little too commanding? Shut up, Oglethorpe. She snuggles firmly next to me as if plugging herself back in, Ferris or no Ferris. The latter fetches us our possets and raises his to our continued health and happiness, as if conceding gracefully. For a horrible instant, I imagine him adding "I broke her in real good for you, didn't I boy," but this only means that I've lost my bearings completely with the guy. What he actually says is "I'll be sorry to leave a lot of things around here but most especially you two. You know I love you both," and withdraws to his Colonel Fender armchair, where once upon a time he used to grow automatically in grandeur. Now as the shadow falls across his cheek suggesting side-whiskers, I can almost see how he did it. But not tonight. Instead he moves his head into the light and yawns prosaically.

"Don't worry, you'll be back someday," I say.

"What makes you think that, old buddy?"

"Because it says so in Waldo's notes. He says nobody leaves the Hamptons alive, no one from our little chain gang anyway."

"Well I'll be damned." Ferris is genuinely flummoxed.

"What notes?" says Cecily.

"Waldo left me some notes," I say proudly; at last I have a secret of my very own. "Now tell me, Ferris," I say, as if playing some immensely powerful new card, "a) what did Waldo mean by making a man of me, and b) *how did he like my novel?*"

Ferris strokes his chin in thought. It seems the old storyteller does not care to be fussed with any more tiresome, narcissistic little questions from the little people out there. He will tell his tale now his own way, or fall asleep in the attempt. The multifarious clocks in the house chime out something late, usually a signal for the Colonel to pull out his pocket watch and check it. But tonight, he dispenses with the flimflam. In fact his style at this moment seems as stripped down as the outside of his house. But this will prove subject to fluctuation as we go along.

"You were a special trahl to him," said Ferris, blending my question into his grand design. "And I'll tell you why in a moment. Now I'm sure Waldo felt like most authors, and farmers too for that matter, that a host of black insects swarms between him and his public. You know the gang—greedy, incompetent publishers, of course, but not just that"—he held up a peaceful hand—"There are also those malicious reviewers, venal financial foundations, and *anyone* else who won't give you money—plus, oh, the movie business, the TV business and the whole educational system; also the highbrow magazines, the lowbrow public . . ."

"How exactly," says Cecily tartly, "did the public come between him and the public?"

"Well, never mind, it just did. Every time the public turned on the dial, it was taking the bread out of Waldo's mouth."

"What about women who wouldn't put out for him?" I ask. "Were they part of the swarm?"

"Oh, he really wasn't so bad about that, as artists go. He figured women should hold as much sway in their field as he did in his. And theirs was the only field that came anywheres near to his in importance, he said. Nikki? I just don't know about her. You'll have to go to someone else on that. Except for that outburst about 'Lucy,' who was fictional anyway, he never once mentioned her to me. As a matter of fact, he didn't really like to talk about his women at all. He thought it was un-gentlemanly. Isn't that so, Jon?"

Surprisingly, "Yes, that's right."

"However, remembering the way she was looking at him the night before the game, I guess something had been going on there. But whatever it was, I must stress that he thought he was doing absolutely the best thing for her *and* Billy *and* the whole wide world. You understand, of course, that he thought of him-self as a kind of saint, and that everyone here is better off for having known him."

I can almost smell sulfur rising through the old floorboards at that one.

"Did he really get off all that guff about insects, or was that just you again?"

"One or the other of us" he says, grinning sleepily and in tipsy triumph. "Yes, that's right."

Oh my, I think we've lost him. Ferris's expressive chin drops, and then drops again. Maybe even the pretense of being the world's greatest drinker can be allowed to lapse now. But then the chin fools me by rising gloriously. Duty calls, and he must finish this cockamamie story somehow, whatever the hell it is.

"From various things he said," says Ferris from way out of right field, "I got the feeling Waldo just couldn't get the new stuff down in book form until he received a signal from some-place that he was still OK, that he wasn't wasting his time. If he'd gotten just one such signal, from the insects out there, he might still be with us. But you both know how it goes when a writer begins to slip, don't you?—hell, it happens to most of us. First your reviews get more condescending and the re-viewers more unknown and incompetent. Then the *publishers* start passing you down the line till you wind up at Outhouse Press—no reflection on you, Jon. And the next thing you know, the younger generation has never heard of you—well, they've never heard of anybody, but try telling that to a drown-ing author. All he's thinking about by then is dragging somebody else down with him, even if it's only a little old lifeguard like you, Jonathan."

I've never heard Ferris talk like this, I didn't even think he cared. But then I didn't know that our New York sidewalks tasted of gold either. The new Ferris will take some getting used to.

"Would money really have helped?" I ask. "I mean as a sign."

"Hell yes!" roars Ferris. "'Money,' he used to say, 'is a lot more sincere than the Nobel Prize.' Over the years he had made out lists of all the 'big boys' as he called them—Dickens, Balzac, the usual—and exactly how much money each of them had made. And he also talked about how much they loved worldly recognition. He figured a little money could buy him some of that too, and he didn't care how tawdry it was. Talk-show recognition, for instance, would have been just dandy. You know, he'd say, you lose your pride about that stuff the moment you see some world-famous author getting away with it without falling at once into international disgrace. Dickens would have done talk shows, said Waldo, Christ he would probably have hosted one of his own. Old Waldo was very persuasive, I must say. Anyway, he was pretty sure his own talent was still there, safe and glittering in his pocket. But he needed a *sign*. Do you understand that at all?" "No," says Cecily flatly. "And meanwhile," adds Ferris, "the Hamptons are a hell of a place to be a failure in."

"He wasn't a failure," I say defensively. "Not yet."

"No, but he was on his way, he'd stepped on the escalator. For example, I'm sure he could already picture, word for word, the obit he got today in the *Times*, not to mention the ones he would have got next year and the year after. You arrive at the size of each by taking the square root of the length of your latest reviews, and dividing by two."

"Jesus, Ferris, you sound as if you've been there yourself."

"Oh, I have, old buddy, I have," he says winking at Cecily to make it seem like kidding. "Don't let my newly unveiled greed for money blind you to my other vices. I also *lust* for immortality every waking minute, like all the boys. Yeah. Busts in

libraries, little old ladies attending readings a hundred years
hence, the whole wash and wax."

As I start to make out in my mind a list of immortal publishers I have known, Cecily says, quite fondly—it's the least
you can do for your finishing school—"I know you fellows
can't help it, but I really think you buy yourselves an awful lot
of unnecessary grief worrying about that stuff. Take me, if you
don't mind. I guess if I really sweat it from here on out, I might
possibly wind up as famous as Charlotte Yonge or even Mrs.
Gaskell—it'll be hard to tell from where I'll be lying by then,
and frankly, I don't know anyone else who gives a flying damn
about the question even right now. So I figure if I don't worry
about it either, poof, there's no question, no problem," she con-
cludes brightly, once more the clever schoolgirl, and very
charming too.

"Oh, why don't you go out and have a baby or something,"
says Ferris good-naturedly, "and leave us guys alone." He
closes his eyes again; where *precisely* is he right now? Give a man
some vectors around here. *"You* Jonathan," he says, looking for
a focus. *"You* almost gave him the signal he wanted by taking his
book, but then you took it back again by paying him peanuts.
Have you . . . any . . . idea, Jonathan, how wounding and
insulting those advances of yours can be?"

"Jesus, Ferris! you've never said anything about advances
before."

"Never came up before, reckon," he says vaguely. *"Any*way,
where was I?" About two-thirds down the second bottle I
would guess. "So anyway, Jonathan. How do you reckon a pan-
handler feels when you hand him a nickel and then wait around
for thanks? *That's* how Waldo felt about you."

"You mean that's how *you* felt."

"Yes, one of us. That's right." He grins again with comatose
glee.

Cecily squeezes my hand, which I take to mean "Let's get out
of this mausoleum."

"Then"—he says loudly, as if he doesn't want us to go and
leave him with his thoughts—"you wrote a *book!"*

"Yes, Ferris?"

"Well, that's it. You wrote a book."

"And did he like it?"

"He said you were a pricky little guy at least, in fact a deep-dyed, truly mean sonofabitch. I guess he was impressed by that. It was more than he expected. I also recall him saying that for a four-eyed bookworm who never seemed to notice anything, you got your people down pretty well."

"Did he include himself?"

"Not specially. He just said you settled some scores around here, and you should be feeling pretty good about that, given your all-round meanness."

"Did"—I fairly beg this time—"he say anything about talent?"

"I think he may have said you were promising. I forget." He waved it away. No more book.

"And did he tell you about the funeral games he had in mind for me?"

"He just said he was working on something. I guess by the looks of it he wanted to reward you and punish you at the same time, though that sounds a little too simple for Waldo—and, of course, he wanted to leave you a better person. Think he did that?"

"I wouldn't have given him the satisfaction. What about you? did he do anything for you?" I ask idly.

It was a casual, halfway-out-the-door kind of question, so I was surprised by the gravity of his response. His chin sank one last time, and then just sat there quivering. "Well we talked a lot about how writers get screwed, you know," he mumbled almost inaudibly. "*You* know—stuff like that."

"And?" I said.

"And I guess he made me see all that a little bit differently."

"*And?*"

His voice sank to almost nothing, and his face looked like the day after Gettysburg. "And he talked me into changing publishers." After one more beseeching look, he closed his eyes for good. Cecily and I could only tiptoe out after that, reaching our hands under what seemed like a hundred ancient lampshades to turn out some lights around here.

As we reached the door, he spoke one more time as if in sleep. "I'm no saint," he said softly.

Well, of course not. Everyone knows there's only one saint around here, and he's gone to his maker. As if to huddle against this particular saint, Cecily and I walk to the car with our arms wrapped tight around each other, like the last survivors of a ruinous storm.

I would like to be able to say that we didn't talk at all for the next twenty-four hours, because in a sense we didn't. There was a stillness between us, an exhausted, grateful peace, that words couldn't pierce. But they did, in a technical sense, occur, randomly and at intervals. Here is one thread that we picked up and dropped over the hours and what seemed like days we spent together.

"D'you think old Ferris would really like to be on a talk show himself?" I murmured at some point. "He might make a great TV character, like," yawn, "Buffalo Bill or something."

She kissed me to remind me of where we were.

"I'm afraid that was just one of his crazy put-ons, darling," she murmured back eventually. "Ferris used to compare his routines to trying on his mother's old wigs when he was a kid (did you know she was a showgirl? before she married down?). He says 'someday I'm going to find me the right wig, and then watch out!' But appear on a talk show? why he'd rather sell, er, Roanoke to the Yankees."

That seemed like a good one to sleep on, so I slept on it. Several centuries later, I awoke to the following:

"I don't think he was *exactly* putting you on," said Cecily. "He was abasing himself, *mocking* himself."

"Why, for God's sake?"

"Because of what he'd done to you, I guess. Changing publishers and all. His 'betrayal.' His 'dishonor.'"

"But I thought that *that* was the put-on—the honor, the whole code of the South bit."

"Are you kidding? They meant *everything* to him. That's what I mean by abasement. He was telling you that his life had become a lie. That he was a clown. That he wasn't fit to be a Southern gentleman, and therefore never had been. You know I didn't even know he'd changed publishers until we were on the way out? That explained *everything.*"

"And you could read all that into one drunken conversation? How can you possibly be so sure about his real Southern honor, sweetheart?"

"I don't know. Little things like top of his class at VMI, battlefield promotion in Korea, more medals than you could pin on the Fat Lady. Some put-on, I would say."

"He never talked about that military stuff," I said.

"Of course not."

Of course.

"And no hardscrabble either?"

"Oh *sure*, hardscrabble. As far as the eye could see. Very good for the imagination, he used to say. And a drunken white-trash daddy to match the soil, and a miserable, defeated mama with a drawer full of wigs, all going down in the world together. 'You don't think there are *grades* of hardscrabble?' he'd say. 'Boy, let me tell you, there's worse and then there's worse again. And then it starts getting really bad.'"

"I guess he just lied to me about all that. Honorable lies, I'm sure."

"Yes, that's right. Honorable lies. He began to bet *everything* on his imagination to get him out of there. And when it did, *you* know, by way of scholarships, and military courage (which he considered his greatest feat of imagination) and finally literature, he thought his imagination had some kind of magic to it, and he decided to trust it with his life. And it was *that* which he felt he had betrayed when he sold his gift, his magic carpet, for cash."

"Was he that desperate for money too, like Waldo?"

"He needed it, I guess, but, no, not like Waldo. Money just didn't bother him, at least not when I was around. He said he could always turn his place into an antique store for people who didn't know any better. And besides, he said, it was ignoble even to talk about that stuff, and as a matter of fact he never did again."

"You mean to tell me that all that hardscrabble had never once turned his thoughts to money, even as a kid?"

"No, that's funny, isn't it? Maybe the meanness and vulgarity of rich people look even worse from down there. Whatever. He could see no glory in getting the stuff, and not much more in keeping it."

It's true, he didn't even read his contracts before signing. "I trust you, my man," he'd say (the memory almost made me cry). So *why?*

I didn't ask and she didn't answer, and it must have been an hour or so before she spoke again.

"I begged with him to stop seeing Waldo," she said out of the blue. "You know, Waldo and all his rich writers' talk. You'd suppose Ferris would have been immune to such malarkey, and oh he was, he was, for the longest time. 'Waldo, old man,' he would say patronizingly, 'do you know what the trouble with you is, ol' buddy? Trouble with you is you began life with a bestseller so you got all the goodies on the first go-round, and now you miss them something awful. And maybe (I'm just guessing) the worst of it is that while you still *had* the goodies you probably felt you had to defend them—against, you know, highbrows, and schoolteachers and maybe even your own maggoty old conscience in there. So you started drawing up those ridiculous lists, and thinking you're Balzac and all, and now you're trying to make *me* think I am too, for company.'"

"I couldn't have put it better myself. What was there left to say?"

"With Waldo? Plenty. And Ferris was always fascinated with him, if not with his ideas. He thought he was a real writer, and whatever he said deserved respect. He called it once again, 'The Authority of Imagination.' He's *very* romantic about writing, you know."

You might suppose that this was Ben Jonson talking about Shakespeare, but in this profession, God bless it, you don't have to be major to *feel* major. A single jolt, like a power surge, runs undiminished from top writer to bottom, killing only those who touch it.

"Anyhow," she said "Waldo kept hammering away about glory and manhood and not ending up like Billy van Dyne, and Ferris just kept on listening, and Waldo would talk about little old ladies who turn out novels like wall samplers and get paid in stamps, and then back to lords of the earth, and grubby little advances from greasy little publishers . . ."

"Here!" I put up my hand.

"And I don't know if any of it worked, or none of it, but Ferris was mesmerized by the whole performance. I didn't get to see all of it, because we were kind of off again, on again, as you may recall (and if you don't, don't bother). But you saw the result for yourself. By the end of it, I do believe that Ferris would have doctored that softball himself if Waldo had asked him to."

"He didn't, did he?" I asked quickly.

"Not that I know of. But he did hide it for him afterwards, I understand."

"Anyway, if he feels so bad about me, why doesn't he just come back to me now? He can't have signed anything yet."

She frowned. "I guess he must have given his word to Waldo."

"Jesus," I said softly. "That's so sad."

Cecily nodded, and we embraced, silently within the silence. And then she brightened, as if a nice thought had struck her. "You know, it may not have all been quite as one-sided as I tell it. I mean, I guess that it was really no accident that they both chose the Hamptons to live in. I know that Ferris talked about the beautiful countryside." "And about being close to his publisher, don't forget that." "And God knows, Waldo went on and on about the fishermen, and the bay constable and all, but there's one rule out here that all the talk in the world can't repeal, and it's a rule that allows absolutely no exceptions that I know of."

"And what is that, dearest?"

"It is that *no*body in the arts, or maybe out of them either, *ever* came to the Hamptons in search of oblivion. And" she paused for emphasis, "Ferris came out here just as much as any of us."

And with that settled for now, we returned clear-minded to our serene uncluttered contemplation of each other and of this extraordinary surprise gift the year had given us simply for surviving it.

26

THANK GOD, you don't have to worry about everything—otherwise nobody would survive twenty-four
hours. So the next day, or to be strict the day after
(Cecily doesn't like the personal stuff), I decide not to worry
about publishing. Ferris will be a sad loss, but more for himself
than his books, and as for Spinks I'm too dazed right now to
think of him as a business property. At any rate, old Prescott
Williams presumably has enough money to keep so modest a
tub as Williams and Oglethorpe afloat without any books at all,
just expenses. And in the eye of history, a bad year looks pretty
much like a good one at a small quality house.

Thus sedated with sophistries and half-truths, I enter the
Building That Doesn't Count bright and early, i.e., a good solid
10:15 on, let's be frank, Wednesday morning. Any trouble I'm
going to get will come, as always, from Sam Welman: first the
usual bush league heckle over time wasted; and then a grilling
about Spinks, manner of death, and is it good for Williams and
Oglethorpe.

But hey, what's this? Sam isn't here yet either. I have, I realize, never seen his office empty before, and I am not surprised
to learn that the anal twit leaves his desk naked as a baby when
he goes home at night. Ooh boy, is he going to hear from me
about this one. There are rules for humorless drones, dash it
all, and punctuality is most of them.

"Where is Sam?" I trot impishly down the corridor, making

sure everybody hears. "Has anyone seen Sam?" I wheel into the ancient Prescott's office in a mock fret. "I really need him. Something just came up."

I fully expect Prescott to say "Sam who?" or possibly to express amazement over anything "coming up" around here.

But no such thing. Indeed, unless my eyes deceive me, there is something like fire in his. Hard to tell with one so moribund, but I could swear old Prescott is actually angry.

"Mr. Welman," he says stonily, "is no longer with us."

Eh? Just like that? how long have I been asleep anyway? "What on earth happened? he quit or what?"

"In a way, you might say he quit. Yes. Or let's say that we reached an understanding."

"Wasn't that kind of hasty? I mean by our standards."

"Yes well, it was 'our standards' that most seemed to upset Mr. Welman. He started out complaining again about your absenteeism, and I said, funny, I hadn't noticed it. (I fancy that shook him, eh?) And he said well, it was a scandal in the business, which I quickly took leave to doubt. Anyhow, since I myself had just arrived for the first time shortly after lunch yesterday, the whole thing seemed to have gotten off on rather the wrong foot, I thought.

"So I asked him if perhaps there was some more fruitful matter we could discuss before I got on with my business, and he with his, and he began to talk about modernizing plant, whatever that is—do we have 'plant'?—and about bringing our whole list into the twentieth century. I must say I was taken aback by that one. Doesn't the young idiot realize that I was born in 1903?"

Was I supposed to laugh at this? mercifully, yes. We both did, indeed—little dry chuckles, you should have heard us.

"So I told him that true distinction in literature was timeless, and that if he was uncomfortable with it, well, the town was littered with twentieth-century publishing houses, coming and going all the time, and he was quite welcome to try any one of them.

"This, I fancy, sobered him up a bit. Because the town, one may suppose, is also littered with Sam Welmans, all hustling around in a great big circle, and it was clearly a much better plan for him to sabotage *you*, Jonathan, on the spot, and have this whole little place all to himself, with only a senile old fool standing between him and his scrofulous 'twentieth century.'"

A smile over "senile"? No. No smile.

"So he said that you were letting the list go to hell, and I disputed this. I actually named several authors of yours whom I particularly admire—Percy Salmon, Jack Vines, Elizabeth Dudley, William van Dyne, and Ferris Fender. I think he was surprised that I knew any names at all."

I feel this deserves another chortle, this one of absolute incredibility.

"Well, Sam at last says, 'Not one of those people makes any money for us,' and that of course was the point at issue here. I answered that I believe Cecily Woodruff makes some money, and that I understood we have high hopes in Waldo Spinks, and that our backlist is still the pride of the industry, and he said in a very ugly tone, 'In that case, why can't you afford to pay me a living wage?' and I said, 'You mean a *high*-living wage, I suppose? Well as to that, we just can't and that's all there is to it.' And then he said, 'Then how come you can afford Jonathan and his house in the Hamptons?' and I said, 'Because I can only afford one of you, and Jonathan knows how to read.' And one thing led to another and he called me a fossil and I called him a cad, and I said that you, Jonathan, were at least a gentleman, and he made a rude noise."

Well, I sympathized with Sam on that one. Me—a gentleman? Prescott must have been reaching for anything he could throw at young Welman by then: fossils can be touchy.

At any rate, the mad compliment might now make it easier for me to announce our latest body count. But first—surely, he needed his nap? I hadn't heard him talk so long or consecutively in aeons.

No, he didn't need a nap, thank you, he was quite revved up by now; and it occurred to me that Prescott might be one of those multitudinous old men who act senile simply because it is less trouble than not. (I imagine this fact must also have surprised the hell out of Sam as he went about his messy little coup.)

"Now we must talk about the *future!*" announced the old man, eyes practically blazing.

"A replacement for Sam, you mean?"

"Well, that too of course. I rather thought my grandson Prescott V might like to give it a try someday. His mother tells me he reads a lot. And perhaps another day, dare I hope it?, your son Alan might be persuaded to give it a thought too? That would be grand." Now this is the Prescott I am used to and can handle. His eyes fuzz for a moment as he browses among this further perpetuation of names, this tiny league of gentlemen (I remember a cousin of my own called Emily who I might throw in there—she reads up a storm), but then he remembers 1903, and all it stands for, and he says firmly, "But all that can wait. For the moment, I've decided we can do very nicely without Sam's salary, however humble he may have found it himself, and that perhaps, if I took a greater professional interest myself, we could weather this quite handsomely by ourselves with the help of our invaluable in-house editors [three semiliterate fly-by-nights]. After all it's shaping up as quite a small but solid Spring list, isn't it?"

It was as if an old armchair had suddenly spoken. I was supposed to work with *this?*

"Well, I'm sorry to say its slightly smaller than we thought. We seem to have lost Ferris Fender over the weekend."

"I see," he said neutrally. "And pray, how did that happen? I thought you had devoted a great deal of time to Mr. Fender."

Eh? How's that again? Prescott never used to know what *anybody* did with his time, including himself. This was a terrifying development. "Time, well yes, I gave him some of that, but unfortunately I couldn't match it with the equivalent in money. Those tiny advances of ours keep us living dangerously with a lot of our people. There's a limit to how often you can say 'quality house, quality house.'"

"I see." He paused. "I suppose perhaps we really *should* try to be a little bit richer," he said, as if we were talking about putting in a new bookcase. "Which alas means, at the moment, simply squeezing a bit more out of our winners to spread around to the others." (This degree of Marxism was old hat with both of us.) "What news then of the new Woodruff opus? She's another of your protégées, isn't she? How is her book coming along?"

Now I was approaching the hard part. "Well, not very well. In fact, she says she doesn't want to go on with it at all. She says she's changed, that she's a new woman, and that she can't write one more word of twaddle, to use her word for it, if her life depended on it." That was our other strand of conversation that night.

"But she's *got* to," he squeaked. "We have a contract."

I spread my palms (I don't know why, I just did). "She insists it just won't come, Pres. I'm sorry, and she's sorry, but what she wants to do most right now is experimental fiction."

"Oh my God," cried the old upholder of standards, almost rising to his feet, as if to see whether Welman might still be in the building after all and might be talked into staying. He finally calmed himself, perhaps fearing, as I did, a stroke of some kind. "Well women are fickle," he said [how true, sir], "and at least we've got the Spinks," and with that he closed his eyes; his little adventure in opening them had not worked out at all well so far. "I guess that'll do for now, Jonathan. But after lunch I want to hear about *everybody*."

That's twice now that I have been dismissed by people closing their eyes. Could this be a trend? or is that what it takes to get rid of me these days?

As I chew moodily on my unworthy corned beef on rye, I review Waldo's notes on this: "The big gag, I need hardly tell you of all people, about your guy 'Jonathan' is that he never really pays attention to anyone. As soon as he learns enough about a character to make him or her sound either ridiculous or insignificant, he freezes him or her in that state forever. So he is constantly being surprised by everything. It's a great comic technique, because he isn't a stupid man in other respects."

Would that this technique were intentional. Waldo seems, for his part, to be gradually achieving the status, for me, of a sound in a music box. When I figure I have heard enough of him, I gently lower the lid. Well, it works this time. Now—what the hell has old Prescott been taking anyway?—monkey glands? Or is this just a truly spectacular, record-shattering example of "Jonathan's" inattention?

One thing Prescott obviously *has* been taking is an earful of Sam Welman's rat poison. All that stuff about how I spend *my* time with *my* protégées could only have come from the green-eyed nerd himself (or is it possible even to oversimplify Sam?). In fact I am beginning to wonder whether that final showdown with Welman was really quite as one-sided as Prescott now describes it. Having cottoned at last to the old boy's foxiness, I can now see no end to it, and I picture him playing a double-game with Sam, which the latter finally lost by one small move.

There is no doubt that Cecily was what hurt the most. Having at last captured my very own pet bestselling author, the first thing she does is quit on me. And I couldn't even object. "Have you given this enough thought?" I asked her inanely. I mean how much thought would it take? If a girl doesn't want to write twaddle, or be in any way shape or form a twaddle peddler, she knows it all right, in a flash. "Are you sure you can afford this step?" I asked from under the covers, where I had taken refuge. "I hope so," she said defiantly, "but frankly it doesn't matter. I'd go on welfare rather than write one more word in that horrible lisp."

In the circumstance, it seemed a little heartless to ask if she'd given any thought to whether *I* could afford this step. Instead I said meekly, "You know, I sort of liked your stuff." "It *was* kind of cute wasn't it?" she said avidly. "In fact, I honestly don't think anyone else could have done it better." "Perfect of its kind," I barely breathed into her starry-eyed contentment. "But a woman must move on!" Clunk.

As we snuggle about randomly the next morning, she says, "Don't you think my public will follow me into experimental fiction?" "Sure they will, honey, the public is always doing things like that." Fact is, she is cordoned off from irony by sheer laugh-out-loud bliss. I'll say no more about it, but this is a real love affair, after so very long, perhaps forever, for both of us. So when she says, "And we'll both be rich and own our very own sand dune and everything," I almost answer in baby talk. To hell with sales sheets, to hell with twaddle, long live *this!*

At that moment, it hardly seemed important at all.

But now I have to shut the Cecily music box regretfully, too, and face some actual music. My immediate hope is that Prescott has been dosing himself cockeyed on warm soup or whatever it takes to put a senior citizen to sleep in the afternoon. His dream of doing his own publishing, of driving the train himself, has to be played out to the nerve-racking limit; but when it is over, he will be more than glad to pay Sam Welman's salary to someone, anyone, who will take his engine back.

However, as I saunter towards my fate, I suddenly find it just as easy to imagine Sam Welman waiting up there with the old man, demanding a retrial. Dramatic new evidence. Dramatic old evidence too, no doubt. There would be a certain symmetry to getting fired at the end of such a year—the kind of symmetry that almost insists on itself. I decide it's a good thing I'm not worried about publishing today; otherwise I could feel pretty upset about all this.

As it turns out, neither of my apparitions quite comes true. When I walk in, Prescott's head is not laid out on the desk and Sam is nowhere in sight. I think that Prescott *has* been taking something all right—maybe freebasing a little speed, or whatever the old folks are onto these days; at any rate, he seems a lot less logy than me.

"The list, the list," he chirps, like a Scoutmaster spotting a rare butterfly.

The list it is, by George, and I go through it in a slow, businesslike monotone, stalling on the Spinks case until the exhilaration of the imaginary drugs has, I hope, worn off and Prescott returns to normal.

But Waldo cannot be gainsaid forever. The second time I bypass his name, a glint appears in Prescott's good eye informing me that the jig is up.

"What about the Spinks?" he says, at his most gravelly.

"Yes, well," I say thoughtfully, caringly, "his death has complicated things, of course."

"His *death*? What do you mean his death?" He quivers with indignant alarm.

"Didn't you see it in the *Times*?"

"No. I must have missed it. Why doesn't anyone tell me anything? Waldo Spinks *dead*? No. Quite impossible." All this and more comes out in a jumble. "No! I don't believe it. I won't accept it," and on.

"Yes, he died just last Friday. Of a brain tumor, I believe." I talk clean through him. "Why do you suppose I was out there for so long?" (never mind the other times I was out there so long, concentrate on this one, you fool). "I was just trying to wrap things up for him [hah!]. I must say I'm amazed that *Sam* didn't tell you anything about it."

Prescott suddenly looked blank. After all that giddy excitement, what was Waldo to him anyway?

"Well, we've still got the book," he said, as if he has already accepted and dismissed Waldo's whole life and death in one hysterical flurry. I could see that if you really were swine enough to wish to wear this good man out, you didn't do it by boring him—he could always beat you at that game—but by exciting him.

"Well as to the book—yes, you're right, we think we've got the book."

"What do you mean *think?*" he said, fighting his rising voice for dear life.

"Well, he left this curious will requesting that the book not be published. Now or ever."

"So what? We've got a contract."

"But he didn't *want* it published."

"What difference does that make?"

"I don't know. A man's wishes should be respected, don't you think?"

"Why?" asked Prescott. "You said he was *dead*, didn't you?"

"Yes, he's dead all right. I'm positive about that."

"Well then, what does it matter what the fellow wishes?"

"I guess that's the whole point about wills, that it does matter. And the other point is that wills are not entirely a private matter."

"They aren't?"

Oh Lord, how did I get into this? "The thing is, sure we can go ahead and publish, but if it comes out that we're doing it over the author's dead body so to speak, what does that do to our precious principles?"

"To hell with our principles," says Prescott, pounding the desk feebly.

"Then again, I'm Waldo's executor. I didn't tell you that? I'm sorry, Pres. All this must come as a shock to you. Anyhow I am, and as such I'm supposed to see that the will is carried out faithfully."

"What is this, Gilbert and Sullivan?" he says, returning with strange gusto to the period before his own. "You are the Lord High Publisher and the Lord High Executor at the same time? Refuse the damn job, man. Nobody *has* to be an executor."

We both fall silent. Perhaps what he just said about principles has caught up with him. As for me, my feelings about Waldo lie a bit too deep for wrangling. He wanted something done, he trusted me to do it. Next question.

Prescott crumples first. The strain of occupying a false position has been too much for him. "Jonathan, you know how much this house means to me, don't you? And I suppose I'd do *any*thing to keep it alive."

"Why, are we dying?"

"You know, Jonathan, for a clever man you really can be quite dense. Why do you suppose I released Sam this morning?"

Bad fellow. *That's* why. I just stare helplessly.

"I appreciate your dreaminess, Jon, in its proper place. But don't you know *any*thing about our bookkeeping? Have you no notion of what inflation and galloping illiteracy are doing to this business?"

"Of course I have. But I thought that *you*—"

"Would pay for it all out of my own pocket?" he shoots back instantly. "No, thank you very much." He stiffens and it is like a thousand mustaches bristling. This is undiscussable territory, so I can't very well ask him how he's fixed these days, or whether I might lend him a couple of bucks to tide him over.

Fortunately, rich men barge in and out of this territory all the time. "Handouts of that kind only serve to keep unhealthy companies unhealthy," he intones. "Besides which I have no personal intention of leaving the Williams estate one penny poorer than I found it," he says with addled pride, like some old general describing how he routed the fuzzy wuzzies in '02. "I consider that a sacred obligation."

So much for doing *any*thing to keep the company alive. What fascinates the peasant in me is that he doesn't even pause for this commercial break, or bother to explain it. These are the rules of the game—surely I know that by now? Like the Padgetts with their endless fundraising benefits, his good deeds are not even on speaking terms with his own capital. Confusing them would be muddleheaded, dash it.

"What are you laughing at, Jon?"

"Nothing." The giggle dies bubbling in my throat. "Indigestion," I add.

Now that he's put on his show, he returns to the crumpled mode. "You know I've often thought about retiring from this business. Selling the company while it's still worth it, and sailing off Connecticut with my son, and being a country gentleman for the first time in my life. But I love the place too much."

"I understand," I say with honest admiration. How often do you see perfection in *anything?*

"So, I'm afraid we must stay within our limits, you and I, but we'll soldier on for a bit, eh?"

Oh, stop thinking you're English, for just five minutes sometime. "What about the Spinks?" I ask bluntly, seizing the moment.

"Do what you think best about that," he says slyly. The one thing he cannot afford to lose now is me, and he sees quicker perhaps even than I, that the Spinks case might just have to lead to that.

So it looks from here like a grim winter for both of us, far worse than Valley Forge for instance, what with our thin ra-

tions and our deserting authors, and scarcely the cloth to bind
our poor books with, let alone our wounds. But, yes, General
Williams and I will soldier on.

And it may not be all that bad at times. Because when the
rigors of the battlefield become simply too much for flesh to
bear, the general can always repair to his twelve-room apartment in the East Eighties, and I to my country seat in the
Hamptons. I will have to work a bit harder than I care to for a
while to shoulder Sam Welman's load of frenzied phone calls
and ill-judged projects, but Lord knows the woods are full of
potential young helpers, pouring out of English departments
every June, the greatest supply of coolie labor in the West, begging only to be called assistant editors. Surely I can find one of
them cheap enough even for Prescott.

So if you throw in the raise that my partner unaccountably
offers me on the way out (I'll never understand these people),
this has been, as recent days go, a goddamn jubilee.

What remains of the week is devoted to drowning Waldo, or
as they say in Washington, commencing the drowning process.
He had conspired to make this easier for me by spending so
much overtime on revisions that his book had run over this
season and well into the next—valuable drowning time gained.
Of course, the poor bugger was still striving heroically to get
me and the others down exactly right, but now he isn't going to
get any of us down at all. His delays mean we hadn't even
started beating our little tin drum for it yet. So all I have to do is
advise *Publishers Weekly* and other collectors of trivia that our
publication date is still completely up in the air. Waldo, at the
last minute, had expressed certain dissatisfactions with it, and
we need time to ponder some suggestions he'd made to me blah
blah blah—in fact, I tell them whatever comes into my head,
just so long as it isn't newsworthy. All you have to do is murmur the phrase "technical difficulties" and you'll put the keen-
est sleuth in the business straight to sleep. Mildred Struthers,
his agent but my friend, proves the easiest of all. "Frankly, I

hated the book, and never understood why you took it." Well, the heart has its reasons, Miss Struthers.

Perhaps a year from now, a few straggling curiosity seekers will ask once more whatever became of the Waldo, and I'll have to think of something else. "Difficulties with the estate" is another good sleep inducer. Or I could simply divulge the will.

Speaking of which, I have no doubt at all that the will could still be broken in a hundred ways. And that if anyone squawked about ethics, all we'd have to say would be "We did it for literature," and all Grub Street would sing our praises. So why *was* I deep-sixing the book? I'm not dead sure to this day. By now, you probably know as much about my motives as I do. It's safe to say right off the bat that I have never had a relationship remotely like my one with Waldo, so there were no rules to go by. With a friend, I'd know what to do, or with an enemy— but with a *Waldo?*

The reasons I gave Prescott are certainly true as far as they go. But there always has to be more, I suppose. For instance, there is no getting around the fact that a perfectly scabrous, soon-to-be-published portrait of me has been left at my disposal, and I am disposing. Waldo undoubtedly planned it exactly so, with I in my quandary and he in his cap and bells, and in fact as I sit here at my chaste desk brooding about it, he seems to escape from his music box and even now is standing directly behind me (if I look round, he'll simply dart to one side and make me look silly).

I thought I had gotten over the sweats for good, but I should have known that you can't perform an act of this deadly seriousness, obliterating a man's whole book, without one more good bout of the ague.

"And there's another thing," says Waldo, Otis, me, "that I'm sure you're too pure to think of yourself, so I'll tell you myself. You have just gained one other immense advantage, which of course you richly deserve. You now have the only game in town, the only novel to come out of our little group alive. *And* you have my notes on how to improve it. Congratulations, Otis."

"That is unworthy of you, Waldo," I mutter stiffly. But it is true enough, I guess. Come to think of it, I do have his notes to steer my hand. *And* I have his manuscript. *And* if there are any working notes relating to his own second novel to be found, his piggy little executor gets those too. So we shall work on this together, Waldo, shan't we, you and I? It will be a joint undertaking, which is really what I do best anyway.

I suddenly let out something between a cackle and a football cheer, vaguely directed at the space directly between my shoulder blades. "Damn right, I've got the only game in town, *Waldo*," using *my* fictional name for *him*.

Prescott peeps in. "Are you all right Jonathan? I thought I heard voices."

How many?

"*Raised* voices."

The cleaning lady tried to bite me. No. Too farfetched. She's a big woman and her escape would have been spotted. "Radio?" I say. Sounds good. "Yes, by all means, radio," I add heartily. "I mean I had it on just now. Hoping to get some news and all that."

Prescott is already bored. It turns out he never was much interested in my voices. "What would you say to some lunch?" He had just wanted an excuse to visit.

Your "Jonathan" character is constantly being surprised by everything.

"Lunch it is," I say meekly.

Winter
and Out

27

THIS is the weekend of Alan's visit and I feel a boyish eagerness to see him, of a kind I dimly remember feeling, when I was very small indeed, about seeing my father, before he became so dry. And I feel the same sort of anxiousness about how to please him. Does he want to see people? and if so, what kind of people? My age? Young? Exceptionally short, fat, anything special? Whatever I decide, he will say, "You needn't have bothered, Dad." But bother I must.

The one person he's going to meet, whether he likes it or not, is Cecily. In the past, I have felt so crushed by his image of me as a ravening adulterer, that on his rare visits I have done my unlikely best to imitate a sorrowing hermit crab. I must say, it never seemed to impress him much: he probably thought I was holding my breath until he left, at which point other people's wives would come tumbling out of closets like clowns.

But now that Alan has a girl of his own, he may have let his teenage puritanism out a notch or two for his sinful old father. And Cecily is at least a plausible female for a grownup to be seen with, compared with some I've known. Anyway, there is no getting around her.

I don't think my style is suited to happiness, so I'll cut those two golden days to the bone. It turned out that both Alan and Cecily were so eager to like each other that it didn't seem fair to all those people who have to make friends the normal way. Cecily would have liked anybody who walked in the door claiming to be my son, while Alan was apparently just worn out from disapproving of me; his mother and her creep had liberated him from those duties, and he seemed happy to meet me all over again, as a father without a past. Thus does one end of a marriage tend to fly up as the other one bangs down, on the fixed mathematical principle that having two lousy parents at the same time begins to reflect on you.

At that, I might not have gotten away with a Mavis, although the war in his soul would have been horrible to see. Alan so manifestly wanted me not to have a creep to put alongside his mom's creep that he was ready to see good in just about anybody. And Cecily had a quality much prized in grownups for its rarity and shock value, i.e., complete openness. I know you can't really say "hello Alan" more or less openly than other people, but that's how it sounded. Cecily has, this particular day, a soul like a clear mountain stream. But I digress.

Alan's girl, a pale, intelligent-looking creature named, strangely, Gladys, has no part in this scene. Alan would probably like me to like her, but it is no big deal; there is bigger game afoot, and she knows it, whether or not she knows what it is. I think of her that weekend as someone forever peeking into a room wondering whether to enter; or more precisely, squinting into a camera to take pictures of the three of us. A camera is a great hiding place and she seized every excuse to use it, clicking away long after, I suspected, her film had run out.

I still have the pictures—blank records of perfect happiness, or as much of it as my lungs will hold. Since Gladys simply didn't get the point of us, she couldn't capture essences, and you just see three average citizens standing in front of the Pequod Lighthouse or anything else that looked distinguished, or holding up fish (we borrowed three of them at the Pequod dock and made like Hemingway. You don't have to be really funny, or in fact have any sense of humor at all, if you're happy enough).

When it is all over, Alan embraces me warmly and I am surprised that his bones are not still a child's; it has been a long time between touches. He hugs Cecily and she hugs enthusiastically back. If three people can will a happy ending, we so will it. Whether we can get it, who knows, but we tried.

"I think your girl is neat," he said.

"So's yours."

"No, I mean really. She suits you, Dad."

I am so pleased that I almost announce an engagement, but feeling this good is not a usual condition for me, and I feel slightly dizzy and unsure of myself. Cecily, standing by the car with Gladys, smiles back at me: you'll get used to it, she seems to say. But then, she probably doesn't know too many Presbyterians.

How deep does her incandescent friendship with Alan go? As with wartime romances, there is such a flurry of need that depth hasn't come into it yet, hasn't had time. But few hard feelings came from those romances either. Even an Oglethorpe, girding himself for drought and famine, can see no doom in the sky today.

As we wave our next generation good-bye in a conscious Grant Wood sort of way—this being a pose every God-fearing American must want to strike at least once, a dyed-in-the-wool Mom and Dad—I reflect that a *good* stepmother is hard to find, on paper or anywhere else, and that all three of us appreciate and value this—Alan's eyes glint back, at once beseeching and commanding: "Now don't anybody screw up on this"—and will stoop to any artifice to keep our little legend going. I squeeze Cecily as if she was my last sixpence, and she squeezes back for her own good reasons. I don't know—maybe a relationship based, like this one so far, on willpower alone may eventually prove just as sturdy, even as intense as a real one; in any case, it seems to suit our three temperaments better than anything else we've tried.

And now it's time to start retiring Cecily to the private life, which even fictional characters are entitled to now and then. The other characters resume their accustomed places at the big table at Jimmy's, so that I can more easily point at them like a lecturer with a stick. The van Dynes, as if waking from a dream, return almost completely to normal. Nikki's flirtation is like a landmark by now; it impresses strangers, and would leave a terrible void if it stopped. And Billy seems none the worse for it—good God, she couldn't be *posing* for him in a Spinksian sense, could she? I hurry on. Billy on the next chair frets as much as ever about his art and his claims to greatness, and of course about how I am butchering his chances with my pinchpenny publishing methods. ("Jesus, only one measly ad, even after what they said in *Publishers Weekly.*" "Word of mouth, Billy. Great word of mouth.")

In fact, if there is *any* word of mouth, I haven't heard it. His book came out in October to respectful reviews, but somehow even his friends managed to miss them. ("An obscure paper called *The New York Times* buried it on page three," he tells them bitterly.) So he is as invisible as ever, although, in the gawky ranting flesh, he has actually moved up a notch as writer in residence at the Big Table. (There are incidentally other writers at other tables, no doubt stewing up their own stories, but they'll have to wait till next time.)

Archie Munson tends more and more to leave us and sit by himself at the bar, nursing some private burden of grief, which will no doubt seem more and more obscure to onlookers as time goes by. Already, as Jimmy's new Happy Hours and early-bird specials swirl around him, he looks like some Conrad outcast out there on his stool; perhaps we at the table are not so very different, as our ranks thin and the saloon changes character under our noses.

"Ranks thin" is right. As well as Waldo, Ferris is not with us for now, but is actually trying out his Southern Strategy in that land of promises. It is my guess that the money down there will prove real, but the readers won't. Lots of rich little boys would love to finance a Southern Revival, but unless the revival contains an awful lot of religion, music, and football, I suspect that it will only play in the English departments. Like most revivals. Speaking of which, though—there are rumored to be many mouth-watering chairs in such departments all over the Sunbelt for Ferris to browse among to his heart's content. And it's good to see the old colonel on the move again. (Actually, Ferris has not made it past New York yet: he sent me a postcard from the South Street Seaport saying "Gittin' there, boss.")

Anyway, I expect him back any day along with Pete Simmons and all our other strays, simply because Waldo's notes say so. Incidentally I have become quite seriously enmeshed in these notes. But more of that in a moment.

Cormac Burke, our wild Irish peacemaker, has scared up a species of weekend touch football marathon, into which Archie Munson gratefully hurls himself. It somehow seems *safer* than softball, especially with Cormac in charge. For instance, whenever Archie, or even the sainted Cecily, show the faintest signs of taking the game seriously, Cormac's Doberman, Edgar, comes trotting onto the field, to take his position quietly alongside the boss. So it's best to keep things light. Then at other times, children will wander randomly onto the field only to find themselves playing willy-nilly. So you never know what you'll run into out there—whether it be four dogs and six children, or two senior citizens and a man with an artificial leg.

The latter would mean that Cormac's parents and brother have dropped by on a visit, and let it be said in passing that Cormac's one-legged brother, Kevin, plays the most vicious game of any kind of football I have ever seen anywhere. All rules are off for him—for who would enforce them? even the Doberman backs off as Kevin bounds over small bodies and knocks down strong women. "He's entitled," mutters Cormac, from flat on his back, one day, after his baby brother has leveled him real good. (It seems the lad lost the leg in Vietnam and is still searching for it in every scrimmage. I wonder if he plays softball?)

Sometimes, when *I'm* down and gasping, Cormac comes over and growls, "Get up MacGregor—I'm on to your game." So I figure he has doped out everything that happened last summer—probably the easiest job of reporting he ever did. But he knows a family secret when he sees one. And besides, he has been translated to the journalist's Valhalla: he is writing a book and will never have to do any real reporting again. (It's called *The Troubles I've Seen*, if you're interested.)

And so, we glide all too swiftly into winter once again, with Jimmy forever polishing glasses and the days slamming down shorter and shorter. For two stingy weeks the colors are lovely, and then you find you have to look down to see them, and the next thing you know, they're clinging to your rake like wet oil rags; and you look up, and the trees are stripped.

The fire at Jimmy's comes to life again, and we return to its banks with caution: can it be trusted this time, or will we see mad visions again? The first frost cleans out the last and most tenacious of the Summer People; water is turned off in their houses and phones are disconnected, and the rest of us crouch down in our bunker and start dreaming, cautiously, of summer all over again. The dreams may be bad at first, but a winter without them would be beyond bearing.

I, of course, return to experiencing all this in quick takes as a weekender, and thus resuming automatically my sense of being only half here, at most. So far, Cecily and I have maintained a two-house romance, in deference to our respective crotchets, but the winter could easily change that. Finding cranky reasons to live apart for even a moment while the pipes freeze all around you seems desolately bleak. And then, playing the selfsame game with city apartments—I don't know, I think you get on each other's nerves just as soon with all this shuffling about.

Domestic arrangements, I understand, are not literature: I'm just putting the pieces back on the board where they belong. Before Cecily and I decide where to settle, the first snows fall, which reminds me of something. A question which hasn't nagged at me at all since this time last year promptly starts nagging again: to wit, who the hell swept my driveway last winter and arranged those fresh flowers for my return? Without much hope I place an ad in the *Hampton Crab* and go on about my business. No one answers, of course. Bonnackers are leery of the phone. Handymen, for instance, either show up or they don't, but either way they don't phone. So to hell with it.

Then one day, a square, blocky woman whom I seem to see everywhere—weddings, funerals, publishing parties—looms up the very driveway in question.

"Who are you?" I protest.

"I," she intones biblically, "am your neighbor," and then, as if to cool this powerful statement, she adds "Mavis Braddock."

Mavis is obviously not used to having her name goggled at or wept over like this. What is it to her that I have finally met a real Mavis, and am free?

She decides to overlook it, as New York behavior, no better than it ought to be, and barrels on rather testily. "I had to chuckle when I read your ad, or rather when Doreen read it out loud at the beauty parlor. We all had a good chuckle over it."

"*Why* in Heaven?"

"Well, it just seemed like a funny thing to advertise about. How much do those things cost anyway? I mean, why didn't you just ask?"

"Are you saying"—I point inarticulately—"you? And the flowers as well?"

She smiles quite demurely for a big woman. "What else are neighbors for, Mr. Oglethorpe?"

Suddenly the air all around her glows and throbs with kindness. There is kindness everywhere.

"Mind you," she adds, "this year'll be a little bit different. My son will be in the snow-plowing business, and it'll cost you fifteen dollars."

Never mind about that. In fact, all the better. I couldn't feel I really *belonged* out here if I wasn't charged something.

"It'll be a pleasure, Mrs. Braddock—and listen, don't you think you and I should get to know each other maybe a little bit better, being neighbors and everything. Maybe you and your husband would like to come over to dinner one night."

At that she begins to back uncertainly, never taking her eyes off me, all the way down the drive and out of my life. Don't ask *me*.

Epilogue

AFTER that I didn't even *bother* to look for the postman. There are some things it is better for us not to know, Dr. Manchu.

But that was all several years ago. For months after that I continued to noodle with my novel until, on a fine May morning, I suddenly got scared of it. It dawned on me that there were too many real people in there and a real suicide, and I don't have the guts to handle dynamite. So I tried moving the plot to California and even to the south of Spain, and then I tried turning the characters into lawyers, schoolteachers, even ministers—anything to hide them. (To this day, I hope that none of you can guess where this story *really* took place, or who these people actually are.)

I also went as far as I could with Waldo's notes, but it was never quite far enough. They were tantalizing—partly best Sunday-suit efforts to show that he could *so* edit, and partly hints that only he could make use of: applied to my text, they looked like a patchwork quilt.

It hardly seems worth making fresh enemies over a book that doesn't quite work, and in fact, and fortified by Cecily's ardent discouragement, I had just about given up on the whole bloody business when, almost an exact year from the day Waldo died, I received a package containing his complete notes and a partial text for the missing book.

If hair really can stand on end, mine made it a mile. How the hell did the thing get here? The postmark was smeared beyond recognition, and the stamp only said U.S.A., although I prefer to think it came from our nether regions. Anyhow, to my pounding heart, it was like hearing Blind Pew knocking on the door of the Admiral Benbow tavern, as overture to *Treasure Island*.

Well, everyone has his own idea of treasure, and this was mine. I suddenly had my helper now, and in full flower. Waldo's previous notes had been tethered dully to my book, like a kite attached to an anchor, and could only flap prettily in its radius. Now he was on his own, winging his way lustily through the wild blue yonder.

Then and there, I began collating his text with mine, and then applying his notes to both at once. By some strange miracle of implosion, the whole thing suddenly began to swell alarmingly, like a magic mushroom, until it threatened to overflow my study and pour down the streets like lava.

In no time, I found that the combined text had so fused in my mind that I scarcely knew which was his and which was mine anymore. I must admit I was shaken to discover that he had actually outlined several scenarios for his death, each quite different from the others, and including one in which he only pretends to die and turns up in a place to be named later—possibly Korea, as a tour guide. Next to all these he scribbled, perhaps regretfully, "corny" and "impractical." Too bad. It's still the ending I prefer to believe myself. So I wrote them all out anyway, in every spare moment I could steal from real life.

At first Cecily seemed remarkably patient with my mad hobby, but as I burrowed further and further into it like some unhinged alchemist, I thought I began to note a certain coolness. (I only *thought* I noted it, my attention being what it was by then.) *Never mind, my dear,* I muttered to myself, *I'll be with you as soon as I finish this next folio but one.* Until one day she snapped.

"Jonathan darling," she said, storming into my sanctum and folding her arms fiercely, "either that book goes or I do."

Calling this amorphous mass a book at all startled me for a moment. "You mean—all this, this work?—for nothing?" I gurgled.

It must have seemed like a lot to ask, because after a painful pause, she said, "Well publish *something*, it's your job after all, and then get rid of the rest immediately. I refuse to be upstaged for one more day, and in my own house, by a maggoty, evil-minded old corpse." With that she slammed out of the study vowing in a rising voice not to return until I'd destroyed every trace, vestige, or echo of "that foul Satanic creature from *our* house."

"I didn't know," I addressed the still shuddering door, "that you felt so strongly about him, dear." Oh never mind.

As it turned out, Waldo proved immediately helpful on both ends of her ultimatum. For one thing, he had taught me all about how to burn paper, knowledge that doesn't come easily to an Oglethorpe, and so, largely thanks to his own inspiration, his written remains should make a lovely blaze out there in this year's snow when I torch them a few minutes from now or, to be precise, as soon as I've written, or remembered, the last sentence in our book.

As for Cecily's other proviso, Waldo positively went out of his way to help me on that one. Somehow, with the old boy at my side or just behind my back, I suddenly found I had lost all inhibition about publishing (perhaps he would call that "making a man" of me). So—out of the many hundreds of pages Waldo and I have worked on together, I have selected a narrative which I *think* most closely resembles my own, and that's what you're looking at now. But if it isn't *quite* mine, who's to know.

By this time tomorrow at the latest, I will honestly be able to say "Waldo—c'est moi."